Based on an incredible true story

THE LAST SHAMROCK

A novel of the Great Depression

Jim Pitts

The Last Shamrock

A novel of the Great Depression

Copyright © 2016 by Jim Pitts

Cover by Georgia Ann Pitts

ISBN: 1523953063
ISBN 13: 9781523953066
Library of Congress Number: 2016902185
CreateSpace Independent Publishing Platform
North Charleston, South Carolina
Printed in the U.S.A.

Cover photo: Bridie O'Driscoll, New York City, circa 1905

PROLOGUE

At the height of the Great Depression, an ex-New York chorus girl throws open the doors to homeless ragtag refugees, castoffs, a few criminals and fifteen feisty children at an abandoned convent in Texas---"a clean, dry place where the rent never comes due."

Bridie O'Driscoll's guests include an ex-convict with no last name, a once-wealthy widower with three sons, a gun-toting ex-speakeasy owner and his wife, several orphans, a pimp and his very young prostitute, lonely women and their children, an affable alcoholic doctor, a farmer and his able wife.

In their daily quest for bread, work and a little dignity, the unlikely residents of All Saints Convent and Girls School shovel manure at the stockyards, do book-keeping, pick cotton and unload railroad boxcars. They also run a poker parlor in the nuns' dormitory, bootleg whiskey from a still in the basement and pursue other enterprises sometimes just beyond the pale of the law.

"Let's not judge others whose sins differ from our own," Bridie tells her wary parish priest as life at All Saints becomes a little less saintly.

Mingling faith and fairies, Bridie turns "on hard days" to the magic of her gold shamrock, hocking it for food, coal and other temporal needs. Won in a dancing contest at a county fair in Ireland, the three-leaf clover—crafted by fairies, she believes, from a rainbow's gold—had once gotten her to New York and a new life as a Broadway chorus girl. Yet the charmed shamrock fails to save her from an unforgiving church that destroys her marriage.

"We'll manage," the indomitable Bridie O'Driscoll tells her adopted clan as they make their way through America's darkest decade to the advent of World War II.

Guests of All Saints Convent and Girls School
Early 1930s – Early 1940s

George O'Driscoll, railroad dispatcher
    Bridie O'Driscoll, George's wife, ex-Broadway chorus girl
    Josephine O'Driscoll, 15
    Anna O'Driscoll, 9

Martin (no last name), former inmate at Sugar Land State Prison

J.P. Quin Quinlan, widower, ex-oilman
    Jonathan Quinlan, 16
    Matthew Quinlan, 10
    Roger Quinlan, 7

Edwin and Lynn Brant, speakeasy owners, bootleggers, arsonists

Wally Cox, farmer, ex-cowboy
    Ollie Cox, Walter's able wife
    Cory Cox, 8
    Sissy (Ollie May) Cox, 7

Julie Bryant, cousin of Walter Cox, forlorn wife of a missing husband
    Juliana Bryant, 8
    Jeremy Bryant, 7

Elizabeth Wellington, distressed wife of a missing husband
  Gabi Wellington, 9

Shirley Roberts, contented wife of a missing husband
  Buster Roberts, 8

Sam and Sandra Scott, pimp and prostitute, respectively

Doc Cooper, physician, affable alcoholic

Richard Levitz, 10, abandoned child

Brandon Reynolds, 8, orphan

Frank Feldman, 9, orphan

Zelda Griffin, 4, daytime resident

Bonnie and Clyde (goats), Mulligan (yellow mutt), Q.C. (Quinlan's cat)

Dedicated

to Bridie O'Driscoll,

who lived this story,

to Josephine O'Driscoll,

who told it so well,

and to Georgia,

who insisted I write

most of it down in these pages.

WHEN THE WHITE HOUSE BURNED

I t was a violent fire.

Burning debris crashed through upper windows, sprinkling sparks across the sprawling first-floor roof. Wood shingles, crisp as dried leaves, erupted in flames. Towering columns of smoke twisted like tornadoes into the night sky. Dancing flames ripped jagged patches of light in the darkness.

Two men, silhouetted against the orange inferno, sat at a table on the lawn. They smoked cigars and played blackjack by the light of the fire. The player lifted a fat jug from the table, took a lusty swig and passed it to the dealer.

Beneath an ancient oak, a piano player hunched over a Steinway upright. His fingers raked the ivory keys. He shimmied and shook, rolled his head, chomped on a giant cigar. Impromptu singers gathered around him, swaying in halting harmony with their song and their alcohol levels.

The residents of All Saints Convent and Girls School had a grandstand view of the burning Victorian mansion perched on a bluff on the far side of Rosen's Pond. "We might have sold tickets," Bridie O'Driscoll said, watching from the back porch of the convent across the tops of pecan trees rising from the hollow around the pond.

Men in double-breasted tuxedos and women in fringed evening gowns danced on a patio under a canopy. Some gripped bottles of liquor "to steady themselves against the forces of gravity," Bridie chuckled.

"Look!" shouted Anna, Bridie's youngest daughter. "The pond! It's on fire!" Like a black mirror, the pond reflected the flames from the White House, as the three-story mansion was called in Rosen Heights. In the pitch of night, the pond looked like a boiling pit of fire.

"The gates of hell opening to swallow up all them sinners over there," said Wally Cox, sipping a glass of dark liquid he identified as iced tea.

"They'd outdance the devil," Quin Quinlan said.

Quin felt the faint beat of the music as the dancers' frenzied steps and missteps sizzled to the crackle and pop of burning wood. In his silk bathrobe and leather slippers, he tapped his right foot to the distant music and sipped from his engraved silver flask.

"Whatcha got in that flask, Mister Quinlan?" Anna chimed in.

"Roses, little Anna, liquid roses."

"Whatcha doing with 'em, Mister Quinlan?" she said, returning her line of their familiar duet.

"Smellin' 'em, Miss Anna. Never forget to smell the roses while you can."

"Well then, Mister Quinlan, don't swallow 'em all first."

As a smattering of "The Charleston" wafted his way, Quin Quinlan slipped the flask into the pocket of his silk bathrobe and broke into song and dance.

Picking up the tempo, Anna mimicked the dancers with a two-step and a "jiggly jig," as she called her dance. She and Mister Quinlan shuffled among others gathered on the porch to watch the White House burn.

"'Tisn't a celebration we're witnessing, you know," Bridie said.

"Depends whether they get away with it," Quin said, quitting his dance to light a cigarette.

"I'm giving 'em the benefit of the doubt," she said.

"There's no shadow of a doubt, Bridie; their furniture and other belongings are scattered across the lawn a safe distance from that burning house." With intense curiosity, Quin had spent much of the day watching movers cart furniture from the great house and arrange it across the lawn. The musicians showed up at dusk, just before guests began to arrive.

"Look at them snookers," Martin said, who'd emerged from his basement lair to watch the biggest house fire he'd ever seen.

In bowlers and tails, four men stood around a pool table, taking turns at snooker and passing a bottle among themselves.

"Some show," said Elizabeth Wellington, standing behind the screen door in the kitchen. "It hardly seems real."

"Like a Charlie Chaplin movie," said Josie O'Driscoll, Bridie's redheaded teenager.

"More like a bawdy vaudeville show," Wally Cox said, tugging a bag of Bull Durham tobacco from the pocket of his faded blue denim shirt.

"Where's the bawdy part?" Shirley Roberts asked, sitting on the back porch steps. "Please tell me."

"I was talkin' about them half-naked showgirls prancin' around like circus horses," Wally said, rolling a cigarette into a compact cylindrical shape.

The showgirls pranced in scanty stage dress, wending their way among knots of people scattered on the White House lawn. They deftly balanced trays on the palm of one hand and served drinks in crystal glasses. A drunk sitting in a tree periodically plucked a glass from a passing tray.

"Whatever their professional calling," Quin said, "you can bet those girls are serving the finest spirits you'll find in this town."

Indeed, the White House promoted its liquor as "the best of the bottle—European brands smuggled directly up from Mexico." It also distilled its own popular booze. What guests didn't drink, the White House sold in town, to the discontent of other bootleggers. Every bottle came with a measure of hometown humor—a label proclaiming "President's Choice" above a pen-and-ink drawing of the White House, the one at 1600 Pennsylvania Avenue in the nation's capital.

Tonight's special guests (by invitation only) sipped from crystal glasses that winked like summer lightning bugs in the light of the flames. They'd been invited to a "farewell lawn party, music, free booze and a spectacular bonfire." Some watched from overstuffed leather chairs and sofas—taken from the house along with pool tables, pianos, mirrors, chandeliers, Persian rugs, lamps, beds, drapes, risqué paintings and a menagerie of erotic statues.

"Looks like a Paris flea market," Quin Quinlan said.

Crowds soon began to pour out of the Hackberry Grove Dance Hall next to the White House to see the fire. They gathered in the street and danced to the beat of the lawn party music, flickering in and out of view in the shimmering light of the fire like figures in a kinetoscope.

If the Sisters of Charity had ignored the spicy life "over there," the convent's new occupants found the view as entertaining as Saturday night vaudeville. Quin often sat on the back porch smelling the roses in his silver flask and watching the parade of guests arriving at the White House.

"Come see our well-wheeled neighbors," he'd call out as they arrived in Cords and Cadillacs, Pierce-Arrows and Chrysler Imperials, and a Duesenberg roadster from Dallas, reputedly the only one in Texas.

Uniformed chauffeurs opened car doors to discharge gentlemen and their ladies under the *porte cochère* on the circular drive. Hostesses, young and pretty, greeted men who arrived solo. And the White House lights blazed all night as guests danced, dined, gambled and cavorted 'til dawn.

From time to time, Wally suggested, "Let's sic the cops on 'em, Bridie."

"Now, Wally, they're our neighbors, after all. And they're doing no harm other than to themselves."

Besides, Bridie's husband, George, said the Fort Worth police wouldn't raid the White House if J. Edgar Hoover himself called them from Washington.

"Two city councilmen and that police captain who goes to your church are White House regulars," George O'Driscoll reminded Wally once or twice a month. "Why, the Baptists will soon outnumber the Catholics over there."

"But they'll never outdrink 'em," Quin assured Wally, who'd recently taken on religious airs after his church made him a deacon.

The White House stood beyond the long arm of the law and the damnation of preachers who railed against it throughout the long, dry decade of Prohibition, well before Bridie and her guests took up residence at All Saints. Now, on this moonlit evening, they watched the Taj Mahal of Texas speakeasies disappearing in a boozed-up celebration of fire and smoke, music and dancing, singing and cheering.

"I'd say their still blowed up," Martin said. It was hardly news anymore when the fire department cited a faulty still as the source of a house fire.

"Is our still going to blow up?" Anna asked.

"Shush, child," Bridie frowned.

"Don't worry, little Anna," Martin said. "I keep a steady eye on your dadda's still."

"Yeah, Mr. Martin, he says that's why you're asleep down there most of the day, because you—"

"Don't be impudent, Anna," Bridie said.

"I do test the quality of the product now and then," Martin said.

It was obvious to Bridie that Wally Cox had been testing Martin's booze all evening.

"Where are the firemen at a time like this?" Julie Bryant wondered. She'd come out on the porch bare-footed, her buxom little body wrapped tightly in a gray blanket. Wally gulped his drink, wondering if his cousin Julie wore anything under the blanket...and vividly imagined that she did not.

Juliana Bryant leaned against her mother, watching the fire in sleepy silence. Jeremy, her younger brother, bounded down the back steps.

"Dammit, Jeremy," Shirley Roberts yelped, gripping her left hand. "You stepped on my poor fingers, you little bas—"

"Oh...sorry, Mrs. Roberts," he called, en route to the seesaws.

"She said 'dammit,' Mama," Anna said. "Are you gonna wash Mrs. Roberts' mouth out with soap for saying 'dammit'?"

"Say it again, Anna, and you'll see whose mouth gets soaped."

The light of the moon lured the younger kids to the swings and slides on the playground. After their curiosity wore off, they gave the fire scant attention.

Matthew Quinlan spun the merry-go-round faster and faster and then proceeded to push his little brother, Roger, Richard Levitz and Brandon Reynolds off into the dirt. The oldest Quinlan brother, Jonathan, came flying out from under the back porch to console Roger and to whack Matthew with a stick. Quin Quinlan jumped off the porch and snatched the stick from Jonathan to swat his middle son's butt. Mulligan, the yellow Labrador-collie, joined the chase as Matthew darted around trees, swings and slides to escape his father's stick.

Awakened by Matthew's full-throated screams and Quin's winded curses, Bonnie and Clyde emerged from the utility shed where the two goats slept with Wally's chickens. When his father ran out of breath, Matthew ran up the fire escape to avoid Richard's and Brandon's wrath.

The two street-savvy orphans took up long sticks and pursued him. The goats, hooves clanging on the steel steps, followed them. Jonathan Quinlan crawled back under the porch to sit on his Ward's catalog and to sneak another cigarette.

When Matthew reached the top of the fire escape, he took a last look at the third-floor windows of the burning White House with some regret. Several months past, Wally Cox had hastily trotted off to the nearest bathroom and left his cherished World War I brass telescope on the fire escape. Matthew, on his way down, picked it up to see why Wally regularly focused it on the White House, especially at night. What the boy saw in the windows in the house of ill repute clearly illustrated his dad's sketchy story of the birds and the bees. The telescope gave Matthew a bird's-eye view of what men and women do to make babies.

Most customers at the White House left the lights on to take advantage of the rooms' mirrored walls and ceilings. And some engaged in a range of erotic activities omitted from his dad's sterile and hurried story of the procreation process. Recently Matthew had begun selling telescopic views to other schoolboys at the rate of a penny a minute.

Now, as the sound of Richard and Brandon's footsteps clanged up the fire escape, Matthew disappeared inside through an open window.

The kids on the playground halted their play when they heard bells and sirens. "Fire trucks!" Bridie said. "Took their good time getting here."

"A vital detail of the plan," Quin said.

A lone fire truck rumbled up the street just as the east wall of the White House fell with a thunderous clap.

"Their still's blowed up for sure now," Martin said.

The explosion erupted in a shower of flames and debris, sending the White House's patrons staggering back across the lawn.

"Whatta show! A bunch of GD drunks celebrating a house fire," Shirley Roberts said, standing up to get a better view.

The fire truck rolled up to the White House, the bell on the hood clanging with alarm. As if someone had shut a music box, the piano under the oak tree suddenly stopped, singers fell silent, dancers halted.

Suddenly a short, bald-headed man in a tuxedo stepped from the crowd and fired three ear-splitting pistol shots into the night sky. He raised a glass and led a farewell toast to the White House amid a round of cheers.

"Why, that's Edwin Brant himself," Bridie said.

"Who's Edwin Brant?" Julie said.

"The head gangster," Quin said.

The crowd began to thin out as chauffeurs arrived with cars. The street dancers from the Hackberry Grove Dance Hall boarded the last streetcars to downtown Fort Worth.

Shirley and Julie herded kids back inside the convent.

"Wally," Bridie said, "see if they're needing a place to stay."

"What's 'at, Bridie?" he said, rolling another cigarette.

"The Brants may have no place to stay the night."

"That would be the only flaw in their grand plan," Quin said.

"You mean ask 'em to spend the night...here?" Wally grumbled, rolling cigarette paper around the tobacco. He ran his tongue along one side of the paper and pressed the two edges together, sealing the little cylinder of tobacco.

"They're neighbors, Wally."

"Those White House people are bootleggers. Whores. Criminals."

"Now, Wally, let's not be sitting in judgment on those whose sins differ from our own."

"What if they put a match to this place, too?"

"Tell 'em we've no insurance," she said with a laugh. "Their name is Brant, Mr. and Mrs."

"If I forget, I'm sure any cop can tell me," Wally mumbled, going down the steps to his Dodge pickup.

"Especially the cops on Mr. Brant's payroll," Quin said.

BRIDIE'S INMATES

"Still awake, I see," George said, as surprised to find Bridie up so late as she was to see him home so early.

"Is it you're broke already, George, right after payday?" she asked, assuming he'd skipped his usual nightcap at Harold's Place.

"Never mind my pocketbook," he said. He tossed newspapers on the table and hung his hat on one of the coat pegs along the wall. "Just saw Mr. Baxter up that light pole taking down the power line to his house again."

"So the meter reader's coming tomorrow," Bridie said. Mr. Baxter's little crime, she believed, was just retribution for the light company's lack of charity toward those needing more time to pay unjust and past-due bills.

"A venial sin at worst," she called it, meaning Mr. Baxter wouldn't go to hell if he got fried alive for stealing a little electricity.

"Venial or not, I'll not be climbing an electrified pole in the dark o' night," George told her whenever she had no money for the light bill.

"Your dinner's on the stove," she said.

"The freight trains were full o' chaps again today," he reported, loosening his tie. "They latch onto moving trains with one hand, holding their bags of belongings with the other. One lad they found on the rails, right leg cut off."

"Killed, was he?"

"They took him to Saint Joseph's. Blood all over the tracks."

Bridie smelled the soot in George's clothes—an iron-like scent of coal and smoke from the trains that chugged past his window in the switchyards of the Fort Worth & Denver Railroad. Like most European men, he still wore a coat and tie when he went out the door to church, to work or to change a tire.

"Still feeding that mangy old cat," George said, glaring at Quinlan's gray-and-black-striped feline lapping up a bowl of milk next to the icebox.

"Let's not begrudge Q.C. a drop o' milk," she said. "He earns his keep feasting on our mice." The three-legged cat's left eye bulged like a yellow marble from his deformed face, his right eye a blind slit. A twisted snout gave him a permanent snarl, revealing razor-sharp teeth in a fixed smile of evil contentment.

"Tommy sent money today," she said, "so I got you a pork chop for dinner."

"That brother of yours will be in the poorhouse, if not the jailhouse, soon enough. Tramping about Nevada all these years looking for gold between bar-room brawls and hiding out from the sheriff."

"You never know when Tommy might have a big gold strike again."

"Or when Saint Patrick might return to Ireland," George said, taking a bottle of beer from the icebox. "Whose big-arsed Packard is it I saw out back? One of your inmates rob a bank?"

"Their house burned down. They're here just for the night, I think."

George put the bottle of beer on the table with a thud. "Someone's house burns down and they turn up here. I suppose your sister sent them, like all the rest of the ex-cons, orphans and derelicts she sends our way."

"She's innocent this time," Bridie said, chuckling. "These are our neighbors from across the way. The White House burned down tonight."

"The White House? Burned?"

"To the very ground."

George went to the door and opened the screen. In the silvery moonlit night, he saw two men standing around kerosene lamps guarding all the goods disgorged from the White House before it burned. One of them toted a shotgun.

"The Brants, having no place to go, took shelter here," Bridie said.

"Not the White House Brants?"

"The same—Edwin and Lynn Brant. You'll meet them tomorrow."

"I don't care to meet them tomorrow or next Christmas, Bridie. Bloody 'ell, the Brants run the richest speakeasy in town. There's gambling over there. And for God's sake, it's a bawdy house to boot."

"No one knows what they did over there, George—surely not yourself."

"Mark my words, Bridie. You'll let some scoundrel in someday who'll kill us all some night."

"If we've nothing else, we have space."

"You know, Bridie, the cops found a corpse down in that pond before we moved to this place—a man, shot through the head."

"They were finding corpses all over Ireland when you left, George."

"The cops questioned this Edwin Brant character about it."

"He wasn't arrested."

"The Brants, broads and booze," George said. "Shall we change the name of the place from All Saints to All Sinners, I ask?"

Bridie looked up at the tall, handsome Irishman she'd married in County Tipperary so long ago: his large hands gripping the back of a chair; his broad-shouldered, six-foot-two frame looming over the table; blue eyes sparkling; coal-black hair gleaming in the glare of the ceiling lights.

"How many inmates do we have in this asylum now, Bridie? Twenty? Twenty-five?"

"The Brants aren't likely to stay."

"Once they're in, they never leave," George said, shoving his supper plate—pork chop, boiled potatoes, cabbage—into the oven and striking a match to light the burner.

Turning to the table, he caught Bridie's warm brown eyes admiring him and the shy smile that so attracted him when they'd collided on the cobbled footpath in Clonmel. Their short, sweet courtship had led to a passionate marriage that produced three daughters in three years. The petite, nimble figure of the professional dancer she'd been had never ceased to rouse him.

So George looked away and said, "Going up to change clothes while my supper warms in the oven."

"I love you, George," Bridie called as he went down the dark hallway to the staircase.

His milk bowl empty, Q.C. slipped silently down the hallway. Wally Cox believed Q.C.—long, slender, muscular, thirty-seven pounds—had been fathered by a bobcat under a full moon. "A witch's cat if there ever was one," he said.

Bridie glanced at the headlines of the newspapers George had picked up at the Santa Fe passenger depot. "These'll wait 'til morning, Mulligan," she told the dog, pushing the papers aside. The big yellow mutt had returned to the kitchen after Q.C.'s departure. He followed her as she got up from the table and went down the hall to bed.

Discovering a "ghost mouse," Bridie returned to the kitchen carrying a dead mouse resting on a dustpan. Quinlan's cat stripped his prey of every last morsel of meat, innards included. The remains consisted of a tiny white skeleton, tail and head, its eyes fixed in eternal surprise. Richard Levitz, one of the orphans, came up with the name "ghost mouse."

Bridie tossed the little skeleton into the backyard and returned to her room. She lived in the nun's library, between the kitchen and a classroom occupied by Shirley Roberts and her son, Buster.

George returned in a white T-shirt, black trousers and slippers. He took another bottle of beer from the icebox, retrieved his supper from the oven and sat at a table.

"Go away, you flea-bitten beast," he shouted at a goat butting its horns against the screen door. Without looking at their fixtures, he couldn't tell Bonnie from Clyde. The goat turned and clopped across the back porch.

Finishing dinner, George fired up a cigar and sat down with another beer to read the discarded newspapers. "Good God," he said, scanning a front-page story:

Dry Agent, Rum Runner Die
in Bloody Daylight Ambush

A fusillade of bullets fired into prohibition agent Mike Malone's car killed him instantly as he returned from a liquor raid. Other dry agents in the car fired back with machine guns, killing one of the assailants. Two other gunmen escaped, police said.

George sighed, thankful he'd decided to forgo his nightcap at Harold's Place on the way home. It wouldn't have been safe no matter what Harold was paying the police captain who drank there. The cops would be raiding speakeasies for a week, reporters and photographers in tow.

George mildly regretted violating the Constitution of his adopted country. Yet, he reasoned, distilling a few bottles of liquor was hardly a sin. Crimes weren't always sins. Indeed, in Ireland, crimes against the British Crown counted as blows against the devil. In the confessional, the penance for the killing of an English soldier was often three or four Hail Marys for the soul of the departed.

So when Martin offered to distill a little whiskey in the basement, George bought a small five-dollar distillery at Walton's Hardware "to let the freeloader earn his keep." To his astonishment, it was the finest whiskey he'd tasted since he'd left Ireland.

"An old Kentucky recipe," the laconic Martin mumbled.

On Saturday nights, George tithed a bottle of booze to Father Nolan after poker at the Knights of Columbus Hall. (Although he no longer had much use for the "church on Earth," he kept the faith and his card-playing friends at the Catholic men's club.) More recently, George had been selling a few bottles to fellow knights and to a bootlegger who hung out at Walton's. It was easy money. He was thinking about expanding the distillery.

Finishing the paper, he picked up his brother-in-law's letter from the table where Bridie had left it.

General Delivery
Round Mountain, Nevada

Dear Bridget,

I have a little cabin here for $5 a month and do my own cooking. I find enough gold to keep going for now. My claim is ten miles from town, so I don't see anyone for months. But I have a dog and do not miss people at all. No need to send Irish World as I get it every Monday by mail for $2.50 a year. Moving around so much I did not get it for a while.

I am sending cheque for $62.10. Pay as much of it as you can on Josie's piano to save the 8 per cent interest. Would be sad to lose it now she plays so well. I would like to hear her play "O'Donnell Abu."

Most of the banks in the state are all busted. I hope the bonds at that Texas bank are not in default. It would be a big loss. That's all we have for the future.

Enclosing a dollar for Josie and Anna. I don't know if I will be able to see you at Christmas but will if I possibly can.

> Your loving brother,
> Tommy
> Erin Go Bragh

"Ireland forever." George read the Gaelic aloud. He didn't care that Bridie had removed the check. The more money Tommy sent, the less George gave her. A feisty, nervous, unsociable little man, he'd wandered into town once, bought them a house with cash and left abruptly without saying goodbye.

George finished his beer, turned off the kitchen lights and went down the dark hall. He paused outside Bridie's door and turned the knob. It was locked. At the click of the knob, Bridie flinched and dropped her rosary beads. She listened, tears in her eyes, as he climbed the stairs to his room.

Q.C. crept along the wall in the dark room, once the office of Sister Angelus, mother superior of All Saints. The three-legged cat deftly jumped onto his favorite couch. Curling up for the night, he detected a movement.

Q.C. tensed and judged the distance to his prey on the floor just below the edge of George's bed. The thing moved. Q.C. sprang. He secured his hairy victim in curled claws, sank teeth deep into warm flesh, and ripped skin and muscle for the taste of blood.

Both hooves caught Q.C. full in the gut and sent him flying against the wall, squalling like a wounded wildcat. Bonnie banged her horns against slats and bedsprings to escape with the remains of her tail.

"Burglars!" George shouted. He jumped out of bed and ran for the door. "God'am burglars! Call the police!"

He sprinted down the hall, Bonnie's hooves beating close behind him. George flew down the stairs three steps at a time until he came face to face with a half-naked man holding up his drawers with one hand, a chrome-plated .45 automatic in the other.

"Halt or I'll shoot!" the stranger shouted, pointing the pistol at George.

Bonnie bolted past George, knocking the gunman to the floor. His pistol fired, the explosion echoing through the convent like thunder in a teacup. George fled back up the stairs.

Bonnie reached the kitchen and ripped through the back screen door.

George went out the open second-floor window, through which the goat had gained entrance. He ran down the fire escape to his car, threw open the door and jumped inside. Reaching into his pocket for his car keys, he found himself in his shorts.

After a while, Bridie came out to the car. "Come inside, George. All's well."

"Where's that naked burglar who tried to shoot me?"

"Mr. Brant's gun went off accidentally. He's embarrassed."

"Edwin Brant, from the White House?"

"Yes, George. Come in now. He's sorry the gun went off."

George got out of his car and crossed the campus, his drawers rising like a white flag as he mounted the fire escape and disappeared through a window.

THE KITCHEN MOB

"George still here after last night's shooting?" Quin Quinlan said, taking his chair in Bridie's kitchen.

"Indeed," Bridie said, pouring him a cup of coffee. "And the Brants are asleep on the floor in the auditorium."

"On the floor?" Quin asked. "At last the decline and fall of our not-so-noble neighbors."

"They have a mattress and sheets," she said, pouring a bowl of cream for Q.C., who was impatiently swishing his tail.

"Shouldn't feed my cat, Bridie. Diminishes his appetite for our mice."

"I saved a drop for you, poor man," she said, handing Quin the cream pitcher. "Martin just skimmed this fresh off the morning milk."

"Thank you, Bridie. And thanks to your cows, Wally. Cream in one's morning coffee's an amenity I'd truly miss."

"It's a rum-runnin' Packard Eight," Wally said. "Bootleggers' favorite car."

Holding the screen door open, Wally drank a glass of milk and studied the Brants' navy blue sedan parked under a tree. "Nothing on the road can touch it at full throttle...except o' course that Cadillac Sixteen of yours, Quin."

"Like Will Rogers says, we're the first nation to drive to the poorhouse," Quin said. A relic of his recent past, his dusty Cadillac was parked under the *porte cochère*, a swallow or two of gasoline left in the tank.

Wally joined others at one of four kitchen tables and helped himself to the newspapers George had brought home the previous night. "Here's yesterday's *Fort Worth Press*," Wally said, pushing the paper to Quin. "I'll check the he'p-wanteds in this here other one."

"See the story about the man they found hanging from the Vickery Street railroad bridge," Bridie said. "Left a wife and three kids."

"Last week it was a man who stepped in front of a train," Quin said.

"I'd take the train myself," Wally said.

"Good morning, all," Julie Bryant called out, nudging open the door with a curvy hip as she emerged from the basement. She held a serving tray with three bowls of porridge and three slices of toast prepared in

25

the basement kitchens that once served the grand dining room where nuns and students took their meals. A mumbled chorus of sleepy "good morning"s resounded in reply.

"I see the kitchen mob's scheming against the world again," she said cheerfully, crossing the spacious room.

Jonathan Quinlan suspended a forkful of scrambled eggs over his plate as he tracked Julia Bryant across the room like a bird dog pointing a dove. She felt the boy's brown eyes boldly sweeping her body, head to foot and foot to head, a coy smile on his face.

"Josie, get Julie some milk," Bridie told her budding redheaded teenager.

"I'm fixing my breakfast," Josie said, rattling a spoon against the pan of porridge on the four-burner stove.

"I'll get you some milk, Julie," Jonathan said, his six-foot athletic frame rising nimbly and eagerly from the table. Everyone looked askance at the brash boy addressing a married woman by her first name. Josie, who'd long yearned for his attention, was disgusted with him.

Ignoring Jonathan, Julie turned to his strikingly handsome father, his head of wavy salt-and-pepper hair bent over his newspaper, and said, "See anything in the help wanted ads, Quin?"

"Not yet," Quin murmured.

If the long-grieving widower had seemed not to notice the pretty brunette—petite figure, ample bust, early thirties, two kids and a long-missing husband—his eldest son had taken to manifesting his emerging testosterone levels by brazenly flirting with her.

Jonathan placed three glasses of milk on Julie's tray. "I'll take this to your room, Julie," he informed her.

"No, Jonathan. I've got to feed Juliana and Jeremy and get them dressed."

"Later," he said, his voice low and lusty, looking all too deeply into her aqua blue eyes.

Julie turned away, scanned the tables to see if anyone had noticed and said, "Let me know if you come across any ads for women's work."

"Nothing yet," Wally said.

"Uh...yeah, I will, Julie," Quin said. "I sure will."

Looking up, Quin caught Jonathan fixated on Julie's bodacious body rippling her dress as she walked quickly to the door. Though taken aback by his son's blatant awakening to the opposite sex, Quin watched Julie with new appreciation as she disappeared into the hallway.

"It's so hard to find women's work," whined Elizabeth Wellington, a timid, plump woman sitting next to Ollie Cox, who was darning socks at one of the tables. "I tried the hotels like you said, Bridie, but they didn't need maids."

"It's all right," said Ollie, a thin, wry woman with brownish-blonde hair, yellow eyes, calloused hands and flinty, sunbaked skin. "You'll find something soon enough, girl." She put aside her darning needle and took Lizzy's hand.

Wally asked, "George mention any work in the rail yards, Bridie?"

"No. He was so beside himself about the Brants being here, and then…"

"And then" Quin said, "he thought the devil had come for him."

Everyone cackled as if George were still running down the hall in his shorts, yelling, "God'am burglars!"

"Maybe that'll cure that old goat from coming in again," Wally said.

"Bonnie or George?" Quin asked.

The phone jangled like a fire alarm. Five-feet three-inches tall, Bridie stretched to reach the mouthpiece that protruded from the phone on the wall.

"Hello. Oh…Sister Alexis….'Tis indeed a blessed day, Sister….Yeah, yeah. Sure. Julie is here." Elizabeth Wellington waved and pointed to herself. "Fine, Sister. I'll give Julie the word. And would ye have anything for Elizabeth today?...Maybe next week, you say. Okay. Bye now, Sister."

Bridie turned to Josie. "Run up and tell Julie she's wanted for a full day's work at the hospital laundry."

"I'll tell her," Jonathan said.

Though Josie had just put two hard-boiled eggs on the table next to her bowl of porridge, she beat him to the door. "I'm going," she snapped at Jonathan.

"Tell her I'll look after Juliana and Jeremy and give them lunch," Bridie called to Josie.

On the second-floor landing, Shirley Roberts emerged from the bathroom under the staircase still in her bathrobe, a hairbrush in her right hand. With blue eyes and good teeth, Shirley was almost pretty when she smiled.

"Good morning, Josie dear," she said, pulling at her faded pink bathrobe. Though stout and big-boned, Shirley was tall and carried her weight well. Quin called her the Amazon woman, but not in her presence. In reference to her missing husband, she called him "that naked bastard I beat bloody with a broomstick when I caught him in the sack with my neighbor's wife."

"Good morning, Mrs. Roberts," Josie said. "I'm on my way to tell Julie Bryant the hospital called her for a day's work in the laundry."

"Good for Julie!" Shirley said, still brushing her short blonde hair. "Got to get dressed for work, Josie," she said, hurrying down the stairs.

Other than George O'Driscoll, Shirley was the only All Saints resident who held a full-time job. And Bridie said Shirley "earns a man's wages, ten dollars a week at Kress's, and intends to send her studious son, Buster, to college."

As Josie passed Quin Quinlan's room, a radio voice seeped under his door. Matthew was listening to his dad's Atwater Kent radio.

Down the hall Julie Bryant threw open her door. "Heard you coming," she said. Josie told her about the laundry job.

Jeremy waved, a piece of toast in his hand, a milk mustache on his lip. Their classroom was furnished with hospital beds Bridie had borrowed from Saint Joseph's. Les Bryant's last letter was postmarked Chicago, Illinois. It contained no return address and no money. Juliana and Jeremy said their dad would send for them when he found work.

Bridie told Josie and Anna not to ask the other kids about their missing daddies. "It only makes them cry."

When Josie returned to the kitchen, Clyde Markum was on the phone. He'd come up from his dairy on the side of the hill to call his veterinarian. In his straw hat, overalls and loose pullover feed-sack shirt, he was declaring, "Cows are the dumbest bastards on earth."

Anna sat in Josie's chair at the table. Shattered, empty shells of two hard-boiled eggs lay next to a bowl of porridge. As she leaned her head into the bowl, spooning up hot porridge like a starving stray cat, Josie pressed her sister's face into the warm mush. "Have it all, and I hope it's full of lumps."

Anna's mouth opened to let out a scream, but her voice stuck in her throat under the oatmeal.

"Anna, close your mouth and wipe your face," Bridie said, coming in from the back porch. "You're to eat your porridge, not wear it."

"Say again, dammit!" Clyde Markum snapped, glaring at Bridie, the phone hard against his ear, dried mud and manure flaking off his knee-high boots.

Julie Bryant strode briskly through the kitchen. "On my way to Saint Joe's, Bridie," she said, stopping at the back door next to the phone. "Gotta run. It's almost a mile to the streetcar, you know."

Picking up the cue, Quin said, "I'd love to take you, Julie, but I'm not sure there's enough gas to get us there."

"Oh, thanks anyway, Quin," she said pleasantly, hurrying out.

"No, dammit, I can't hear ya," Clyde Markum barked into the phone when the screen door slammed behind Julie. "An enema. Yeah, doc, I done it before. Stick the hose up the cow's ass, turn on the water and a get outta the line of fire."

Bridie's face reddened. Quin chuckled behind his paper. Anna smiled to inform the room she'd heard every forbidden word. She and the other kids, including Jonathan, stacked their dishes in the kitchen sink and went outside or down the hall.

"Thanks for the phone, Bridie," Clyde Markum said, hanging up the receiver. "The wife sent ya some feed sacks and a few eggs there on the table."

"Tell her I said thanks, Clyde," Bridie called as he went out the door. Clyde mounted Myrtle the mule and trotted downhill to his dairy farm. "Poor man. All those cows to milk and kids to feed."

"Ol' Clyde's not gettin' much for his milk an' eggs these days," Wally said, folding his newspaper. "Not a lick o' work here." Out of Bull Durham, he chewed on a toothpick. "Could pick cotton if we had gas to get up to McKinney."

"Not me," Quin said. "I can make more money at home playing with my pecker. Oh, sorry, Bridie."

Washing dishes at the sink, Bridie pretended not to hear what she didn't want to hear.

"Let's go down to the Texas and Pacific and see if there's any boxcars to unload," Wally said. "They pay twenty cents an hour."

"Enough gas in your truck?" Quin asked.

"Think so, if we coast down the Northwest Twenty-Fifth hill."

"The boys'll be okay, Bridie," Quin said, decked out for a day of labor in fresh khakis and brown brogans. "I've threatened Matthew, not that he ever listens. And Jonathan'll take care of little Roger."

Bridie knew that Jonathan would leave Roger with her and go off to see his friends. Josie knew they'd be smoking cigarettes, drinking bootleg booze and oohing and aahing at the half-dressed women in the ladies' lingerie section of Jonathan's Ward's catalogue.

Jonathan had bragged to Josie that he'd been hopping freight trains to and from Austin, pocketing the train fare his dad sent him to come home from school once a month. "It's enough to buy a quart of Blackie's best hooch," he said. She'd heard all about Blackie the blacksmith, the neighborhood bootlegger.

"See ya later, sweetie pie," Wally said, kissing Ollie on the cheek. She looked at him warily, still cool after his latest iced tea binge. He grabbed his Stetson and paused at the door. "I'll patch this screen with that goat's hide when we get back this evening," he said and went out to his pickup with Quin.

"Wait," Shirley Roberts called out from the back porch. "I need a ride to the streetcar stop." When the truck backfired like a cannon, she stumbled halfway down the back steps. "Double damn you, Wally Cox," she gasped, hanging onto the handrail. "Stop that laughin'. You too, Quin, you double S.O.B, you."

Ollie Cox gathered up her sewing basket and the feed sacks Clyde Markum had left on the table. "These'll make good shirts for the kids," she said.

Elizabeth Wellington held her face in her hands. "I just can't find work anywhere, Bridie. Luck's against me."

"We'll manage, Lizzy," Bridie said. "Nothing's so bad it couldn't be worse, you know."

"Anna says you have a lucky shamrock. That's what I need—luck."

Bridie took the gold shamrock from her apron pocket. Glowing like sunshine, it covered the palm of her hand.

"Are the real ones that big?"

"About the size of your thumbnail, Lizzy. With their little white flowers, the three-leaf clovers grow in Ireland, though you'll find four-leaf clovers elsewhere. Here now, I have some that came just yesterday from Delia Walsh, a girl I grew up with in Ireland." Bridie fished an envelope from her apron, opened it and poured little brown leaves on the table. "They've turned brown since Delia mailed them fresh five or six weeks ago, but you can see their size and get an idea what they look like."

"Yes, I see the three leaves, Bridie."

"Sad that they've lost their color and the little white flowers that make them so pretty," Bridie said.

"I can see how they'd be beautiful. And you say they bring you luck?"

"The shamrock's always protected the Irish against curses and evil spirits, sickness and invaders, and all sorts of things."

"Do you really believe all that, Bridie?"

"The English surely did, Lizzie. They feared the power of the shamrock enough to ban our wearing them."

"Wearing them?"

"We pinned 'em to our clothes like jewelry on saints' days and wore them to weddings and wakes. Our lads wore them fighting the English. And when it became a hanging offense to wear the shamrock, we put the crime to rhyme:

"O'Paddy dear, an' did ye hear the news that's goin' round?
The shamrock is by law forbid to grow in Irish ground!
Ireland's the most distressful country that ever yet was seen,
For they're hangin' men and women there for wearin' o' the green!"

"Oh, Bridie, I love it. Let me hold your shamrock."
Bridie laid the gold shamrock in Lizzie's hand.
"What's it ever done for you, Bridie? Really, now?"
"Took me to America. See what it says on the back: 'First Prize, Dancing, County Tipperary Fair, 1899.' I was eighteen, and winning it gave me the courage to go to New York to dance on Broadway."
"You, a New York chorus girl?"
"Believe it or not, Lizzie, I danced on Broadway back in 1901. A few years later, I made it to the Ziegfeld Follies. And I even modeled clothes for Charles Gibson himself."

"So you met George in New York, then?" Lizzie asked, rubbing her hand over Bridie's magic shamrock.

"After eight years, I went home to Clonmel. I met him there on the street after Sunday Mass. So my gold shamrock brought me both luck and love."

Lizzie said, "We could sure use some luck now."

"And a load of coal for the winter," Bridie said.

THE PRIEST AND THE DEPUTY SHERIFF

After a cursory rap at the back screen, a man in a black suit, black hat and Roman collar stepped inside, the door creaking shut behind him.

"Well now, if it isn't Father Nolan himself," Bridie said, her face alight with delight and a broad smile. "My second favorite priest after the Pope."

"Good day, dear Bridget," Father Nolan said, taking off his hat, which uncapped a hoary head of silver-white hair. "Looks like you're busy getting lunch together."

"No, Father Nolan, but you're just in time for breakfast with George."

"Breakfast at high noon...and with George O'Driscoll....Not today, thanks."

"Well, you know, Father, he works 'til midnight, so he gets up wanting breakfast midday. And a bit of a tussle here kept us up later than usual last night. How about a peanut-butter sandwich? And I'm just making a pot of tea."

"If you don't mind, Bridie, I'll have a beer," Father Nolan said, going to the icebox.

"He keeps it behind the block of ice," Bridie said.

"George does brew a good bottle," the priest said. Taking a seat at the table, he cast a wary eye on the very large gray-and-black-striped cat sleeping in a windowsill. "You go ahead with his breakfast."

"He won't be down for a bit yet," Bridie said. Sitting down with a cup of tea, she noticed that Saint Patrick's pistol-packing priest, as the papers dubbed him, was unarmed today.

His church, the city's largest, towered over the seedy remains of lower downtown's old Hell's Half Acre—a neighborhood of smoky pool halls and domino parlors, dingy two-bit hotels, and smelly whorehouses, greasy cafes and the Salvation Army Center. Sporting badge and gun, Father Nolan regularly arrested thieves pilfering the poor box and stealing gold candelabra right off the great marble altar at Saint Patrick's Church.

"Say, who is that grubby-looking, short meatball of a man on the back porch massacring a catch of fish with a knife?" Father Nolan asked.

"You mean Martin? I thought you'd met him by now. Been here awhile. He caught some perch in Rosen's Pond. We'll have them for lunch."

"He looks awfully familiar. How'd he turn up here?"

"Sister Vee sent him."

"I should have known. Scraped him up off the street someplace."

"Why would you be saying such an uncharitable thing?" Bridie said.

"Because I know your sister. And I remember him now, this Mr. Martin of yours, standing in front of my church one morning, pondering the pilfering of my poor box."

"What is the poor box for if not for a poor man like Martin?"

"It's charity, Bridie, to be given to those in need, not to be taken by thieves at their leisure for drink and whatnot."

"Remember, Father Nolan, Christ forgave the good thief on the cross at Calvary."

"I forgive them their sins and arrest them for their crimes," Father Nolan said, laughing and almost choking on his beer. "I'm a man of two hats."

"And two hearts," she said.

"You do know, Bridie, I'm duly deputized by the county sheriff himself?"

"So we've read in the papers," she said disapprovingly. "What would the Pope say about one of his priests carrying a gun?"

"His Holiness has never mentioned it to me," Father Nolan said. "And by the way, I remember seeing your Mr. Martin wandering the seamy streets in Hell's Half Acre."

"Martin's his Christian name. He gave no other."

"I doubt he's Christian," the priest said. "Not a Catholic, for sure. He's probably an atheist or even a Baptist. Not smart enough to be a Jew."

"I wouldn't know, Father," Bridie said, shrugging her shoulders.

"No, you wouldn't, Bridie. You take in all kinds of riffraff. But you should take in Catholics in this Catholic convent ahead of others. How many of the faithful live here now?"

"They're all God's children," she said. "Does it matter how they go about believing in Him?"

"Heresy! Pure heresy!" the priest declared. "You're as irreverent as your holy sibling, Sister Vee. But you didn't answer my question; how many Catholics live here...or would you know?"

"They're eight of us since Quin and his three boys moved in."

"Ah yes, Mr. Quinlan, the oilman. Used to be a big donor to Saint Pat's," the priest fondly recalled. "Before he lost everything."

"Like everyone else," Bridie said.

"Not nearly as much as Quin Quinlan lost," the priest said, finishing his beer. "Used to send his oldest boy to that expensive boarding school down in Austin, you know. Then he lost his wife and all his money, too."

"Jonathan's still down there at Saint Edward's High School. Comes home weekends about once month."

"So Quin still has money and not putting a penny of it in my collection basket at Sunday Mass. And he lives here rent free."

"The Sisters of Charity didn't ask me to collect rent, Father Nolan."

"Neither did they ask you to throw open the doors to every panhandler who comes down the street."

"You sound like George," she said, laughing at him.

"Well now, George has his good points, though not a great many. What was the tiff you mentioned kept you all up last night?"

Relating how Bonnie had spooked George and sent him scrambling down the stairs, Bridie said, "And then Edwin Brant's gun went off accidentally.'"

"Edwin Brant? From that house of sin across the pond? What was he doing here in the first place?"

"The White House burned to the ground last night, Father. Edwin and Lynn Brant took shelter with us."

"Well, thank God for the fire, but heaven forbid, Bridie, you haven't let the Brants in here? He's a gangster."

"Remember, the Lord said, 'What ye do for the least of them, ye do unto me.' Besides, they're only staying a night or two."

"Did by the grace of God that other sinful place burn, too?"

"The Hackberry Grove Dance Hall's unscathed. Another beer, Father?"

"No, I'm leaving before Al Capone or Machine Gun Kelly comes down the hallway here," he said, watching Q.C. stretching himself on the windowsill, scouring the room with his good eye.

"The poor cat's looking for something to eat after napping all morning."

"That's what worries me," the priest said. "Oh, the reason I dropped by is to let you know I'll be sending you a gentleman in need of a room for a night or two. His name is Phillip Marstiller. Didn't think you'd mind, Bridie, if you still take in Catholics."

"And no room for him at that priestly palace you live in," Bridie said, an amusing smirk on her face.

The priest ignored her, took his hat and got up from the table. "If you can find out this Martin fellow's last name, I'll check him against the police records."

"I'll do nothing of the kind, Father."

"I'm going to drive around the block to see the ashes of the White House and give thanks to the Lord for its demise," the priest said as he turned to leave. "Try to get George to Mass next Sunday, Bridie."

"I try every Sunday," she said as the screen door slammed behind the priest.

Bridie stifled a smile as she imagined the shock on Father Nolan's face when he encountered the menagerie of erotic statues standing on the White House grounds like refugees from Sodom and Gomorrah, untouched by the fire.

THE BEGGAR'S BANQUET

"Almost everyone's out looking for work, George," Bridie said, scrambling eggs at the stove. "And Julie's got a day's work at the hospital laundry. Maybe their luck's changed for the better."

"Maybe better enough to find another place to live," George said. "At least the Brants'll be gone when I get home tonight. And who's this young lady?" A brown-eyed little girl with light brown hair sat in a chair on a dishpan at the table.

"Stella Griffith's little Zelda. Stella's cleaning rooms at the Westbrook today. Zelda, won't you say hello to Mr. O'Driscoll?" Zelda waved her spoon, flinging oatmeal all around.

George waved, muttering, "Whole damn neighborhood's moving in."

Bridie placed a plate of eggs and a piece of toast on the table for him; then she wiped Zelda's face with a towel.

"Seems all we eat here—eggs, milk and butter—day and night," he said, spreading Ollie Cox's hand-churned butter on his toast.

"And where would we be without Wally's cows and chickens?" Bridie said.

"Come on, Mulligan," Zelda told the yellow dog under the table. "Let's go play." They exited through the hole Bonnie had ripped in the screen door during her accelerated exit the previous night.

"By the way, George, we've no coal for the winter."

"Told you, Bridie. I'll not be providing warmth or sustenance to all these freeloaders living here. I have business in town this morning. Going to Walton's Hardware, the bank and the Roosevelt Garage to get the clutch adjusted on the Chevy."

Finishing breakfast, George put on his hat, shook his head at the hole in the screen and went out, the door slamming behind him. He got into his "glass car," as Anna called his 1927 Chevy, their first car with glass windows instead of curtains.

Bridie was relieved he'd be gone. It was her custom to serve new guests "a decent lunch to make them feel at home." To make it special, she called it a "luncheon." George called it the "beggar's banquet." With a fresh supply of money from Tommy, she phoned

Mr. Harrison and ordered a large ham, a quart of ice cream and a loaf of bread.

"Here, Anna, take this to Harrison's Grocery and pick up my order," Bridie said, handing her a dollar. "Get yourself a penny's worth of candy, and bring back the change." Anna flew out the door. "Tell Mr. Harrison I'll be giving him a piece of my mind now if you come back with last week's bread," Bridie called after her. "And ask if he won't spare Mulligan a bone. Hear me now, Anna?" Her skinny little daughter's gangling figure rounded the corner of the building.

"Morning." Lynn Brant yawned as she entered the kitchen.

"Lovely," Bridie said, admiring her hand-stitched silk housecoat and Hollywood slippers topped with pompoms.

"It's all I could find in the tumble of things we brought over last night."

"There's coffee on the stove," Bridie said.

The madam of the White House had arrived from the great fire looking like a moneyed middle-aged matron, from art deco shoes to a Clara Bow turban hat.

Lynn took a cup from the bookshelves along the wall. "I'm really sorry about Edwin's gun going off last night, Bridie. I'm just thankful it wasn't his machine gun."

"'Twas that bloody goat caused it all," Bridie said.

"I sure hope it didn't scare your poor husband outta his wits."

"Neither of us mentioned it at breakfast this morning."

"Edwin will apologize to him," Lynn said, pouring a cup of coffee. "At least I got to meet your beautiful daughters, Josie and Anna."

"It did stir everybody out of bed."

"So where is everybody this Saturday morning?" Lynn asked, taking a chair at one of the breakfast tables.

"At work or looking for it. Most of the kids went out to play or down to Mr. Markum's dairy to ride their donkey."

"What about the nuns, Bridie? Where are they?"

"Oh, they're gone. Left some time ago. No one has money these days to send girls to a boarding school like this. The nuns asked me to look after the place until happier days return."

"But I see the playground full of kids over here all the time. So we thought the school was open. And adults coming and going. Where'd they all come from?"

"We have plenty of kids living here, all right, and those from the neighborhood come to play with them on the swings and slides. You see, people still come to the door thinking the nuns will give them a sandwich or something. I do what I can, and I offer some of them a room until this thing is all over." Like President Hoover, Bridie believed this thing called the

Great Depression would end like a bad thunderstorm, as abruptly as it began.

"When Wally Cox came over and invited us to stay the night, he said the place was about full," Lynn Brant said.

"The man can't see beyond the brim of his big hat, Lynn. We've three floors and a basement. Enough room for the British army, not that I'd let them in."

"Well then, Bridie, would you mind if we stay until our insurance pays off?"

"Take our welcome as long as you like, Lynn. As I tell everyone, All Saints is a clean, dry place where the rent never comes due."

Trucks from the White House soon started arriving at All Saints. Neighbors watched from front porches as burly men paraded into the convent with furniture, lamps, rugs and an endless number of boxes and barrels. "Looks like enough silverware and china to fill Windsor Castle," Bridie said.

Like a stage manager, Lynn Brant directed the movers: gaming tables and paintings (wrapped in plain brown paper) to the basement, a pool table to the science laboratory, teakwood furniture, drapes and a red rug to the bishop's parlor, a canopied bedroom suite to her and Edwin's room.

Balancing privacy with proximity to the three privies in the convent, the Brants took two rooms on the third floor. Even if it was a breathless climb, it was the least populated and offered a bathroom with the only bathtub in the building. Edwin Brant also took a storage closet and padlocked the door. At the foot of the stairs, he tossed a fifty-cent coin into the coffee can with its crayon label, "Let there be light," where residents deposited spare change to help pay the next light bill.

Up the staircase, Edwin pondered a large hand-lettered sign tacked to the wall on the second-floor landing:

Fear Not. The Lord Is With Thee.

Bridie had put it up after the light company had shut off the electricity the first time. "A house prayer for gamblers," Edwin mused, envisioning a casino in the nuns' dormitory on the third floor. He stood aside as a herd of noisy, laughing kids stampeded through an open window from the fire escape and dashed down the stairs.

"Damn kids," a mover cried, wrestling a dresser up the stairs.

"For heaven's sakes, Edwin," Lynn called as he ambled down the steps, "do something with these kids. Take them for a drive. Anything before a piano or something falls on one and—"

"And we *don't* have insurance for that," he said.

Without asking, Lynn replaced the small breakfast tables in Bridie's kitchen with a regal teakwood banquet table and twenty-four matching chairs, their cushions embroidered with Louis XIV's royal coat of arms.

"Grand enough for a bishop," Bridie said, admiring the table that reached right across the former classroom.

"And we have gold candelabra, Spanish silverware and silk table linens to go with it for holidays and other occasions," Lynn said. "We'll throw a party."

"Where are those kids?" Bridie wondered, looking out at the empty playground. "Pray God they haven't gone down to Rosen's Pond and drowned."

She found them in the science laboratory. Edwin Brant was bent over a pool table taking aim at the cue ball.

"Now, what's this you're teaching these children, *Mister* Brant?"

"Ballistics and geometry by way of an ancient and honorable game of skill," he said. Small and wiry with alert blue eyes, the diminutive Mr. Brant looked like a bald-headed Napoleon, his pate shiny as polished glass. "It's a combination of art and science, skill and a little luck." He pointed his cue stick to "The Rules of Eight Ball" he'd written on the classroom chalkboard. "Today's lesson."

"But no lessons, Professor Brant, in the unholy art of gambling."

"Ah…if only I knew the art, Bridie. If only I knew the art."

Anna returned from Harrison's with bread, ham and a beefy dog bone. In midafternoon, Bridie invited the Brants into her kitchen.

"Irish linen?" Lynn asked, stroking the tablecloth that covered one end of the new banquet table.

"I brought it from Ireland."

Josie chipped ineptly at a block of ice with an ice pick and admired Lynn Brant, whose fading beauty lingered in sharply etched facial features, a perfect nose and a strong jaw. Wisps of gray laced her lustrous blonde hair

"Here, Josie, let me do that," Edwin said, taking the ice pick from her.

His softly fuzzy voice and warm smile put Josie at ease. She had seen the notorious Mr. Brant occasionally at a distance—on Sunday afternoons down at Rosen's Pond, shooting beer bottles with a shiny pistol.

"What a lovely lunch," Lynn said, peeking inside the pots on the stove.

"The peas and sweet potatoes are fresh from Ollie's little garden," Bridie said, slicing the loaf of bread. Ollie complained that the sterile soil produced more rocks than vegetables.

Edwin stepped back from the massacred block of ice to admire his handiwork. Josie picked up ice chips scattered round the kitchen.

"Men undo more than they do," Lynn sighed, helping Josie collect ice chips from the floor.

"Look, Bridie," Edwin said, "no need having chipped ice all over the floor. We stored several refrigerators in your basement. I'll have the movers bring one up, one that actually makes ice in little trays, too."

"An electric icebox," Bridie said. "Why, we'd really be uptown. Thank you, Edwin."

Anna entered the kitchen, noisily took a chair at the long table and announced, "I washed my hands."

"A breakthrough in world hygiene," Josie said, distributing glasses of ice at the table. Anna stuck her tongue out at her sister.

"What's this mile-long table doing in our kitchen?" Anna wanted to know.

"Gives you plenty of elbow room," Edwin said.

Bridie filled her Waterford crystal glasses with tea. A drink foreign to her when she came to Texas, iced tea had become "as essential against the heat as holy water against hell," she said every summer.

"Now some broth," she said, ladling steaming soup into bowls.

Anna giggled when she saw Mulligan's bone at the bottom of the pot. She'd been warned to stay quiet. "It's not a dog's bone 'til it's given to the dog," Bridie had told her.

Inviting everyone to take a seat, Bridie and her daughters abruptly bowed their heads and made the sign of the cross. "Bless us, oh, Lord, and these thy gifts which we are about to receive from thy bounty." Edwin and Lynn Brant glanced at each other and bowed their heads.

"Where'd you get the giggly juice, Mr. Brant?" Anna asked as he poured something other than iced tea from a bottle he had under the table.

"Rescued from the fire. You know how it is, kid. Someone has to drink it."

"Yeah, the nuns say it's a sin to waste anything with all those people starving in China."

"Starving and thirsty," he said, sipping the liquor.

After finishing his lunch, Edwin refilled his glass and lifted a Romeo y Julieta from his shirt pocket. Anna slipped the embossed gold band from the cigar over her index finger. Blue smoke scented the table with a sweet, aromatic fragrance.

"Bridie," Edwin said, "maybe I shouldn't bring this up at the table, but I found what looked like a murdered mouse this morning on the third-floor landing. The little thing had a tail, a head, a skeleton and nothing else."

"A ghost mouse," Bridie said, explaining how Q.C. stripped his prey right down to the skeleton.

"If you think that's spooky, wait'll you see Q.C.," Josie said.

"Also," Edwin asked, "what's with that schedule of times and dates and names up on the third floor? Tacked to the bathroom door? Do we need a reservation to use the bathroom?" He chuckled, exhaling cigar smoke.

"The bathing schedule. We've only the one bathtub in the whole place, so not everyone can bathe at the same time, you see. So there's—"

"Mr. and Mrs. Cox bathe at the same time," Anna said. "I've heard them in there splashing around together."

"Saves water," Lynn interjected.

"Didn't save any water," Anna said. "It was splashed all over the floor and the walls like they'd been wrestling or something in there."

"Don't talk with your mouth full, Anna," Bridie said icily. "So, Edwin, with only one bathtub, baths have to be scheduled, especially on Saturdays."

"I see," he said, his eyes slanted toward Anna in anticipation of more revelations about the bathing habits of Mr. and Mrs. Cox.

"Just write in your name and the time you'll be bathing," Bridie hurried on. "And it's polite to wash out the tub after yourself."

"But if you leave your soap up there, people will use it all up," Anna warned, scraping her pudding bowl clean.

"Love your red hair, kiddo," Lynn said to Josie, turning the talk in a new direction. "And by the way, just who are our fellow tenants or whatever we're called here?"

"Inmates!" Anna blurted. "That's what Dadda calls 'em. Bloody inmates and derelicts from—"

"Watch your tongue, Anna!" Bridie said.

"Your dadda?" Edwin frowned.

"He's the man you almost shot last night," Lynn said. "The girls call their daddy Dadda."

Edwin bowed his head. "I'll apologize to him soon as we meet."

"Our dadda left this morning to see his bootlegger and his banker," Anna said.

"The only prosperous people left in America," Edwin said. "And you can't be too sure about those bankers anymore."

"So now that we're one of the inmates," Lynn said, "will you introduce us to our fellow jailbirds sometime, Bridie?"

"At Sunday dinner. Couple of times a month, we gather here in my kitchen and cook and eat and talk all afternoon."

"And Dadda and the other men pass around the hooch," Anna said.

"No!" Edwin said, clapping hand over heart. "I'm shocked. On Sunday! And in a holy place like this!"

"Yeah, they do," Anna giggled. "And Mr. Cox sneaks upstairs and sips from that hot water bottle hanging on the end of his bed."

"Ah…the old hot water bottle trick, eh? A dead giveaway to any rookie dry agent. I'll have to give Mr. Cox one of my hollow walking canes."

"He could sneak a sip in church with that," Anna said.

"The men do sip a bit," Bridie said. "'It's the strangest law, this prohibition against spirits. No home in Ireland is without whiskey and holy water." It was her preface to all discussions about a law that had left an entire society fixated on finding its next drink.

"You know, Bridie, no one would ever suspect a still in a place like this."

"You and George will make good soul mates," she said nervously.

"Or cell mates," Lynn said sharply. "Just forget it, Edwin. We're outta all that business for good. Remember and remember why!"

"Out of it, Lynn, but closer to it than you think."

"And what's that supposed to mean?" she said.

Taking his bottle from under the table, Edwin said, "If Bridie doesn't tell you about the business in the basement, I'm sure Anna will."

"No, we're not allowed to talk about our still," Anna said.

JULIE'S LAMENT

Drained after ten endless hours in the hot, steamy hospital laundry, Julie sat limp on the back porch, watching the younger kids blow off energy on the playground after dinner.

She smoked and vaguely listened to the clamor of childish chatter, pleased with the dollar and a half she'd earned. It had been a day of surprises, the job in the laundry and then Sister Mary Xavier's hinting of part-time work clerking in Saint Joseph's emergency room.

But the day's biggest jolt was coming home to find that Edwin and Lynn Brant had moved into All Saints. Although Julie wasn't Catholic, she wondered what had possessed Bridie to let the proprietors of Fort Worth's most infamous, most exclusive whorehouse move into a Catholic convent.

Everyone knew that Bridie seemed to accept the world and everyone in it as God's creations, regardless of past or present imperfections. Those who raised questions about fellow residents knew well her familiar mantra: "Let's not be judging those whose sins differ from our own."

Julie, however, was in no forgiving mood about the would-be sins of Jonathan Quinlan. She wondered if anyone in Bridie's kitchen this morning had noticed his making a pass at her. Time had come to quash the boy's one-sided romance before his misguided overtures got any more out of hand.

Julie partly blamed herself for kindling Jonathan's juvenile infatuation. Knowing they'd lost their mother, she had taken a matronly interest in all three Quinlan brothers when they moved into All Saints. She talked to them as if they were her own, reaching out with a pat on the back, a hug, a smile, an encouraging word. They hung out in her room with Juliana and Jeremy whenever their dad's drinking put him in a foul mood. But Jonathan's interest in her had graduated from adolescent admiration to lusty glances and now to callow advances.

As she pondered exactly what to say to Jonathan, curses and screams erupted from the playground. She snuffed out her cigarette and ran down the back steps.

Matthew Quinlan and Richard Levitz had squared off in a "sword fight." The other kids cheered them on. Confiscating their weapons—two pointed pickets from a fence—she threatened to send them to bed early.

Jonathan came out the back door as Julie returned to the porch. "I'm about to put your brother and that Levitz kid in chains," she said jovially, taking a chair and resting her feet on the porch railing. "If Bridie had heard them, she would've washed out their mouths with soap."

"Tell Matthew if he gives you any more trouble, I'll kick his...his you-know-what," Jonathan said.

"Watch it or she'll be washing out your mouth with soap. Going back to school tomorrow, Jonathan?"

"Yeah, gotta catch the old four o'clock train," he groused. He watched her pretty face flicker in the flame of a match as Julie lit another cigarette. Feeling his eyes scanning her semi-prone body, she took her feet off the railing and put them back on the floor.

"Got a spare cigarette, Julie?" Jonathan said.

"No, Jonathan. You're seventeen, you're in high school, and you're a football player."

"I never smoke in Austin," he said, stung by her rebuke.

"Be sure to say goodbye to Juliana and Jeremy before you leave tomorrow."

"You can count on it," he said huskily. Jonathan often played Old Maid cards with her kids, letting Juliana win enough to keep her interested. She fairly drooled over him. And he was Jeremy's idol after teaching the boy to kick a football and showing him pictures of himself in his number 41 jersey.

"Going out tonight?" Julie said.

"We're playing penny poker over at Robert Fuller's house." Jonathan was tempted to boast that, en route, he was picking up cigarettes and bootleg liquor from his stash down by Rosen's Pond.

"Have fun and be careful," Julie said as he went down the steps.

Though he cringed at her motherly tone, the quarterback for Saint Edward's' undefeated team knew that Julie Bryant was as taken with him as all the girls were back in Austin. She was just playing hard to get, the way of all women, a challenge he was ready to tackle.

The next afternoon, Julie told Juliana and Jeremy to go play at Mr. Markum's dairy on the side of the hill, where they rode the donkey with the Markum kids. "I get to ride Jack-the-ass first," Juliana told Jeremy.

"It's Jack the donkey," Julie said.

"Well, Mr. Markum calls him Jack-the-ass," she said. "And something else when Jack's bad."

Julie planned to be firm without embarrassing Jonathan or puncturing his budding male ego. Having grown up with four brothers, she understood how a seventeen-year-old boy might have taken her casual warmth and friendliness as more than motherly affection.

With curly black hair, warm brown eyes, an aquiline nose and a pearly-white smile, Jonathan was a Hollywood-handsome kid. She wondered if she'd said too much, having told him more than once, "You'll soon be even more handsome than your dad, if that's possible."

When Jonathan knocked, Julie opened the door. She didn't smile. "Where are the kids?" he asked, looking round the room.

"They'll be back soon, Jonathan."

"Running late, so give them a hug for me," he said.

With apprehension, she accepted his gentle hug and said, "Jonathan, listen. We've got to talk."

"I know, I know," he whispered, suddenly enveloping her in both arms, lightly kissing her neck and sighing in her ear.

Julie felt Jonathan's unyielding strength, his iron shoulders and his flat, firm torso pressing against her body as she struggled and pushed at him. "Stop, Jonboy. Stop it now!"

At the sound of her shrill voice, Jonathan let go and stood away, towering over her, his face ghastly pale.

"What do you think you're doing?" Julie's face was red with anger or embarrassment (Jonathan wasn't sure which).

"I thought…," he said. "I thought you wanted to talk…about us. I want you, Julie. I—"

"Go catch your train, Jonathan," Julie said, her voice thin and cold. "And forget this ever happened. Go."

As he went out the door, he whispered, "I love you, Julie," as if it were their secret.

Julie collapsed in a chair, tears running down her cheeks, her hands shaking. "Oh God, how did this happen?"

BRIDIE'S ORPHANS

"Jesus, Mary and Joseph! When I came in last night, I thought I'd stumbled into a bloody bordello, I did!"

"And how would you be knowing about bordellos, George O'Driscoll?" Bridie asked, serving him a plate of scrambled eggs, toast and ham left over from her banquet for the Brants.

"And for God's sake, where did you get this massive table, Bridie? It must've come from Buckingham Palace."

"The Brants brought it along with other furniture from the White House," she said.

"Just wait'll the nuns see this place," George said. "They'll think the devil's moved in, and they won't be far wrong. Have you seen the parlor, I ask? Looks like hell's waiting room with that red rug and the gaudy furniture. I can't believe you let the likes of the Brants move in."

"Shush now, George," she whispered, sitting down with her newspaper. "They'll be hearing you up on the third floor."

"Looks like they've taken over the whole convent. A billiard table in the science lab. A piano under the staircase. Harlots' furniture in the parlor. Have they put gaming tables in the chapel yet?"

"They won't be staying long, George. Only until their insurance pays off."

"Arson. I knew it. The insurance will never pay up. And they'll stay forever, like all the rest of the vagrants hanging out here. On the other hand, Bridget, arson is a crime that will get them a place to stay—a place called prison. And what's this?"

"Why, George, it's an electric icebox, of course," Bridie said, standing back to admire the new appliance. "Edwin Brant had the movers install it yesterday."

"Electric icebox?" George said, studying the tall, white enamel box. "You mean electric refrigerator. You can't pay the light bill half the time now."

"But we won't be buying ice anymore, George, and Edwin said the icebox...refrigerator...will keep your beer colder."

"Well, he's probably right about that," George said, his voice softening.

"Sister called yesterday from Dallas," Bridie said, taking advantage of this mellow moment to deliver some news.

"Don't tell me. You're holy sister's sending more ex-cons from Huntsville."

"An orphan. He'll be on the bus from Dallas."

"Another of those little street urchins. We always know when your beloved sister moves from prisons to orphanages by the kind of misfits she sends over here. Thank God there's no leper colony in Texas."

"The Dunne Home is brimming over with the little fellas, George."

"And this place is brimmin' over with derelicts from everywhere. We'll soon be in the street ourselves."

"It's not as if we're paying rent here, George."

"Neither is that parasite living in our house over in Bessie Street. When'd he last pay the rent?"

"He's disabled, ye know. A hero from the Great War."

"Another hero on the dole. He'll die before we collect from the bastard."

"Maybe he has life insurance," Bridie said, laughing at her husband's random fits of rancor—his habit of periodically lashing out at ex-convicts, orphans, disabled veterans, Jews, Baptists, Negroes, Mexicans, the unemployed, the insane and others blocking his path to the American Dream.

"You're laughing at me again. You don't take me seriously."

"No, George, not always."

He gulped a final swallow of coffee, stood up from the table, took his jacket and hat and started out the door.

"The lad's name is Frankie Feldman. He'll be on the two-thirty Greyhound."

"Feldman? She's sending another Jew?"

"He's a child of God, and she turns none away. She's sending money to help with the other boys she's already sent us."

"Money? So she's been playing the horses again, has she?"

"And returned with another bag of money."

"Surely the bishop doesn't know one of his nuns is working the racetrack?"

Seeking new sources of revenue for the orphanage, Sister Vee posted herself at the entrance to the Arlington Downs Racetrack, situated halfway between Fort Worth and Dallas for the convenience of the citizens of both cities.

"May the luck of Saint Patrick be with ye," the rosy-cheeked little nun called to the crowds. "And may you share your good fortune with our little orphan boys at the Dunne Home Orphanage."

Some race fans bought futures in the luck of Saint Patrick as they entered the grounds. "Say a little prayer for my horse, Sister," they'd say, dropping coins and the odd dollar into the open black bag at her feet.

But it was after the races when she bagged the big money. Grateful winners—especially those who'd been drinking—shared the good luck she had blessed them with as they went in. Even some losers, repentant over their prodigal ways, dropped offerings into her bag. "Say a prayer for me, Sister, and say it before I get home."

With no competition from other churches or the Salvation Army, Sister Vee held a tainted corner on an otherwise untapped source of charity. And before the first racing season ended, she upped the odds in her favor even more by taking an orphan to the races.

Properly attired for the occasion in tattered and patched clothes, George Salih, frail, skinny, his bare feet in sandals, held the black bag and smiled meekly at the passing throngs. Sister Vee's daily take rose substantially as the happy horse crowds filled the pale boy with hot dogs and his bag with greenbacks.

"Your sister's the only one I've ever known who never loses at the track," George said.

"Now, don't forget the lad at the bus station," Bridie said.

"But take in no more inmates."

"No, George, not today."

Searchlight, Nevada

Dear Josie,

Found your welcome letter in the package and the cookies were very good. I would very much like to hear you play the Irish tunes. Can you play "O'Donnell Abu" yet? I am enclosing a cheque for $50. It will help to buy your violin. Also a dollar for Anna.

We will have lots of fun when I go to Fort Worth. You and Anna can have all the ice cream and soda pop you want. Give the cheque of $64.13 to your dear mother. Tell her not to write as I may be leaving here at any time.

See you Christmas, if possible.

Love,
Your Uncle Tom
Erin Go Bragh

THE GOOD JEW

After the White House burned, little else remained of Sam Rosen's once-popular White City Resort and Amusement Park. To entice visitors from downtown Fort Worth to stay the weekend, he had built a stately Victorian mansion at the edge of his park.

He coated it in white paint—blinding bright in the Texas sun—and called it the White City Hotel, complete with restaurant and bar. Everyone else called it the White House. It stood mirage-like on a bluff overlooking a small hollow of pecan trees and the pretty pond Sam created by damming up a stream that ran down to the broader Trinity River Valley.

Sam's White City Resort and Amusement Park was an extension of Rosen Heights, a working-class community of houses, schools, grocery stores, filling stations and a variety of churches, the latter on land given them by Sam Rosen. And in 1906, the Sisters of Charity of the Incarnate Word opened All Saints Convent and Girls School on a choice plot Sam Rosen had set aside for them. A stone wall enclosed the imposing three-story building on three sides, leaving a view of the pond and the new White City Hotel on the opposite bluff.

Sam, with steely indifference, ignored the Ku Klux Klan's bigoted babble that his gift "to these Roman nuns is more proof of the Jewish–Catholic conspiracy to create a one-world government"—even if Catholics and Jews regarded each other with as much disdain and damnation as the KKK heaped on both "foreign" religions.

For their part, grateful if graceless Catholics called Sam Rosen "the good Jew." And the Sisters of Charity prayed fervently for their benefactor's conversion to Catholicism "to save this Jew's soul from the eternal fires of hell."

Firm in his own faith and a pragmatic businessman, Sam had no quarrel with how others worshipped, and he was pleased when Father Bob Nolan invited him to the dedication of All Saints. "We would be honored, Mr. Rosen, if you would join us and perhaps say a few words," Father Nolan said.

"I speak no Latin," Sam said.

"English will suffice," the priest said, chuckling into the phone. "I do apologize for the late notice. It's this Sunday."

"I'm free Sundays."

After the ceremony, Sam reported to his wife, "A monsignor prayed in Latin, a priest burned incense, nuns sang, and a bishop consecrated the land and blessed our little pond. Thanks to these Gentiles, Rosen Heights has its own Holy Land now."

"Something new for your ads, Sam," Betty Rosen said of the weekly newspaper advertisements that drew prospective residents to his development.

Rosen Heights expanded rapidly on a broad plateau overlooking the flood-prone Trinity River Valley. Across the wide valley, downtown Fort Worth huddled on another plateau behind the Palace of Justice, as cynical citizens dubbed the extravagant pink granite courthouse. A monument to taxpayer debt, it stood on Trinity River Bluff one-hundred ten feet above the river, where the old wooden fort once commanded a view of the valley and the farms below.

Sam Rosen, said even by Gentiles to be as honest as God, never envisioned his White City Hotel becoming a speakeasy, not even for Fort Worth's honorable elite. As downtown built up, however, fewer and fewer people trundled out to the amusement park on Sam's Rosen Heights streetcar line. Fewer still stayed overnight at the White House.

Prohibition took an even greater toll on Sam's hotel, at least before he sold it. If the Eighteenth Amendment to the Constitution had shut it down, this strange new law had inspired less savory entrepreneurs to buy the White House for a song from the Rosen Heights Land Company.

To Sam's dismay and embarrassment, the new owners, Edwin and Lynn Brant, remodeled the mansion to fit their seedy designs (guest bedrooms with mirrored walls and ceilings, a casino in the basement, erotic statues and nude paintings everywhere). Within months, it reopened as a speakeasy in the early days of the nation's noble experiment (as President Hoover famously described Prohibition). The Brants' shady enterprise quickly pole-vaulted to social and economic heights the hotel had never known as a legitimate business.

Though chagrined that his hotel had become a house of debauchery, Sam took some consolation that a religious community—thanks to his generosity—thrived as a balancing moral force on the opposite bluff. All Saints taught young girls the virtues of virginity and the power and glory of God in the strict religious regimen of boarding school life. And a fair number of them took the veil and the vows of the nunnery themselves, in keeping with the sisters' hopes and prayers.

Despite All Saints' almost thirty years of success, its days were numbered. Although the school's bawdy neighbor across the pond continued to prosper, the Great Depression forced the nuns to close the doors at All Saints—or almost close them.

Sam Rosen's land deed required them to keep their convent school "continuously occupied for fifty years." After praying for divine guidance, the Sisters of Charity reasoned they met the terms so long as "anyone" occupied the convent. Legal, if not moral, scholars might have agreed with them.

Thus they asked Bridie O'Driscoll to "keep All Saints continuously occupied until happier days return." In light of the hard times and assuming the sisters would reopen the school someday, the good Jew of Rosen Heights kept his silence, even after Bridie turned the abandoned convent into "a refuge for street urchins, beggars and other freeloading derelicts," as her husband characterized those unfortunates who came knocking at the door seeking charity from nuns no longer there.

But if Sam Rosen saw justice redeemed when the White House burned to the ground, he was aghast when its seamy owners took up residence at All Saints. "I have somehow facilitated the merger of good and evil," he told his wife, throwing up his hands. "Just who is this Bridie O'Driscoll that lets such people in the door, anyway?"

MARTIN AND THE DEVIL

B ridie looked around warily for the source of a
strange, disturbing noise: a mechanical moaning
that became a quaking rumble invading the convent,
rattling windows and echoing like thunder. A Texas
tornado crossed her mind as she reached for her rosary beads hanging next to the stove.

A river of coal and thick black dust thundered
down the chute to the bin in the basement. The con-
cussion blew open the furnace door and fanned the
flames in the burner.

Gripped in the headlock of an alcoholic haze,
Martin sat straight up in his cot to find himself
smothering in a dark cloud of choking dust. He
coughed, barely able to breathe. Flames leapt at
him in the darkness, the furnace itself cloaked in
a mushroom of boiling coal dust. Martin, gripping

a half-empty Mason jar of whiskey, wondered how he'd been killed.

"I'm sorry, God!" he screamed, recoiling from flames dancing wildly in the blackness that enveloped him. "Don't put me down here with the devil."

Martin stumbled up the stairs toward a ray of light where Bridie had opened the stairway door to the basement to investigate the hellish noise below. Black as soot, Martin shot past her, yelling, "No, God! I ain't gonna steal no more cars!"

He bolted through the kitchen like black lightning. The screen door flew off its hinges as he exited and leapt from the back porch. "Please, God, don't let him get me!" he cried, looking over his left shoulder for the devil.

"Saints preserve," Bridie said, heading up the hallway to see who was rapping at the front door.

"Yes, my good man?" she said to a stranger covered in coal dust, standing at her door. He handed her a sheet of paper.

"So ye're the one who scared the wits out of us." Her grin faded as she studied the invoice from the Stockyards Coal & Firewood Company.

"I'm sorry. I've no money, not a penny."

"The nuns always pay when we deliver coal."

"I fear the nuns have long gone, sir."

"Pay now or you'll be in a lot of trouble."

"I'm very sorry, sir. You'll have to take it all back."

"How can I get coal out of a basement?"

"Did I ask you to put your coal in my basement?"

"I'll call the cops," said the man, taking a step towards her.

"Call the deevil if ye like," Bridie said, slamming the door.

"The Lord provides in strange ways," she shrugged. "Thanks be to God and my lucky gold shamrock we'll have heat and hot water for the winter."

Suddenly Bridie feared that Martin, drunker than usual from testing a new batch of product from the still, had run all the way to Rosen's Pond and drowned himself.

After he collided with the merry-go-round, Martin lay there dazed, spinning slowly as he stared at the most heavenly blue sky he had ever seen. He had escaped Satan's grasp. Between thumb and finger, he rubbed his Saint Christopher's good luck charm and promised again never to steal another car.

"Come in, Martin, and I'll make some hot tea and give you an aspirin or two for your head," Bridie called from the back porch as a coal truck groaned down the driveway. "We have coal from heaven…or somewhere."

Much to Bridie's bewilderment, Martin lived in the basement between the furnace and the coal bin instead of taking one of the convent's vacant rooms. He fired the furnace, milked Wally Cox's cows, did other chores and ran George O'Driscoll's still "to help pay my keep."

Martin slept on an army cot below a ventilation window big enough to squeeze through. The backpack under his cot contained his clothes, a wad of cash, brass knuckles, a switchblade knife and a loaded .44 automatic.

Martin had never left the campus since his arrival. He gave little Anna a nickel tip to buy his cigarettes at Harrison's Grocery. All Saints was a safe haven from the police and Jesus H. Cortez. The cops wanted to put him in jail, and Jesus wanted to cut his throat.

A state trooper in a Ford cruiser and a deputy sheriff in a clunky Dodge had cut him off on a country road en route to Waco. Martin drove his beloved stolen Packard, fully loaded with Duke Hamilton's bootleg liquor, into a ditch. A shot rang out as he scrambled under a barbed wire fence and crawled into a field of tall, green corn. After an hour in the sweltering heat swatting swarms of mosquitoes, the exhausted, sweat-drenched cops gave up the chase.

Martin slipped into a barn during the night. He discovered storage bins filled with apples, corn and potatoes. He found cases of liquor under the potatoes—all of them from his abandoned Packard. He ate two apples and a raw potato and downed a quart of liquor.

He awoke next morning looking down double barrels of death—both hammers of a twelve-gauge shotgun cocked back like rattlesnake fangs, the safety off, a boy's finger firmly on the trigger.

"That thing could go off," Martin moaned, wondering whether his head or his stomach hurt the most.

"Yes, sir," said the shoeless teenager, who'd crept into the barn with high hopes of shooting the fox that had been killing his pa's chickens.

When the boy's pa showed up, compromise had been simple. If he called the sheriff, Martin promised to rat on the farmer, who'd stolen the liquor from his Packard while the cops were chasing him through the cornfields.

"You can't drink all that rotgut, anyways," Martin said.

"Never touch it," the farmer snapped. "We're Baptists. Gonna sell it."

"Ever been to jail for bootleggin'?"

They trucked the whiskey to its original destination, a speakeasy behind a Dr. Pepper plant in downtown Waco. The farmer pocketed his half of the cash, drove Martin to Fort Worth and dropped him off late at night at the Greyhound bus station. Neither had asked the other's name.

"Nineteen cents," the waitress said, serving Martin the blue-plate special: fried chicken, mashed potatoes, gravy, green beans, roll and a slice of apple pie. A pretty Mexican teenager—jet-black hair, rosy cheeks—knelt on her knees scrubbing the floor as Martin finished dinner and turned to his pie and coffee.

"Enjoying your last supper, *amigo?*"

Martin dropped his fork—the deep, familiar voice activated his adrenal glands as if someone had put a knife to his throat.

The scrub girl laid her brush aside and stared unabashedly at the towering stranger's face: swarthy as bronze; high cheekbones; long, angular jaws; ivory-white teeth; eyes black and hard as obsidian. She hoped for a nod, maybe a smile.

Jesus Hernando Cortez rested his rangy, six-foot five-inch frame on the stool next to Martin. "What we gonna do with you, Senor Martin?" he said, tilting his cowboy hat back, revealing a mane as blue-black as gunmetal. "Been looking for you since yesterday."

Martin hastily explained to Jesus that he was on his way to see Duke Hamilton with the money. "I can give you half now and—"

"Half, *amigo*?" the tall, statuesque Mexican said, teeth flashing like fangs beneath a luxuriant long-horn mustache.

"Look, it's a long story, Jesus. The cops got my Packard, and some farmers got half the money because—"

"Farmers!" The Duke's hit man laughed.

"I'll steal another car and get the rest of the money next month when I—"

"Know what happened to the last gringo cheated the Duke?" Jesus said, clamping a black cheroot in his white teeth. "He went swimming in the Trinity River. The poor hombre, he could not swim. To save him from drowning, somebody cut his throat."

"Tell the Duke I'll bring the money tonight," Martin said foolishly.

"*Adios, amigo,*" Jesus said, firing up the cheroot with a match, its flame illuminating the rage in his coal-black eyes. Going out the door, he called, "*Que el Dios tenga merced por tu alma.*"

Martin turned to the Mexican scrub girl. "What'd he say?"

"The beautiful man, he blessed you, *senor.*"

"Blessed me?"

"*Si, senor.* He say, 'May God have mercy on your soul.'"

Surveying the dining room, Martin rose from the stool on short, hammy legs; head and shoulders tilted like a charging bear; long, beefy arms dangling down his blocky, truncated torso almost to his knees. Bent slightly forward like a hunchback, he appeared shorter than his bulky five-foot frame suggested.

Martin dropped a silver half-dollar into the scrub girl's soap bucket and bolted through a swinging door at the end of the lunch counter.

"Can't come in here, mister!" a cook yelled.

Martin swept through the kitchen and out a back door. At the Salvation Army Hotel on Commerce Street, he got his bag from the night desk clerk. Outside, he spotted a lone taxi at the curb. "Take me here," he demanded gruffly, pushing a slip of paper in the driver's face.

"Well, shit, man, lemme read this first," the startled cabbie said, taking the paper and turning on the dome light in the cab. "Hmm...out in Rosen Heights, on the north side beyond the stockyards."

Martin piled into the back seat.

"Whatta we lookin' for?" the cabbie said, starting the taxi. "House, business, hotel?"

"Boarding house, I think," Martin said.

The plump little Catholic nun who visited the inmates at Sugar Land State Prison Farm had given him the address just before his release. "It's a place you can stay until you get on your feet again, Martin," she had told him, her smoothly rounded words rolling off one another in the melodic lilt of her Irish brogue. "Just say that Sister Vee sent you." She abruptly hung a sterling silver chain and Saint Christopher's medal around his neck. "This will protect you along the way."

"Like a lucky charm?"

"Something like that, Martin," Sister Vee said, a pert smile on her rosy face.

Fondling the medal, Martin now recalled some of the nun's clever little stories, which she called "para-bulls" (something like that) and read from a book of gossip. Martin liked Sister Vee because—unlike the other Bible thumpers who preached at the prison— she never threatened the inmates with the eternal fires of hell if they didn't take up the ways of the Lord.

"All saints are sinners," she told them in her warm, lovable accent. "And all sinners are saints. All ye need do is find the saint in yereself."

Saint Christopher had brought Martin luck by landing him a job delivering whiskey for Duke Hamilton, Fort Worth's most infamous bootlegger. But, he wondered, why had the saint let him down today?

"Looks like a hotel to me," the driver said as the cab stopped. "That'll be six bits, my friend."

Martin gave him a dollar and stepped from the cab.

"Sorry, got no change."

"It don't matter," Martin said. As the cab turned and departed, its headlights scanned a rock wall along the wide avenue. A dark, rambling building loomed behind it.

To get off the street, Martin felt his way along the wall. It ended at a bluff overlooking a pond shining like a silver dollar under the full moon. He made his way down the slope and sat against a pecan tree. He smoked and watched the moon and the stars.

Just after dawn, eight or so cows waded into the pond to drink. As the sun inched higher, Martin shaved in the muddy water. Late in the morning, he made his way through a minefield of cow patties and followed the rock wall back up to the street. He looked warily in all directions.

The address on Sister Vee's penciled note—Bridie O'Driscoll, 2115 Belle Avenue, Fort Worth, Texas— matched the number on the iron gate. Martin followed the flagstone walkway across the shaded lawn.

A husky yellow dog, tail wagging, trotted over and sniffed the cow shit on his shoes. "It's okay, ol' boy," Martin said, patting his head. He and the mutt went up the steps to a porch. Martin knocked on the massive mahogany doors, waited, knocked again.

A flock of sheep and a lone shepherd looked down at him from a green pasture in stained glass above the doors. Letters etched in the granite archway read, "All Saints Convent and Girls School." Martin sighed, thinking neither Jesus nor the cops would look for him here.

A comely middle-aged woman slowly cracked open one of the great doors and peered out at him. A dish towel over her shoulder, a mop in hand, she wore house slippers, a baggy cotton dress, an apron around her slim waist, gold-rimmed glasses and a quizzical frown on her face. Though they were about the same height, she titled her head and looked down her nose at the short, bulky bear of a man. His massive shoulders, long ropy arms, thick trunk and powerful legs would have better fit a person twice his height. He reminded her of a misshapen midget at a circus sideshow.

"Well now," she said, "you don't look like a bill collector." The woman's voice echoed Sister Vee's musical lilt, her rounded words rolling rhythmically one off the other.

"Sister Vee sent me. I'm Martin."

"I'm Bridie O'Driscoll," she said.

"You know Sister Vee?"

"Indeed. She's my older sister. And how do you know Sister Villlanova, Martin? Sister Vee as you call her."

"Oh...," he mumbled. "I met her along the way somewheres. Didn't know her very long."

"Long enough, I see, for her to introduce you to Saint Christopher," Bridie said, nodding at the silver medal hanging from his neck.

The yellow dog followed Martin inside.

THE FRONT

E dwin Brant tossed his .45 automatic on the seat, piled into the Packard and started the engine. The big, powerful car lumbered down the drive and out the gate, neither hesitating nor sagging under its great load. He and Martin had packed the trunk full, removed the rear seat and stacked cases of President's Choice from floor to window.

It was a pity, Edwin had argued, that Martin distilled the finest whiskey in Texas only to have George O'Driscoll drink it, give it to priests and sell a few bottles to friends at the Knights of Columbus Hall, the Catholic men's club where he played poker on weekends.

"It's as good as any liquor I've ever had," Edwin told them.

"Kentucky's best," tight-lipped, enigmatic Martin said.

Edwin proposed a larger, more lucrative operation. "I'll buy a drugstore to market the product," he explained.

Like other drugstores, his was licensed to sell liquor for medicinal purposes. Hoodwinking inspectors was a matter of bookkeeping and bribes. As *Life* magazine wryly observed, drugstore to drugstore is the shortest distance between two pints.

Walton's Hardware legally sold a full range of distilleries in the shadow of the Palace of Justice, the regal pink granite county courthouse where District Attorney Monty Stewart prosecuted legions of bootleggers five days a week. The only snag in Edwin's plan was Martin. He refused to go to Walton's to select pieces and parts to build a large commercial-size distillery. "I ain't leavin' this place for nobody for no reason," he said stubbornly, without explanation.

"Jesus H. Cortez won't touch you," Edwin told him, aware the enforcer for Duke Hamilton was after Martin for shortchanging him in a bootlegging deal.

"Oh...you know about Jesus and me?"

Edwin nodded. "What counts, Jesus knows about me."

Martin spent several hours at the store selecting vessels, pipes, pressure gauges and other parts from an array of distillation equipment. He assembled the new still in a far corner of All Saints' basement and stepped up production. He used a formula engrained in his memory like the old family recipe that it was.

"Making a few bottles of spirits for yourself and a few friends is one thing," Bridie had warned George, "but running a bootlegging business will surely land you in jail, if not the rest of us as well."

"Didn't they just let the jolly good U.S. Senator from Jolly, Texas, go scot- free after finding a distillery on his ranch?" he said. The press had made hilarious hash hamming up the town's name after the raid at the senator's nearby "jolly-juice farm," as reporters dubbed the place.

"Senator Sheppard denies knowing the still was on his property."

"That's what I'll say, Bridie, when the dry agents come for me. 'Forgive me, sir, for I knew not there was a still in my basement. The Sisters of Charity must've left it down there when they abandoned this godforsaken place.'"

Lynn Brant had refused to sleep with Edwin for a week, so he promised her he'd "get outta this business" as soon as the insurance paid off the White House fire. She reminded him that their life at the Taj Mahal of Texas speakeasies had become tense and dangerous, balancing business between corrupt cops, who wanted more payola, and bootlegger gangs, who wanted a slice of the profits.

Lethal, overdressed entrepreneurs from Kansas City had wanted the White House itself. They promoted their own products in cocky voices, wooden smiles and angular bulges under hand-tailored coats.

An obliging host, Edwin Brant returned their smiles, his crystal ocean-blue eyes revealing nothing as he studied each of them. He drank their fine whiskey, laughed at their bad jokes and told them good war stories. They flinched when the .45 automatic suddenly appeared in his right hand (from a rack under the table).

"I had it chrome plated when I came home from the war," Edwin said, fondling it with affection. "I added the pearl handles, of course. Isn't it just beautiful?"

Edwin also showed them the medal General Blackjack Pershing had pinned on his chest at the Arch of Triumph in Paris. They noticed the dried blood on his bayonet. The men from Kansas City passed the medal and the bayonet around the table. Edwin held the .45, loaded, a ready bullet in the firing chamber.

"Yeah, they say I killed more Germans than anybody else in our regiment."

"But that was a long time ago, that war," a short, heavyset thug who called himself Ace Anthony said, staring at Edwin across the table. A fedora he never removed shadowed his bulldog face. "Maybe ya lost your touch by now," he added. Wiggling uncomfortably against the seams of his silk suit and adjusting the bulge under his coat, he handed the bayonet back to his host.

"At thirty yards, I miss a beer bottle about one out of ten shots with this," Edwin said, patting the .45. "At twenty yards, I never miss. So, yeah, I'm slipping." He lifted his chin and looked down his face at the bulldog. A metallic click broke the ensuing silence as he sheathed the bayonet in its steel scabbard.

The Kansas City men in their Italian suits cut directly to business.

"You take this here good European whiskey, and we cut it about thirty percent with water. Hardly anyone notices and we all make money." They smiled in unison at their brilliance and their generosity in offering to cut him in on their operation, their first step, he knew, to taking over the White House.

Edwin delivered the reply he had prepared before they arrived: "Gentlemen, I'm afraid I've spoiled my customers. They're the kind of people who don't mind paying good money for the good stuff, undiluted. Our European whiskey comes via Mexico—it's cheaper than this liquor you bring down from Canada." He paused. "Must be because Mexico's a little closer?"

As the out-of-towners left the White House empty-handed, the bulldog pulled the fedora down tighter on his head. "We'll be in touch, my friend."

"It was nice of you to come all the way down from Kansas."

"Yeah, and you'll be hearing from..." The bulldog fell silent midsentence as the light in Edwin Brant's ocean-blue eyes glazed over like ice, turned to marble and looked through him the way a blind man does— as if he were not there anymore.

Packing his .45 automatic and a machine gun on the floorboard, watching over his shoulder and keeping an eye on the Packard's rearview mirror had drained some of the good from the good life the Brants had built up during the nineteen twenties.

A black Dodge had followed Edwin across town one night. It was parked next morning a block from the White House under an elm tree on Northwest Twenty-Fourth Street. A blue ribbon tied in a big bow around a red stick of dynamite appeared on the running board of Edwin's Packard. An explosion in the pond between the White House and the convent killed some fish and awakened half of Rosen Heights one night.

Then came the phone call. "Ace Anthony here, Edwin. We're comin' down next week to offer you a new and final deal."

"Don't waste your time, Ace," Edwin said. "And don't bother me again."

A week later, the police found a dead man in the pond behind All Saints. The bullet had entered the right eye and exited the back of the head. The victim wore a silk suit and an empty shoulder holster. They found a crushed fedora on the pond's muddy bank. The papers called it a "mob job" after the coroner removed a small fish lodged in the unidentified victim's throat.

"Who's the stiff in the lake?" Lynn asked after police questioned Edwin.

"No idea," he said, somewhat truthfully. And it hardly mattered. He knew there would be others. Chicago, Kansas City and Fort Worth had a surplus of hard-boiled hoods—cheap, dangerous copycats of John Dillinger, Machine Gun Kelley, Bonnie and Clyde, Pretty Boy Floyd.

"We've never had trouble here until this," she said. "So what's the story?"

"They say the man couldn't talk, Lynn, with that fish in his throat."

She studied her man's face and peered into his alluring blue eyes in search of something reassuring. He feared she was about to demand the dark facts, something she'd never done.

Affable and gregarious, Lady Lynn had always managed the White House and welcomed their customers like old friends. As the lady of the house, she presided over the lounge rooms, the dining rooms, the kitchen and the ever-popular mirrored "guest rooms" upstairs. Her dirtiest duties encompassed watching over the hostesses, seeing the girls didn't take too much time off during their monthlies. And she saw to it they paid Doc Cooper for their periodic exams in as much whiskey and warm flesh as he could handle.

Edwin had shielded her from the underside of the business—paying the cops, dealing with bootleggers, bankrolling politicians' campaign funds, keeping employees honest, especially those running gaming tables in the basement casino. He supplied judges, politicians and other high rollers with their favorite needs, however simple or quirky. And when there was a disturbance, he quelled it quickly, quietly with whatever force was required. Lynn had only a vague notion of her husband's darker duties.

Edwin studied her fondly, recalling how strikingly pretty she had been at twenty-five—a smoky blonde, slim, willowy and smart. Short, bald and broke, he'd had nothing to lose when he asked her to dance. Maybe she'd liked his uniform, his war medal and the stories he told her about wartime Paris.

"The French people loved us."

"The French girls, you mean," she replied.

Lady Lynn was still on the slim side, still somewhat willowy and, he thought, still…

"Okay, Edwin," she said, breaking up his reverie. "I don't wanna hear about it. But this business is getting scary. We've talked about getting out, and now's the time…while we have a little money and before we get hurt."

Striving to please the only woman he'd ever loved, Edwin promised her a legitimate life forever after. And on a clear, sunny day in the fall, he had all the furniture moved outside. He threw a lawn party that lovely moonlit evening and burned the White House to the ground.

Edwin hadn't revealed that their funds were not as flush as Lynn believed them to be. She was not involved in the stiff payoffs and other underground "taxes" it took to run the White House. Mainly, she didn't know about Edwin's waning luck with the horses at Arlington Downs. Short of cash, he'd offered Quin Quinlan an investment opportunity in the drugstore venture.

"You can't lose," Edwin told him.

"Thing is, I can't afford to lose," Quin said. "As a businessman myself, I think you have a reasonable chance of success, but I can't risk my promise to Marion to send our sons to Notre Dame."

So Edwin sold the land where the stately White House once stood back to Sam Rosen. "You guys always win," Edwin said, disappointed in the sales price.

"You didn't think so, Mr. Brant," Sam said, exhaling the light blue smoke of a La Gloria Cubana. "Not when you purchased the White House from me for a song, as they say, back in twenty-one."

Sam Rosen fell silent, squinting at Edwin through the veil of their cigar smoke in his modest frame office at Northwest Twenty-Fifth and North Main. "I would've offered you more if that great house hadn't been destroyed in the unfortunate fire, though not as much as you hope to get from the insurance company."

Edwin pitched his plan to open a new drugstore with a pharmacy if he could only get a loan. "It'll be on the southeast side, so it won't compete with your Rosen Heights Drugstore."

"And what do you know about drugstores?" Sam asked, an angry edge to his voice. "Other than most are fronts for bootlegging? Is that what you're up to again? I never would have sold the White House if I'd known you were going to turn it into a bordello and speakeasy."

"Mr. Rosen, I have a reputable partner—a physician, Doctor Cooper—who'll manage the pharmacy and hire a licensed pharmacist," Edwin said. Sam nodded. Known as the benevolent Czar of Rosen Heights, there was little he didn't know about the neighborhood and the people who lived in the houses he'd built there. He knew that Doc Cooper was an affable, white-haired gentleman who drank a little too much and had patronized the White House. He also knew that Doc Cooper took care of the sick whether they paid him or not.

And Edwin Brant knew that Captain Samuel Rosen, Commander, Company D, Second Regiment, Texas Voluntary Infantry, was a veteran of the

Spanish–American War. A Russian immigrant, Sam was immensely proud to have "served as an officer in the Army of the United States," as he liked to put it, in perhaps the only breach of modesty he ever allowed himself. He'd smoked Havana cigars as a symbol of victory ever since he'd returned from Cuba.

So Sergeant Brant looked Captain Rosen in the eye, veteran to veteran, and said in a sincere, contrite voice, as if confessing his sins to a priest, "This is a chance for me to lead a good, honest life, Mr. Rosen—the best chance I've had since I came home from the Great War. All I want is to live up to the honor that came with this medal." Edwin took the World War I Bronze Star from his pocket and laid it on the desk.

Sam took the medal in his hand and studied it carefully. He nodded and gave it back to Edwin. "All right, I'll take a chance on you," he said.

Edwin was less concerned about the heavy note on his newly opened New York Drugstore after George O'Driscoll landed the lucrative Knights of Columbus account. Edwin knew nothing about the Catholic men's club except that its members consumed untold crates of President's Choice at their weekly poker games, dinners and dances held in the honor of one saint or another.

"How do they get away with serving all that booze?" Edwin asked George.

"There are nearly as many cops in the Knights of Columbus as there are in the Ku Klux Klan," George explained.

Edwin told Lynn that the drugstore would survive as a legitimate business if Prohibition unfortunately ended, a campaign promise made by the Democrats' presidential candidate, Frank or Frankie something Roosevelt.

With a marble-topped fountain serving Cokes, banana splits, shakes and an array of ice cream flavors, Edwin's drugstore also featured off-the-shelf medicines, cosmetics, popular dry goods, magazines and a pharmacy.

A pharmacist filled prescriptions and hawked a plethora of over-the-counter cures: Texas Fig Syrup for Sluggish Intestines, Dr. Warner's Tonic to Revive the Entire Masculine System, Castoright for Diarrhea and Constipation, Dr. Cristobal's Imported Spanish Salts for Kidneys that Hurt, AspirinPlus ("Better for Colds than Whiskey") and other nostrums of the age. On whispered requests, they also sold rubbers, as customers called condoms.

Doc Cooper kept afternoon hours in a clinic behind the pharmacy, where he treated patients and wrote prescriptions—a great many of them for medicinal whiskey for those suffering back pain and other elusive symptoms. While still keeping his usual morning hours in his old office at the back of the

Rosen Heights Drugstore on the North Side, the doc complained to Edwin, "I used to work mornings and drink afternoons until I got this second job with you."

"You should thank me for keeping you sober until sundown," Edwin said.

With profits from the drugstore and the rich Knights of Columbus account, Edwin hoped to buy the old Hackberry Dance Hall, the last of Sam Rosen's White City Amusement Park next to the burned White House. Beyond dancing and a big band, the new Hackberry would become a high-end speakeasy, casino and bordello. *If only the damned insurance company would pay up*, Edwin thought as he turned off Vickery Boulevard to New York Avenue, a tree-lined street of small green lawns and modest, well-kept frame houses.

Two men read newspapers in a Ford V-8 Roadster, half a block beyond the New York Drugstore. Edwin shifted the Packard to second and took the pearl-handled .45 in his right hand. The roadster suddenly lurched from the curb and sped directly toward him. A tall, thin man in a long black raincoat stepped out of the early morning shadows, a cigar in his mouth, a tommy gun cradled in his left arm. As "Mad" Maddox Moran braced the machine gun against his shoulder, the roadster made a squealing, tire-smoldering U-turn and fled.

"I shoulda riddled 'em," Maddox said, "but I didn't want to draw no cops to our business here. I don't think those boys'll be back for a fountain Coke today."

"Not 'til their mommy changes their diapers," Edwin said. "I'll catch up with the bastards. They're Duke Hamilton's boys."

YIDDISHE KOP

Elizabeth Wellington turned up the sidewalk at 312 Northwest Twenty-Fifth Street. Inside the white frame building, she joined a line of men and women in a narrow hallway. As they filed into a small waiting room, redheaded Miss Maggie welcomed them like old friends. When someone exited the office behind her desk, she nodded to the next person. "He's waiting for you right in there."

Beyond the door sat Sam Rosen, known in the Jewish community as a man with a *Yiddishe kop*— loosely translated for Gentiles as "smart thinker." Entering his office, Elizabeth found a short, well-proportioned man hunkered down behind piles of paper and file folders stacked on a desk sprinkled with cigar ashes.

"Come in, come in please, and take a seat," Sam told Elizabeth, dusting cigar ashes from his shirt and pants as he stood to greet her. "I'm Sam Rosen." He wore a warm smile, bowing slightly as he reached across his desk to shake her hand.

"Elizabeth Wellington," she said softly, taking a chair in front of his desk. She thought him remarkably fit for a man in his sixties, sporting a stylish mustache and a pate of silver-gray hair retreating across his broad forehead.

"What can I do for you, Mrs. Wellington?" he asked. Sitting again in his swivel chair, puffing contentedly on his Havana cigar, he sized her up as shy, embarrassed, about thirty. She was pleasantly plump and deliberately plain with no lipstick or rouge to spiff up her anemic white face and sad gray eyes.

Elizabeth sat quietly, looking at the floor, saying nothing. Many began this way, in stony silence. If their whispered speech was barely audible at times, Sam often knew their stories as well as he knew the people who brought their troubles to his cluttered desk. Most of them lived in the houses he had built in Rosen Heights, many of them workers in the nearby stockyards and meatpacking plants. The lucky ones still worked part-time now. The others had lost their jobs.

They needed a little money—to get a sore tooth pulled, to get the car fixed or the lights turned on again. Others needed time—"a few more days"—to pay rent or mortgage to the Rosen Heights Land Company. For most, coming through his door was a soul-breaking confession of failure and humiliation. Not a few cried at Sam Rosen's desk.

"My husband's looking for work in another city," Elizabeth began, haltingly measuring out her words in a bleak monotone. "I haven't worked in a month. Now my daughter, Gabi, is sick and needs medicine." She wiped her eyes.

"Now, now, Mrs. Wellington, these are tough times even for good, hard-working people like us," he said, his words carefully chosen to allow people to forgive themselves of the blame they carried inside. "How much do you need for medicine to make your Gabi well again?"

"Seventy-five cents."

"Take two dollars in case she needs more. And you pray and I pray, and your little girl will get well again," Sam said, his charming Russian accent ringing with Slavic sounds. "I understand you live up there in the convent with Bridie O'Driscoll."

"I do, Mr. Rosen. So you know Bridie?"

"I know she's taken in all kinds of people there."

"Oh, she takes in anyone."

"So I've heard," he said. "That Brant couple still there?"

"Edwin and Lynn. Yes, they are. You know them, Mr. Rosen?"

"I know about them," he said ponderously. "Otherwise, how are all those people getting on living in that drafty old convent?"

"We manage, as Bridie says. Believe it or not, a truck came recently and dumped a load of coal into the basement, so we'll have heat and hot water this winter. Bridie thanks God and her lucky gold shamrock."

"A lucky shamrock," Sam said. "Whatever works. Anyway, I'm happy the place is being put to good use, for the most part, at least. I was there when the Catholic bishop came from Dallas to inaugurate All Saints."

"Oh, really, Mr. Rosen? When?"

"Back in '06, over a quarter-century ago. I'll meet Bridie O'Driscoll sometime, I'm sure. And you come back to see me, Mrs. Wellington, if Gabi needs more medicine or anything at all." Sam stood up and shook her hand.

"I just don't know how to thank you, Mr. Rosen."

"I'm glad I can help," Sam said. "Miss Maggie will take care of you out there at her desk." Miss Maggie gave Elizabeth two dollars and wrote out the interest-free due bill.

Elizabeth described Gabi's symptoms to Doc Cooper in his office at the back of the Rosen Heights Drugstore. His patients called him the "morning doctor" in recognition of his sobriety until about noon, when he went up to Riscky's for the nineteen-cent lunch special.

In the afternoon, he read and drank until the words became fuzzy. Then he closed his book and drank until he passed out—his routine since his wife died in 1930. Nowdays, however, he spent afternoons prescribing medicinal whiskey across town at Edward Brant's new drugstore.

"So, sounds like the same cough Gabi had last time," Doctor Cooper said, writing out a prescription. "Let's hope it's not whooping cough."

"I'm sorry I can't pay you today, Doctor Cooper," Elizabeth said as he handed her the prescription.

"Don't worry about it, Mrs. Wellington. I didn't even see the patient."

Elizabeth gave Gabi a slug of cough medicine the pharmacist had whipped up. She also rubbed yellow ointment on her daughter's bony chest. Anna told Gabi she smelled like "an old, dead fish."

"Mr. Rosen was more worried about Gabi than money," Elizabeth said.

"If he were Catholic, we'd call him Saint Rosen," Bridie said. "There's not many who haven't knocked at his door." Even Edwin, she recalled, wondering what business he had with Mr. Rosen. She had seen his Packard parked at the Rosen Heights Land Office.

"I've never been so broke so long, Bridie," Elizabeth said, tears in her eyes. "And Gabi needin' shoes and...."

"We'll manage," Bridie said, taking her hand as she sat down at the long table in her kitchen. "Nothing's so bad it couldn't be worse."

"I couldn't even pay Doc Cooper this morning."

"Not to worry," Bridie said. "He'd rather have a bottle of whiskey than a bag of money. We've plenty of President's Choice in the basement."

"I just can't take another dime from you, Bridie."

"You know, Lizzie, this very morning I heard they let women make men's work clothes at Williamson-Dickie. Eileen O'Reilly works there now, bringing home six dollars, fifty-three cents every Saturday night. She said they're looking for a seamstress, too."

"Why, I'd be rich…if I could sew."

"Just tell 'em you love to sew. Surely you will once you learn how."

"Oh…I can try…I guess. But Gabi's sick and—"

"I'll look after Gabi. Go now and get dressed."

When Elizabeth returned, she pirouetted into the kitchen, modeling a cotton dress with a red floral print and a once-stylish hat.

"Dave gave me this hat on our tenth anniversary. How do I look?"

"Fresh and fit, Lizzy. Just don't look so sad. Smile." Bridie pressed two dimes into her hand for carfare.

"I have some money left that Mr. Rosen lent me."

"Ye'll need lunch," Bridie said, easing her out the door. "And remember the song 'Let a Smile Be Your Umbrella.' Show them a happy face."

"Let me kiss your gold shamrock for luck."

Bridie fished it from her apron.

"I'm sure to get the job now," Elizabeth said, kissing the shamrock.

"Off with you now. And don't forget your umbrella, love."

Elizabeth frowned. "But the sun's shining, Bridie."

"The song, Lizzy. The song 'Let a Smile Be Your Umbrella.' Smile, smile, smile."

JONATHAN AND MRS. BRYANT

Jonathan was weary and nauseous as the boxcar rattled over the rails, thick black smoke streaming through the open doors from time to time.

He and several others had hopped aboard the boxcar around midnight as the train chugged slowly up a steep hill south of downtown Austin. Men already aboard were asleep, heads resting on their belongings. Now, as sunlight seeped over the horizon, the locomotive picked up speed, pulling a hundred freight cars at a steady forty-five to fifty miles an hour.

It had been a restless night as Julie Bryant roamed his mind like a recurring song, one he couldn't shake if he'd wanted to. Her soft, supple body had burned itself into his vivid memory ever since he'd hijacked her friendly farewell hug as he was leaving for school last time. He'd latched himself to her and brushed his lips against her sensuous neck.

Julie had pushed him away, rebuked him and addressed him as "Jon-boy," as if he were a mischievous little brat. Yet if she'd been truly upset, she would have told his dad. She'd accepted his ill-begotten embrace, Jonathan decided, like a stolen kiss that becomes sweeter with the passing of time.

Julie plagued him like a fever. He thought of her and little else day and night—during class, during the state high school wrestling tournament in Houston and even during football games.

Brother Marcos had kicked him in the butt when Saint Edward's lost by a touchdown to Saint Joseph's in San Antonio. "Where've you been, Jonathan?" he yelled. "You mucked up the last three plays."

If his coaches and teachers were giving up on him, Jonathan had given up on the nubile nymphs at Saint Alice's Academy for Girls. They came to Saint Edward's' home games and cheered for the team, particularly its handsome quarterback. But after embracing Julie Bryant, he gave up pursuing schoolgirls who teased with sumptuous kisses yet rejected his breathy vows of love and slapped away his wandering hands.

Jonathan Quinlan, age seventeen, was in love with a mature thirty-two-year-old mother of two. Jonathan and Julie—J & J—embedded in his mind like an omen of the future, his and hers, theirs.

When the train clattered to a jolting stop, a horde of men jumped from railcars and dispersed like frightened jackrabbits across the Santa Fe rail yards. The feared, hated railroad bulls gave chase, several firing pistols into the early morning sky. Slow runners were caught, beaten bloody and thrown off railroad property.

A tall, broad-shouldered guard, cursing and swinging a baseball bat, ran directly at Jonathan. Saint Edward's' star quarterback hit the ground in a practiced roll, clipping the bruin at the knees, slamming him face first into the dirt like a felled tree.

Jonathan deftly rolled to his feet and kept running, his overnight bag tucked under his arm like a football. The dazed guard held a handkerchief to his bloody nose as he watched the boy racing up Jones Street. Jonathan laughed. If only Julie Bryant had seen him in action.

He walked briskly up Commerce and cut behind the pink granite courthouse to the bridge that slanted down to the river valley. He stuck out his thumb and snagged a ride in a pickup driven by a shirtless, white-haired farmer wearing overalls, a straw hat and thick glasses.

"The smell's worse than ever," Jonathan said as they trundled up North Main past the meatpacking plants and acres of cow pens.

"That's 'cause there ain't no breeze today, sonny," the farmer curtly informed him. Jonathan got out at Northwest Twenty-Fifth Street and walked up the long hill to cleaner air. With train fare his dad had sent him, he bought cologne at the Rosen Heights Drugstore and a pack of Lucky Strikes at Harrison's Grocery. Then he stopped by Rosen Heights' only blacksmith's shop.

Blackie stood six-foot-three, a hairy hulk of a man, three hundred pounds, dirty, bearded face and a smile broken by several missing teeth. He shoed horses, repaired cars, fixed flats and ran a package delivery service out of the cluttered shop behind his house.

"Hey, Jonathan, ain't seen ya in long time," Blackie said, looking up from a red-hot horseshoe he'd been pounding into shape with a heavy hammer. "What kin I git fer ya today, boy?"

"A quart of hooch," Jonathan said.

"Blackie's best for three bucks or the rotgut fer a dollar?"

"I just have a dollar this time."

Jonathan took his purchases to his old cave at Rosen's Pond. Pondering his plan, he smoked and took a sip of rotgut, gasping as the fiery liquid burned its way down his throat, torched his esophagus and scorched his stomach.

As his innards cooled, he recast his approach to Julie, having already developed and discarded several scripts. It had to be different from the fumbled, impulsive move he'd made last time. When nothing romantically suave came to mind, he decided to tell her the God's truth: "Julie, I love you and can't quit thinking about you."

He bolstered his courage with more rotgut and hid the bottle in a box at the back of the cave. Fortified with whiskey and romantic notions, he crossed the playground to the back door.

"Oh, Jonathan, you're home again…at last," Bridie said, rising from her chair and hugging him. "Been a while. We missed you."

"Lots of football practice, Miss Bridie."

"At least you got in early with the day ahead of you," she said, frowning in the wake of his whiskey breath.

"School holiday today, Miss Bridie," he lied. Reading Jonathan's forged letter from his father, Brother Thomas had given him permission to go home a day early. "Tell your father we send blessings on his birthday," the dean said.

"You're looking good, Miss Bridie," Jonathan said.

"Thank you, Jonathan. How was the train?" she said.

"I slept most of the way. I'd better drop by and let Dad know I'm here."

"He's moved to the third floor. You'll find him all the way down the hall in the last room on your right."

"Why move? Those old classrooms are all about the same."

"Oh, he said something about wanting to be near the fire escape and that Matthew and Roger needed a room of their own," Bridie said without conviction.

"All right, Miss Bridie. I'll drop by to talk after I've had a bath."

Jonathan knocked once and opened the door to his dad's new room, filled with the same ornate furniture from their old house in Ryan Place.

Quin stood by a window in his shorts, smoking a cigarette and drinking a mug of beer. In his early forties, he had the figure of a younger man, stomach still fairly flat, lean limbs, square shoulders, a head of wavy black and gray hair.

"You're home early," Quin said, smiling as he crossed the room and hugged his son.

"Yeah, Dad, school holiday," Jonathan said, holding his breath and turning his head to hid his whiskey odor.

"I see you have a window to the fire escape now."

"The room's been vacant, so why not? What's on for the weekend, Jonathan?"

"Hanging out with some of the guys."

"How about studying and bringing up your grades?"

"I'm back on track, Dad," Jonathan said, scrutinizing the room with renewed interest.

"I may have gotten carried away in my letter, but your grades were below par on the last report card."

"Aced a physics exam last week and got an A-minus in English."

"You know it was your mother's last wish that you go to Notre Dame."

"I'll get in, Dad."

"Not just get in, Jonathan, but in with a scholarship," Quin said, sipping his beer. "I have enough to cover about two years. We need that scholarship."

To change the subject, Jonathan said, "Kind of early for a beer, isn't it?".

"Early, Jonathan, depends on what time you get up. It's almost 10:30."

"Going to let me have a cold one, too?"

"One, if it's not too early for you."

Going to the refrigerator, Jonathan paused at Quin's desk. The framed degree hung above it on the wall: "Colorado School of Mines Has Conferred Upon Joseph P. Quinlan, The Bachelor of Science Degree, Geology, June 1, 1915." The familiar picture of his mom and dad sitting in a swing together was no longer on the desk.

"That's George O'Driscoll's home brew," Quin said. "Very good."

Jonathan opened his bottle and took a deep swallow. "I'll take it with me, Dad. Need to get a bath."

"Sit down, finish your beer, tell me about school," Quin said.

Jonathan put the beer bottle on the desk. "Who's the woman?"

"Woman!" Quin said, startled. "What do you mean, woman?"

"Come on, Dad. Lipstick's all over the place, the beer glass on the coffee table, those butts in the ashtray, earrings on the nightstand next to the bed. I don't care. I knew this would happen. I'll get over it. You're not a priest, after all. But where's the picture of you and Mom that's always been on your desk?"

"Look, Jonathan," Quin said softly, his tone contrite and understanding. "Your mother is the only woman I've ever loved. She was a beautiful girl and a beautiful person. I'll never forget her, never stop loving her, never get over losing her. But it's been over three years, and...and I got lonesome. Julie's lonesome, too, and we enjoy being together. It's nothing more than that right now. So please..."

Jonathan paled. "Julie....You mean Julie Bryant?"

Quin nodded, reaching for cigarettes on the coffee table. "We've kept it quiet because of her kids. They still think their daddy's coming home someday. And if Matthew or the other kids find out about us, they'll tell Juliana and Jeremy. They don't deserve to be hurt like that. So please...."

When he looked up from lighting his cigarette, Jonathan walked out, leaving the door open. Quin shrugged, knowing it would take time for his son to accept another woman in his dad's life. It would be easier, of course, because Jonathan already knew Julie as a decent person and a good mom.

Next morning, when Quin found Jonathan's room empty, he sent Matthew down to the cave by the pond. "Tell him I need to talk to him, Matthew."

"What's he done this time? Are you going to kick his butt? "

"Nothing, Matthew, nothing. Tell him everything's okay."

Matthew reported back that the cave was empty. "No sign of Jonathan," he said, omitting the empty quart bottle he'd found.

Saturday night, Quin told Julie, "He must've gone back to Saint Edward's."

"But he's always stayed until Sunday," she said warily, sitting on the edge of the bed, pulling on her night-gown and slipping on her slippers.

"Teenagers," Quin said, buttoning his pajama top. "I'll bet he has a serious girlfriend in Austin. That would explain why he hasn't come home for so long, too. Let's have a nightcap and a smoke before you go down."

After pouring their drinks, Quin sat next to Julie on the couch, put his arm around her shoulders and told her what had happened when Jonathan had come to his room that morning.

"I couldn't lie to Jonathan. It'll take him a little time to get used to the idea that I can't live my life alone…and neither can you. At least you're no stranger. He knows you and likes you and Juliana and Jeremy. I'll talk to him next time he comes up from Austin."

"We'll work this out, Quin," Julie said quietly, kissing him as she got up from the couch. "I need to get back before my kids wake up."

Julie threw on her housecoat and went out the window and down the fire escape to her room, frightened that she had come between father and son. She decided to console Jonathan without telling Quin that his son was jealous of the woman his father was sleeping with.

THE AFFAIR

Their affair began like an accidental fire set off by a flaming match tossed carelessly into dry weeds. On a whim, as they walked up the stairs together one balmy afternoon, Quin said lightheartedly and as neighborly as he could, "How about a drink, Julie?"

"Oh...I don't know," Julie said, nonplussed and uncertain.

"It'll be all right," he said whimsically. "Just a drink."

"Well, why not, Quin?" she said, regaining herself.

Julie entered his room and abruptly stopped. She felt she'd stepped into a mirage—an oasis of opulence in the desert of the Great Depression. She was astonished by a space so beautifully decorated, fully furnished and sectioned off in separate living areas.

Teakwood bookshelves along one wall led to a sitting room defined by a long couch, three overstuffed lounge chairs organized around a teakwood coffee table, bejeweled Tiffany lamps on end tables. A stately dining room table for twelve, matching sideboard and floor lamps, occupied another area. An armoire hid a bedroom suite from the rest of the room. A desk, matching chair, desk lamp and filing cabinet filled a corner of the room. Elegant Persian rugs covered the hardwood floors.

"Oh my God," Julie said as Quin closed the door behind them. "It's like a palace. The paintings and mirrors and all…"

"Stuff from my old house," Quin said, shrugging. "None of it worth anything now. Sit anywhere, Julie. I'll mix some drinks."

Taking a seat on the couch, she studied the eight-by-ten picture of Quin and a beautiful young woman sitting in a swing together. His late wife, she assumed.

Quin took ice from a refrigerator and filled two glasses at the teakwood bar with President's Choice and 7Up. He sat next to Julie on the soft leather couch. "Cheers times three," he said, nodding as their glasses clinked together.

"Cheers," she said, tipping the glass to her lips. Quin admired the lingering bloom of youth still aglow in her pretty face.

"I haven't tasted liquor in a long, long time."

"Wish I could say the same myself, Julie," he said, laughing quietly at himself.

She knew from his sons about his fondness for the bottle and the foul mood it cast over him at times. "He misses Mom," Jonathan had told her.

"Everybody needs to let go and let down now and then," Julie said languidly. "Mind if I have a cigarette, Quin?"

He offered her a Chesterfield from a silver cigarette case. He took one himself and gave her a light from a jeweled lighter on the coffee table. She leaned back on the couch, kicked off her shoes and coiled her lovely long legs beneath her.

"This is relaxing and so quiet for a change," Julie said, holding the drink in her left hand, a gold wedding band on her finger. "It's nice to get away from everybody, though I do love all these people at All Saints."

"Well, most of them some of the time," Quin said, laughing and wondering how he'd looked past this slim, busty, sexy woman for so long. "It's hard to escape from the crowd in this place,"

"The inmates, as George O'Driscoll calls us," Julie said.

"I don't think we've ever talked—just the two of us, I mean," he said.

"Just hello, goodbye," she said.

"Wally's your cousin, isn't he?" he said, struggling for conversation.

"He is. That's how we got here. Wally told Bridie about me and the kids, and she sent him to pick us up right away. Quin, I hate to think where we'd be if we hadn't come here."

Their halting conversation moved slowly from weather and news to their common interest in kids and how they were doing in school and the hardship of bringing them up alone.

"It's like being handicapped," Quin said. "No matter what I do, I feel like I'm missing something, overlooking something with them. There's no one to check with anymore, no one around with a trusted second opinion or a better idea."

"I know it wouldn't be the same for you, Quin, but I had four brothers, so I know about boys if you ever want to bounce ideas around. You know, just talk things out."

"Don't be surprised if I take you up on that," he said, patting her lightly on the shoulder. Trolling for a comment about her husband, he added, "I think you're pretty much in the same boat, Julie?"

"I worry about Juliana and Jeremy, Quin, if something should happen to me. And that aside, where do we go from here? What's next? It's so scary being alone. I just don't...," she said, snuffing out her cigarette as words caught in her throat and pearly tears welled in her blue eyes. "I'm sorry."

Taking Julie's right hand, Quin kissed her lightly on the lips. Though she didn't kiss him back, she hadn't turned away.

"I should finish my drink and go."

"Julie, I hope I haven't scared you away...or anything," he said. "I just...like being here with you."

"It's okay," she said. "But our kids—yours and mine—will be home from school any time now. I'd better go."

"I so enjoyed talking with you, Julie," Quin said, walking her to the door.

She smiled meekly and went out. He watched her go down the hall, her slim body amplifying her well-rounded hips. Closing the door, he said, "God dammit," cursing himself for moving too soon, too fast.

When she knocked the next afternoon, Quin opened the door and said, "I'll mix us a drink, Julie." Taking her left hand and leading her into the room, he saw she'd shed her gold wedding band.

As she approached the long leather couch, Julie saw that the picture of Quin and his wife was gone from the desk.

"I'll get the drinks," he said, still holding her hand.

"Both of us have been lonely for a long time, Quin." In a wink, she slipped off the shoulder straps of her dress and dropped it to the floor, unveiling her resplendent nude body. She stepped out of her shoes and kissed him.

The next day, Quin moved up to the third-floor room with a window to the fire escape—"For safety's sake," he told Bridie.

Julie's room on the second floor also had an exit window to the fire escape—giving her stealthy access to Quin and avoiding the risk of encountering residents in the hallway.

From her first-floor room in the former library, Bridie listened to Julie's late-night footsteps clinking lightly on the fire escape, its steel frame a telegraph of the traffic it bore. She'd hear Julie returning an hour or so later. The liaisons occurred after her kids were asleep—Juliana and Jeremy in her room and Quin's boys, Matthew and Roger, in theirs.

Rationalizing her religion, Bridie reasoned Quin the widower was "free to see a woman." She fretted fleetingly with his seeing a married woman. Yet wasn't it likely her "long-gone husband," as Julie described him, was long dead? What Quin and Julie did—if indeed they did—was between themselves and God, was it not?

Whatever they did, Bridie reminded herself not to judge those whose sins differed from her own. And on the upside, she wondered if anyone else had noticed that Julie was so much happier and that Quin drank so much less since he'd moved to the third floor.

THE MEN FROM
NOWHERE

"**M**ornin', Father," the bewhiskered man mumbled, a gallows grin of yellow, broken and missing teeth gracing his gaunt, grimy face. In tattered coat and patched pants, he smiled, toes protruding from mismatched footwear—a boot and an oxford.

"Father's arse, man," George said, sizing up the rogue at his door as about forty, dirty brown hair, able-bodied if somewhat thin, yet fit to work if only he would. "What is it you want?"

"Ah, nothing, Father, nothing at all, but I'd work for a meal, Father."

"Do I look like your father?"

"Uh, no, Fa…I mean, sir. No, no, I reckon not."

Standing beneath a cross, a flock of sheep and shepherds depicted in stained glass over the door to a convent, solemn-faced George O'Driscoll, in black pants and dark shirt, might easily have been mistaken for a man of the cloth, one whose daily discourse with the Almighty had been interrupted by this trespasser.

"I jest thought," the stranger said.

"When you were coming down the street, did you see the white cross atop this building?" scowled the "holy man" in the doorway, his index finger pointing sharply skyward.

"White cross, oh, I did, Father….I mean sir, I seen it, Sir Father," the hobo stammered. "It's a real pretty cross."

"Then be on your way before I nail your arse to it as an act of contrition for your many sins," George warned and slammed the door.

As the bewildered visitor backed slowly down the steps, a one-eyed cat, with black and gray stripes, studied him from a first-floor window, teeth snarling in its twisted snout. Q.C. looked straight through him. Black crows roosted on the white cross to which the mad priest had threatened to nail him. A large goat, its horns gilded in sunlight, peered down at him from the roof.

"Good Gawd Almighty," he gasped, bolting through the gate, wondering why that gun-toting priest at the big downtown church had sent him to this place. He stopped to adjust the switchblade in his boot before heading down Belle Avenue in search of a stout drink.

"Who was that, George?" Bridie wondered.

"Another crooked Bible salesman," he groused, sitting down to breakfast. George was seldom home to drive off those who came calling at All Saints for handouts. Despite his warnings that "you're going to let someone in one day who'll kill us all some night," Bridie turned none away.

George wasn't alone in his misgivings about some of the characters who found their way to All Saints. Sitting in Bridie's kitchen, Julie Bryant wondered aloud about Edwin Brant's reputation.

"The man sells a few bottles of whiskey to keep body and soul together, so let's not judge those whose sins differ from own," Bridie said, Julie's liaison with Quin Quinlan on her mind.

"Well," Julie persisted, "I hear things like he's an upstanding member of Fort Worth's underworld and...."

"Come now, Julie. Edwin's good to us, and what he does is between himself and God."

"And between himself and the cops," Quin laughed.

Most who came to the door were gypsies, as Bridie had called such wanderers in Ireland. They ate whatever she had to offer, thanked her and drifted off again—men from nowhere going nowhere.

"You might at least feed them on the back steps," George said.

"I don't feed Mulligan on the back steps."

"They pass through the rail yards by the trainloads, day and night," George said time and again. "You can't save 'em all, Bridie."

"Given half a chance, people will save themselves. And remember, the Lord said, 'What ye do for the least of them, ye do unto me.'"

"I worry more about what they'll do unto us," he said.

Perhaps the least of those who had come to her door arrived on a warm summer night. He wore an ill-fitting secondhand suit, a gold pin in a faded red tie, polished winged shoes on his feet.

"Name's Sam Scott, ma'am," he began, removing a new fedora and bowing rather too gallantly. His showmanship amused Bridie. Standing erect again, he looked like a wrestler—broad, powerful shoulders; thick neck; beefy chest; long arms dangling down his short, muscular frame.

"Sister Vee said you might help us," he said, fumbling with a Saint Christopher's medal she'd hung around his neck at Huntsville State Prison. "Sandy's out in the car. She's been sick, and I'm outta work."

"Well, Sam, bring her in for a spot o' tea and a bite to eat."

Sam returned with a tall, slim young woman. She nodded and averted her eyes when he introduced her. Sandra Scott's blonde hair, dark-red lipstick and heavy makeup masked a pretty face drawn hard by fatigue. Painted eyebrows arched darkly over blue eyes.

Bridie thought how much prettier the girl would be if she washed her face and if someone had taught her to cut her broken fingernails, to comb her hair properly, and other refinements mothers teach daughters.

"Come, Sandy, sit down here," Bridie said, helping her to a chair at the kitchen table. "Sam says ye're not feeling well, dear. Would ye like an aspirin and a glass of water?"

"All I need is a cigarette. And a beer, if you can get one in a place like this."

Sam asked for a glass of milk as Bridie gave the girl a beer.

Bridie served them a couple of boiled eggs, cabbage and boiled potatoes smothered in Ollie Cox's butter. Sandra Scott smoked Lucky Strikes between bites as Sam Scott talked and lit her cigarettes.

Bridie guessed Sandra to be about twenty, young enough to be Sam's daughter. His stringy black hair sported strands of gray. His emerald green eyes scoured the room, shifting left, then right.

"Look!" Sam said. "A mouse, over by the door."

"We've our share of them," Bridie said.

"I guess the little bas-...ah...little creatures don't eat much." He laughed at his joke.

"But Sam, it's a skeleton with eyes and a tail!" Sandra said.

"That's how Q.C.—Quinlan's cat—leaves 'em," Bridie told her.

The girl pushed her plate away. "I could use another beer."

Sam was a likable sort, Bridie thought, his thin lips pursed tightly across a mouthful of large and perfect teeth. He grinned easily and talked a great deal, yet revealed little about himself and deftly slipped past Bridie's motherly questions.

"And what kind of work would ye be looking for, Sam?" Bridie asked, getting Sandra a beer from her electric icebox.

"The accounting profession," he said, without claiming to be an accountant or that he would like to become an accountant or knew anything about accounting.

"We've a friend at the stockyards who sometimes has bookkeeping work for one of my guests. So perhaps...."

"Any more of that milk, Bridie?" Sam Scott asked, raising an empty glass, his fingers festooned with rings, a cross crudely tattooed above the thumb.

Sam parked his four-door Lincoln touring car out of sight behind the laundry house. He and the girl slept on a mattress in the auditorium. The next day, they moved their things to a second-floor classroom.

Bridie gave the Scotts a double bed, one the Brants had stored in the basement, a table and two chairs from the nuns' dining room. They put their belongings on the bookshelves and hung their clothes on the coatracks along the wall.

"Where'd that new couple say they're from, Bridie?" Lynn Brant asked, stirring her coffee the next morning.

"From Dallas," she replied, at the stove boiling rice for the kids' lunch.

"Might keep an eye on 'em."

"Because they're from Dallas?"

"Reason enough," Lynn laughed, lighting a cigarette. "And who's this Sister Vee that keeps sending you orphans and characters like this Sam guy?"

"My oldest sister, she is. Mary Josephine, she was, before leaving Ireland for a convent in Texas as a young girl to take the veil."

"How young, Bridie?"

"No more than fifteen."

"Seems awfully young to leave Mom, Dad and country."

"She cried all the way to America."

REDDY KILOWATT

"Can I sleep down here, Miss Bridie?" Frankie Feldman cried, standing in her doorway. "They said the devil's gonna get me," the new boy from the orphanage told her.

Bridie made him a pallet of blankets on the floor and went upstairs to threaten Frankie's roommates. Richard and Brandon had told him candlelight attracted the devil, who carted small children off to hell after they fell asleep.

"Frighten that child again and I'll be carting you both off," she warned them. She blew out their candle, leaving them in the dark.

Flickering candlelight created dancing shadows that frightened the younger kids. Squeaking doors, creaking floors, echoes and other spooky little noises—real and imagined—conjured up haunting images. Bridie feared a fire from the candles.

Sleeping with his door ajar, George O'Driscoll erupted in devilish laughter when Shirley Roberts stumbled down the dark stairs returning from the second-floor bathroom. (Flushing of the nearby toilet annoyed him.) She threatened to climb back up the stairs and do things to George that Wally Cox said slaughterhouses wouldn't do to a cow.

"Are you going to wash out Mrs. Roberts' mouth with soap, Miss Bridie?" Richard Levitz snickered at breakfast next morning.

"That'll take a lotta soap," Anna said, cracking a hard-boiled egg on the table.

Dan Donovan offered no hope when Bridie phoned about work at the stockyards. "Nothing here, Bridie. Ranchers can't get enough for their cattle to ship 'em to the meatpackers. They're shooting 'em by the thousands. So most of the stockyard pens here are empty, and Swift and Armour are laying off more men at the meatpacking plants."

Bridie hung up, looked across the kitchen at those at the table and said, "Nothing."

Quin shrugged, got up from the table and went to his room.

"Might as well work on my truck," Wally said. The back door slammed behind him.

Quin donned his London suit, grabbed his hat and walked past his Cadillac to catch a streetcar on Northwest Twenty-Fifth. At the Greyhound station downtown, he found a discarded newspaper in the waiting room. At the W. T. Waggoner Building, he tucked the paper under his arm and went inside.

Quin slowly paced the familiar lobby, checking his pocket watch as if waiting for someone. An elevator door opened.

"Goin' up, Mr. Quinlan, suh?" the porter said.

"No thanks, Jenkins. Just waiting for someone."

"Nice seein' ya again, Mr. Quinlan."

No one happened by and took him to lunch. Back on the street, he looked up at the eighth-floor window that had been the view from his office.

At the Westbrook Hotel, Quin patted the Golden Goddess's ample ass and took a seat in a lounge chair. The busty nude statue still reigned over the luxurious lobby where Quin had once speculated in oil fields and wildcat wells, talked about discoveries and listened for strands of truth in rumors and lies exchanged by men who became millionaires and millionaires who became paupers. He and other oilmen had once consummated their deals by kissing the goddess's smooth marble buttocks for good luck.

"Well now, if it isn't Quin Quinlan!"

Quin smiled and stood to shake hands with W. T. Waggoner, Jr.

"So good to see you, W.T. How've you been lately?"

"Better than I deserve, Quin. And how are those boys?"

"Fine, fine, W.T. Jonathan's in boarding school down in Austin. Roger's at Saint Ignatius Academy, over there next to Saint Patrick's Church. If I can just keep Matthew out of jail."

"Oh, he'll be all right, Quin. Usually one in every litter like that. But I'm glad things aren't so bad for you. So many of our old friends are just down and out and can't seem to get up again. Heard about Van Dyke, I guess?"

"You mean Thomas Van Dyke? He was so young. I was taken aback to see the obituary in the paper. Then I heard he'd gassed himself."

"Sad," W.T. said. "Sarah found him in the kitchen, the gas oven turned on full blast. The rest of us need to keep goin' and get through these times."

"Well, W.T., I'm looking at a couple of prospects, but plenty of room for anything that might come along. I mean, if you hear of anything…"

"I'll sure keep you in mind, Quin. Waitin' for somebody?"

"No, just left a meeting and thought I'd glance at the paper."

"Take care of yourself, Quin. I'm running late. Let's go to lunch sometime."

Quin patted the Golden Goddess on the rump as he left the hotel.

Bridie held her nose against the stench as the street-car trundled past two hundred acres of stockyard pens, slaughterhouses and meatpacking plants. She got off on North Main, blessing herself against the curse of the white neon cross on the KKK Building across the street.

Bridie threaded her way through Zinn's North Main Pawnshop past jumbles of tools, toolboxes, furniture, an icebox, a rolled-up rug, a gray cat sleeping on a couch.

"Nice to see you again, Mrs. O'Driscoll," Julius Zinn smiled.

"Good day, Mr. Zinn," she said, opening her purse.

"What brings you my way today?"

"My light bill." She handed him her gold shamrock.

As Julius Zinn assayed the shamrock, Bridie waited under a curious thicket of life's furnishings suspended from the ceiling—bicycles, chairs, car wheels, tires, tubes, suitcases, a wicker baby carriage, a pair of crutches.

"'County Tipperary Fair, 1899.'" Julius Zinn read the inscription on the shamrock. "First prize. Hmmm…for dancing, no less."

"I was eighteen."

"I've rarely seen gold as radiant and lustrous or craftsmanship as fine."

"'Twas made by the fairies in Slievenamon Mountain back home."

"It seems to glow…as if there's light inside."

"The fairies crafted it from a pot of gold at the end of a rainbow."

"You don't say," Julius said. The pawnbroker polished the clover's three leaves with a soft cloth. "Hmmm…I swear, it feels warm to the touch."

"It doesn't warm to just anyone, Mr. Zinn."

"I can offer you a handsome price for this."

"No, Mr. Zinn, it's not for sale."

"I gave you a fair price for the Waterford crystal."

"I'll not be selling my shamrock," Bridie declared, looking down her nose at Julian Zinn behind his counter—a glass case of wedding rings and watches, brooches and bracelets smartly displayed on her mother's Irish linen…and a brass telescope engraved in German.

"I understand," he said, going to his safe. He returned with some bills in his hand. "Your shamrock's in my safe."

"I'll be back, now, so don't be selling it before the thirty days are up," she warned. Signing the loan agreement and taking the money, Bridie said, "How much is that telescope, Mr. Zinn?"

"Oh, so you like the telescope. Three dollars," he said, taking the telescope from the glass display case. "I just put it out as the kid didn't come back for it after thirty days." He handed it to Bridie.

"A kid brought this to you?" Bridie said, frowning as she examined the treasured World War I telescope Wally Cox had brought home from Flanders Field.

"Yeah, a kid about nine or ten. Handsome little devil, black wavy hair, innocent brown eyes. Smart, too. Said he found it, but I think otherwise. I can let you have it for two fifty."

"I'll give you a dollar and the rest later," she said.

"All right, Miss Bridie. And when you get the rest, come in and pick it up."

She returned the telescope and one of the dollars she'd just borrowed from him and hurried out to continue her journey.

The streetcar rumbled up the North Main bridge, rising like a ramp to the majestic pink courthouse. The town's iconic landmark, it overlooked the Trinity River valley on one side and the red brick streets of downtown Fort Worth on the other.

But for my shamrock and Tommy's checks, we'd all be down there, Bridie imagined, looking at people huddled around campfires under the bridge and along the muddy riverbank. Women washed clothes in the river. Shoeless, half-naked children built castles of mud on the shore. The river people lived in abandoned cars and huts built from scrap wood and cardboard.

The streetcar trundled around the courthouse and past the infamous hanging tree on the front lawn. At the Texas Electric Building, a cardboard man—a bolt of red lightning for a body, a blinking light bulb for a nose, a silly smile for a mouth—greeted her with a sign proclaiming, "Reddy Kilowatt—Always at Your Service."

"Always ready to cut off your electricity, he is," Bridie told the clerk as she slapped down her delinquent payment.

Going home, she found Quin sitting at the back of the Rosen Heights streetcar. "So what brings you to town this afternoon, Bridie?"

"I went to see an old friend, Quin." She knew by the stack of books on his lap that he'd been to the library and by the alcohol on his breath that he'd been to a speakeasy.

The streetcar trundled noisily across the bridge over the river people and down North Main into the valley. "Biggest cow patty in Texas," Quin said as they tried to hold their breath past the stockyards and slaughterhouses.

The lights at All Saints had been turned back on for three days when a letter from Bridie's brother arrived.

Denver, Colorado

Dear Bridie,

I just got back to Denver. I did not do any good. I know you must need money badly. But nearly all the mines in the state are closed. Even coal mines are working only two or three days a week with the men making just enough to pay their board. There are about 20,000 idle men here and nothing doing. I have been a little sick and this has held me back. I'm sorry I have no money. George should at least give you money for the kids. Only in years to come will we realize how lucky we were for the years before this thing whatever it is took our jobs and everything else.

Your loving brother,
Tommy
Erin Go Bragh

"Any money, Mama?" Josie asked, taking the letter from Bridie.

"No, he's on hard times, too."

"Why does Uncle Tom always write 'Erin Go Bragh' after his name?"

"'Ireland Forever' was what the lads said just before they attacked the English. Tommy left Ireland after they came looking for him one night."

"What did he do exactly, Mama?"

"There was an ambush on the Waterford Road…. No, 'tis best forgotten now, love."

JUDAS

"You're always sayin' nothing's so bad it couldn't be worse, Miss Bridie."

"Oh, God o' mercy, Martin, you frightened the life out of me."

He stared at the noose in her left hand, the other end of the rope tied to a wooden beam, as she stood precariously close to the edge of the concrete steps.

"Oh no, Martin, this isn't for me," she said, holding up the noose, smiling wanly to suggest the folly of the macabre scene he'd discovered in this shadowy corner of the basement.

After chasing Bonnie and Clyde out of her kitchen, Bridie had come down to see if the two goats had gotten in through the double freight doors in the basement. She knew that Edwin Brant and Martin

139

unloaded ingredients for the still at night. They'd probably forgotten to close the doors.

She'd crossed the dank cavern of support columns, nests of electric wires, mazes of water pipes, discarded furniture and stacks of boxes and barrels the Brants had moved into the basement after the White House fire. Small windows sent rays of light angling through the musty darkness. A naked light bulb glared in Martin's space between the furnace and the coal bin. A narrow cot, trunk, chair and table furnished his needs. Finding the freight doors shut, Bridie went up the steep concrete steps and jiggled the latch. The skeleton of a mouse indicated Q.C. had been at work.

Turning to go down the steps, she saw the rope. It was tied around a heavy crossbeam, the rest of it coiled atop the beam. She pushed the rope off the beam and fell backwards as a hangman's noose uncoiled like a snake in her face.

"A man could slip it around his neck and jest step off the side of them steps," Martin said.

"Someone here, under our own roof."

"Lost his courage," Martin said.

"Or left the grim task for later...to care for some unfinished business first?"

"Or to take a few snorts of something to work up his nerve?"

"I can't think of a soul here who'd commit the unforgivable sin."

"Unforgivable, Miss Bridie?"

"The sin of Judas, Martin. 'Better that he had not been born,' Jesus said after Judas hanged himself."

"Served the stool pigeon right, squealing to them Romans about Jesus," Martin said, recalling the gospel story Sister Vee had told the inmates at Sugar Land Prison.

"God gives life, and only God can take it," Bridie said, reciting the teachings of her faith. "We must bear the burdens we're given in this life."

"You mean take our lumps," Martin shrugged. "The rich and the lucky don't never hurt at all."

"We never know how much people are suffering, Martin. We're all the same here at All Saints, yet someone among us is on the verge of this." She ran her fingers over the rope's coarse strands.

"Elizabeth Wellington's always sad and cries a lot."

Bridie nodded. "Let's keep this to ourselves, Martin."

He came up the steps, cut the rope from the beam and went back to the still he operated for Edwin and George.

Upstairs, Bridie made a cup of tea as she considered the suicide prospects among her guests one by one, face by face. Everyone read the papers about the mounting number of suicides. The police benevolently recorded many of them as accidental deaths to shield families from shame. The press reported only the most spectacular ones: a man who hanged himself from a railroad trestle, another who stepped in front of a train, and a bank clerk who blew out his brains on the courthouse steps, a note in his pocket telling his wife his insurance policy would pay off their mortgage.

Sipping the hot tea, Bridie pondered the faces of the residents of All Saints, remembering things they said, the tone of their voices, and recalling their moods for signs. For what signs, she did not know. Yet she did know:

About George's anger over their moribund marriage, his outrage at the Catholic Church and his exasperation with God. Yet Father Nolan had seen him now and again sitting alone in Saint Patrick's Church.

About Quin's depression, his flashes of wrath at everything over the death of his young and beautiful wife, and the subsequent loss of his business, prestige and pride in the great Crash of '29—losses he steadily diluted with alcohol.

About Wally's forlorn longing for the soil, just a patch of ground big enough to scratch out a living raising vegetables and keeping a few cows. Ollie said he sometimes drove out west of town alone and looked at the farm he'd lost to the bank, its fields fallow, idle and as useless and ruined as Wally Cox himself.

About Edwin Brant and Sam Scott, Bridie felt they lacked any sense of loss about their wayward lives, immune in good times or bad to what happened around them or to them. The two scofflaws blithely rejected society and heavenly redemption to ply their schemes against the laws and mores of ordinary men. They were too much about themselves to take their own lives.

She worried Martin might be right about downhearted, wimpy Elizabeth Wellington, except that she loved Gabi far too much to leave her alone in the world. Ditto for Julie Bryant with Juliana and Jeremy to care for, Shirley Roberts with Buster under her wing, and Ollie Cox with Cory and Sissy.

Perhaps that's why almost all suicides were men. They could leave the children in the care of their women and leave their insurance money to redeem their dignity. By the same token, she decided that, having no woman to look after his three sons, it was unlikely Quin had gone to the basement with a noose in hand. Besides, the handsome widower was secretly in love with Julie.

Sandra, on the other hand, lived with Sam Scott—reason enough to hang herself, Bridie thought. She wondered where they went every evening at dusk, returning just before dawn, their footsteps a familiar tapping pattern on the fire escape that passed her window.

Bridie finished her tea, no further enlightened about who among them had taken three destructive steps—buying the rope, making a hangman's noose, attaching it to the basement beam. Taking up her rosary, she threaded the beads through her fingers on behalf of this suffering soul, whoever it might be.

ALL SAINTS' POKER PARLOR

M ulligan pulled himself up from the kitchen floor to greet the priest, who'd tapped lightly at the back door and let himself in.

"Ah, so it's you, Father Nolan," Bridie said, looking up from her kitchen stove at his wrinkled, friendly old face, hair as stark white as his Roman collar.

"Blessings, Bridie," he said, rubbing the yellow dog's head.

"I'm just making a pot o' tea, Father. Would you care for a cup?"

"No thanks, Bridie. I'll have something a little more spirited upstairs."

"I see you're sporting neither gun nor badge for this occasion."

"Might scare off the clientele," he said, stroking Mulligan's back.

"Mike Long's already up there, decked out in his spiffy police uniform, gun, badge and all," Bridie said.

"Well now, with both the law of the land and the law of the Lord at the tables, we should have orderly and perhaps lucrative games tonight."

"I heard some of the others going up the fire escape already."

At Bridie's behest, tonight's players had been asked to come and go via the fire escape "so as not to disturb the children or embarrass the women going up and down the halls in their bathrobes."

"I'm not one to take fire escapes unless there's a fire, Bridie."

"Indeed, what would the neighbors say if they saw a priest sneaking up our fire escape to the nuns' dormitory in the dark of night?"

"Scandalous," Father Nolan said. "Come along, Mulligan," who followed him.

Edwin had converted the nuns' dormitory into a poker parlor after he and Quin lost a few dollars to George O'Driscoll one rainy Sunday afternoon. "Where'd you learn to play?" Edwin said, forking over a five-dollar bill.

"Back in Clonmel," George said.

"Clon…what?"

"Clonmel, where we lived before coming to America. Seldom missed Saturday night poker at Moran's Pub."

"I didn't catch any tricks, George, but you must've had a few cards up your sleeve somewhere."

"No tricks, Edwin. It's all about schoolboy math. Credit goes to my cruel and unusual math teachers at the Christian Brothers High School. A wrong answer got you a smart swat across the arse with a wood paddle."

"Look, George, I've been thinking about this ever since I got here. Let's set up a poker parlor in that big room up on the third floor."

"The nuns' dormitory?"

"Yeah. You and I'll deal for the house. Make a little money."

By invitation only, the first poker games tonight drew a full house. Father Nolan and George had invited the best players from the Saturday night poker tables at the Knights of Columbus Hall. Edwin Brant recruited high rollers from his old clientele at the White House. Some, like Captain Long, had been regulars at both places. Players were promised honest poker and free booze.

Mulligan flopped down on the floor as Father Nolan took a chair at George's table with a lawyer named Pat Galyon; Chris Garson, a wealthy westside car dealer; Zim Zadi, a retired county judge, and Randy Hallman, a retired salesman.

"Didn't know I'd be playing against the Lord," Zadi said, nipping off the tip of a hefty cigar and clamping it between his teeth.

"Unfortunately," Father Nolan said, "you'll soon see He's not in my cards, Judge Zadi."

"Just call me Zee."

"As in zero," Chris Garson chuckled, piling stacks of fives and tens on the table, rolling up his sleeves and unwrapping a cigar.

"At least we're not playing against the cops," Galyon said, nodding at Captain Long's table across the oak-paneled room.

"Lady Luck's all in the cards, gentlemen," George said, deftly shuffling the deck.

Randy Hallman eyed Chris Garson's double stacks of greenbacks and surmised he might be in over his head. Cigar smoke built like storm clouds as dealers dealt the first hands and players placed bets. Besides George, Edwin and Captain Long, the other dealers had dealt for the White House before the great fire. Quin, a preeminent poker player at the Westbrook Hotel during the oil boom, had declined to deal for All Saints. "I love the game, Edwin, but as I've said before, I promised their mother I'd send our boys to Notre Dame."

Wally Cox had built the crescent-shaped bar facing a panoramic window overlooking the campus and Rosen's Pond. Like the poker tables, the leather-covered bar stools once accommodated guests at the White House. Lynn Brant poured liberal quantities of beer and booze for players, serving dealers from whiskey bottles filled with Bridie's tea.

"So nice to see you again, Lady Lynn," Chris Garson said, smiling and standing to give her a hug. "Been awhile."

"We've missed you," she said. "How's Melody?"

"Long as I keep her in expensive cars, she lets me out once in a while to play poker. Edwin treatin' you all right?"

"I whip the ol' boy in line now and then," she grinned.

Other former White House guests stood to greet Lady Lynn as she made the rounds, keeping their crystal glasses topped up with President's Choice.

George saw him first, leaning languidly against the door, surveying the room as he lit a cigarette. A fedora shadowed his face. Though short, he filled the doorway with his bulky, muscular frame, thick neck and bullish shoulders. George shot a troubled glance at Edwin's table as Sam Scott sauntered into the room. When Sam had heard about the poker parlor, he said he'd drop by to play a hand or two.

"It's a private club, and the tables are full," Edwin had said curtly.

"Must be afraid o' losin' your shirt...or your ass, Eddie Boy."

"Call me Eddie Boy again, you sawed-offed punk, and I'll—"

"All right, all right, forget it," Sam said.

Captain Long intercepted Edwin before he got to Sam.

"Back to your table, Edwin," Long said in the steely voice of authority cops use to intimidate scofflaws, drunks and bad dogs. The room fell silent.

"All right," Edwin said, deferring to the big Irishman towering over him. "Just get him outta here."

Captain Long gripped Sam's right arm. "You gotta leave, buddy."

"Whatever you say, Mr. Policeman," Sam said, sneering.

Later in the night, Lynn Brant served steak sandwiches courtesy of Dan Donovan, who'd had a good month trading cattle at the stockyards' Exchange Building. "I'll throw in a side of beef for a place at one of the tables," he'd told George.

Wally Cox carved the beef and grilled the steaks. "Nothin' better than mesquite-fired Texas beef," he said.

By ten-thirty or so, the games had separated winners from losers, the latter lingering over drinks at the bar. Dan Donovan teetered precariously on a bar stool long after he'd folded his cards for the night.

"One for the road, one for the ditch and one more for no reason at all," he called out, holding up his glass for a refill. Lynn coaxed him from the stool to a leather lounge chair. "Thank you, Lady Lynn. This is more comfortable."

"And closer to your destination, Dan."

"My destination?"

"Yeah, the floor," she grinned, pouring him another drink.

The dealers closed out the last hands just before two o'clock.

"So when's the next game, George?" Chris Garson wanted to know, his piles of fives and tens having grown appreciably over the evening.

"Every Friday night," George said.

"And you can play Saturday nights at the Knights Hall," Father Nolan said.

George had played the cards to tithe about ten percent of his table's pot to the priest. And at Bridie's request, Edwin kept Doc Cooper from losing his shirt, though not rewarding him any "courtesy wins."

"Now another one for no reason at all," Dan Donovan called as he zigzagged toward the bar.

"You're goin' with me," Long ordered.

"You gonna arrest me, Cap'n Mike?" Dan smiled like a naughty boy.

"No, Danny Boy, but I am haulin' your drunken ass home so I won't be on the streets when you are."

"What'll my neighbors think about a police car bringing me home?"

"Damned if I know." Mike guided him toward the door.

"Don't hurt 'im," Chris Garson called. "He's my best customer. Totally wrecks a new Cadillac about once a year."

Lynn yawned as the last players waved on their way out. "How'd we do, Edwin?"

"It was a good night, Lynn."

"Except we're dying for a drink after all that tea," George said.

"It kept you sober," Lynn said, handing glasses of President's Choice to George and Edwin, who were counting the night's take.

"Never mix whiskey with poker," Edwin said, gulping his drink. "If you have to shoot some cheater, you'll probably miss."

George was never sure when Edwin was serious. But he knew the poker parlor would soon provide enough cash to start an honest business of his own.

Bridie had been awakened by the metallic clatter of feet on the fire escape and the murmur of voices as the poker players descended to the campus and found their way to the street. She fell into a deep slumber, dreaming George had won enough to give her a few dollars for new dresses for Josie and Anna.

She didn't hear the kitchen door slam behind Father Nolan, followed by a scream and, "You ungodly horned beast, you," after he tripped over Clyde, asleep on the back porch.

Just before dawn, Bridie awakened to the ring and ping of Sam and Sandra Scott's footsteps on the fire escape as the reclusive couple returned from wherever they went every night.

SLICED BREAD AND
WATER

"Let there be water," Wally Cox commanded, turning the handle. The faucet shook and rattled, coughing up sporadic pockets of air and rusty red water.

"You've worked a miracle or robbed a bank," Bridie said, opening a letter at the kitchen table.

"The miracle of the shovel and the pipe wrench," Wally said, wiping his sweaty brow. "I dug down and ran the pipe under the meter. Soon as the lines clear, we'll have good water again."

"Oh?" Bridie said, raising an eyebrow. "So you didn't pay the water bill?"

"It's God's water, not the city's."

Opening the refrigerator, Wally looked quizzically at Bridie.

"George'll never miss it," she said.

"One or two won't hurt." He took a cold bottle of beer. "Where's my Ollie?"

"You needn't worry," Bridie said. "Your beloved wife's with Martin, filling washtubs down at the pond."

Ollie had been boiling water on the big stoves in the basement kitchen for drinking and washing dishes. Few at All Saints had bathed since the city cut off the water. Carting water to flush the toilets had been an endless, backbreaking chore shouldered by Quin, Wally, George and Edwin.

Sam Scott joined the water brigade after Edwin knocked on his door and said, "If you want bathroom privileges here, you're going to help haul water up from the pond."

Wally plunked himself down at the long table with his beer. "That electric icebox sure keeps 'em cold." He lifted a bag of Bull Durham from his pocket. "We can quit haulin' water now," he said, rolling a cigarette, "before we all get cholera or somethin' worse from that pond."

"Tommy sent a check," Bridie said, holding up an envelope. "More than enough to get my shamrock out of hock. And just in time."

She folded her brother's check on a bank in Tonopah, Nevada, put it in her purse and went to cash it at First National downtown. Taking the streetcar home, she got off at Zinn's North Main Pawnshop.

"How nice to see you again, Mrs. O'Driscoll," Julius Zinn said.

"Likewise," Bridie said, exchanging a wad of greenbacks for her gold shamrock four days before her loan expired. "And I'll give you the dollar and a half I owe on that telescope, too."

At Harrison's Grocery, she splurged on a festive dinner after a month-long diet heavy on eggs and scant vegetables from Ollie's rock-infested garden.

"We're all going to turn into chickens, Bridie," Quin had been telling her. "Every day it's eggs—eggs fried, eggs scrambled, eggs poached, eggs soft-boiled, eggs hard-boiled, but eggs all the same all the time. We ought to fry one of those chickens now and then."

"Then we'd soon have no eggs, Quin."

"Cherish the thought, dear Bridie. Cherish the thought of no eggs."

As Bridie pondered the offerings in his meat case, Mr. Harrison peeped over the shelves at two small boys circling a cedar barrel of pickles. "You boys get away from them pickles and go on outside. Damn kids steal a pickle and run straight out the door."

"Boys will be boys, won't they?" Bridie said.

"That Matthew boy from your place is the worst. Takes a bite outta of a pickle and tosses it back in the barrel. It's disgusting."

"I'll speak with Matthew. How much is your ham, Mr. Harrison?"

"Twenty cents a pound, Mrs. O'Driscoll."

"Rather dear, is it not, Mr. Harrison?"

"I've got chuck roast for thirteen cents and ground beef for seven."

"All right, Mr. Harrison, I'll take the ham, if you'll spare a bone for Mulligan."

"I've got Vigo dog food, four cans for two bits."

"The poor dog lives off table scraps and the odd bone, Mr. Harrison. And I'll have a loaf of that new kind of bread, though it's not as fresh."

"Same bread, just sliced now, Mrs. O'Driscoll."

"At what price, Mr. Harrison?"

"Same price, Mrs. O'Driscoll—five cents."

"It smells so fresh when I slice it myself."

"I think sliced bread's here to stay, Mrs. O'Driscoll."

Matthew paled when Bridie took the telescope from her purse. Though at first he denied stealing it, she stretched the truth a little and told him that Mr. Zinn had identified him as the boy who'd brought the scope to his pawnshop.

"Are you going to tell Mr. Cox or my dad?" Matthew asked.

"Not if you'll pay me the two dollars and fifty cents I gave Mr. Zinn to get the telescope back for Wally."

"You know I don't have any money, Miss Bridie."

"Get a lawnmower and cut people's grass. Anything honest will do."

"I'll try," he said.

"And don't forget to tell the priest you stole a telescope and took a bite out of Mr. Harrison's pickles when you go to confession Saturday."

Matthew went out the door without replying.

Bridie sent Wally to Harrison's in his truck to pick up the ham, a basket of vegetables, sliced bread, candy for the kids and a bone for Mulligan. The ham was eaten and, thanks to Wally, baths were taken late into the night as water coursed through the pipes again.

Bridie was washing supper dishes when Wally sailed into the kitchen with his long-missing World War I bronze telescope. "Look, Bridie, what I found in my truck just now!"

"Oh, so that's where you lost it—in your old truck!" she said.

"No, no, Bridie. It was on the dashboard right square in front of the steering wheel. I couldn't've left it there all this time. I just can't imagine how it got there."

"The thing is you got it back, Wally."

"I gotta go show this to Ollie," he said, hurrying down the hall.

After drying the dishes, Bridie polished her gold shamrock and put it on the shelf in her room. She admired it for several minutes. Then she sat on the edge of her bed and read the letter that came with Tommy's check.

Bishop, California

Dearest Bridie,

Received package of gloves with socks. They fit all right. Enclosed find cheque for $64.30. I trust you will do all right now. George should at least help support the children.

I am working 40 miles out of town up in the Sierra Nevada but don't know how long the mine will be open. I fear it will be a long while before times get better. Do the best you can. You needn't worry about me. I get along.

Your loving brother,
Tommy
Erin Go Bragh

P.S. Give a dollar to Josie and Anna for ice cream.

MEADOWS OF HONEY

"Lunches made and bagged," Lynn Brant announced.

Names scrawled in crayon identified the brown paper bags lined up at the back screen door: Josie, Anna, Richard, Brandon, Frankie, Matthew, Roger, Sissy, Cory, Juliana, Jeremy, Gabi, Buster.

Lynn put away the gallon jar of peanut butter, poured a cup of coffee and sat down between Gabi and Anna at the kitchen table. She lit a cigarette as Josie herded two sleepy-eyed orphans into the kitchen.

"Where've ye been, Josie," Bridie asked, "for it's almost time to go?"

"Clyde was asleep in the boys' room. Someone left the window open to the fire escape again."

"Pray God that goat's not in your dadda's room," Bridie said, wondering which kid had left the window open despite all her admonitions.

"I pushed Clyde out on the fire escape and shut the window, Mama," Josie said, spooning up a bowl of porridge at the stove.

"I hate this ol' porridge," Richard whined. "And my toast is burned."

"Eat now before everything's cold," Bridie said, moving around the table, filling glasses with milk and topping up a bowl on the floor for Q.C. As Quinlan's cat slipped along the wall to his milk bowl, Mulligan abandoned his place under the table, nosed open the back screen door and went out.

Matthew shoveled down his porridge as the other kids took their places at the table. Zelda Griffin sat next to him, pouting to go to school with the big kids.

"Ahhhh!" Richard shrieked. He stood up in his chair, gripped his throat and pointed accusingly at his bowl of porridge. He grasped the bowl and sent it flying down the table, mushy oats splattering Zelda as it skidded off the table.

"Are you possessed by something, Richard?" Bridie yelled, putting down the bottle of milk to console Zelda.

"Damn you!" Richard shouted as Matthew laughed aloud and sprinted out the back door with his lunch bag.

"Mind yere language, Richard, before I wash yere...no, no!" Bridie cried as the boy bolted for the door, seizing a butcher knife from the bookshelves.

"That little bastard put a beetle in my porridge!" Richard yelled, seeking another suitable weapon after Josie wrenched the knife from him.

"You don't like porridge, anyway," Anna said, laughing at him.

Q.C., his big yellow eye cast on the commotion, lapped up his milk.

Zelda screeched, her face pale as a bewildered black beetle caked in porridge lumbered slowly up the front of her yellow dress.

"Get it off her, Brandon!" Bridie cried.

Brandon Reynolds took the beetle between finger and thumb. En route to the back door, he suddenly lurched at the table and thrust the bug at Anna. She screamed and threw her soft-boiled egg. He dropped the beetle when the egg struck him in the face.

"Oh, shit!" Brandon cried, wiping egg from his face as he rounded the table to beat Anna.

Fearless, she raised her bowl of porridge to launching position. "Come and get it, you little shrimp!"

"Back to your chair, Brandon, this instant!" Bridie ordered. "And I'll be washing your mouth out with soap. And you, Anna, put down that bowl and eat your breakfast in peace. And you, Richard, sit down and eat your toast and eggs. I'll take care of Matthew."

"So will I, soon as I catch the little son of a—" Richard said before Bridie cut him off: "Enough, Richard, enough!"

"Shoo, Q.C., shoo," Lynn Brant ordered as the crippled cat stalked the battered beetle on the floor. "Poor bug," she said, tossing it outside. A crow swept down from the roof and flew off with the beetle in its beak.

Trouble had come to the table when Matthew started having breakfast with the other kids. Rather than everyone preparing separate breakfasts on school days, Ollie Cox said it would be cheaper and easier to serve standard fare every morning. Although Quin had warned her, Bridie invited Matthew to the kids' breakfasts anyway.

"Better than he gets from me every morning, Bridie," said Quin, whose boiled eggs cracked and filled with water. "But when he gives you trouble, just whack hell out of him. I do."

"Finish eating, and be off to school now," Bridie said, cradling teary-eyed Zelda in her arms and wiping porridge from her dress. "And bring those lunch bags home this afternoon."

Ollie Cox had also organized the standard brown-bag school lunches: peanut butter sandwich, hard-boiled egg and, if available, half an apple.

"Peanut butter's cheap and something Catholics and Jews can eat any time," Ollie said, mindful of the

Jewish aversion to pork and of the various meatless days for Catholics. "Thank God Protestants got no religion when it comes to eatin'."

The thirteen kids took their books and sack lunches and walked along Belle Avenue. They separated at Northwest Twenty-Fourth, some going to Sam Rosen Elementary and others to Mount Carmel Academy. Roger Quinlan took the streetcar downtown to Saint Ignatius Academy.

After Sister Vee sent Frankie, the second Jewish boy from the orphanage in Dallas, Bridie had paid a visit to the Rosen Heights Land Company.

"I need your advice about what's kosher in food and education for my two Jewish lads," she told Sam Rosen after introducing herself, though he seemed to know all about Bridie O'Driscoll and all the people who lived with her at All Saints Kibbutz, as he called it.

"Well now, Mrs. O'Driscoll," he said, amused by her dilemma and pleased by her thoughtfulness, "if a Catholic orphanage took them in, the boys'll become good Jewish-Catholics or good Catholic-Jews. What's kosher these days is that they eat at all, though the less pork perhaps the better. And we'll spare my rabbi the details of what I've just said."

Bridie was especially pleased that Sam had begun taking Richard Levitz and Frankie Feldman to the synagogue on Saturdays and other Jewish religious days.

Though at first they protested getting up Saturday mornings while the other kids slept in, Sam coaxed them to the synagogue with promises of candy, ice cream and other suitable bribes.

Otherwise Bridie took Sam Rosen's unorthodox advice to do her best for their temporal needs. She sent the two Jewish boys to the Catholic school and tried not to feed them too much pork or ham—on the rare occasions these delicacies graced her sparse kitchen table.

"Thank God I never had children, Bridie," Lynn Brant sighed, washing breakfast dishes at the kitchen sink. "Where did that little one in the yellow dress come from?" she said as Zelda ambled out the back door with Mulligan.

"Her mother's cleaning rooms at the Westbrook today, so Zelda stays with me. Her no-good, drunken husband walked out sometime ago. Now she's behind on her house payments to Sam Rosen, though he never throws anyone into the street who's trying to do the right thing."

"Oh him," Lynn said. "We bought the White House from Mr. Rosen."

"Mornin', Julie," Bridie said as Julie Bryant stepped into the kitchen.

"Mornin', Miss Nightingale," Lynn said, admiring her crisp white uniform.

"Just call me Florence," Julie said, primping smartly in the uniform that came with a promotion to full-time clerk at Saint Joseph's emergency room.

"Busy at Saint Joe's?" Bridie said, mopping porridge from the floor.

"Lot of kids with rickets and pellagra from not eating right or not eating at all. So where's Quin...and the others this morning?"

"Quin's at the stockyards," Bridie said, not deceived that Julie's broad inquiry about "the others" had attempted to hide her liaison with the resident widower.

As Julie's high heels tap-tapped across the kitchen to the back door, Bridie continued, "Quin's bookkeeping for Dan Donovan, while poor Wally's shoveling you know what out of the cow pens down there today."

"And all the little monsters are gone to school to terrorize their teachers," Lynn said.

"Thanks for feeding my two," Julie said. "Gotta run and catch that streetcar." The back screen slammed as she went out and waved to Zelda playing on the merry-go-round and to Ollie yanking weeds from the dry, hardscrabble soil of her vegetable garden.

Lynn finished drying the dishes. "Whew, whatta morning." She lit a Pall Mall and sat down at the table. "How'd you ever end up here in this big convent in the first place, Bridie?"

"Oh, we were living over in Bessie Street in a house. My brother Tommy bought it for us after his big gold strike, and—"

"Gold strike!" Lynn said.

"He's been prospecting for gold since he came over from Ireland. He hit a big one and bought us the house for thirty-five hundred cash. Imagine that! When the nuns had to close this place, they asked me to look after it until this depression thing is over. I couldn't say no, my sister being a nun and all."

"Just like that, huh? What happened to the house?"

"Well, George wasn't happy about it and still isn't. I told him we could save some money renting the house. He's always looking to make more money. So we did, but the renters seldom pay up."

"Throw the bums out, Bridie, and rent to somebody else."

"That's what George says. I just can't throw them into the street. The poor man's a disabled war veteran. He lost his job. They have kids. They pay when they can."

"Ever wish you were back in Ireland, Bridie?"

"Sometimes, Lynn, when I think about those soft, misty days and our lovely little town by the River Suir, the green hills all around us. I dream of friends going to the shops, dropping by for tea in their little houses, going to the market and the county fair—all without me now."

"A town? A city?"

"Pretty little river town as old as the green hills themselves. Called Clonmel, meaning 'meadows of honey' in Gaelic."

"Meadows of honey—oh, how truly beautiful, like a fairy tale. Surely, Bridie, you miss your old home at times."

"It's like childhood, Lynn. You remember the best times and you'd love to go back, knowing there's no way. Once in a while I dream of it and my two daughters, little Norah and baby Brigid, buried at the foot of Slievenamon Mountain."

Bridie removed her glasses and wiped her eyes. "My last link is my gold shamrock." She took it from her apron pocket and rubbed it fondly. "I was so worried when I hocked it last month that I might lose it. It got me to America, you know."

"All right, Bridie, you've been promising to tell me how you got out of Ireland and came to this godforsaken outpost in Texas. So how about it?"

"Over a spot o' tea."

"I'll even try a spot," Lynn said.

"And afterwards I'll read our tea leaves," Bridie said, putting a kettle of water on the stove.

"Reading tea leaves! Where did you get that, Bridie O'Driscoll?"

"My mother learned it from the gypsies, who got it from the fairies."

"Oh, now I want to hear it all, Bridie: the fields of honey, the tea leaves, gypsies, fairies, that gold shamrock you're always polishing, the whole shebang."

THE FORBIDDEN
SHAMROCK

Well, Lynn, one day in Clonmel, I got this letter from Tommy in America about his first big gold strike:

"Those shamrocks you sent I sprinkled over me diggings and what luck they brought, dear Bridie. 'Tis a vein of gold promising to reach all the way to China. The least I can do is send you ship's passage to America."

I went running through the narrow, cobbled lanes to Delia Walsh's little house in William Street.

"We'll soon be dancing on Broadway," I told her as she opened the door. "Remember those shamrocks I sent Tommy? Well, he sprinkled them over the ground he was working and struck gold. And now he's sent money for ship's passage to New York."

"And you'll never see Clonmel or me again," Delia cried, wiping her watery eyes.

"Why, Delia," I told her, "you're coming with me, of course, for we both outdanced Ireland's best. And there's money enough here to take the two of us to New York. See for yourself." I handed her Tommy's money order in the envelope, postmarked Elko, Nevada.

It had been two years since Delia and I danced our way to first place at the County Tipperary Fair against high-steppers from as far away as high-flutin' Dublin. Mobbed by throngs of handsome, strapping lads and sassy, rosy-cheeked lassies, the grand fiddler claimed to have outfiddled a gypsy to gain possession of the most coveted prize ever offered at Ireland's ancient fairs.

"'Tis crafted by fairies from a rainbow's gold— gold that brings fairies' cures and life's luck to the one who possesses it," he said, holding up a gold shamrock that covered the palm of his hand. A wave of aahs and oohs rolled across the crowd. "Yet ask not how the gypsy man came by the magic shamrock, for the answer surely bears a fairy's curse."

"Oh my, a fairy's curse," Lynn said, laughing aloud.

No one laughed, Lynn, for the story was out: a gypsy—as only a gypsy might—had slipped a potion in a fairy's drink and then slipped the shamrock from his little pocket up on Slievenamon Mountain, the place of the wee people.

"*Wee people?*"

They're the bad angels, Lynn. Lost their wings and fell to earth never to return to heaven. That's who the fairies are, you see—fallen angels with evil powers and curses to lay on anyone.

While priests threatened excommunication and the fires of purgatory and hell, we Irish never quite gave up blending our Catholic faith with fairies, myth, witchcraft and pagan places like magic water wells, ghosts and the like. Indeed, Delia and I had skipped school to catch glimpses of the trial of Michael Cleary, who burned his beloved wife to death to exorcise fairies from her young body. I'll never forget the children's evil little rhyme:

> Are you a witch?
> Or are you a fairy?
> Or are you the wife
> Of Michael Clearly?

"*So you're serious,*" *Lynn said,* "*that people really believe in witches and fairies?*"

Oh, indeed, Lynn. And to ward off witches and fairies and their curses, Delia and I drenched ourselves with buckets of holy water from Saint Patrick's well and went forth to dance for what some—including my own mother—were calling the forbidden shamrock at the County Tipperary Fair of 1899.

"Was your mother at the fair, Bridie?" Lynn asked, lighting another cigarette.

She was there but wouldn't come near the gold shamrock at the dancing contest for fear of the curse. Sad because Delia and I both smartly outstepped the girls from Tipperary Town, Cashel and Currick-on-Suir in the final circles of the competition. When the two of us took to the last dancing circle, friend against friend, the fiddlers never fiddled finer or faster in feverish fury to separate the best of the best. Yet when they rested their fiery violins, the judges lamented they had only one first-place prize. In truth, they said, either of us was as good a dancer as the other.

I just went up on the stage and called out, "'Tis ours together, Delia." Everyone applauded and hooped and hollered as the fiddlers struck up music that set the crowd dancing and singing. I hugged Delia and said, "We'll always share the luck of the gold shamrock together."

"Its curses as well, to be sure," someone called out.

"Did that worry you, Bridie?" Lynn said.

Delia insisted that I be the keeper of our shamrock. What she kept was a bowl of holy water from Saint Patrick's well in her bedroom window to ward off any fairies passing by in search of our shamrock. I never worry a wit about those wee people, having faith the shamrock will protect me. And two years later, it got me to New York. I begged Delia to come with me.

"Oh, Bridie, if only I could, but ye know I'm to marry John Butler come this summer."

Other than Tommy, only Delia knew I was going to New York to become a Broadway chorus girl. My parents thought I'd take a job as a respectable house-maid, like my sister Polly, who worked for a rich family in Manhattan.

"What was the problem with dancing on Broadway?"

You see, Lynn, while dancing is as Irish as singing in pubs and at church, in the eyes of mothers, fathers and parish priests, chorus girls aren't much better than prostitutes.

Thanks to Tommy's Nevada gold, I felt like the no-bility laying down twenty-five pounds British sterling for a first-class cabin aboard the *Teutonic,* a White Star Line steamer sailing out of Southampton. I'd never been out of County Tipperary, so sailing over smooth summer seas was like going to the moon.

And after eight days, the fabled city rose on the watery horizon. Lynn, it was to me like the resurrec-tion of the Roman Empire. I can still see those tower-ing ten- and twelve-story buildings standing shoulder to shoulder scraping against the blue sky. Of course, I joined the mob on the deck to wave, bow, cry and throw kisses to the Statue of Liberty.

I fairly floated down the gangplank into the New World and...

"At that island where all the immigrants—"

No, Lynn. At the time the ship landed, first-class passengers like me disembarked at the Battery in Lower Manhattan. Second-class and steerage passengers went on to Ellis Island for the much-feared medical exam. A fair number got turned back for tuberculosis and other things. Me, I wasn't stopped or asked a single question.

"A new world and a new life," Lynn said.

At first it was a bit shocking. Following my sister's hand-drawn map, I lugged my bag through noisy streets jammed with horse-drawn cabs, carriages, carts, trolleys and bicycles—more people than I'd ever seen at a county fair. I almost got run down by a horseman as I stopped in the middle of the street to look at a black man on the corner. I'd heard of black people, of course, but I had never seen one in my life.

"And what did you think?"

He looked to me like all other men, just black, that's all. Tell no one now, Lynn, but I did wonder if the black would rub off if I touched him.

"You didn't!" Lynn said, *chuckling as much over Bridie's innocence as her ignorance.*

I did, but I've never understood why white people here mistreat them so.

"Go on with your story," Lynn said.

I continued on my way, fanning myself against the heat and longing for those frequent mists that cool our summer days back home. And the closer I got to the Lower East Side, the stench of horse manure and spoiled garbage piled in the streets would've gagged a maggot. I would've given anything for a breath of Clonmel's fresh air. Barefooted, half-dressed kids played in the dirty streets, their mothers clumped down on the front steps of unpainted old tenement houses.

Polly lived in two and a half tiny rooms on the third floor of a dank, creaky tenement house, a smelly community toilet at the end of the dark hall. She had fared better living in a maid's closet at a mansion in Lexington Avenue where she worked. She'd moved to this cramped cold-water flat when she married John Curtis, an Irish bartender and boozer. He was none too happy to see me.

In her modesty, Bridie didn't tell Lynn she had muffled her ears at night to shut out the moans of the newlyweds in a bed that squeaked and rattled, its headboard banging rhythmically and then wildly against the thin wall.

After resting up a few days, I sprinkled myself with a jar of holy water I'd brought over from Saint Patrick's well, kissed my gold shamrock for luck and took a streetcar to the theatre district. I soon learned Broadway was no county fair where any girl with a flair for dancing had a chance at the finals and hopes of taking home a prize. Auditions for new Broadway productions drew droves of stagestruck actresses and dancers—young, pretty professionals who got most of the parts. A few who'd danced out their days kept trying, more from habit than hope.

"All that rejection must have hurt, Bridie."

No, no, like all chorus girls, I knew absolutely every morning I was only a step or two from a place on stage and fame's limelight. I'd be back next day in another line of girls waiting endless hours to dance two minutes for a couple of stone-faced directors.

"And what was Polly saying about all this?"

Oh, I've never lived such a lie in my life, Lynn. I scanned the newspaper ads for live-in maid's positions "in one of the better neighborhoods," as Polly advised. "Irish girls have a reputation as reliable servants. Ye'll be given a uniform, meals, a warm place to sleep and a little spending money. What more to ask?" She couldn't understand why I hadn't found a "household position," as she called that life of drudgery she lived as a housemaid.

Then one day, boom! I landed a role with a line of chorus girls at the Bowery Theatre on West Thirty-Second Street, off Broadway a bit. Just in the nick of time, too, as my money was running out paying my share of the groceries and buying John Curtis a few beers to keep him from throwing me out.

I told Polly I'd gotten a job dipping strawberries in chocolate at a candy factory. I told her it was night work as the candy was delivered fresh every morning to expensive shops in Fifth Avenue.

"What a sweet little lie, Bridie!" Lynn said.

But when I reached into the cabinet above the kitchen stove for my gold shamrock, it was gone. Choking with tears and torn with grief, I couldn't imagine what had happened to it.

"Stay here, Bridie," Polly said.

She returned an hour or so later. "I found John playing poker at Duffy's Lounge," Polly said, handing me the shamrock. "I made him borrow against his pay to get it out of the pawnshop. He'd hocked it for gambling money."

When John came home, he said, "Ye needn't have worried, Bridie. I'd only borrowed your little shamrock 'til payday."

Wanting to keep the peace, I gave him a sisterly hug and told him if God could forgive him, surely I could. But after that, I slept with the shamrock and kept it in my purse.

The Bowery was a rowdy, noisy place—a working class saloon with a stage and a three-piece band, usually half drunk. So I kept going to auditions at other theatres. Next thing I knew, I was in the chorus line at the New Amsterdam. I couldn't believe I'd made it, Lynn, from the Tipperary County Fair to Broadway in New York City, New York!

Clapping and smiling, Lynn said, "All on your own talent."
That and my shamrock. Over the next couple of years, I sang and danced at the Knickerbocker and the Metropolitan. I even got a few cameo roles in major productions. I went for any role that was decent and moral—none of those sleazy castings of half-dressed girls hanging out of their clothes, you know.

Having little to do after morning rehearsals, I got really bold, Lynn. I tried out as a model for Charles Gibson, the designer of women's fashionable clothing.

"Sure, I remember Gibson," Lynn said.

I dressed for the audition, showing up in the latest Gibson girl fashions, hair piled in chignon, lacy shirt-waist, flowing skirt, the whole bit. And Mr. Gibson himself gave me a smile and a nod.

"I'm not at all surprised in the prime of your beauty, Bridie. You must've been a doll."

Wait, Lynn, I'll show you something.

Lynn poured the last of the tea and fired up another ciga-rette. Bridie returned from her room with a framed picture.

In a moment of vanity, Lynn, I had this made of myself and sent it home to my mother. My papa had gone to heaven by then.

Lynn studied the photo of a poised, comely young lady in the bloom of youth, trim and fit as a dancer, a pretty mellow face, softly arresting eyes, flawless skin. She also saw that de-spite a few wrinkles and stray strands of gray hair, Bridie had held her own over the years: still spry and petite, a youthful twinkle in her eyes, a warm smile and a quick wit.

"Must'a been a bunch of boys trailing after you?"

A few—nothing serious. American boys were a bit pushy and demanding. And Irish lads, like many back home, tended too much to the bottle, if you know what I mean?

"Oh yeah, I know all about pushy men who drink too much. And Polly never discovered your act about working at a candy company?"

Now and then I'd leave a box of candy on the kitchen table, telling her I brought it from the candy maker where I worked.

"How deceptive of you, Bridie," Lynn said.

But I forgot one night after the show to wash off the heavy stage makeup, Lynn, and next morning, Polly was shocked. You see, like a lot of Irish girls, we never wore makeup. So I simply confessed.

"My God and heaven forbid," Polly said. "What'll Mum be thinking, with one daughter a nun and the other a common—?"

"God forbid, you won't be telling her, Polly," I said.

"But showgirls are indecent and sinful, Bridie."

"Let's not be judging those whose sins differ from our own," I told her. Though she never exactly approved, she knew my paycheck was more reliable than John's, and she was pregnant by then.

I sort of redeemed myself as the only chorus girl dancing on Broadway Saturday nights and singing in Saint Patrick's Cathedral Sunday mornings. Polly had been singing in the choir there for some years and got me an audition. Like her, I knew all the religious songs in English and Latin from singing at church back home.

"And you had the voice, the talent, Bridie."

I had my lucky shamrock is what I had, Lynn. My biggest break came in '06 when I danced my way to a spot with the Anna Held Girls. And just a year later, I made the cut as one of Anna Held's fifty dancers in the new Ziegfeld Follies. The *Times* called the Follies the greatest show of the new century when it opened on the roof of the Jardin de Paris on Broadway and 44th. Tickets went for two dollars and fifty cents—the highest ever in New York.

"You made the big time, Bridie, like so many never do, you know."

I was still a chorus girl, Lynn, but a chorus girl in the big leagues. Yet year by year, stardom fades. And I watched younger dancers replace older ones, who became ushers, ticket sellers and backstage maids. Many ended up with a brood living with a drunken husband like Polly's John.

I saw the handwriting on the wall, Lynn. I loved the theatre, the lights, the music, the crowds, the applause. The glamour of it all was heaven on earth. Yet I was twenty-seven and still a chorus girl, but my theatre days were numbered. Also, I was sharing a small room with two-year-old Patrick when Polly got pregnant again. I thought I'd finish out the winter season and go home.

"To Ireland?"

To Ireland to find an Irish gentleman, Lynn.

But coming home from the theatre on a bitterly cold night, I found John Curtis passed out drunk in the snow outside our tenement house. Fearing he'd freeze to death, I shook him until he came around. The drunken fool wanted to take me to a pub for a beer. When I turned to walk off, he grabbed me.

"Give your dear ol' Johnny Boy a little kiss now, Bridie."

I swung, called him a drunken Irish bastard and ran up the steps.

"It'll be black by morning," he cried, sprawled in the snow. "What'll I tell Polly about me poor eye?"

Of course, I never told Polly. And we cried together a week later when I boarded the *Lusitania* on a voyage to Queenstown and home, where I met George.

"Well, Bridie, a sort of happy, sad ending."

I lived my girlhood dream, Lynn, but I never saw Polly again. She died a few years later. I've always thought her John had something to do with it. I'll never know. Anyway, Lynn, that's my life on Broadway story, and we're fresh out of tea.

"One more thing, Bridie," Lynn said. "Did the so-called curse of your lucky gold shamrock...well, did it ever come down on you?"

It didn't keep me from burying two lovely daughters in Ireland.

She omitted the awful curse that had befallen her marriage to George O'Driscoll.

Tybo via Tonopah, Nevada

Dear Bridie,

Tybo is a lead mine with some silver, set in a narrow canyon with lots of pine and cedar juniper and wild flowers and ice cold water in the streams all summer. They are trying to keep it going as they have put $2 million into it over the last few years. The nearest town is Tonopah, 75 miles from here. It's a silver town and about dead.

I need several more paychecks to strike out on my own again. I have a stake in Clonmel No. 1 near a place called Jarbidge. Pray it's that vein of gold I've been looking for these many years. The one that runs to China. I hope to see all of you next Christmas.

Give a dollar to Josephine and Anna to get ice cream and soda pop. Did you receive three shares of Edison stock a few months back. Worth $111 a share before the crash. I told the bank to send them to you. Let me know about this.

Your loving brother,
Tommy
Erin Go Bragh

P.S. Almost forgot to thank you for the package. You might have put a letter in it. The shirt is warm and the socks almost fit.

JONATHAN'S REVENGE

"I admire you, Jonathan. I'm proud of the grades you make and the athlete you are. And I care about you and Matthew and Roger. And—"

"And you're dating my dear old dad," Jonathan said, sulking, head down, staring at the floor. "Or is dating the right word?"

"Jonathan, I'm about twice your age with two kids about half your age. How would you like living with those two?" Julie said. She laughed lightly. "No one will ever replace your mother, but I'll always be here for you, somebody you can trust. It's time you—"

"Yeah, you might even be my stepmother someday," he said, emitting a harsh, bitter laugh.

"Jonathan, please. Even if I didn't know your dad, it's time you quit doting on me and find yourself a girl more your age."

Sitting opposite each other on chairs in the middle of her sparsely furnished room, Julie touched Jonathan gently on the arm. "As a mature woman nearing middle age, I'm flattered that you even noticed me. I really am. But we're an age apart. Always will be. If you care for me at all, Jonathan, let me love you...love you like a brother."

"That's not how you love my dad, is it?" he said, hot tears running down his cheeks.

"Jonathan!" Julie shouted when he bolted and pounded down the hall.

She closed the door to her room as others on the floor opened theirs to investigate the noise. She wondered again if she should tell Quin about his son's heartfelt crush on his father's lover.

Home for fall break, Jonathan retreated to his cave down by the pond, smoking Camels and drinking Blackie's best bootleg whiskey. The rest of the week he nodded when spoken to. He ate alone, leftovers he'd asked Bride to leave on the kitchen stove. He entered and exited his room via the fire escape.

"He's probably having girl trouble in Austin," Quin said when Julie asked if he'd noticed the profound change in his son. "It's the fate of young love. He'll live through it."

Julie was relieved several days later when Jonathan smiled and spoke to her—until she realized whose room he was leaving.

"Hi, Julie," he said, a cocky half grin on his face. "How're things?"

"I'm fine, Jonathan," she said softly. "We missed you lately."

"Oh," he said, his grin fading to a slight smirk. "I've been, uh…well, Julie, you might say I've been getting acquainted with our newest resident." He nodded at the door to the Scotts' room, rocking back and forth on his feet.

"Sam and Sandra Scott?" she said.

"No, not the Sam character. The pretty one, Sandra. She's an entertainer at those nightclubs out on the Jacksboro Highway. You must know her?"

"I know about her, Jonathan," Julie said, aware that the girl was a stripper at expensive men's clubs. Lynn Brant also had told her that Sam Scott booked Sandra for after-show dates with high-dollar customers.

"I just met Sandra," Jonathan said. "We hit it off from the beginning. I'll be coming home more often now that we're friends. A lot more often, Julie."

"What about Sam Scott?"

The boy laughed. "He's not my type."

"Listen to me, Jonathan. I know what you're telling me, what you're doing in there, and—"

"Jealous?" he said. "Sandra's very pretty...and young, isn't she?"

"What you're doing is dangerous, Jonathan. Sam's not a kid, and Sandra's no high school chick."

"She's almost twenty-one, Julie. You said to find a girl closer to my age."

Julie stared blank-faced at Jonathan, humiliated that he was toying with her. It was his moment of revenge. And for better or worse, Julie realized, his hands-on education with a striptease artist at least ended his obsession for her. If there was no need now to tell Quin that his son coveted his mistress, should she inform him Jonathan was sleeping with a professional whore at All Saints Convent and Girls School?

Julie reached out and jiggled Jonathan's loose belt. "Better buckle up before you lose your pants."

"Oh," he said, buckling the belt. "Guess I forgot... afterwards, you know."

"Try not to catch something you really, really don't want...while you're at it, you know," Julie said, turning and walking away.

It occurred to her that Sandra wasn't so bad for Jonathan. Whores were a growing-up thing for some boys. Her two older brothers had broadcast their whorehouse escapades to all their high school friends. One of them practically advertised that he'd gotten the clap. *That would be a true growing-up experience for Jonathan Quinlan*, she mused, chiding herself for smiling.

SANDRA

Jonathan had met her on the fire escape. She was picking her way down the steep steps in a blue evening dress and high heels, gripping the railing and focusing on her feet.

"I'll give you a hand," Jonathan said.

He reminded her of boys she'd dated not long ago in high school.

"Oh...I'll be okay," she said, as he took her hand.

"I'm Jonathan Quinlan."

"Sandra Scott."

"You always take the fire escape instead of the stairs?"

"Yeah. Sam don't like me to mingle with all these people. You live here or just visiting?"

"Second-floor room at the end of the hall."

"Oh, we're neighbors," she said, smiling. "We ought to visit sometime."

"I'd like that."

"I've gotta meet my manager right now," she said.

"You mean Sam?"

"Yeah. Come by in the morning after his Lincoln's gone."

Sam left the convent around ten every day. "He plays pool and poker at those parlors downtown on Main," Sandra told Jonathan on his first visit. "He picks me up in the evening and takes me to work at the clubs."

Sandra offered Jonathan a beer. "Sam won this electric icebox in a pool game," she said, handing him a bottle and opening one for herself. He gave her a cigarette. She sat next to him on a couch Sam had won in a poker game.

"It's lonely here all day," she said, her eyes locked on his. "I'm so glad you came to see me."

"I couldn't wait to see you again." He touched her arm. The heat between them was palpable and raw.

"Jonathan, you're so handsome," she gushed. "So nice and polite, so sparkling and young."

If Sandra took him as some high school sweetheart from the past, she was also weary and disgusted with men sporting unkempt mustaches and unwashed beards that raked her cheeks. Men reeking of cigars, cigarette smoke, chewing tobacco and snuff and alcohol and whatever they'd just eaten. Ugly, potbellied, hairy guys old enough to be her daddy or granddaddy. Boastful, boisterous strangers who acted as if she were their girlfriend and wanted to kiss her in the mouth with their tongues and make damn sure they got their money's worth.

Without another word, Sandra kissed Jonathan lightly on the lips, held him gently, and slowly ran her fingers through his thick, wavy hair. She sighed as Jonathan folded his muscular arms around her. He kissed her deeply and ran his hands down her back, around her waist and over her breasts. He kissed her bare shoulders as she unzipped her dress, unbuttoned his shirt and proceeded to undress them both.

In his arms, she was back in high school with clean, eager boys, clumsy and overly considerate at first, wanting to please her, not wanting to hurt her as they shared their bodies, discovering heavenly bliss, mistaking torrid passion for love.

"You were wonderful, Jonathan," Sandra whispered, lying naked beside him on the couch, smoking a cigarette.

"It's never been any better," he said, running his hand over her flat stomach. "You have the most beautiful body I've ever seen."

Sandra giggled, fairly sure he'd never seen a nude girl and that she'd just relieved him of his virginity.

Their morning routine continued until he left for school again. On that last day, he brought his suitcase and stayed until midafternoon. "Jonathan, you'd better go," Sandra said. "Sometimes Sam comes back early."

"I'm not worried about Sam," he said. After taking down the railroad bull in the Santa Fe rail yards, Jonathan had no doubt he was stronger and more agile than grown men.

Sandra abruptly sat back on the couch and looked directly at him. "Jonathan, don't fuck with Sam. You don't know him. Promise me you'll stay away from him."

Jonathan shrugged. "Okay, Sandra. But who is Sam, really? Is he your—"

"Like I said, he's just my manager, Jonathan. Sam takes care of my entertainment contracts. I use his last name so men at the clubs think I'm married and don't mess with me."

"I see," he murmured, looking curiously at the double bed across the room. "Until next week," he said as they kissed goodbye.

"Now, don't be running around with those Austin high school girls," she said. "I can tell, ya know."

Going down the fire escape, Jonathan froze as Sam Scott mounted the steps to his and Sandra's room.

"Afternoon, Jonathan," Sam said, smiling.

"Hi, Mr. Scott. How are you?" Jonathan mumbled in a faltering, squeaky voice.

As Sam reached out and shook hands with him, Jonathan saw the pistol inside his coat.

"Looks like you're goin' off for a while," Sam said amiably, nodding to Jonathan's suitcase.

"Oh, yeah," the boy stammered. "Back to school again."

Sam touched the brim of his hat with two fingers. "Have a good trip, Jonathan."

"Yes, sir. Thank you, sir."

THE SOUND OF MONEY

Waiters in white coats sailed across the marble floor serving coffee, soda pop and sandwiches. The swaggering sounds of swing echoed through the crowded lobby as two orchestras served up "Zulu Wail" followed by "Bashful Baby," hit tunes that set people to tapping toes and swaying in rhythm.

A smiling, jolly man in a white cowboy hat, handmade western boots and an Italian suit applauded. He stood on a marble-topped table where customers normally filled out deposit slips. He harangued the dubious crowd with assurances that "this is the safest bank in the world."

A few waved at the renowned publisher of the *Star-Telegram*, whose editorials assured readers the Great Depression was an illusion: "a ridiculous spectacle brought on by idle gossip, unfounded rumors and hysteria."

Others laughed at the cowboy atop the table tapping his boot to the music. Most ignored Amon G. Carter, a.k.a. Mr. Fort Worth. Undaunted, he urged them to "dance away your troubles" as the dual bands struck up George Gershwin's "Rhapsody in Blue."

"May I have this dance, madame?" smiled a tall, rangy man, wisps of white hair sparsely ringing his baldpate.

"Why, indeed, Mr. Connell. I'd be honored."

"The honor's all mine," replied the city's best-known banker, an ex-cowboy who'd never quite lost his campfire drawl. "Just call me Wilson, and you are....?"

"Bridie O'Driscoll. Just call me Bridie."

"Well now, Bridie, with a name like O'Driscoll and an accent like that, you'll dance a jig around me," laughed the lanky, lantern-jawed banker.

Their feet took up the tune as they swirled gracefully in rhythm around marble columns, between mahogany desks and leather chairs. The crowd cheered. Others took partners and joined the six-foot six-inch bank president and his little dancing partner. Anna drew a round of chuckles and light applause as she performed her own dance.

The man on the marble table danced with himself, puffed on a Montecristo cigar and clapped his hands. Mounted above the row of teller cages, the head of a longhorn steer—nine-foot horns spread like wings—gazed contentedly over the growing lines of anxious customers.

People outside hoped to get inside before all the money was gone. They lined the sidewalk and spilled into Houston and Seventh streets, blocking traffic and ignoring red-faced cops shouting, "Move! Move on! Get outta the way!"

Men with tense faces and women in tears talked about neighbors left penniless by the recent failure of the Texas National Bank. A distraught bank clerk had blown out his brains with a pistol at high noon on Main Street. Despite Amon Carter's *Star-Telegram* stories that stock market troubles in the East benefited the West, the talk around town slowly turned to speculation and rampant rumor. Hearsay became "fact." Fear bred panic.

And on this chilly Wednesday afternoon, Lillian Reckard, a friend from her old neighborhood, phoned Bridie O'Driscoll. "There's a run on the First National," she said and hung up.

Bridie grabbed her purse, donned her Sunday hat, dashed out of the door and down Belle Avenue. "Come along, girls," she called when she saw Josie and Anna walking home from school. "Let's not miss the next streetcar." Her mission was to rescue brother Tommy's bonds, his now near-worthless stocks and almost sixty dollars in a rainy-day savings account at First National.

As the word spread, men walked off their jobs. Women left supper on stoves and children in back-yards. Drivers abandoned cars in traffic-jammed streets and ran toward the towering First National Bank, a pillar of the town's cattle and oil economy, the repository of life savings and next month's rent.

Tom Yarbrough, the bank's vice president, called Sheriff Red Wright to "come on down here and help with this mob." The sheriff put the crowd at upwards of a thousand "fairly frantic folks." He called the Texas Rangers.

"What is your suggestion, Ranger Hickman?" the bank vice president demanded of the steely-eyed law-man, a .45 Colt six-shooter on his hip, a silver star on his lapel, a blackjack protruding from his back pocket.

"Well, Mr. Yarbrough, I suggest you give these folks their damn money a sight faster than you're doin'— 'afore this stampede gets completely outta hand," Ranger Tom Hickman said. "That's what I suggest, Mr. Yarbrough."

Sheriff Wright busied himself handing out a sup-ply of newly arrived hot dogs. "Got any mustard, Mr. Sheriff?" Anna asked.

"Sure, little lady, right over there with them on-ions and ketchup at that first teller cage," he pointed. "Jest he'p yourself." Neither the high sheriff nor the Texas Ranger "noticed" booze generously served by bank clerks to soothe the distraught nerves of male customers.

When the man on the marble table had sent out for live music, two big bands came running, one from the Texas Hotel and the other from the Westbrook. "These folks need to hear the sweet sound of money," he told the musicians. They served up "Ten Cents a Dance" and "I'm in the Market for You."

Between tunes, Amon Carter announced that bank passbooks were good for free admission to the Majestic Theatre. Two hundred customers stampeded down the street to see William Boyd in *Officer O'Brien*, a new talkie.

"If you got any more tricks like that, Mr. Carter, now's the time to pull 'em outta your hat," Ranger Hickman advised.

By the time Bridie had closed the savings account and retrieved Tommy's stocks and bonds from a safe deposit box, waiters were serving ham sandwiches, coffee and cold soda pop.

"Excuse me, Bridie," Wilson Connell said, checking his pocket watch as the bands played "Singin' in the Rain." "I've enjoyed the dance, but I've got to help out my friend Amon for a minute."

His timing was on the mark. A convoy of Brinks armored trucks from Dallas nudged through the throng on Houston Street. Uniformed guards armed with tommy guns emerged from the trucks. The music stopped as they pushed through the lobby with canvas bags—marked "Federal Reserve Bank"—into First National's vault.

Like an auctioneer at a cattle sale, Amon Carter bellowed from the tabletop, "Yippee, li'l dogies! Six million, seven-hundred-fifty thousand dollars coming through before your very eyes." He looked slowly round the lobby, gathering the attention he expected as Fort Worth's self-appointed spokesman.

"Almost seven million greenbacks," he continued, "deposited here as an expression of the Federal Reserve's faith in this great bank of ours. But as my friend Wilson Connell will tell you, your bank doesn't need that extra money to cover your accounts. Climb on up here and talk to these folks, Wilson."

"I wouldn't want to steal your thunder, Amon," the soft-spoken banker said. The crowd chuckled. "I'll simply say this," he began, leaning on the table as if talking to neighbors over the back fence. "Our doors will be open tonight until the last customer has made the last withdrawal. But if you leave your money here, it's as safe with me as it has been since I joined the First National back in the 1890s."

People looked at one another to see if strangers standing next to them believed the words they wanted so much to believe themselves.

"Maybe Wilson Connell's right," Bridie whispered.

Scattered murmuring, shuffling of feet and nervous coughs rippled timidly through the crowd—until Amon Carter pulled the last trick from his white hat, "Pappy" Waggoner himself.

"Let's stop this money stampede," the laconic, tobacco-chewing Waggoner said, a thirty-dollar Stetson tipped back on his head. "Your money's always been safe here. It still is. If you have any doubts, I'll take over your deposits at any time and pay you in cash. Now, ya'll go on home, hear?"

"Whoopee!" Carter shouted. "Our own Uncle Waggoner has done what our Uncle Sam won't do—guaranteed your bank deposits."

Most people fell in line to redeposit their money.

"So whatta ya say, Bridie?" Wilson Connell said, returning to his dancing partner.

"I say you talk as well as you dance," she laughed. "Now, if you'll excuse me, Wilson, I must open a savings account."

"We never closed 'em, Bridie. We thought most of you folks would be back. So just redeposit whatever you took out."

Campfires dotted the riverbanks as the streetcar crossed the Trinity Bridge. "I never thought about people being down there at night," Josie said.

"But for the grace of God, your Uncle Tommy and my lucky shamrock, we'd be among them," Bridie said.

Anna, mustard and ketchup on her coat, fell asleep before they passed the Ku Klux Klan Building, its electric cross illuminating the ten-hundred block of North Main. Josie trembled, never forgetting the night the KKK burned a cross at All Saints when she had boarded there in the first grade. Bridie gave her a hug.

"Not since the Ziegfeld Follies in New York, Josie, have I danced to the music of a professional orchestra. What fun it was. Not a word to your dadda about it, either. 'Tis our little secret."

George O'Driscoll laughed over the front-page story in the paper:

Jury Summons Bank Customers
After Panic Run on First National

"Amon's paper says the grand jury's hauling in the first thirty customers who made withdrawals. They've arrested a truck driver for slandering a bank and questioned a plumber about making the first withdrawal. They'll be coming for you anytime now, Bridie."

"'Tis a witch hunt," she said, pouring George's coffee.

"Better hide your broom, then, Bridie. And with money in hand, you actually gave it back to them, did you?"

"'Tis as safe as the crown jewels, George," Bridie said dubiously.

The news story dismissed the run on the town's biggest bank, declaring "the whole affair turned into a sort of jollification."

George shook his head. "But this must be a mistake," he said. "Says they served sandwiches and coffee as two—not one, but two—full orchestras played in the lobby."

"'Tis true. And they were grand."

"Yes, Bridie, so was the orchestra that played on the decks of the *Titanic*."

Jarbidge, Nevada

Dear Bridie,

I had to leave the Tybo mine when they laid off 100 men. I am in a place called Jarbidge. I may have to leave at any time as this new prospect does not look very good. Silver fell to 40 cents an oz. Most of the silver, copper and lead mines are about shut down.

In Tonopah you can buy a four-room furnished house for $250. In fact, you can buy at your own price. A married man that follows the mines is in a bad fix and no place to go.

Farms are vacant, the banks are closed and half the towns in Nevada look like graveyards after dark. When chickens are cheaper than eggs, you know something has gone very wrong.

Too bad I had to leave Tybo as I was in hope to be able to visit you this year. I am enclosing cheque for $41.88. Do the best you can. We may never see times as good as they were.

Your loving brother,
Tommy
Erin Go Bragh

BLACKIE

Edwin Brant sauntered into the kitchen, a slight smile on his thin, angular face, an open bottle of President's Choice in his right hand.

"Oh, it's yourself," Bridie said, turning from a pile of dishes in the sink.

"How are things today?" he asked, taking a glass from a bookshelf and pouring himself a drink from his bottle. At five-foot-two, wiry and of slight build, he was about the same height as Bridie.

"Fine, just fine, Edwin," she said, drying her hands with a towel. "Would you like some ice for your drink?"

"No, thank you. Care for one?" he said, offering her the bottle.

"I had my morning quota before breakfast," she said.

"We need to talk about young Matthew."

"Uh oh," Bridie said, pouring tea from a pitcher into a glass of ice. "What's he done now? Let the air out of your tires, poured water down your gas tank, hocked your hubcaps…or worse?"

"You know me, Bridie. It's against my upstanding underworld ethics to rat anybody out, but I'm making an exception in this case," Edwin said, dapper in a dark suit, open collar, sporty black and white shoes, the signature bulge under his left arm.

"Out with it, Edwin."

"The boy's a bootlegger."

"You jest," Bridie said, taking a chair at the banquet table.

"Afraid not," Edwin said, sitting across from her.

"For God's sake, don't tell Quin," she said.

"No, I don't want to get the poor kid murdered," Edwin said, lifting a Romey y Julieta from an inside pocket.

"That's the meanest kid I've ever known," Quin said time and again.

Bridie attributed Matthew's troubles to anguish and anger over his mother's death. Although Jonathan still grieved for her, he was old enough to reach some understanding of his loss. Little Roger didn't remember her. Matthew was old enough to feel the pain and too young to understand why God had taken his mother from him.

"He's angry with God and the world," Bridie told Quin.

"And I'm angry with Matthew," his father said. "I'll straighten him out yet."

Edwin explained, "Bootleggers use kids to deliver their packages 'cause the cops hardly ever stop 'em. They use women, too, because you all can hide the stuff under your dress, in case you're interested in a job, Bridie." He smiled and fired up his cigar. "Matthew's running hooch at a dime a bottle for Blackie the blacksmith."

"A competitor of yours?" she said, chuckling.

"No, my customers won't touch that rotgut he sells."

"I've heard of Blackie. What's awful, Edwin, is this Prohibition thing is corrupting children and everyone else one way or another...even this holy place."

"Well, as a kid, Matthew's not likely to get caught, but if he does, he could end up in reform school, not to mention getting himself a police record."

"God help him."

"Probably not," Edwin said. "But we can. You talk to Matthew, and I'll have a word with this Blackie fellow." He winked and slapped a blackjack against his palm.

"No, Edwin, I'll handle this. I know just what to say to Mr. Blackie. And believe you me, I'll have a talk with Matthew."

"Oh, now, Bridie, don't be so hard on Matthew. The boy's just trying to make a dime."

"A dishonest dime," she said, adding, "but this explains how he paid back the money he owed me for the telescope." Bridie told Edwin how she had recovered Wally Cox's war trophy that Matthew had hocked at Zinn's Pawnshop.

"You see, Bridie, Matthew's an entrepreneur. He'll be a successful businessman someday."

"A businessman like yourself, Edwin," she said somewhat accusingly.

"Now, now, Bridie, everyone has a calling in life." Edwin decided not to reveal Matthew's other enterprises. "Anyway, let me know if Blackie gives you any shi...uh, trouble."

Donning her church hat and dress, Bridie walked briskly down Belle Avenue in the splotchy shade of elm trees on this sunny afternoon. Radio music drifted from open windows. Halting piano notes escaped from a strenuous lesson under way in Aunt Lucille's music parlor.

At the Ralston house, a clarinet set Bridie to prancing in time with a rendition of John Philip Sousa's happy, high-stepping "The Liberty Bell" march. Rick Ralston, an aspiring musician, lived in the house. His father, Felix Ralston, and his cow lived in a barn behind the house. Neighbors said Felix couldn't stand the music and preferred the barn to his house and the cow to his son. The police no longer responded to their complaints. Neighbors and police alike hoped the son soon achieved his ambition to play at Carnegie Hall in New York City.

Bridie turned up a driveway, marked by a crudely hand-painted sign: "Blacksmith. Horseshoeing, Car Repairs, Flats Fixed." She found Blackie bent over an anvil, hammer in hand pounding a red-hot metal rod. The glow of a coal-fired furnace reflected in his eyes.

"Oh, I'm sorry, ma'am. Didn't see ya. What kin I do for ya, Mrs....?" Blackie's hulking six-foot-six, three-hundred-pound frame was bent slightly over an anvil.

"Bridie O'Driscoll. Just call me Bridie."

"Oh yeah. You live in that Catholic place up the street," he said, a maw of crooked and missing teeth opening across his bearded face.

"That's right, Mr. Blackie. I see ye're busy, so I'll be to the point. Matthew Quinlan's been making deliveries for you, and it must stop."

Blackie averted his eyes and grinned sheepishly. "Well now, Miss Bridie, I been teachin' that boy to weld broke car springs and axles and to shoe horses. Things like that. He likes workin' here. Sometimes he runs an errand for a dime."

"I know all about the dime, Mr. Blackie."

"Cops don't never shake down kids, Miss Bridie," he said, laying aside his hammer.

"But if he is caught...and he will be someday...he'll be in serious trouble."

"You his mommy or somethin'?" the blacksmith said, the whites of his eyes glaring from his soot-covered face.

"Do you know Jesse Martin, the new district attorney, Mr. Blackie?"

"A friend of yours, Miss Bridie?" he said, towering over this puny dwarf of a woman talking to him the way no man dared.

"I delivered campaign circulars for him during the last election. I've my citizenship papers now, I vote, and I know where his office is."

"I guess you gonna tell him about that still Matthew says is down in your basement," Blackie said, trumping her district attorney card.

"Whatever you hear is in the basement, Mr. Blackie, it belongs to Edwin Brant," she said, dealing her ace of spades.

"Now look, Miss Bridie," he said, raising hairy, gorilla-size hands in a gesture of surrender. "I ain't wantin' no trouble with that man. What'll I tell Matthew?"

"I'll talk to Matthew."

"I'll jest have to find somebody else to deliver my stuff, ya know."

"But no other children, Mr. Blackie. Hire some of the idle men in the neighborhood to do your bootlegging. They could use a dime. Good day, Mr. Blackie."

ONE SUNDAY
AFTERNOON

B ridie sifted flour, rolled dough, molded it into pie
pans and layered a bowl of sliced apples in the
piecrusts. She sprinkled them with sugar and cinnamon and blanketed them with a thin sheet of dough,
which she buttered and sprinkled with cinnamon.

"Careful not to let them burn now, Martin."

"Save me some of them little piecrust rolls," Martin
said, taking the pies to the big ovens in the basement
kitchen.

Bridie sprinkled cinnamon and sugar over the left-
over pie dough, rolled and cut it into small pieces and
popped them into the oven of her small stove.

"What about this tubful of potatoes?" Lynn Brant asked, tearfully peeling onions in a cocktail dress, high-heeled shoes, a pearl necklace and one of Bridie's aprons.

"Ollie's doing the potatoes. Wally doesn't want 'em Irish-boiled, as he says. Let's shell the peas and peel the carrots."

Bridie had gone to six o'clock Mass to get a jump on preparing the feast of All Saints, as she called the periodic Sunday gatherings of all the residents. Pooling their money, they'd come up with four dollars, including ninety-seven cents from the light bill can at the foot of the stairs. Then to everyone's astonishment, George threw in another greenback. "The ol' Scrooge must've seen Marley's ghost last night," Quin Quinlan said.

Five dollars had filled the Brants' Packard to overflowing with vegetables and fruit at the Jones Street farmers market.

"I just love a party," Lynn said, taking a knife to the carrots.

Bridie sat down with a cup of tea to shell the peas, the start of a day's work for the women—who sifted flour, beat batter, rolled dough, peeled, cut, chopped, shelled, cooked, stirred, poured, minded the children and served up the late afternoon lunch.

For their part, the men smoked, drank, read the papers, argued sports and politics, told Hoover jokes and cursed the government, talked about jobs and bootleggers and speakeasies and the invention of night baseball, and called out to the women to do something about the unruly kids running and shouting through the halls.

"I hear a car," Lynn said, whaling away at the carrots with a paring knife, peelings flying.

Quin, his three sons in their Sunday suits and Jericho Donovan with her two children bounded through the back door.

"How was Mass?" Bridie asked.

"Short and sweet," Jonathan said, home from school for the weekend. "A three-minute sermon."

"Three minutes too long," Matthew groused, thumping Roger's left ear.

"Leave him alone!" Jonathan shouted, kicking Matthew in the butt.

"You boys stop that fighting and go change your clothes, hear?" their father ordered, pretending to unbuckle his leather belt.

Jericho's daughter, Margaret, gaped in open-mouthed worship of Jonathan Quinlan, "the handsomest boy in the world," she confided to Josie O'Driscoll, who compared him to Jimmy Stewart.

Quin sat down to read the *Fort Worth Press.*

"I'll give you a hand with those peas," Jericho said. She'd phoned Bridie Saturday morning after Dan

Donovan came home and began breaking up the furniture. "And he's gone out for more booze."

Bridie sent Edwin to pick up Jericho and her children at their mansion on Grand Avenue, a fashionable neighborhood on the Bluff.

"We're going outside to see Bonnie and Clyde," Margaret Donovan said, heading for the backyard with her brother, Dan Junior.

"Be careful those bloody goats don't get in as you go out," Bridie warned. "And take these piecrust rolls and share them with Zelda." She kept three of the little sweets for Martin.

The Coxes returned from the First Baptist Church of Fort Worth, their kids and Julie Bryant's two children in the bed of Wally's pickup. Ollie grimaced as Lynn Brant whacked away half a carrot in a single stroke.

"Lynn darling, you'll cut yourself," she said, taking the knife.

"These poor carrots do seem to be shrinking," Lynn said, slivers of peeling spangled in her hair like sequins.

The acrid aroma of wood smoke and the pungent scent of roasting meat wafted through the tall windows, thrown open to catch the breeze this warm, sultry Sunday. Mulligan sat in the shade, nose raised to the teasing scent of the carcass slowly browning over the coals.

Turning the carcass on a spit, Martin nodded to silver-haired Father Nolan as the priest—who went unarmed on the Sabbath—emerged from his car, loosening his white dog collar as he went up the back steps.

Watching Martin turn the beef, Cory Cox told Buster Roberts and Jeremy Bryant, "That's Willie he's cookin'."

"Naw, can't be Willie," Buster said, recalling how they'd hand-fed the little calf after its mother died. "Willie's down by the lake."

"Not anymore he ain't," Cory said.

"Is that really Willie you're roasting there?" Jeremy asked Martin.

Martin nodded. "God Almighty," Buster cried. "I'm not eatin' Willie."

Seething with lust, Jonathan sat in the windowsill of his room with an eye on Sam Scott's Lincoln. Sandra had warned him, however, that on Sundays, Sam often slept late and didn't go to the downtown pool parlors until midafternoon. His attention suddenly turned to the sweeping metallic lines of a new Ford swinging into the driveway.

Forgetting the Lincoln for a moment, he marveled at the sleek black Deluxe coupe as it darted round back and rocked to a dusty halt in the shade of a tree. A scrawny kid popped out on the driver's side. An elfish, rosy-cheeked nun emerged from the other door, her stark white wimple brilliant against her black robes.

The kid driver was unloading a trunkful of bats, baseballs and gloves when Jonathan sauntered up to the car. The nun handed out Snickers and boxes of Cracker Jack to kids swarming around her.

"Whose car?" Jonathan asked, not bothering to introduce himself.

"Sister Vee's, I guess," said George Salih, who'd been "promoted" from the nun's beggar boy at the racetracks to chauffer at age twelve.

"Just like Bonnie and Clyde's, isn't it?"

"Yip, with a hot V-8 under the hood."

"So, how'd you get to drive something like this, little as you are?"

"Sent twenty-five cents to Austin and got this back in the mail," the kid said, whipping out his driver's license.

"'George Salih, birthdate February 16, 1920.' I'd like to get that address in Austin. I'm Jonathan Quinlan."

Richard Levitz, hands stuffed in his pockets, sidled up to Sister Vee. "Seen my daddy lately, Sister Vee?"

"No, Richard," she said, kissing the boy's forehead. "He's working so he can find a place for the two of ye to live."

"Would you tell him I need to see him? That I'd like to see him?"

"I will, Richard."

"Tell him I love him."

"I'll surely tell him, Richard...next time I see him," she said, wiping tears from her eyes as the boy wandered off.

Sister Vee smiled wanly and turned to her young driver. "George, get up a game of baseball with these kids."

"What about the girls?" Josie asked. "What'll we do?"

"Why, play ball, Josie, play ball," Sister Vee said.

Taking a bat, the short, sprightly little nun tossed a ball straight up, gripped the bat with both hands and slammed the ball as it came down. Wide-eyed kids watched it sail out over the playground.

"All right, let's choose up sides," George Salih said.

Jonathan worshipped at the Ford coupe, raised the hood to ogle its V-8 engine, sat behind the wheel, fondled the gearshift, ran his hands over the dashboard. He pictured himself flying down the road at eighty miles an hour with Sandra Scott sitting next to him.

Martin wiped sweat from his forehead as Sister Vee hurried toward him at the mesquite fire.

"So, Martin, ye still have the Saint Christopher medal," she said, taking his hand and clapping him on the shoulder.

"Always, Sister," he mumbled. He'd hung the medal from his neck after Bridie told him she was coming. "I'll never hock it, neither. I still know some o' them stories you told us at the prison, too."

From within her robes, the nun produced a black book, its chafed leather cover engraved in faded gold letters: *Book of Gospels.* "You'll find all those parables in this, Martin."

"For...for me? Are the story para...para-barrels, whatever...ya told us at the prison in here?"

Sister Vee nodded. "Indeed they are," she said as Bridie dashed down the back steps and hugged her. The nun gave her a large box. "Shoes and shirts for the orphan boys ye're looking after for me, Bridie. And here's a few dollars to help feed them."

"Oh, no, we're managing all right here."

"Take it, Bridie dear. 'Tis from my collections at the racetrack. Better ye have it than the bookies at Arlington Downs."

They went inside.

"Where'd you get all the baseball booty, Sister Vee?" George O'Driscoll wanted to know.

"The good merchants of Dallas are kind to our orphan boys, even if you have to push them a little harder these days."

"And that new Ford, steal that from 'em, too?" Edwin Brant asked.

"The Ford man in Dallas, Ed Marr, bless his soul, lends us a new car every year. Now, if ye'll excuse me, I'll help the lasses with lunch, being as ye lads aren't budging off yere backsides today."

"It's Sunday, Sister Vee, a day of rest for all good men," Quin said.

Edwin passed a bottle of President's Choice down the table. Wally sipped a tall glass of iced tea.

"Ye wouldn't have a wee bit of sherry?" Sister Vee inquired.

"A wee bit of the best coming right up," Edwin said.

"To Mr. Brant, our blessed benefactor," Father Nolan said, raising his glass to the table.

"And to our good health," Edwin said, passing around a box of El Productos. Matches flared, sending up a sharp scent of sulfur as cigars ignited and rings of blue-gray haze mushroomed over the smokers.

"Well now, if it ain't Nurse Nightingale," Wally said as Julie Bryant came through the door, her crisp nurse's uniform amplifying her slim yet buxom figure.

"How'd your midnight shift go?" Bridie inquired, pouring Julie some iced tea.

"Awful, just awful. Family of eight brought in with food poisoning. They'd shut off their electric icebox to save on the light bill."

"The papers keep warning people about that," Shirley Roberts said.

Julie continued, "The little girl won't make it through the day."

"God be with her," said Father Nolan, blessing himself.

Quin sat like a wooden Indian as Julie gently massaged his right shoulder. Catching herself, she jerked back as if she'd burned her fingers, looking around to see if anyone had noticed. Bridie wondered if she had hocked her wedding band, its impression still ringing her finger.

"I'll go change and give you ladies a hand," Julie said. Bridie and the other women filed down the stairs to boiling pots and hot ovens in the basement kitchen.

George launched into his much-dreaded job-finding lecture. "Always ask for work, never a position," he droned on. "You have a position, the position of being unemployed. Work is what you want."

"Yes, Professor O'Driscoll," Quin said.

He likened George's Sunday lectures to eating stale Cracker Jacks to get the prize at the bottom of the box. The reward at the end of his condescending little talks was often a few days' work in the rail yards. If there was no prize in today's lecture, there was a bombshell.

"As for myself," George said, "I've resigned as dispatcher at the Fort Worth and Denver Railroad." He drew deeply on his cigar. "Going into business for myself."

His announcement elicited silence, followed by cautious congratulations—the kind given a fool for leaving a steady job in the depths of the Great Depression.

"Ya think your old job's still open?" Wally asked

"You've already resigned?" Father Nolan frowned.

"I'll be going into the auto parts business tomorrow morning."

"Well now," Quin said, "seems to me with nobody buying new cars these days, everybody needs parts to keep their old ones going."

"That's how I see it," George agreed.

"Ought to be a winner, I'd say," Quin said.

"A toast to George's success," Edwin said.

"As for the rest of us working stiffs," Wally said, "it won't be long now to cotton pickin' time again."

"As I've said before, I can make more money at home playing with my pecker," Quin said. "Excuse me, Father Nolan."

Jericho Donovan and Ollie Cox came up from the basement with bowls of radishes and sliced cucumbers.

"Anything goin' on at the stockyards, Jericho?" Wally called, his speech slightly slurred.

"Nothing," she said. "The cattle business has driven Dan to drink more than usual—to give you an idea just how bad things are at the stockyards."

Ollie snatched Wally's glass of iced tea from the table. "You've got to carve that calf, remember?" she whispered in his ear.

Adorned with Lynn Brant's china, silverware, silk tablecloths and napkins, the banquet table was dressed for a feast.

"Looks like dinner at Versailles," Quin said as Lynn added three silver candelabra, six white candles in each.

"Now we'll have to watch our table manners," Wally said, lamenting the loss of his iced tea.

Ollie went out on the porch, poured out Wally's tea and called the kids from their ball game. "And wash your hands and face before you come to the table."

The ballplayers stampeded up the fire escape and through an open window on the third floor to the only bathroom with two water faucets, one at the sink, another at the bathtub. After a free-for-all water fight, they clambered down the staircase, shouting and laughing.

"Godammit, cut out that racket before I come out there. Don't you kids know people are tryin' to sleep?" A door slammed, then opened again on the second floor. Sam leaned over the banister and yelled down the staircase. "And I mean it, dammit!" The door slammed again.

"No, Edwin!" Lynn cried when her husband stood up, overturning his chair.

"Please, Edwin," Bridie added. "It's Sunday, after all."

He shrugged and returned to the table. "Thought I'd just invite them for dinner, Bridie. They never come out of their room."

"I asked them to join us. I think they were out a bit late last night."

"All night every night," George said.

"Was that Mr. Scott doin' all that cussin'?" Matthew asked.

"Yeah, he needs his mouth washed out with a lotta soap," Anna said.

"How exactly do you go about washing out somebody's mouth out with soap, Miss Bridie?" Richard asked, scooting a chair out from the table.

"You and Anna sit down before you find out firsthand."

Everyone sat back to watch Wally carve the carcass in the middle of the table. Then Father Nolan said the blessing.

"Amen and let's eat," said Zelda, sitting in Bridie's lap and wielding a spoon.

Julie, who'd changed to a loose-fitting housedress, sat between Jeremy and Juliana and cast stealthy glances down the table at Quin. He winked. Jonathan observed their exchange with indifference.

"How did you cook these potatoes, Ollie?" Lynn wondered.

"They're cowboy potatoes. Put 'em skins and all in a covered iron pot, bury 'em in the hot coals of your campfire."

"How's Gabi?" Bridie asked Elizabeth Wellington.

"Still coughin' but better, I think. It's whooping cough. Doc Cooper's just leaving."

Black bag and fedora in hand, Doc Cooper—shaggy white hair flowing to his shirt collar—came through the door and bowed deeply in mocking ceremony to the table.

"Top o' the mornin' to you, Bridie. Or is it *ye* or *thee*?"

"'Tis afternoon. Take a chair, Dr. Cooper, and have a bite."

"And a swallow or two," Edwin said, splashing President's Choice into a whiskey glass.

"Been awhile," Lynn said, giving the doctor a hug.

"So nice to see you, Lady Lynn. I do miss those easy evenings at the White House."

Quin stood and rapped his whiskey glass with a spoon. "Now that everyone's here, I have an announcement. Jonathan is going to Notre Dame for sure. He's won a football scholarship that covers his tuition for the entire four years."

"Here, here," George said, standing with glass in hand. "Cheers to Jonathan!" Glasses were raised in the boy's direction.

"What about it, Jonathan?" Quin said, beaming proudly. "A few words for the table."

"Well, first of all, I don't have a drink to join this august crowd," Jonathan said, grinning broadly.

Quin nodded an okay as Edwin poured the boy a short glass of President's Choice.

Taking the glass, Jonathan raised it to the table. "The Notre Dame scouts have been talking to me for about a year. Two weeks ago, I got a letter offering the scholarship. One more season at Saint Edward's and I'll be off to join the Fighting Irish."

Everyone drank up.

Julie Bryant walked around the long table and gave Jonathan a hug and a kiss on the cheek. "We're all so proud of you, Jonathan." She teared up when he gently returned the hug and kissed her lightly on the cheek (the way a son kisses a mother, she thought).

"We all love you," Julie said, returning to her chair to a round of applause.

The men smoked their after-dinner cigars as the women cleared the table and made coffee to go with Bridie's apple pie. As she put a kettle of water on the little stove to make tea, a car skidded into the driveway, sped around to the back of the convent and crashed into something.

"Not my car, I hope," Edwin said.

"It's Dan Donovan," Wally said from the back door. "Jest redesigned the whole left side of his Cadillac against the big oak."

"Tell him we've left," Jericho said, running down the hall and up the stairs.

Bridie went to the back door and watched Dan throw open his car door and zigzag across the playground.

"Send that squaw out here!" he yelled, gripping the handrail at the foot of the steps, shirttail hanging out, hat tilting on his head. "I'm gonna give her a good beatin' if she doesn't get home and cook my dinner."

"Come back tomorrow when ye're a better man," Bridie called from behind the screen door.

"I came for that squaw woman you've got in there, Bridie, and I'm gonna have her," he raged, his face red with anger and alcohol. He stumbled on the first step, fell and started crawling up to the porch.

Bridie flew out the kitchen door and across the porch, a butcher knife in hand. "Set foot on this porch, my good man, and I'll slash yere bloody arse and pray to God for yere poor soul."

In a dense fog of alcohol, Dan halted halfway up the steps on hands and knees. A loud crack, like a gunshot, had split through his head when the screen door slammed shut. He looked for the harsh voice that drove pins of pain through his throbbing brain. A murky figure stood at the top of the steps, its eyes glowing red and yellow and white fire as the afternoon sun reflected off Bridie's glasses. A large knife appeared in his vision, its blade gleaming on and off in the sunlight like a neon sign.

Dan lost his balance and rolled down the steps. He sat up, shook his head, regained some vision. "Oh, it's you, Bridie. I'll be back." He staggered to his car, backed it into another tree and weaved out the drive.

Bridie went down the steps, picked up his hat and dusted it off. She returned to a hoopla of cheers.

"Carrie Nation's got nothing on Bridie O'Driscoll," Quin laughed.

"A sobering performance," Edwin said.

"Ol' Dan'll become a teetotaling Baptist now," Wally said.

Father Nolan wanted to know if she'd write his yearly fire-and-brimstone sermons for Lent.

"I cannot believe what I did out there," Bridie said.

"Neither can Dan Donovan," Quin said.

After pie and coffee, the men grew groggy, the kids grew cranky, and the women grew tired of them all. Bridie packed Sister Vee off to Dallas. Ollie gave her a brick of butter. Edwin slipped her a bottle of sherry.

"Almost forgot Tommy's letter," Bridie said, handing her an envelope. "He's working on some great dam out in Nevada."

George Salih gunned the V-8, fanning Jonathan's jealousy, and spun the tires as the Ford coupe bolted out the driveway.

Jonathan had watched Sam Scott's Lincoln all afternoon in burning anticipation of spending an hour or so with Sandra before he went back to Austin. But Sam, sleeping off a hangover, never left. Jonathan had spent most of Saturday with her. And he'd gushed out the news about his Notre Dame football scholarship.

Sandra mustered an anemic smile. Her lukewarm congratulations caught in her throat. "When, Jonathan?"

"Well, it's a long time off, Sandra," he said, deeply touched that she cared so much for him.

"How far off?"

"Oh, about a year," he said, kissing her teary eyes.

For the first time in her life, Sandra looked into her future—a mirror that reflected the present. Sam Scott was it. She had no other place to go. Jonathan's scholarship cast a glaring light on her dark prospects.

When he left, she broke down, sobbed uncontrollably and collapsed on the floor. Sam slapped her hard when she refused to work the clubs Saturday night, the most lucrative evening of the week. Then Jonathan left Sunday without a chance to say goodbye.

Her overnight guests tucked away—the Donovans on the third floor, Doc Cooper passed out in the bishop's parlor—Bridie climbed wearily into bed.

It had been a happy day, except that George had quit his job without the slightest warning to her. *Perhaps I'll get rich* his only thought, his only care, neglecting all else: herself, their beautiful daughters, his own soul.

Was it her fault? The question haunted her, always in her lonely bed at night. Father Marconi in the confessional had assured her over and again it was not her fault, not her wrong, certainly not her sin. Father Nolan said it was the will of God and…

Clank. The sound interrupted Bridie's reverie. Another metallic *clink, clank*, then a heavy, sure-footed thud. She'd learned to distinguish among the medley of light clinks, little clanks and clumsy thuds playing the fire escape like a xylophone: not Quin's heavy footsteps, not as stealthy as kids sneaking from one floor to another, more careful than goats seeking an open window, and not the muffled footfalls of Wally's stocking feet as he slipped down to the basement to share a sip with Martin.

Bridie recognized the rhythm of light-to-heavy footfalls of a man and a woman—Sam and Sandra Scott, stepping out for the night. Moments later, light, rapid footfalls played delicately up the steps—the metallic melody of Julie tiptoeing up to Quin's room.

Where would we be without a fire escape? Bridie wondered. *'Tis a better escape than a noose, to be sure.*

KNIGHTS OF THE NIGHT

"We're just gonna shake 'em up a little, Betty Lou. Ya know, sorta put the fear o' Gawd in them black-robed ol' ladies."

Short, bulky, square-framed, the tobacco-chewing man in his Saturday night Stetson and dirty western boots handed Edwin Brant a five-dollar bill for a bottle of President's Choice.

"Oughta be funner than scarin' the tar outta niggers," he went on, chortling in a hoarse horselaugh and looking to Edwin for his change.

"All thumbs tonight," Edwin apologized, putting on a fool's smile as he slowly gathered the coins he'd dropped behind the counter and eavesdropped on his customer's conversation.

Couples on the dance floor swayed to the gentle rhythms of "Till We Meet Again," the band's signature sign-off at the Hackberry Grove Dance Hall, the last of Sam Rosen's once-popular amusement park. Edwin had bought the dance hall with a second loan from Sam. Like Edwin's drugstores, it was another hedge against the approaching demise of Prohibition and his bootlegging business.

"Kin I go with you, Ned?" Betty Lou asked the cowboy.

"Klan business, baby," he said, taking his change from Edwin. "No dames allowed."

⇒╪ ╪⇐

The residents of All Saints listened in anxiety to Edwin's story. "It's kind of a test of new Klan members, I think."

"An initiation rite," Quin added, sitting next to Julie, leaning against him and holding his hand. Except for Sam and Sandra Scott, all the adults had gathered at the banquet table in Bridie's kitchen.

"God help us!" Bridie said. "Let's call the police."

"Might as well call the fox to save our chickens," Wally said.

Edwin explained, "At least one city councilman, a couple of police captains and no telling how many street cops are Klansmen."

"We see 'em at our church, those two police captains," Ollie said.

George said, "You can count on the cops getting here well after the KKK raid is over and done with."

"Whatta they gonna do here, anyways?" Martin said.

"The last time the Klan came, they set fire to the grass, broke some windows and burned a cross out front," Bridie said. "That was back when Josie was a boarding student here. In the end, they harmed no one."

"Right, Bridie, these bully boys just want to scare the hell out of some nuns," Edwin said. "But I have it from a friend in the Klan that they're planning on burning that white cross up on the roof just for fun."

"They might come inside," Elizabeth Wellington gasped.

"We'll scald 'em with buckets of boiling water when they come up the fire escape," Ollie said, her tense face red with anger. "We'll catch 'em off guard because they'll think the nuns are hidin' somewheres."

"Now you're talking, Ollie," Edwin said. "We'll set an ambush for 'em. I've got a plan."

"Now, Edwin, we're not going to…you know, do anything bloody or worse," Lynn said. "Nothing like that."

"No, no, Lynn…," he started to explain.

George cut in. "What we need are some knights of our own. I'm sure I can recruit some fellows at the Knights of Columbus Hall."

Quin laughed. "The Knights of the Ku Klux Klan versus the Knights of Columbus. Let's call Hollywood and remake *The Birth of a Nation*."

"If we do that, there'll be some broken bones before it's over," Edwin said. "The Ku Kluxers will come armed with baseball bats and boards. O' course, we've got Doc here to heal our wounds."

"Sure. I'll set up a battlefield infirmary," said Doc Cooper, who had taken a room at All Saints. "I'll bring bandages and splints from the office just in case."

Wally fired up a freshly rolled cigarette and leaned across the long table. "Well, I fer one don't wanna get hurt."

The table fell silent. Wally Cox stood six-foot-three, big boned, his body hard from a lifetime of labor and hard-luck living, his arms long, his leathery fists like sledgehammers, his calm hazel eyes unflinching. No man had ever called him a coward. "Nobody needs to get hurt, not even them Ku Kluxers," he said. Everyone listened, nodded and chuckled as he laid out his plan.

They came like ghosts on a moonless Saturday night, parking their pickups along Ephraim Avenue where the White House once stood. White robes marched silently down the slope, around Rosen's Pond and up the near side of the hollow to All Saints.

The women gathered the kids behind locked double doors in the chapel. Shirley Roberts guarded the door, a butcher knife hidden in a dish towel. "Let the bastards come," she said.

Gabi Ellington and Sissy Cox had fallen asleep on the altar. The other kids slept on church benches. Matthew sat on the fire escape, furious he'd been denied a role in the coming battle.

Bridie sat in the confessional, the gold shamrock in her pocket, a board across her lap, a rosary threaded through her fingers. Ollie watched out the window, a baseball bat over her shoulder.

The Ku Kluxers assembled along the edge of the campus. On a signal from the lead Klansman, the hooded ones broke into smaller groups. Just as they finished lighting their torches, Edwin fired his chrome-plated .45 automatic.

Mounted on mules, Wally Cox and Clyde Markum hooted and hollered like Indians, spurred their mounts and stampeded a herd of thirsty cows across the campus toward the pond. The Klansmen's flaming torches reflected in the eyes of the shadowy bovines thundering out of the night directly at them. Black-robed nuns sprang from behind bushes and trees, screeching like banshees as they charged from all directions, baseball bats and boards raised above their veiled heads.

Tossing their torches, the white-robed figures fled as horned animals romped toward them, followed by a mob of screaming black-robed nuns. As the Klansmen scattered, fiery rockets arched into the night sky, exploded and blossomed above them in a sparkling display of pyrotechnics eerily reflected in the pond.

"What the hell?" Martin said, halting to watch a rocket lift off the roof of the convent and streak like a fiery arrow across the sky.

"That's got to be Matthew up there shooting off some bottle rockets he stole somewhere," Quin speculated, somewhat proud this time of his wayward son.

"Them guys'll probably call the cops themselves," Martin laughed as he took off his white mask and removed the black veil from his head.

"They'll be ashamed to go home," Edwin said. "Run off by a bunch of nuns. Nobody'll ever believe a herd of wild cows came after them, either."

"No casualties on either side," Wally reported as he and Clyde Markum rode up on their mules.

"All our cows are drinking at the lake," said Clyde, who'd added his milk cows to Wally's herd just before sunset. Mounted on Clyde's mules, the two riders had held the thirsty cows in a corner against the rock wall.

"We caught a Klansman after he slipped on a fresh cow patty," said Father Nolan, who supplied the black cassocks and nuns' veils to members of the Knights of Columbus, who'd volunteered to take on the Knights of the Ku Klux Klan.

"And when the boys ripped off his robes, he thought some depraved nuns were about to make a steer out of 'im," Wally laughed.

"We threw 'im in Rosen's Pond," Martin said.

"Time to celebrate with a little President's Choice," Edwin said.

Sitting at the head of the banquet table in her kitchen, Bridie looked up from the Sunday *Star-Telegram.* "I can't believe such good news. The Klan's headquarters down on North Main burned to the ground."

"Imagine that," Wally said.

"There's a front-page story about it in the *Press*, too," Quin said, sipping his morning coffee and smoking a cigarette.

"Couldn't have happened to a nicer bunch of people," Edwin said.

"The fire department thinks it was arson," Bridie said.

"Right," Quin said. "They say somebody saw three men there around two in the morning—a small, short guy in a fedora with a shorter meatball of a man and a tall, lanky cowboy in a western hat."

"Not much for the cops to go on," Wally said.

"Says they were in a late model Packard Eight," Bridie added.

"Edwin, you just traded yours for that new Cadillac Sixteen," Quin said.

"Yes, and it's a very fine automobile," he answered curtly, getting up from the table and putting on his fedora. "I've got to go over to the drugstore for a while." The screen door slammed behind him.

River Camp
Boulder City, Nevada

Dear Bridie,

There are 3,000 men registered here in the little town of Las Vegas to work on the new Boulder Dam. There is a doctor and I was afraid of not passing his exam, but he was in a great hurry and took little notice of me and they sent me on to the River Camp to work in the tunnels. They are trying to call it Hoover Dam, but the name does not stick.

The river is always muddy. Lots of families camped out and drinking the dirty water. It's very bitter. Hundreds more come every day from all over the country. It's terrible for people facing poverty and no matter what we do now it's too late to save ourselves.

We have a fine dining room at the camp where 1400 of us eat at one time. We also have a good room and key for each. But the wages were cut again and the work made harder. I will mail this with a money order for $51.92 when I go into Las Vegas.

Your loving brother,
Tommy
Erin Go Bragh

THE AMERICAN WAY

"If it hadn't been Norwegian steel, it would have snapped in half," George said, adding, "and there you'd be with a broken wrench in your hand. I'll be in Fairfield Tuesday. Now, what else besides spark plugs for the Ford and the crankshaft for the Chrysler?"

Bridie looked warily at her husband when he hung up. "You told the poor man he's lucky his wrench bent?"

George chuckled, returning to his breakfast. "Made him feel better, Bridie. I'll sell him another one. Spanish steel instead of Norwegian this time. It's the American way."

"And what happened to your face, George?"

"Battle scars from doing business with Jews." He gently touched his split lip. His leg hurt, too, the teeth marks still visible.

Though Josef and Felix Rubinstein said George O'Driscoll didn't know "a spark plug from his pecker," the brothers had quickly seen the lucrative merits of the "big Irish bastard's idea." And the Irish bastard had some cash, a scarce commodity in the 1930s.

George had checked out the Rubinsteins. Allied Auto Parts on lower Commerce Street was the biggest car parts house in Fort Worth. It was also losing ground as competitors sprouted up all over town to cash in on the mushrooming demand for auto parts as people struggled to keep their aging cars running. He offered the Rubinsteins a whole new market—a dozen small towns strung along Highway 75 between Fort Worth and Houston. These were the "big small towns," he explained, where farmers did their Saturday business, their wives did their shopping, and their kids went to the double feature at the picture show for nine cents.

The keys to the auto parts market in country towns were the frustrated garage owners and service station mechanics. They ordered parts "from big-city dumb-asses in Dallas and Houston who send the wrong ones on the Greyhound a week later," mechanics told George.

"We can supply all these towns," he told the bald-headed, bright-eyed Rubinsteins, miniature men weighing about a hundred pounds each in crisp white shirts, black bow ties, black trousers and black oxfords.

The tall, broad-shouldered Irishman and the five-foot, gnome-like Rubinsteins struck a deal in a round of handshakes and smiles. The Jewish leprechauns, as George called them, would sell him parts at a discount and teach him about wheel bearings and carburetor repair kits, mufflers and piston rods.

George sputtered along Highway 75 in his '27 Chevy, calling on garages and service stations. Mechanics liked his pitch: "Order from me and pay when I deliver the parts—the right ones."

Soon, even after removing the spare tire, there was just room enough in the coupe for George and his car parts when he left Fort Worth Monday mornings. He stayed nights in drafty, cold-water tourist courts, studying parts catalogs and eating bologna sandwiches.

When George discovered mechanics needed tools, the Rubinsteins had a supply of third-rate Japanese-made wrench sets, shoddy pliers and brittle screwdrivers. "Jap junk," Fort Worth mechanics called them.

"We've dumped about as much of this stuff around town as we can get away with," Josef Rubinstein said. "Just don't mention it was made in Japan."

"Norway," George said. "Norwegian steel—best in the world."

Josef chuckled. "I swear, George, you're almost too smart to be a cabbage-headed Irishman."

Returning to town on Friday evenings, he met with the Rubinsteins to tally their books over a bottle of whiskey. Undaunted by a complicated scheme of price discounts based on a slippery, sliding scale of dollar sales and volume, George had politely corrected a small math "error" weighted in Allied Auto Parts' favor. His partners nodded with chagrin and with new respect for the spud-masher's math, a discipline beaten into him by Ireland's most militant educators, the Christian Brothers.

"We're probably the only people in town making any money these days," Felix boasted every week as they closed the books.

"We're so smart, our heads hurt," George replied faithfully.

"C'mon, George," Josef always laughed. "We'll take ya to the Saddle and Sirloin for a plate of juicy calf fries"—touted on the menu as "those proud delicacies that separate the bulls from the cows."

And Felix always added, "You can pretend they're fish balls, or just forget it's Friday."

"And I'll order you lads the Jewish special, a pound of pork pricks."

The first bump in their burgeoning business came six months into the partnership.

"So why get greedy now, George?" Felix wanted to know. "You're making money."

"Perkins'll give me thirty percent of sales," he bluffed.

"Ol' Pop Perkins is crookeder than a New York Jew—or an Irish Catholic, if that's possible," Josef said. "He sells stolen stuff. He'll steal from you, too."

And so would you, George thought, *if you were a little better at math.* He played his ace of spades. "Felix, you and your little brother make anywhere from sixty to two hundred percent on these parts. Everybody does. I want forty percent plus expenses."

Felix tried mightily to stifle himself when his Herculean temper dwarfed his diminutive five-foot, hundred-pound body. Yet it enraged him that he and Josef had done so much for this ungrateful foreigner, who had come to them not knowing a spark plug from his pecker.

"Listen, you goddam Catholic fish-eating son of a bitch…"

The reserved, somber George O'Driscoll broke out in tearful laughter in the face of the most creative cursing he'd heard since leaving Ireland. Dumbstruck by his demeaning laugh, Felix threw whiskey in his partner's face, an act that violated George's solemn Irish dignity and dissolved his self-control.

"Why, you sawed-off little bastard!" The six-foot-plus mackerel eater yanked the miniature Felix from behind his desk and tossed him like a sawdust doll through the paneled wall of his own office.

The two leprechauns caught up with George briskly crossing Commerce Street to his car. Like a couple of bantams attacking a bear, Josef tackled as Felix flew up to beat George about the head. A crowd from the nearby Salvation Army Hotel cheered them on.

"Look at that big-assed bully beatin' up on them midgets!"

"But they's two of them!"

Felix's face turned red, then blue as the Irishman's big hands clutched his throat. George cursed and released his grip on Felix's windpipe when Josef's teeth sank into George's left leg. Fists flew until the combatants surrendered to exhaustion.

The street crowd dispersed, disgusted no one was killed or even needed an ambulance. "Somebody oughta call the cops on them creeps."

Josef hugged a fire hydrant and pulled himself up from the sidewalk, his nose bleeding. Felix sat on the curb, nursing his neck. George leaned against his Chevy, face bruised, lip split, leg aching.

"C'mon, George," Josef moaned. "Let's go in and have a drink."

"Forty-five percent and expenses," George said.

"You told Felix forty."

"Forty-five and I'll double sales in three months."

"How?"

"Never mind," George said. "I'll do it."

"All right, dammit, forty-five percent, but nothing doin' on expenses."

"You're the boss, Josef," George said. "Let's have that drink."

JONATHAN'S CASKET

The Santa Fe railway cop spotted him high-stepping briskly over the rails. It was the kid who'd clipped him months ago below the knees, leaving him face down in the dirt with a bloody nose.

Crawling from under a string of parked freight cars, Jonathan saw him just as he swung the baseball bat. "You bastard!" the cop shouted, missing the boy's head by inches.

Jonathan rolled back under the freight car and out the other side. The end of the half-mile-long string of railcars became his goalpost. The cop ran along the other side of the cars to head him off. Jonathan beat him to the end by six car lengths.

To his surprise, the railroad bull pursued him beyond the rail yards and up Jones Street. Saint Edward's' quarterback shifted into a hundred-yard dash mode. When the bull lagged a block behind, Jonathan shot him the finger and disappeared around the corner toward Commerce Street.

He decided to walk the six miles out to the convent. He needed time to think about how he was going to tell Sandra what he'd done. He had to tell someone what had happened on the train.

Jonathan was relieved that Sam Scott and his big-ass Lincoln were gone. Sandra, in bathrobe and slippers, stood on the fire escape smoking a cigarette, her golden hair glowing like a halo in the morning sun. She waved both hands wildly. Her smile faded when she saw his face: drawn and somber, no hint of joy at seeing her.

Jonathan kissed her on the cheek. "Sandra, let's go inside." In her room, he grasped her in his arms, kissed her deeply and suddenly began to shudder as if suffering convulsions.

"Jonathan, Jonathan," Sandra said, leaning back in his arms to see his grief-stricken face. "What's wrong, darling? What is it?"

He drew her back to him and clung to the tender young body under her thin bathrobe. "God," he cried, "I need you."

Sandra gave him a knowing smile and silently led him to the couch. "I'm all yours."

"I need a drink," Jonathan said, trembling. "I really do."

"Okay," Sandra said wanly. She went to a table cluttered with whiskey bottles, glasses, an overflowing ashtray. "What's going on, Jonathan?"

He took the glass from her, his hand shaking. They sat on the couch. Jonathan wrapped his arm around her thin shoulders. "Something awful happened on the train. I did something…something very wrong," he said.

Jonathan took a long swig from the glass and began telling her:

He'd caught the freight train in Austin, tossed his overnight bag into a boxcar and sprang like a jackrabbit through the open door. Behind him, a tall, stringy, white-haired old guy struggled to pull himself aboard. Jonathan extended a hand and yanked him inside like a bag of laundry.

"Ya got a hell'va grip, young man. How old are ya, anyways?"

"Seventeen," Jonathan said, sitting down on his overnight bag against the wall. He took a pack of Lucky Strikes from his shirt pocket.

"Couldn't spare a weed, could ya?" a toothless fellow traveler asked. Jonathan eyed his half-empty pack of Luckies. He started to beg off when he noticed the man's left trousers leg, tied in a knot where his knee used to be.

"Bull threw me off a train comin' outta Savannah couple years ago," the cripple explained. "Cut it clean off."

Jonathan grimaced, holding out the pack of Luckies.

"You know, kid," the cripple said as Jonathan gave him a light, "ya look just like that movie guy. Know who I mean?"

"Jimmy Stewart," Jonathan said, accustomed to the comparison.

"Yeah, that's him. Jimmy Stewart."

"Hey, Jimmy Boy, I'll take one of them cigs, too," a short, heavyset passenger called gruffly from the far side of the rumbling, rattling boxcar. A bulky, broad-shouldered man, he glared at Jonathan, eyes blood-shot, face unshaven, bulbous nose alcohol red.

"Guess I can spare one more," Jonathan said.

"One, hell. I'll just take that whole god'am pack, boy," the man said. He tilted a torn straw hat back on a head of dirty, wiry brown hair. "And let's see whatcha got in that little suitcase while I'm up." He wobbled to his feet, reeking of alcohol and foul odor.

A slip of black soot and hot cinders streamed through the boxcar. Jonathan glanced at the wide-open door. Too late. A rocky terrain swept past in a vista broken by telegraph poles, trees, boulders, bridg-es and barbed wire fences. Outside the other door, the silvery rails of the southbound track glinted coolly in the shadow of the northbound Santa Fe freight.

"I need my bag," Jonathan said. "Just socks and stuff, you know."

"Give me the bag, dammit."

Vulnerable in his sitting position, Jonathan made the sign of the cross and sprang to his feet. Three years' experience on Saint Edward's' wrestling team clicked on like a live electrical circuit. His adversary swayed as he gathered his balance. To Jonathan's surprise, his mind was clear and focused. He had a plan and no fear, none at all.

The switchblade snapped open with a metallic click as menacing as a coiled rattlesnake's warning. Jonathan paled, fear surging through his body, heightening his mental alertness. The other men sat in the shadows against the walls, watching and waiting.

Jonathan had no intention now of wrestling a man with a knife. Wearing an ill-fitting, buttonless old sports coat over blue denim overalls, no shirt, a brown brogan on one foot, a black oxford on the other, Jonathan's grizzly opponent said, "For the last time, gimme that god'am bag, you little shit, you."

Poised to lunge, he hunkered low, knees bent, shoulders forward. He waved the silver blade in a hypnotic arc, left to right, right to left. Silence hung between them like a transparent curtain.

Like a lineman waiting for the football to snap, Jonathan looked past the knife and focused on the man's tense posture, intently watching his face, his neck muscles, his jugular vein for the slight ripple that often signaled an opponent's forward movement.

When the man with the switchblade lunged, Jonathan dived, clipping his assailant sharply just below the knee, tossing him forward face-first to the floor...except there was no floor outside the door...and he plunged into the dusky evening without a sound.

Jonathan looked aghast at the broad, empty space beyond the open door. He felt sick to his stomach, searching the eyes fixed on him from round the boxcar.

"The sumbitch got what his ass deserved, pullin' a knife on a kid," said the one-legged passenger. The others grunted in general consent.

"You think he made it? Maybe he's...okay?" Jonathan said, sitting in the middle of the boxcar where he'd ended up. "I mean, he could've..."

"I think—" The cripple started to speak when the southbound San Antonio Express blasted past the door in a noisy blur. It was gone as suddenly as it had appeared. Everyone stared out the door as the rails rang out the fading sounds of the high-speed passenger train.

"Well now," the one-legged man went on, "he's sure 'nough askin' the chief devil right this minute what in hell hit him," grinning to a round of laughter. "Now, let's see what's in this sack he forgot to take with him."

"That's what I did," Jonathan told Sandra, burying his head against her shoulder. "I killed him," he said, sobbing. "A living human being, a man, a person with a soul like yours and mine. I committed the sin and the crime of murder."

"No, no, you didn't, Jonathan," Sandra said firmly, clearly, wrapping her thin arms around him. "What were you supposed to do? Let that guy run you through?"

"If he just hadn't pulled that knife, Sandra, I was going to put him in a choke hold or break his arm. Something like that, so he'd leave me alone. That's all I wanted."

"He threw himself out that door and killed himself," she said adamantly.

"I clipped him, Sandra, and sent him flying out onto those tracks in front of a passenger train."

"Enough," she said, gently lifting his chin off her shoulder. She kissed him and unwrapped her svelte body from the bathrobe. "I need you, Jonathan. Now."

"Cigarette?" Sandra said afterwards. He nodded. But he'd fallen asleep when she returned with two lit cigarettes. She covered him with a sheet. She went up to the third-floor bathtub to get ready for her evening performance.

At around two o'clock, she woke him up. "You gotta go, Jonathan. Sam'll be here soon. Big night. I'm dancing for the first time at the Top O'Hill Terrace Club over in Arlington. It's a big break for me."

"Dancing? That's what you do?" he said, pulling on his trousers.

"I'm an exotic stage dancer."

"Erotic dancer, you mean," he said, smiling and buttoning his shirt.

"Whatever you say, sweetie," Sandra said, not knowing the word. "And don't torture yourself about that man who fell off the train, okay?"

"I feel better thanks to my Sandra."

When Jonathan left her, he hurried to Northwest Twenty-Fifth Street and took a streetcar downtown to Saint Patrick's Church. He knelt in a pew with other Saturday afternoon confessors ahead of him, thinking out what he would say and how he would say it.

This wasn't the rote confession he'd been making since he was six, when he told of disobeying Mom and harboring selfish thoughts about hiding his toys from his brothers. Taking the church's sacrament of confession had been pretty much a nonevent until the age of puberty opened the door to sins of the flesh.

Required to cleanse their souls weekly at Saint Edward's, Jonathan and the other boys had been instructed in a euphemistic vocabulary. The words sanitized the confessing of such grievous mortal sins as impure thoughts (e.g., pondering the profound mysteries of young girls' budding bodies and, worse, imagining what they would do with a girl in the back seat of a car) or committing self-abuse (masturbation in lieu of a girl's body).

Jonathan knew Father Nolan from his visits with Bridie at the convent but not well enough that the white-haired old priest would recognize his voice through the little black cloth screen that separated the two inside the confessional.

"Bless me, Father, for I have sinned…"

After a while, other sinners awaiting forgiveness began to squirm impatiently and to imagine what sins the young man in the confessional might have committed to be in there so long. It took time to tell what happened on the train and to answer Father Nolan's questions about motive and intent and how Jonathan felt toward the deceased. In a low, comforting voice, he blessed the boy for having the charity in his heart to have said a Hail Mary for the poor man's departed soul.

It was easier than Jonathan had imagined. As the old priest was about to give absolution and bid him to go in peace, Jonathan said, "There's one more thing, Father."

Those still waiting to confess their trespasses heard the angry sharp edge of Father Nolan's thundering voice. To their disappointment, they picked up only a smattering of his words: "sinful embrace…evil woman…Satan…save yourself…fires of hell."

Jonathan, forgiven for killing a man, was thrashed by threats of eternal damnation for committing "the sinful embrace of a woman," the proper Church euphemism for screwing Sandra Scott. And the priest's voice rose to the heavens when Jonathan replied, "No, Father, I don't know how many times," adding with a twinge of male pride, "but it was a lot."

"To gain forgiveness, never again lay eyes on her. Otherwise, young man, be certain to be buried in an asbestos casket to protect you from the flames of hell."

A FRESH GRAVE

Gravel crackled like popcorn under bald tires as Wally Cox edged his rusty pickup to the side of the narrow dirt road, rolled to a stop and shut down the clattering engine. In the distance, he recognized some of the men crowded under the shade tree in front of the house. Others he knew by their trucks, buggies and horses gathered in the front yard.

There were no women or children. This was men's business. And the ones Wally knew were good men, neighbors, church friends, people like himself. So he tried not to dislike them or hate them too much. A deputy sheriff leaned against a Ford cruiser, rolling a cigarette.

The rope dangling from the sprawling oak, arching like an umbrella across the shady yard, raised

Wally's ire. He looked away and swallowed the knot in his throat. The tire that hung from the end of the rope was gone. Sissy and Cory appeared like a mirage, she sitting in the tire screaming, "Don't swing me so high, Cory!" as her barefooted brother pushed her back and forth.

The apparition vanished as a man in a white shirt and a tie stepped onto the front porch. It didn't matter that Wally couldn't hear what the man said. He knew the script. Shortly the crowd followed the banker around the house to inspect the water well and windmill, the barn, fences, the peach and apple orchards and the outhouse.

The man in the white shirt stopped abruptly out in the fallow fields. Turning to his followers, he threw up his arms in bewilderment at the long, wide ditch. Freshly dug to about eighteen inches deep, it was roughly a hundred feet long and thirty feet wide. The men scooped up handfuls of black soil. They sniffed the fecund dirt, tasted it and nodded to one another.

The banker pointed to tire tracks. It had taken Wally and Martin a week to dig up the dirt, shovel it into the bed of his pickup and haul it away. The digging had been easy compared with excavating the sorry hard-rock soil behind All Saints. By the end of the seventh day, they'd filled in the rock-infested vegetable garden with black dirt from the farm.

Ollie had taken off her shoes and walked the length of the plot, smelling the loamy soil, running her fingers through it, tasting it and digging into it with her toes. "I'm almost home again," she'd told him.

The banker led the men out of the fields to the back porch and through the door to Ollie's kitchen. He pointed out the cast iron cooking stove marked in raised letters: Ridgewood—Sears, Roebuck & Co. Wally had mounted it on bricks to protect the linoleum-covered wood floor.

"You could put a six-place family dining table over here," the banker said, pointing to the center of the kitchen. He didn't comment on the flower-patterned wallpaper peeling from the walls. "We'll replace the broken window panes after the sale," he said. "Otherwise, the vandals'll just break 'em out again."

"Does the place have 'lectricity?"

"Not yet," the banker said, "but I hear Texas Electric's on the verge of stringing lines out this way just anytime now," adding, "It does have a good tin roof," as if a roof offset the lack of electricity.

When the men gathered again in the front of the house for the auction, Wally drove away. He soon passed the abandoned roadside vegetable stand where they'd camped after the eviction. He'd pitched a large army tent there.

A friend told Wally, "They're hirin' people to build that new Texas and Pacific passenger depot in Fort

Worth." He was there at four o'clock the next morning and got hired two hours later building wooden forms. The T&P paid him two dollars cash for the day. He bought gasoline and hamburger meat on the way home.

Ollie had already milked the cows when he got there. She cooked hamburger steak and onions in a greased skillet and boiled potatoes. Two cans of ranch-style beans heated up on the hot manifold of the pickup's idling engine. Dining by lantern light in the vegetable stand, they watched the buckets and cooking pans Ollie had put out slowly fill with rainwater.

"We gotta do something before it gets cold," Ollie said.

"It's already hard to stay warm in the tent," Sissy said, scooping up beans with a spoon.

En route from work the next evening, Wally turned off the highway onto a dirt road that led to a farm on the side of a steep hill. The farmer laughed at the pickup slipping and sliding on the muddy road after a late afternoon rain. "I was pretty sure I was gonna have to hitch up one o' my mules and pull your ass outta the ditch," he said when Wally got out of the pickup.

Tall and slender in overalls, a feed-sack shirt and rubber boots up to his knees, the farmer said his name was Clyde Markum. And, no, he didn't need any more cows at any price. "If you give 'em to me, I couldn't take 'em. As you see, there ain't much grass on this rocky hill. And nobody can afford hay."

"Well, guess I'll take 'em to the stockyards and sell 'em," Wally said.

"They ain't gonna give you nothin'," Clyde Markum said. "See the top of that building just over the hill, got a cross on top?" Wally nodded. "Well, there's a good-sized pond down behind it and some grass up a gully where a little creek runs down into the pond."

"Yours?" Wally said.

"No. There's a woman lives there with a bunch of other people, and she probably wouldn't mind if you put your cows down by the pond."

"She own it?"

"It's some kind of Catholic place that closed, and the woman's sorta the keeper now, I think. I really don't know how it works, but she's a nice little lady with a funny accent and a funny name. Bridie O'Driscoll. I use their phone from time to time."

The next afternoon, Wally pulled a borrowed cow trailer behind his pickup and unloaded three or four cows at the pond behind All Saints. He made four trips delivering cows. When he arrived with the last two, Bridie was talking with Ollie.

"Mr. Cox said you live nearby," she said.

"Nearby is what he told you?" Ollie said. "Well, he would say that. Men have that kind of dog-stupid pride.

We live in a tent, Mrs. O'Driscoll, out off the Jacksboro Highway. Like lots of folks, we lost our farm."

When Wally came up from the pond, he said, "The cows'll be fine down there, Mrs. O'Driscoll. Like I said yesterday, I'll be back every day to milk 'em, so if you need milk, just say so."

"Wally, we're movin'," Ollie said.

"Movin'?" he said.

"Mrs. O'Driscoll told me to just pick out a room in there," Ollie said, pointing to the convent. "We're movin' in the morning. They have runnin' water. Indoor toilets, too."

"And heat," Sissy said.

"Whenever we have coal," Bridie interjected.

"Listen, Ollie," Wally said, "you know we got no money to pay that kinda rent...or any rent at all."

"It's all right, Wally. All Saints is a clean, dry place where the rent never comes due. And just call me Bridie."

Bridie was delighted when Ollie asked if she could plant a vegetable garden. "I'll be your sharecropper, and we'll divide up whatever this rocky dirt will produce." Wally borrowed a mule from Clyde Markum and plowed up ground behind the utility shed, which became a chicken house for his flock of hens.

Driving back from the auction, Wally knew there was no hope now of returning to life on the land that he'd cultivated, land that had cultivated him. The farm, his farm—its soil ingrained in his character—was gone, sold at auction to a stranger that morning.

He drove around to the utility shed and parked under a tree. Ollie was stooped over, planting a new crop of vegetables. The familiar soil—its moist, loamy texture rich in her calloused hands—had rejuvenated her. He knew she would coax an abundance of vegetables from the narrow strip of good earth he'd hauled from their farm.

From his truck, Wally saw the dark plot of soil as a fresh grave for the farm he'd just lost forever. He waved to Ollie and went down into the basement to get a tall glass of "iced tea" from Martin's still.

River Camp,

Boulder City, Nevada

Dear Bridie,

Tell Josie and Anna I received the cookies and candy okay. Enclosed find two money orders for $41.50 and $79.33. Give Josie and Anna a dollar.

I trust that you will do all right, if only George will pay for the care of the children. I will do the best I can but may be out of work at any moment as the tunnels are nearly finished. I think they're going to call it Hoover Dam, though nobody here likes it anymore than they do President Hoover.

The dam tunnels where I work are the largest in America—56 feet high and 56 feet wide. The work is so hard that very few men can stand it. Most cannot take the terrible heat and bad air underground. Some become unconscious and never recover. The rocks are so hot they burn your hands. It's the nearest approach to slavery that I have ever seen.

I'm feeling a little better. I go down to the river every evening and sometimes sleep in the wet sands. It's the coolest place.

Although I am not making very much, intend to stay as long as possible as there is not much use of looking for work.

Your loving brother,
Tommy
Erin Go Bragh

BRIDIE'S NEW
DAUGHTER

Q.C. leaped from the stairway in pursuit of a frantic mouse. Bridie watched as the cat chased the mouse into the Scotts' room, its door always closed and locked. She thought perhaps they'd left it open in haste that morning. Sam's Lincoln had shot down the driveway, blue smoke billowing from the exhaust long before the Scotts' usual waking hour.

"Is Q.C. troubling you in there?" Bridie called into the dark room.

"I...I don't think...he's...in here." Sandy's choked reply, broken by sobs, drew Bridie inside. Raising a window shade, she found Sandra curled up on the bed, covering her face.

"Are you all right, Sandy?"

"My teeth," she sobbed. "All broken. Can't go to work like this, you know. That light hurts my eyes, Miss Bridie."

"Your teeth, darling, let me see."

"Over there. On the dresser."

Bridie found dentures, uppers and lowers, front teeth missing, others loose, some cracked and broken. "These cannot be yours, love, at your tender age?"

"Car accident, long time ago. I can't work without teeth, and Sam's so mad, he's gone off somewhere. If he doesn't come back, I don't have any place to go and no rent money, Miss Bridie."

"Rent money? As I told Sam, nobody pays rent at All Saints."

"What? That lyin' son o' bitch."

Looking around the dirty, disheveled room, Bridie said, "I'm afraid he'll be back. His things are here." Beneath a chair piled with men's clothes, Q.C. gnawed the corpse of a freshly killed mouse. "We'll see a dentist about your teeth straightaway."

"The son o' bitch took all the money."

"Tut, tut now, Sandy, nothing's so bad it couldn't be worse. We'll manage." Bridie had seen the advertisement in the *Star-Telegram*:

Upper or Lower Teeth
Just $17.50

Dr. E. Glab, Dentist
Flatiron Building
609 Ninth Street

On the downtown streetcar, Sandra Scott wrapped a headscarf across her bruised face, one hand hiding a black eye, the other dangling a Camel cigarette between two fingers.

"I can't go to work like this, and that'll make Sam even madder," Sandra said.

"And where is it you work, love?"

"Nightclubs, fancy speakeasies. I'm an entertainer. But I've been sick, and Doc Cooper said I needed to stay home and rest for a couple weeks. So Sam's getting madder about it every day that I can't work. Called me a bitch and said I was faking it. Then this morning he hauled off and he hit me hard, broke my teeth, and now he's real mad 'cause I sure can't work without teeth."

"You'd be better off without that man, Sandy."

"Sam didn't really mean to hurt me, Miss Bridie. He just gets so mad sometimes. He can't help it. And I need him. He got me off the streets and gave me a place to live."

"You have a place to live now, Sandra, right here with us."

"I'm afraid of Sam, Bridie, to tell you the truth."

Getting off the streetcar at Ninth and Houston, Sandra said, "What a funny-lookin' building, Miss Bridie. Looks like an iron."

"The Flatiron Building. I watched them putting up the one in New York years ago when I lived there."

"I'd like to see New York, Miss Bridie."

"'Tis the place to be, Sandy, especially when ye're young."

Dr. Glab, a jovial, balding man in his late forties, served up his "fine seventeen-fifty, good-eatin' teeth" on a silver tray. "You can eat anything, just anything at all, with these, young lady—apples, corn on the cob, chew your nails, whatever."

His pretty patient—a slim, smoky blonde with sexy aqua-blue eyes and lusty red lips—explained how she'd fallen down the stairs and broken her dentures.

"You're lucky it wasn't worse," said Dr. Glab. He'd heard more colorful and more credible stories from patients whose dentures were damaged or had disappeared during a night of drinking and carousing.

He smiled, pointed to his own perfect ivory-white teeth and said, "Now, if you want a winsome smile like this, we have these smilin' teeth." Like a shoe salesmen, the glib Dr. Glab presented another silver tray of dentures. "Only twenty-five dollars for these smilin' teeth, uppers or lowers. Or both uppers and lowers for forty-eight fifty—installed and guaranteed."

The cheaper, off-white "good-eatin' dentures" paled next to the finely crafted, brightly gleaming "smilin' teeth."

"Oh, they're so pretty," Sandra whispered. "I don't think we have enough…"

"Beautiful," Bridie chimed in.

"I make them myself," Dr. Glab informed her.

"A work of art, they are," Bridie said, adding, "Have I not seen you at Saint Patrick's, Dr. Glab, with your family?"

"Every Sunday and all holy days," he said, wary of a friendly warm-up as a prelude to requesting a discount.

"Kindred souls we are then. Let's see what's in my purse. Twenty dollars, doctor, and this, my gold shamrock."

Dr. Glab raised an eyebrow, and when he reached out to touch the shamrock, Bridie placed it in his hand. "I won it dancing at the County Tipperary Fair when I was a girl, younger than Sandy."

"A fine piece of jewelry."

"Indeed, crafted by the fairies in the Comerah Mountains above Clonmel." He listened with interest to her delightful fairy tale, how the lucky shamrock had spirited her from a little town in Ireland to dance on Broadway.

Bridie laid her twenty dollars on his desk and assured him she'd be back with twenty-eight dollars and fifty cents to retrieve her beloved shamrock, "for I could never live without it."

Dr. Glab nodded and put the shamrock in his desk drawer, pleased to sell the expensive "smilin' teeth" and confident he'd be paid. But if not, he'd already taken a shine to the shamrock. "Your beautiful daughter deserves the best."

On the streetcar back to Rosen Heights, Sandra said, "You didn't tell the dentist I ain't your daughter when he said I was."

"I was so flattered to have another wonderful daughter, Sandy, my love."

"Thank you, Mom, for the teeth…and everything."

THE NEW DEAL

"They said I cheated on our deal," he said, explaining his bruised face, black eye, skinned knuckles.

"And did you, George? Did you cheat the Rubinstein brothers?" Bridie asked, scrambling eggs for his breakfast.

He chuckled. "There's nothing in writing, Bridie, so, like that guy Roosevelt running for president, I said, 'Look, fellas, this is the new deal.'"

In their signature business dress—white shirts, black bow ties, black pants, black oxfords—the bald-headed, midget-like Rubinsteins, Josef and Felix, had circled the big red truck at Allied Auto Parts on lower Commerce Street.

Their partnership had grown like Jack's beanstalk as George steadily sewed up the auto parts business in country towns between Fort Worth and Houston. His customers now accounted for fully thirty percent of Allied's business.

George's "parts-on-hand" plan alone had boosted sales threefold. From well-kept records, he showed garage owners the list of parts they'd ordered over the last several months.

"If you'd had these parts on your shelves, you could have fixed cars the same day and gotten paid right away," he said. "So why not buy a month's supply at a time?" He even lent them the money at five percent for ninety days in a financing plan underwritten by Sam Rosen. "Two percent to you, George, and three percent to me," Sam said.

If this sharply reduced the number of deliveries, just one order filled his '27 Chevy coupe. George bought the bright-red Dodge truck two months before Christmas. The brothers admired the wooden shelves, racks and built-in covered boxes, all designed to store nuts and bolts, piston rings and fan belts, generators and Spanish-made wrenches.

"A rolling auto parts store, George, just like we talked about," Felix said coldly, struggling to quash his infamous temper.

"Yeah, it's a beaut all right," Josef said, "though red isn't exactly the color I might've chosen, if I'd been asked."

Felix climbed down from the truck. "It's perfect, George, but you might've had the courtesy to talk to us before you hauled off and bought this rig. I guess we'll keep our part of the deal and pay for the truck."

Their deal called for Allied Auto Parts to buy George a truck after the business proved itself. Fearing the Depression might end and deflate the demand for auto parts as people bought new cars, the brothers Rubinstein put him off time and again.

Deciding to take on the risk himself, George spelled out his plan to Sam Rosen. Sam was much impressed with the quick success of George's original idea to cater to small-town garages. "So I see your need for a truck to keep up with all the orders," he said.

Sam knew the Rubinstein brothers as longtime Fort Worth businessmen and members of his synagogue. "They're tough little guys, though," he cautioned. "Just watch out for fast math and slippery numbers." George grinned knowingly and nodded.

With money saved and winnings from All Saints' poker parlor on Friday nights, George had a cache of cash. After a meticulous review of George's books and receipts, Sam lent him the rest of the money for the truck at an interest rate lower than banks or the truck dealer offered.

Shaking hands on the deal, Sam asked, "How's Edwin Brant doing with his drugstore business?"

"So far as I can tell, Sam, he's selling lots of ice cream, fountain Cokes and prescription medicine,"

George said, omitting reference to the store's burgeoning bootlegging business.

"I thought so. He pays me right on time every month. It's gratifying to help someone change from bootlegging and loose women to an honest business." George looked away without comment.

Standing in the street admiring the new truck, George O'Driscoll told the Rubinsteins he'd paid cash for it. Thus he would not be going on the road in their truck as a salaried agent plus commissions and expenses. Also, he said, the customers he'd cultivated along the road to Houston were his—"not yours, not ours, but mine."

George hoped Allied Auto Parts would continue to be his supplier.

"Why, you goddam double-crossing Irish cabbage-headed Catholic crook!" Felix shouted, putting George in a one-legged street dance when he kicked him in the shins.

Josef brought him down with a flying tackle, and before George could get up, both brothers fell on him, flailing with feet and fists until George launched Josef into the path of an approaching police car.

"I'd put my money on the midgets," the cop behind the wheel told his partner.

"I'd put 'em all in jail," said the other cop. Both officers emerged from the patrol car, billy clubs in hand, and ambled over to watch Felix kick George in the ribs.

"You boys havin' a good time?"

"I'm Josef Rubinstein, officer, owner of Allied Auto Parts there." He nodded to his store. "We're just settling a little business dispute."

"That's right, officer," George said, getting up from the redbrick street. "Just working out some kinks in a new deal."

Josef slipped the big cop a five-dollar bill. "You fellas take your families out tonight for steak at the Saddle and Sirloin."

"All right, and you guys get out of the street before you get hit by a car," the cop said, stuffing the crisp bill into his pocket.

Felix brought out the Montecristo cigars. George filled three glasses from a bottle of President's Choice. He told the Rubinsteins road sales would grow a hundred percent. He demanded a sliding discount as sales grew.

"You make more, you want more," Josef complained.

"It's the American way, is it not?" replied the Irishman. "To the new deal." The Rubinsteins slowly lifted their glasses.

MATTHEW'S DEAL

"Somebody put those books in my satchel," Matthew protested.

"Mr. Berry says that *somebody* is you."

"Where's my dad?"

"Lucky for you he's doing bookkeeping at the stockyards."

"You're not gonna tell him about this, are you, Miss Bridie?"

"That remains to be seen, Matthew, depending on what these books are about and whether you stay in your room until I call you for dinner."

Back in the kitchen, Bridie put on her glasses and took one of the gutter booklets, as Mr. Berry called them, from Matthew's satchel. She opened and closed the little booklet in a flash.

Printed on cheap pulp in black ink, the booklet featured crudely drawn cartoon characters having sex in wildly grotesque positions (on staircases and banisters, on horseback, springing from diving boards, swinging from chandeliers and so on) and spewing words not heard in church-going homes.

"Looks like you've just seen a ghost, Bridie," Edwin Brant said, coming through the back door into the kitchen.

"It's Matthew," she said glumly. "The boy's going to the devil."

"I've never heard you speak so harshly of Matthew," Edwin said.

"Mr. Berry himself brought him home from school just now along with filthy little books in Matthew's book satchel," she said, nodding at a book bag on the table.

"Oh, let me see," Edwin said. He took five or six booklets from the satchel and flipped slowly through one of them.

"Mr. Berry called them gutter books, straight from the gutter," Bridie said. "I think they're published by the devil himself."

"Who's this Mr. Berry?" Edwin said, thumbing through another booklet.

"He's the school principal, Edwin. He caught Matthew with this sinful material."

"Oh now, Bridie, just a boy growing up."

"It gets worse, Edwin. Mr. Berry said Matthew's sharing the books with other boys at school."

"Sharing?" Edwin said, laughing. "Matthew's not that dumb. He sells them at school."

"Why, that's worse than his bootlegging, corrupting those nice little boys."

"I can see you've never been a little boy, Bridie," Edwin said. "As I've said before, Matthew's quite the little businessman. He trades George's beer for these books at Champ's Gas Station and sells them to his school buddies."

"You mean he's stealing beer, too? May God forgive him."

"I doubt it," Edwin said.

"And how is it you know all this, Edwin?"

"Champ's is one of my outlets for President's Choice, and I buy gas at the station. Champ told me he'd been trading these little books for good home brew with Matthew, who sells them at school."

"How long has this been going on?" Bridie said.

"Since you cut off Matthew's bootlegging job with Blackie. You forced the poor kid to find another line of work."

"This is all much worse than I imagined," Bridie said, frustrated.

"What are you going to do with these?" Edwin said, holding up the disgusting little books.

"Burn them, Edwin, burn them in the furnace and see what I can do to save Matthew's soul from burning in hell."

"You could feed 'em to Bonnie and Clyde," Edwin suggested, "after I finish reading them." He emptied the satchel and took the books to his room.

Bridie went to see Matthew. "You've been stealing beer and selling sin to little boys."

"They used to buy 'em for a dime, Miss Bridie," he explained. "I sell them for a nickel and make a little profit."

"And you're stealing George's beer from the basement."

"He can't drink all that beer he makes down there, so…"

"Matthew, you've been breaking the Seventh Commandment, 'Thou shall not steal,' among others. To save your soul from the devil and your backside from your dad, you'll be going to Saint Patrick's Saturday afternoon to confess your sins to Father Nolan."

"The asbestos priest," Matthew said, snickering at Father Nolan for warning sinful boys they'd better be buried in asbestos caskets to protect themselves from the fires of hell.

"Asbestos priest?"

"Nothing, just a joke," he said.

"This is no joking matter, Matthew."

"All right, Miss Bridie, it's a deal. If you won't tell Dad, I'll go to confession Saturday," Matthew agreed, thinking a few Hail Marys said in penance beat the beating he'd get from his father.

"We'll catch the three o'clock streetcar," Bridie said. "And I'll see that you go into that confessional when we get there."

"You don't trust me?" Matthew said, smiling mischievously.

"No, Matthew, I don't."

Los Angeles, California

Dear Bridie,

This city sure looks great. All kinds of life here. The beaches are full of people every day with some sleeping out on the sand and living in cars all over the place.

Lot of the public schools are closed. The idle are meeting and marching to the city hall and seizing public buildings to sleep in. Thousands of men working for nothing but their board in government camps.

The freight trains and all the roads are full of idle men everywhere you go. From the trains you see wheat in the fields and breadlines in the cities. It looks like there will have to be a different system. The old order has about come to a close. We don't know what will take its place, but there has got to be some change.

I am leaving in the morning for Seattle to get a boat to Alaska. It's getting harder here to pass the doctor exam but up there they don't care much. I worked on the docks here and am enclosing $40.31. Do the best you can.

Your loving brother,
Tommy
Erin Go Bragh

DEATH AND TAXES

Under a full moon, the white cross atop All Saints cast its shadow over the men coming and going from the campus. They parked their cars half a block away. Sam Scott took their money and directed them, one at a time, to the Lincoln touring car behind the laundry house.

From behind the chicken house, Anna and Irene Markum gawked and giggled as the car began to rock like one of the rides at an amusement park soon after a man climbed inside and closed the door.

"Whatta they doin' in there…dancin' or sumpin'?" Irene wondered.

"Wrestlin', maybe," Anna guessed, having watched men emerge from the Lincoln rumpled, buckling belts, buttoning shirts and lighting cigarettes. As one started back to his car, another came walking toward All Saints. Both girls wondered why Sandra Scott never got out of the Lincoln.

Sam had come up with the "Lincoln plan" to sidestep paying the Jacksboro Highway clubs they'd been working. The nightly take from Sandra's services to high-stakes gamblers at the Flaming Flamingo Club and the nearby Double Deuces would have supported a carefree life if only the clubs hadn't assessed a hefty "tax" on her earnings. If only the Flaming Flamingo hadn't caught Sam cheating on its share of Sandra's nightly income.

"Ya maybe heard o' Benjamin Franklin, Sam?" said Harry-the-Hammer Harmon.

"George Washington's father?"

"Maybe so, but he's famous for sayin' that death and taxes are certain, Sam. And next time you cheat me outta my taxes, sonny boy, you gonna find out just how certain death is. Now, boys, take this runt out somewheres and show him how mad I am."

In a rage, Sam had passed on the beating to Sandra, blaming her "for getting us caught," pummeling her face and breaking her teeth.

Through the warm autumn months, Sam's Lincoln plan had been lucrative enough, though the street customers paid less and never tipped vis-a-vis the better-heeled clientele at the clubs. But as winter approached, Sandra and her clients began complaining about the cold car. "I'm gonna catch pneumonia," she grumbled.

Now, just before Thanksgiving, clients walked down from the corner, up the fire escape and through a second-floor window. Anna and Irene watched from behind the laundry house. So did Bridie.

"Not a word now to yere dadda," she whispered. "I'd never hear the end of it."

"What are they doin', anyway?" Irene still wanted to know.

"I don't think they're wrestlin'," Anna answered.

She had almost thrown up when Matthew Quinlan explained, "You dummy, they're doin' what we see the boy and girl dogs doing together out in the yard and what Mr. Markum's cows do in his barnyard."

"They're up to no good," Bridie whispered as another man mounted the fire escape. "God forgive them all, but this must stop. And stop at once it will."

Sam Scott, shaven and bathed, sauntered into Bridie's kitchen the next afternoon in his bathrobe and slippers, waving a note Bridie had slipped under his door.

"You wanted to see me, Bridie?" he said, thinking she'd summoned him about paying her for Sandra's new dentures.

Sitting at the far end of the banquet table reading her tea leaves, Bridie looked up from her cup. "Sam, I'm sorry, but you'll have to go. You're setting a bad example for the kids. Need I say more about what I observed last night—men trooping up and down the fire escape to your room?"

Sam's smile dissolved, his teeth clenched tight, his eyes hardened. He took a pack of Pall Malls and matches from his pocket. Lighting a cigarette, he shuffled slowly toward Bridie, tapping the table with the gaudy rings that festooned his fingers. The Saint Christopher medal Sister Vee had given him dangled from his neck.

"Your own sister. What's her name now...?"

"Sister Vee, you mean?"

"Yeah, her," he said, fondling the medal. "The nun who gimme this in the prison house. She told us God forgives sinners. So was she wrong about God?"

"Ask and ye shall be forgiven, Sam. Now, go in peace, but go you must."

He abruptly leaned forward, coming face to face with Bridie, and blew cigarette smoke in her face. She recoiled from the smoke and in fear that he was about to hit her.

"Ya know, Bridie, the police might be interested in a little tip about an unlawful business down in the basement of this here house of God."

"If it's illegal, at least it's not immoral."

He laughed. "You can get mad after all, can't you, Bridie? But you don't want me to make that phone call to the police and get all these nice people here thrown in jail, do you? Now, if you'll excuse me, I've gotta get Sandra up. Uh, so she can work tonight."

"Don't worry, Bridie," Lynn said, sitting down at the banquet table with her. "Edwin knows now, and Sam Scott's on his way out. I'm just glad you let me in on what he did."

"I didn't know what else to do," Bridie said in despair. "You're the only person I've told about it all. Edwin won't...you know?"

"No, no, Bridie," Lynn said. "He'll just send Sam packing. That's all."

His .45 automatic bulged under Edwin Brant's coat as he tapped lightly at Sam's door with a blackjack. When Sam cracked the door, Edwin slammed it against his face, bolted into the room and kicked him in the groin. Amid Sandra's screams, Edwin left Sam bleeding on the floor with instructions about his impending departure.

That evening, as Bridie washed supper dishes, Sam limped into the kitchen. She paled at the sight of him—his right eye black, his face bruised, his lip cut, a bandage above his left ear.

"Me and Sandy's headin' up to Saint Louis. Got connections up there. Never meant to cause ya no trouble, Miss Bridie. Never woulda called them cops, neither. Just a joke, ya know. And I'm sorry my cigarette smoke got in your face. Anyways, we're leavin' soon as Sandy gets the car packed. I'll mail ya the money for her teeth."

Sam fell silent, pondering the floor as if checking off what Edwin had told him to say in his apology to Bridie. "Well, I guess that's all." He shrugged and limped back down the hall.

"God be with ye both, Sam," Bridie called.

Just after dark, Sandra, bundled up in a red coat with gold buttons, hurried into Bridie's room. "Goodbye, Bridie." She smiled faintly as they hugged. "Oh, I see you got your shamrock back from my dentist."

"Indeed, by the grace of God and a check from brother Tommy, I paid Dr. Glab in full."

Sandra took the gold three-leafed clover from the shelf over Bridie's bed. "For luck," she said, touching its leaves to her lips. A car honked in short, impatient bursts. "Stay, Sandy, and save yourself. You're safe here with us."

"He's blowin' his horn, Miss Bridie, so I better get goin' before he blows his stack," she whispered, choking back tears as she returned the shamrock. "I'll miss you, Mom," Sandra cried out, rushing into the hall.

Sandra reappeared in Bridie's doorway seconds later. "Thank God, you've come back, Sandy," Bridie said, smiling faintly in disbelief.

"No, no, Mom. I'm sorry. Just please do me a favor."

"Anything, Sandy. Anything I can do for you I will."

"Tell Jonathan I said goodbye and that I'll miss him."

"You mean Jonathan Quinlan?" Bridie asked, astonished and puzzled.

"Tell him...tell Jonathan I'm sorry and that I love him," Sandra said, sobbing as she turned and walked back down the hall.

"God help her," Bridie said, baffled by Sandra's farewell to Jonathan. *Does he even know her?* she wondered, her face grimacing as the unthinkable crossed her mind. *No, she wouldn't have,* Bridie tried to convince herself. *Jonathan's a mere boy, barely seventeen.*

She banished the forbidden thought as best she could, took up her rosary and prayed for Sandra...and for Jonathan, too.

Next morning, grateful nothing worse had happened, Bridie said, "So, Edwin, you put the fear o' God in Sam Scott."

"Wasn't God, Bridie. Something a little closer to earth."

c/o Alaska Road Commission
Valdez, Alaska Territory

Dear Bridie,

Enclosed find cheque for $133.39 and hope you will get along all right until you hear from me again. I finally found work fixing the road that goes up the mountains. It is not so bad as we live in a camp in cabins and have plenty of wood for the stove to keep us warm.

We have a great time with the bears. Five of them come around to be fed and will eat out of your hand. We have a tame weasel and he sure cleans out the rats and mice and is as quick as a shadow. He gets into our beds all the time at night.

I got to Valdez back in the summer. Hundreds of boats were tied up as there is no price for the fish at two cents a pound. Lots of clams on the beach and wild goats, deer and bear in the hills. Lots of wood, too. So you can live cheap. Thank God I found this job before winter hit.

I am looking for gold all the time and someday I may find a lot. Don't write until you hear from me as I may leave here any time. I must run to get this to the supply truck that goes into town every week. Bye.

Your loving brother,
Tommy
Erin Go Bragh

THE RED BANDANNA

Weary hoboes shivered miserably as the Santa Fe freight steamed nonstop through the Fort Worth rail yards.

"Sometimes they do this and hold up on a side track north o' town," someone hoped aloud.

"Yeah, an' sometimes they keep goin' right on to Oklahoma City," someone replied. "An' if you think it's cold here, brother, just wait'll we cross that Red River."

"Wait, hell, I'm gettin' off a'fore my ass freezes to the floor," said a tall, rangy cowboy in a sheepskin coat, leather gloves, knee-high Mexican boots, a soiled Stetson on his head and a red bandanna around his neck. Balancing a bulky duffel bag on his shoulder with one hand, he scrambled up a ladder at the end of the car and opened a trap door to the roof. Jonathan

Quinlan followed him. The cowboy struggled to shove his gear out onto the roof.

"It's that saddle horn sticking out of the bag," Jonathan called. The cowboy freed it and pushed the bag through the door.

He and Jonathan clung to the slick, slightly slanted roof. They coughed on thick smoke from the locomotive, gritty soot collecting in their ears and eyes. A bitter north wind cut like a blade of ice.

"Gotta hurry, boy. She's startin' to pick up a little speed," the cowboy said, stepping down a ladder on the side of the boxcar. "When ya git to the end o' this ladder, drop yore suitcase jest a'fore ya jump."

"Quin, it's Jonathan," Bridie panted, breathless after bounding up the stairs and bursting into his room. "He's at the hospital after falling off a train."

"A train!" he gasped, looking up from his armchair.

"Julie called from Saint Joseph's. The boy's in surgery."

A book tumbled from his lap as Quin bolted out of the chair. He stepped barefooted into his shoes. "Is he okay?"

"Come, Quin, let's go."

He felt for his car keys in his pocket as they ran down the stairs.

"He'll survive, thanks to that red bandanna," the surgeon told Quin in a hospital hallway. "Somebody tied it around his leg and stopped the bleeding."

"Who?"

"No idea. The gravest threat now is infection. Sulfa drugs just aren't always effective." Quin nodded. "I've dosed him up on morphine. He may say things a boy normally doesn't say to his father."

Leaving Quin at the hospital, Bridie took the last streetcar home.

"What a Christmas present," Quin said, squeezing Julie's hand as they sat together in a waiting room. "Why in hell was he riding a god'am freight train?"

Jonathan, his mind mushy with morphine, his speech slurred, answered the question the next afternoon.

"I've been hopping freights awhile, Dad, so I could come home from school more often. I'm pretty good at it. But in the dark, I thought there was one more step at the end o' that fucking ladder." Quin flinched. "When it wasn't there, I went sailing halfway under the boxcar. I'd have laid there and bled to death if it hadn't been for that cowboy."

"Cowboy?"

"The real thing. Stetson, boots, red bandanna around his neck."

Jonathan's limp body thrown over his shoulder, the cowboy had flagged down a pickup, laid him in the back and tossed his suitcase in after him.

"Better get this kid to a doctor right pronto," he told the startled driver. Adjusting his hat, he nodded sharply and disappeared into a windy sleet storm in the night.

"Doesn't look like I'll be playing quarterback next year," Jonathan said, adding under a hollow laugh, "but there's always another season, right?"

"Don't, Jonathan," said Quin. Neither mentioned Jonathan's football scholarship. "I'm sorry I didn't send you train fare, son, but once a month was about all we could afford."

"Oh hell, Dad," he laughed deliriously. "I would've smoked it or drank it or spent it on one of those wicked women down on Sixth Street. That's where half the football team got the clap last year, you know."

"You'll recall I got a heavy letter from Brother Michael," Quin said. "He was very upset."

"Upset we didn't take him with us. He pardoned me because I didn't get 'a social disease,' as he called it." Despite their ridicule, "the Blessed Virgin Jonathan," as they called him, had refrained from joining his teammates in their extracurricular weekend workouts at Austin's infamous whorehouses. For his faithfulness to her, Jonathan knew with certainty he'd gotten the clap from Sandra Scott.

"Anyway, I would've blown the train fare and hopped that freight dead broke. So don't blame yourself."

"I was trying to stretch what's left of the money to send you boys to Notre Dame like I promised your mother."

"Except Matthew. You'll be lucky to keep that little fart out of the electric chair."

Quin laughed. "He is the meanest kid I've ever known. Did I tell you Roger's an altar boy now at Saint Patrick's?"

"At least you've got one son worthy of your name."

Roger turned away abruptly as the nurse changed the bandages on the stump—an ugly, bruised mass of stitched raw flesh, twisted muscle and splintered bone.

"I'm so sorry, Jonathan," Roger said when the nurse left. "What do you want for Christmas?"

"Swipe me a bottle of President's Choice out of the basement. And get me some Luckies. Say, where'd you get that shiner, kid? You look worse than I do."

"Matthew took over the cave you gave me down by the pond. Said it's his now. He goes in there to look at those dirty little sex books he sells at school."

Jonathan laughed. "And you, Mr. Innocent, you're slobbering over those half-dressed women in that old Ward's catalog I gave Matthew."

"Yeah, I kept the catalog in the cave, but Matthew beat me up and told me not to come back."

"That little bastard! I'll beat the living crap out of him."

"I can see you chasing Matthew down the fire escape on crutches, Jonathan."

"Do me a favor, Roger. Just between us, okay?"

"Sure," Roger said, pleased to be taken into confidence by his hero.

"Let Sandra Scott know what happened and that I'm here at Saint Joe's. Don't let anybody hear you or even see you talking to her."

"You didn't know, Jonathan? She left. She and that guy, Sam."

Jonathan paled, staring at Roger as if his brother had told him someone had died. "I didn't know," he finally said. "Where'd she go?"

Roger shrugged. "Who knows? Who cares?"

To break the silence that followed, Roger said, "Did Dad tell you I may have to leave Saint Ignatius and go to public school now, and you won't be going back to Saint Edward's? He says he'll be out of money after all the hospital bills, the doctors and more surgery and something he called physical therapy."

Jonathan tried to sit up, fell back dizzily and slammed his fist into a pillow. "Godammit, why didn't Dad tell me first? I know it's my fault, but..."

"Dad's feeling pretty bad 'cause he promised Mom he'd send us to Notre Dame," Roger said. "I never wanted to go there anyway. I don't even know where Notre Dame is."

⟞⟝ ⟞⟝

It was just after one o'clock in the morning when Julie got off the streetcar and headed up Belle Avenue, beaten from twelve hours in the emergency room. She'd checked on Jonathan just before leaving the hospital.

"He has a ways to go, but he'll be okay if infection doesn't set in," the night nurse had said. Julie was less certain about the boy's father.

Quin had asked her to move to his room several weeks ago. "It would save us a lot of trouble running up and down that damn fire escape," he argued. "They all know about us here anyway."

"Jeremy and Juliana don't," she said. "It would be like telling them their daddy's never coming home. Or that he's dead. I need time to think."

Reaching the darkened convent, Julie climbed the stairs to her room and put her coat and hat on a chair. She checked on her sleeping children and went out the window to the fire escape, bracing against the cold wind and stepping carefully up the ice-encrusted steps.

She knocked lightly against the window, opened it, stepped in and stripped off her dress, ready to jump into Quin's warm bed. "Mrs. Santa's here, darling!"

He lay passed out in his armchair, a cigarette burning in the ashtray, a half bottle of President's Choice next to a copy of *The Thin Man*.

She wiped his face with a damp cloth. "You weren't going to do this anymore, Mr. Quinlan."

He moaned. "It's the end of everything, Julie. Everything's gone."

"No, Quin, not everything. We're together. And Jonathan's going to come through this."

"It's all gone. Everything. I rubbed shoulders with the pontiffs of power—Amon Carter, Sid Richardson, the Waggoners. Then Marion died. The business folded. I lost the house. I live in an old abandoned convent. Now Jonathan. Julie, all the money's gone, and I promised her…"

"Marion knows you're trying, Quin. She still loves you. And so do I," Julie told him for the first time. "Yes, it's all right for both of us to love you. And Quin, it's all right if you…" She hesitated.

"It's all right if I love her…and love you, too?"

"It's all right," she whispered, kissing his cheek.

"I love you, Julie. And I need you now." He reached for her standing there in panties and bra.

"What you need, Quin, is aspirin." She put on her dress. "I'll get a bottle of 'em from my room." She started for the fire escape, turned and went out the door and down the hallway to the stairs.

MIDNIGHT WITH JESUS

"Let me outta here alive, God, and I'll never come back," Martin prayed as he fled Saint Patrick's Church. He trotted up Throckmorton Street and turned off on Ninth Street to bypass the police station and jail.

The Carnegie Library loomed in the dark like an English manor house, Corinthian columns guarding its ornate sandstone visage. He slipped through silent canyons of buildings in empty, dimly lit streets.

A police cruiser lurked at Seventh and Main. Martin darted up an alley. "If I just get back home, I'll never leave again," he swore, angry with himself for going to midnight Mass with Bridie to hear Josie sing Christmas carols in the choir.

He had been to church once before. His pa had decided it was time his boys got some religion, and he took the family to the Tabernacle of the One True God. The preacher and the people prayed in tongues for the new converts and welcomed them to the fold with loving hugs.

Deacon Coleman beseeched them to testify to their new faith in God by taking unto their bosoms live rattlesnakes from a washtub of slithering serpents hissing and rattling. Martin's pa backed away from the tub, shouting, "If I'd brought my shotgun, I'd shoot those damn snakes and you too, you damn fool you!" The family never went to church again.

Bridie assured Martin there'd be no serpents in a church named after the saint who drove all the snakes out of Ireland, a legend Bridie and most Irish took as mystical truth.

Saint Patrick's looked to Martin like the gilded gates to heaven—its colossal columns of granite towering skyward, beamed ceilings vaulting to the heavens, statues of robed holy men praying and stained glass windows picturing saints in all their glory. The tiered marble altar—adorned with silver candelabra, gold chalices, bejeweled ciboria, gilded monstrances—rose like steps to a glittering stained-glass portrait of Christ on the cross.

Martin shuddered as all twelve-hundred-sixty-eight pipes of the organ erupted like musical cannon fire.

The iron music and the haunted chanting of the choir rattled bones and shook souls.

Bells ringing, incense rising, candles burning, priests in golden vestments chanting and all the people singing in Latin from little black books created a pageantry of worship that instilled Martin with a mighty fear of Almighty God. Unlike the Latin prayers, Father Nolan rendered both Gospel and sermon in plain and beautiful English. His telling why the Savior was born among the poor in a stable of animals gave Martin a sense of peace he had not known since he was a boy in Kentucky. He felt a kinship with Jesus.

Leaving him alone in the pew, Bridie stood in line to take the host—the body and blood of Christ—at the altar. As the priest placed the white wafer on their tongues, the communicants bowed their heads and returned to their pews, eyes downcast in humility.

When Jesus came down the aisle, Martin began to tremble, his heart raced, his legs shook. He thought he might collapse. There was no mistaking him—his mane of blue-black hair, high cheekbones, angular jaws, sun-bronzed skin, a luxuriant handlebar mustache. He wore a black western suit, wide leather belt and polished steel-toed boots.

Head bowed, eyes downcast, Jesus H. Cortez turned in at a pew four rows forward from Martin's and knelt in prayer.

Jesus's presence—some said boldness—startled fellow worshippers who knew that Catholic Mexicans "belonged" at San Jose Church, just as Negroes had "their place" at Our Lady of Mercy. Yet every Christmas, Jesus H. Cortez patronized the big gringo church downtown, confessed his sins and entered, however briefly, the state of grace.

The voice of Jesus at the Greyhound bus station echoed in Martin's memory: "Enjoying your last supper, *amigo?*"

Bridie was baffled to find Martin gone when she returned from Communion.

Shivering and chilled to the bone, he reached All Saints as sunlight tinged the eastern horizon on this icy Christmas morning. He saw Wally Cox dragging a Christmas tree up the back steps. He stood it on the porch and went inside.

Wally had left in his truck Christmas Eve to drive 150 miles into the East Texas forests near Palestine. He spotted the big fir tree just the other side of the fence. He didn't doubt the sincerity of signs on the fence posts: "Trespassers Will Be Shot. Survivors Will Be Shot Again."

Right after sunset, he climbed over the barbed wire fence with a saw, cut the tree down and dragged it to his truck. The round trip had taken him all day and half the night.

Martin tended the cows and chickens, left the milk and eggs on the back porch next to the tree and went to bed.

CHRISTMAS DOLLS

"Why'd my daddy give me to the nuns, Miss Bridie?"

Putting her arms around Richard Levitz, she told him once again his daddy was working and saving money to bring him home someday.

"Is he coming to see me today?"

"If he can get time from work, love, he'll be coming this afternoon with Sister Vee. She's bringing Santa's gifts for you and Allen and Frank. Now, eat ye're porridge, lad."

"You'll like my dad," Richard said, spooning his oatmeal for creepy crawlers—a compulsive habit since finding the beetle in his bowl.

Bridie had read her tea leaves and the morning paper before Richard shuffled into the toasty kitchen, its floor warmed by the furnace below. She was relieved to find the milk and eggs on the back porch, which meant Martin had made it home after his abrupt disappearance at midnight Mass. The Christmas tree on the porch left her puzzled.

Richard finished his porridge. "I'm goin' back upstairs, Miss Bridie, an' see if Q.C.'s still eating that mouse he caught a while ago."

It was a quiet morning with the Catholics snoozing in after midnight Mass, the Brants keeping their usual hours, Doc Cooper sleeping off his nightly prescription of President's Choice and the Protestants at church.

Clyde Markum had delivered the Headless Turk, as he called the doomed bird. Bridie had asked him to raise the turkey at his dairy "so the children won't make a pet of him." Ollie Cox had stuffed the big bird and shoved him into an oven in the basement kitchen before leaving for church.

Shirley Roberts, Buster and Julie Bryant's children went with the Coxes to Christmas services at First Baptist. Wally borrowed the Brants' Cadillac to get them all there. "You'll either get arrested by the cops or machine-gunned by some of Edwin's closest friends," George told him.

When Sandra Scott came down from her room, Bridie handed her a paring knife and pointed to a pile of potatoes. Sandra had stepped silently through the back door a few days earlier. "Hi, Mom. I'm home," she'd said, a small suitcase in her right hand.

"Oh, thank God you've come back, Sandy," Bridie cried, tears in her eyes as she hugged her adopted daughter.

"Sam and me split after he went to jail," Sandra explained.

If Bridie embraced her like a prodigal daughter, others failed to roll out a carpet. "So we've got a loose woman running loose in the nunnery again," Quin laughed.

Lynn Brant didn't laugh. "I know her kind, Bridie. Be careful."

Julie Bryant was blunt. "Stay away from Jonathan, Sandra. Otherwise, I won't hesitate to tell Bridie and his dad you've been bedding down with that boy."

"So I guess in a way, you and me are family, Julie, being as you're bedding with his father," Sandra said, giggling.

"Damn you," Julie said, slapping Sandra across the face.

"I'm sorry, Julie. I didn't mean it."

"Well, I meant it, Sandra. You stay away from Jonathan, or I'll get Bridie to throw you out into the street where you belong."

"Please, Julie, please. I have no place to go."

"Just don't go near Jonathan," Julie warned, ashamed that she'd slapped the girl.

"But what'll I do when I see him here in the hall or kitchen?"

"He's in the hospital and will be for a while." Julie told her about the train accident. "And don't be going there to see him, either."

Doc Cooper maintained his professional decorum with his former patient when Sandra encountered him in a hallway. "Oh, Doctor Cooper, I didn't expect to see you here," she said.

"I live here now, Sandra."

"Well, I just…I want to thank you, Doctor Cooper," she said awkwardly, looking around to see if anyone was nearby. "I'm okay now. You cured me."

"I hope you stay that way," he said.

"You wouldn't…I mean, you wouldn't…uh, tell anyone here about my problem?" she said.

"I'm a doctor, Sandra. I never discuss my patients with anyone."

"Thank you, thank you so much, Doctor Copper," she said as he nodded and walked on down the hall.

Helping Bridie with dinner, Sandra skinned the spuds with a skill learned in the kitchens of the St. Louis city jail. Bridie poured Q.C. a bowl of cream and went to work making piecrusts.

By noon, the women of All Saints were chopping, cutting, mixing and cooking. The men lounged around the fireplace in the parlor, drinking and speculating whether Franklin Delano Roosevelt's

New Deal would end the Depression once he took office in March.

Lynn Brant and Elizabeth Wellington decked the halls, the parlor and Bridie's kitchen with Christmas wreaths, bells, stockings and candles that once decorated the White House.

Lynn gave the kids boxes of tree trimmings to decorate the eight-foot fir that had arrived mysteriously on the back porch. Edwin found the forgotten decorations in the basement when he was rummaging through their belongings in search of ammunition for his tommy gun.

After dressing the tree, most of the kids gathered for no reason at all on the second-floor landing, wondering what they might get for Christmas. They wondered why a neighbor, Dean Chollar, got a Shetland pony and why Anna got to ride him and they didn't.

"Because Dean's my best friend," Anna said.

"Dad says it's just a dumb ol' two-dollar donkey," Cory Cox said. "Dean's too dumb to know the difference."

"Whatever it is, you're not getting one for Christmas," Matthew Quinlan told Cory.

"I wanna bike," Richard said.

"Think you're rich or something, Richard?" Matthew smirked. "You're nothin' but a worthless little orphan, you know."

"No dammit, I'm not either! My daddy's coming to see me today."

"We're worthless little orphans," Brandon Reynolds said as he and Frank Feldman came down the stairs. "And we're gonna kick your worthless ass, Matthew."

"It'll take both you little street bastards, if ya can catch me," he said, throwing open a window and scampering down the fire escape. Brandon followed him while Frank took the stairs "to head off the little prick on the playground." Jeremy Bryant closed the window against an icy breeze.

Julie Bryant dragged in, tired and yawning, from her shift at the hospital. "Jonathan was in physical therapy and cheerful when I left," she told Bridie, looking askance at Sandra Scott whittling a potato.

Wally checked the carcass of beef roasting over a mesquite fire behind the laundry house, a barrier against an unrelenting north wind.

"You're gonna run out of beef cows someday," Martin said, stirring the mesquite coals. He tossed Mulligan a beefy bone.

"Then we'll eat those goats," Wally said, nodding at Clyde, standing on the hood of the new LaSalle. "Sooner than later if George catches that one on his car." Clyde bleated and jumped to the ground when Wally whacked him with a mesquite limb.

Before lunch, everyone gathered in the parlor for the blessing of the tree.

"My God," Father Nolan gasped, "I've never seen such...." His blessing faltered when his eye caught a nude Clara Bow doll smiling at him inside a pale blue bauble among the tree's green pine needles.

"We never seen nekkid angels, either, Father Nolan," Jeremy said. A galaxy of other Hollywood stars—Marlene Dietrich and Greta Garbo among them—appeared in their buxom nudity inside red, blue and green baubles dangling naughtily in the limbs.

"For God's sake, Edwin," Lynn cried, snatching the lewd baubles from the tree. "They must've been in those White House Christmas decorations you brought up from the basement."

"Me? You gave 'em the boxes."

"Look, another nekkid angel, up there." Sissy Cox pointed.

"Yeah, look at those boobs," Richard said.

"I've got them all now, Father Nolan," Lynn said, plucking Mary Pickford from a lower limb.

"Not all of 'em," Buster Roberts told her. A movie buff, he knew the dolls were Hollywood stars, not nude angels. "Matthew took Joan Crawford up to his room."

"I'm so sorry, Father Nolan," Lynn apologized. "Please forgive him—my husband, I mean."

"I suppose....I mean, forgiveness is my business," the priest said. "Without it, churches would be empty. Now, let's just get on with the blessing here."

Wrapped in a quilt, Sister Vee arrived from Dallas, teeth chattering in a Ford coupe driven by George Salih, her youthful driver from the Dunne Home Orphanage.

"Sorry we're a bit late," Sister Vee said, warming herself at the parlor fireplace.

"Too bad you missed the blessing of the tree," Quin said.

"Oh, you should see the leftovers the Dallas hotels delivered to the orphanage this morning," she said. "Now, where will I find Richard Levitz?"

"His father's not coming?" Bridie asked.

The nun shook her head and went to find the boy.

After everyone adjourned to the banquet table in the kitchen, Father Nolan blessed the feast. "Amen, and thank God Jean Harlow didn't pop out of the turkey." Sister Vee wondered how much he'd drunk today.

Bridie rapped her glass with a spoon. "Thanks be to God for everyone here. Ollie for cooking the turkey and all of you who gave to this feast—be it a bag o' potatoes, a pot o' peas or a prayer. And to Wally for the fatted calf as well as our freshly cut Christmas tree."

"From whose land it once graced only God, the devil and Wally would know," Quin interjected, raising his glass to Wally.

"And," Bridie went on, "Mr. Markum for fattening our turkey, Lynn for the decorations…"

"Especially the little angels for the tree," Quin said.

Doc Cooper, raising his glass, added, "And thanks to Edwin for the booze."

"We've much to be thankful for," Sister Vee said, sitting next to Richard Levitz, his eyes still teary over his father's absence. "I'm so happy ye're back," the nun told Sandra Scott.

"I don't think I'da got back alive if I hadn't kissed Bridie's lucky shamrock before I left," Sandra said. Julie, sitting between Quin and Juliana, looked down the long table and gave her a mean frown.

After pie and coffee, everyone gathered around the purloined tree in the parlor to watch the kids open gifts. Sister Vee's newest benefactor—Samuel Gibson IV of the All Seasons Hotel—sent Christmas presents for the three Dunne Home boys and all the other kids as well.

"Godammit, Sister Vee, I've wanted one of these all my life!" Richard Levitz screamed, unwrapping a Babe Ruth fielder's glove.

As Bridie and the other women returned to the kitchen to wash dishes, Roger and Josie slipped out to Sister Vee's Ford. George Salih drove them to the hospital to see Jonathan. Josie took him a flat fifty—a tin box of half a hundred Lucky Strikes. Fulfilling his brother's Christmas wish, Roger delivered a bottle of President's Choice.

Sandra was leaving Jonathan's room as they came down the shiny, spic-'n'-span hallway at Saint Joseph's

Hospital. She seemed not to see or hear them when they greeted her with hellos and "Merry Christmas."

Jonathan quickly wiped away a tear as they entered his room. Memories of his love for Sandra had splintered against rocky realities of their relationship. As he saw it, she'd left him to go off with Sam without leaving so much as a goodbye note. Neither could Jonathan forget that morning he was going into Doc Cooper's office as Sam was coming out.

And after the diagnosis, Doctor Cooper said pointedly, "You're the second case of clap I've seen today, Jonathan—and the third at that convent where you're living. I know you're young, but haven't you ever heard of condoms?"

"Uh…you mean rubbers, Doctor Cooper?"

"That's right, Jonathan. Quietly ask the pharmacist at the drugstore when nobody else is around. He keeps them under the counter."

Nausea and depression overwhelmed Jonathan as he reluctantly realized that both he and Sam had gotten the disease from Sandra and that she must be the third person Doc Cooper had referred to.

"Sam's gone, Jonathan," she told him. "I'll never see him again. You're all I have…all I want." She took his hand as he looked up at her from bed in the sterile hospital room. They cried together.

Jonathan discovered he was numb to Sandra. His love for her was nostalgic, their relationship moribund despite lingering memories of their passionate times together when he came home from school.

Sandra yearned for this seventeen-year-old high school quarterback. Possessing him resurrected her youth and innocence and cleansed her of the odious life she'd lived over the last few years.

Jonathan still cared enough for Sandra that he didn't tell her she'd given him the clap. He didn't think she knew. He felt she'd suffered enough in her short, tumultuous and tortured life. That's what Jonathan knew, what he'd learned, when Sandra left the hospital that Christmas afternoon.

GOOD NIGHT, LADIES

The dance started at seven o'clock with "*The Lucky Strike Hour,* live from New York, New York," the host announced. "We'll kick off the evening with Duke Ellington's latest hit, 'Mood Indigo,'" Bridie's new radio blared out.

Girls from Mount Carmel Academy and boys from North Side High School had been invited to the New Year's dance at All Saints. Everyone was asked to bring a record to play on Bridie's new Victrola.

Allen Murphy, Dean Edwards, Harry Mosely, handsome Hardy Lockhart and a motley collection of ungainly boys, hands stuffed into their pockets, lined the wall along one side of the auditorium. They talked among themselves as if they were at a pool hall, casting oblique, surreptitious glances across the room.

Christine Hogan, Zelma Cartwright, Jo' Evelyn Waugh and other prime and proper Catholic high school girls smiled at the gaggle of boys from "their side" of the spacious dance floor and basketball court.

"What are they waiting for, a formal invitation?" Jo' Evelyn complained. "Don't they even know they're supposed to ask the girls out on the floor?"

After the first radio commercial ("L/SM/F/T—Lucky Strike Means Fine Tobacco"), Al Jolson crooned all the way from New York "Let Me Sing and I'm Happy."

"They're just shy like boys are," Sandra Scott said, breaking out of the knot of the girls and swaggering across the floor. She went directly to Hardy Lockhart, the six-foot-four senior who rode wild horses and wrestled bulls to the ground at weekend rodeos.

"I'm Sandra," she said, her voice sultry, her blue eyes lighting up. Like a magnet, her vivacious smile lured Hardy away from the other boys. She pointedly did not ask him to dance.

"I'm Hardy. Hardy Lockhart," the biggest boy at North Side High stammered. "Would you...would you...want to dance, Miss...?"

She nodded coyly. "Please call me Sandra," she said as they moved out onto the dance floor. Though Hardy's cowboy boots slipped easily over the hardwood floor, he danced like a cow. Sandra, however, soon put him at ease and had him in step.

"Well now, Sandra, this is easier than I thought."

"You're a marvelous dancer, Hardy, just a natural."

Surprised that Sandra had come to the dance, Bridie was taken aback when she plucked Hardy from the wall and danced across the floor with him. Though Sandra was older than the other girls, she looked young enough to be one of them. And having dismissed her incipient suspicions of an untoward relationship between Sandra and Jonathan, Bridie was happy to see her relaxed and having a good evening with the nice young men from North Side High.

The young men, jealous that Hardy had corralled the sexiest girl they'd ever seen from Mount Carmel Academy, got up their courage. They did a quick triage of the young ladies' assets across the room and chose their favorite targets. Forgoing introductions, the bunglesome boys blurted out one after the other to the girls, "Uh, wanna dance?"

"Well...I guess so," Christine Hogan said. The others nodded, and the couples scooted out onto the floor. The ice broken, the Grover brothers, Tom and Leo, the suave Lance Lanier and a few others mustered up enough of their emerging manhood to ask for a dance. By the third or fourth radio commercial, everyone was mingling and swinging to Paul Whiteman's high-stepping "Happy Feet."

When *The Lucky Strike Hour* show signed off, Bridie opened the walnut-finished cabinet of the radio to reveal its built-in Victrola. Starting with Tommy Dorsey's "The Music Goes Round and Round," she spun one record after another and kept the crowd dancing.

Bridie had won the Majestic Radio ("all-electric, no batteries") in a raffle at the Majestic Theater, operated by Larry and Mairead Smothers, a girl Bridie knew from County Tipperary. "Must be yere lucky shamrock, Bridie," Mairead said, winking.

Harry Mosely and Mimi Rutherford, Hardy and Sandra and other couples sauntered over to the punch bowl. Shirley Roberts stood guard to prevent anyone spiking the red Kool-Aid from hidden flasks.

Bridie spun the smash hit "Walkin' My Baby Back Home" and took to the dance floor herself.

"Oh, Mama, please!" pleaded Josie, her redheaded daughter.

"Why, your mom dances like a pro!" Harry Mosely told Josie.

To loud applause, shouts and whistles, Bridie moved gracefully in tune the music and out onto the floor embracing a broom.

"You don't need that, Mrs. O'Driscoll," Allen Murphy grinned, tossing the broom aside and joining her on the dance floor. "You dance like Joan Crawford," Allen went on.

"More like Anna Held, you mean," she said, smiling as she relived her glorious dancing days of youth on Broadway.

"Anna...who?"

"Never mind, Allen. 'Twas a lifetime ago."

Josie found herself dancing with the coveted Randle McKnight. By female consensus, he was the second-handsomest boy on earth after Jonathan Quinlan. And Randy knew it.

On the sidelines, the younger residents of All Saints gawked and giggled at the awkward antics of pubescent courtship played out by their youthful elders. Ollie Cox ran them out when Richard Levitz and Anna O'Driscoll shouted, "Let's see ya kiss her!" and "Yeah, smack her right on the lips!"

Matthew led the banished ones to the forbidden basement, where they opened bottles of beer for Bonnie and Clyde. Both goats madly sucked the suds from brown bottles that almost disappeared down their throats.

"Don't let 'em swallow the bottles," Brandon Reynolds warned.

"Fifteen...sixteen...seventeen seconds to Bonnie's nineteen," Matthew counted, declaring Clyde the fastest beer drinker at All Saints.

"Clyde's the fastest," Jeremy Bryant said, "so let's see who can drink the mostest." More beer poured into two mop buckets, one for each contestant, both of whom had to be restrained until the containers were full.

"Let 'em at it," Anna said when the buckets brimmed over with frothy home brew. Cory Cox and Frank Feldman released the goats.

"I'm bettin' on Clyde," Gabi Ellington said.

"Bonnie's got a bigger belly," Juliana Bryant noted astutely.

"Hurry up and open some more before they run out," Buster Roberts said, handing out brown bottles of beer from the shelves.

Lynn Brant and Elizabeth Wellington ran the kitchen, making ham sandwiches and mixing punch.

Edwin provided the ham after selling a truckload of President's Choice out of his New York Avenue drugstore. He and Wally Cox sat out the evening on the back porch. They shared a bottle, puffed on Romeo y Julieta cigars and swapped war stories about their days in France and Belgium.

Martin had taken refuge in the laundry house, reading the *Book of Gospels* Sister Vee had given him. Doc Cooper, self-medicated in unmeasured doses of President's Choice, snored in a stupor beyond the reach of teenagers and big band music. Q.C. limited his nocturnal pursuit of mice to the upper floors. Locked in sexual bliss in his room, Quin and Julie heard nothing beyond themselves. George O'Driscoll had shut his door and his mind to the music and the tramping of feet on the stairs to the bathroom, only a few feet from his room.

So no one heard Jo Evelyn Waugh's delirious screams when—moments after taking a seat in the second-floor bathroom—she spied the skeleton of one of Q.C.'s ghost mice, its tiny eyes fixed on her.

Just as Bridie put another record on the new Victrola, Clyde staggered across the stage looking for another bucket of beer. Swiftly mounting the steps, broom in hand, Bridie chased the woozy goat across the stage. To escape the broom whacking his hairy hindquarters, Clyde stumbled down the steps. He bolted drunkenly across the dance floor to Duke Ellington's bouncy "It Don't Mean a Thing (If It Ain't Got That Swing)."

Hardy Lockhart, the bull wrestler, tackled the horned intruder. Wrestled to the floor, the drunken goat found himself lifted by his front legs, his hooves in Hardy's hands, as boy and beast two-stepped to laughter and applause. Taking the lead, Hardy swayed wildly to the music and the influence of the beer Matthew Quinlan had pilfered from the basement and sold to the older boys. Clyde nibbled at his partner's cotton shirt. Bridie, unaware both dancers were under the influence, laughed until she collapsed in a chair.

When Hardy and Clyde fell down, Lance Lanier and Tom Grover gripped the goat's horns and steered him into the hall. Clyde broke away and bolted for the kitchen, seeking the stairway to the basement and another bucket of beer.

Inspired by Clyde and Hardy's performance, the dancers choreographed their own goat-trot tango.

"May I nibble on your collar?" Harry Mosely asked Margaret Weaver.

"Just don't hit me in the eye with one of your horns," she giggled.

"Don't step on my new yellow hooves," quipped Leo Grover as he and Rose Marie Ralston slipped out onto the floor.

"You smell like a brewery and dance like a goat, you oaf," she said, when he stepped on her foot.

At eleven o'clock, Bridie played the evening's swan song, "Good Night, Ladies." "And good night, lads," she sang. "'Tis the Cinderella hour, and time to call it a night."

Shirley Roberts discovered them in the science lab—boisterous boys bunched around the pool table, laughing, stumbling and guzzling beer. Bridie confiscated the beer.

"Don't worry about these fellows getting home," Dean Edgar said, his breath fuming with alcohol. "I'll take 'em in my car." The son of a prominent attorney, he was the rare high schooler who had his own wheels.

"Indeed, you won't be driving anyone anywhere tonight," Bridie told him, demanding his car keys.

"I'm taking you boys home," Wally informed them.

"Oh no, Mr. Cox," Dean said. "Daddy'll kill me when he finds out I left the car somewhere."

"Ain't that a shame," Wally said, herding the boys out the back door to his truck. "What happened to these goats?"

Bonnie and Clyde lay sprawled out on the porch. Clyde's head hung limply over the side.

"Are they dead?" Bridie asked. She shook Bonnie with her foot until the goat belched a staggering aroma of beer. "They've even corrupted God's innocent creatures tonight."

After the nonresident teens left and the others had gone upstairs for the night, Bridie sat down at the table and sipped a cup of hot tea in the silence that enveloped her kitchen. She was happy that so many kids had come to the dance and pleased that they seemed to enjoy the evening. She wondered why Sandra had left just before it ended. And now heavy footsteps on the fire escape prompted her to wonder where Hardy Lockhart was at the moment.

> Forest Service, Camp A-4
> Juneau, Alaska Territory

Dear Bridie,

I hope you are all well and received letter sent to you on the 20th. Enclosed find cheque for $30 and do the best you can until I see what can be done. I am not making very much as there is very little work.

We are on the edge of a big lake, and a ski plane just landed on the ice with a load of grub. We have a stove in the tent and lots of wood. I got a letter from Mary Josephine and hope to send her some money next month for the boys at the orphanage.

I am all the time trying to find something and never can tell the minute when I may find a fortune. This is practically an unexplored country. You can never tell in Alaska when you're going to stumble onto something. If I can ever make anything we will all go back to Ireland and buy a little place in Clonmel and have a small car to run about in.

I have not seen a paper in months, so don't know how things are down in the States. Must mail this before the plane leaves. Bye.

> Your loving brother,
> Tommy
> Erin Go Bragh

MONA LISA

Jonathan lay stripped to his undershorts as Julie Bryant dipped a sponge in a pan of warm, soapy water. "Time for your bath, young man," she told her patient.

After the latest surgery, Dr. Johnson let him recuperate at home because Doc Cooper and a nurse in training were there to care for him, to guard against gangrene and to administer morphine for pain. Quin was relieved his son was out of the five-dollar-a-day private room.

Julie was washing Jonathan's back when someone knocked. "Come in," she called.

The door opened to a girl with wavy, jet-black hair, sharply sculptured facial features, cherry-red lips and snow-white teeth. She was stunningly beautiful. Her tight white nurse's dress accented curvaceous hips, an abundant bosom rising above a flat tummy and a twenty-inch waist.

"Mo-na, Mona Li-sa," Jonathan said. The name tag over the sloping fullness of Mona Lisa's breast pocket identified her as Mona Lissard, Registered Nurse, Saint Joseph's Hospital.

"My God, Mona, you came."

"Told you, Jon-boy, you couldn't escape Mona," she said, her voluptuous body exuding the carnal virtues of nubile womanhood.

"I'm Julie Bryant. I work at Saint Joseph's. I was about to give Jonathan his daily bath and change his bandages."

"Sure, I've seen you at the hospital, Julie. I'm Mona Lissard from P.T. at Saint Joe's, and I'm here to take care of my patient's therapeutic needs," the registered nurse informed the nurse trainee. "I'll bathe him and bandage his wound, too."

Dismissed by a girl ten years her junior, Julie heard the lock click when she closed the door to "Jon-boy's" room.

"Who's that foxy nurse up there with Jonathan?" Quin asked her. "Is she really his physical therapist?"

"Thermal therapist, I'd say," Julie said.

"She's awfully young," he said, assuming thermal therapy was a new rehabilitation procedure.

"Jon-boy's in good hands, I'm afraid."

"Something I ought to know?"

"No, Quin, nothing your son hasn't handled before."

Sandra Scott had watched the shapely young nurse with sullen interest when Mona Lissard introduced herself and asked Bridie for directions to Jonathan Quinlan's room. A surge of jealous disgust swept over her as Mona sashayed down the hall with the self-assurance of a twenty-three-old who'd never met defeat.

Sandra had had the blues since Stella Griffith had left Zelda with Bridie early that morning. "I'll be cleaning rooms at the Blackstone until midafternoon," Stella said, turning to Sandra, slouched in a chair, smoking and drinking a cup of coffee. "If you're interested in work, Sandra, the hotel's looking for help."

"Cleaning rooms and toilets?" Sandra said. "Like a hotel maid?"

"Seventy-five cents a day," Stella Griffith replied stiffly.

"It's money," Bridie put in.

"Not my kinda money. I can do better than that at ten cents a dance at the clubs."

Stella kissed Zelda and went to the door. Turning, tears in her eyes, she said, "It is hard work, Sandra, but at least I'm not working on my back." The door slammed as she crossed the porch and went down the steps.

When Mona Lisa disappeared up the stairs, Sandra shuffled off to her own room and threw herself onto her bed. "Cleaning hotel rooms! What the hell do they think I am?" Her impulsive question summoned spontaneous truth. "No, no, goddamit. I'm not just a whore!"

With no income, Sandra regularly helped herself to the cache of booze in the basement and pilfered smokes from unattended packs of cigarettes. Martin left half-empty packs around the convent for her. He also moved his stash of cash to a dark corner of the basement.

Whenever Bridie boiled cabbage and potatoes, Sandra drifted down to the basement kitchen to see if Ollie Cox and Elizabeth Wellington were cooking something more tasteful. Ollie had put her to work churning, until cigarette ashes turned up in the butter.

"Sandra's like a house cat slinking around, begging food, swiping cigarettes and whiskey," Lynn said. "Even Q.C. earns his keep murdering mice."

Bridie feared Sandra would return to her old life—"entertaining" at the clubs along the Jacksboro Highway. She wondered what had happened to her and Sam in St. Louis.

Bridie was in bed when she heard footsteps on the fire escape. Not a clumsy goat, not the rapid, noisy steps of children and surely not Julie, who'd recently taken to the stairs on her frequent visits to Quin's room. She listened: two pair of feet on the iron steps: heavy, light, heavy, light, heavy (man), light (woman), heavy (man), light (woman).

Bridie got up and opened her window. The fire escape was silent, though she clearly heard a window slam shut. She chided herself for suspecting Sandy of "doing business again" at All Saints.

ROOSEVELT'S CHOICE

"Thank God and Franklin Roosevelt," Bridie said when Prohibition ended and Edwin shut down the still at All Saints. She shuddered, however, when he invited George to join him in a bigger bootlegging business.

"Listen to this," Edwin said, reading the *Star-Telegram*: "'The city collected $16,000 in permit fees from 259 stores that began selling beer today. Bars have hired hundreds to serve customers.'"

If churches gave thanks for a partial victory, bootleggers rejoiced when Texas allowed the sale of beer, but no liquor, after the Twenty-First Amendment to the U.S. Constitution ended Prohibition.

"These beer bars are a perfect cover for serving bootleg liquor to more people than ever—without worrying about dry agents raiding 'em," Edwin said. "I might even pay that poll tax and start voting just to keep this governor and his mob in office."

He laid out a plan using George's trucks as a cover along his expanding auto parts routes. "I'll buy the next truck. We'll already have a lock on the business even if they start selling legal liquor someday." George laughed. "I didn't mind serving the public interest during Prohibition, Edwin. But I've got a good business going now, and damned if I'll go to jail running moonshine."

Martin, however, refused once again to leave the campus—still fearful of an encounter with Jesus H. Cortez's seven-inch switchblade—to run a new high-capacity still in the basement of Edwin's second Southside drugstore.

"I'll take care of Jesus for you," Edwin assured him. Martin reclutantly agreed to set up the still and tutor a new moonshiner in the art of distilling President's Choice, renamed Roosevelt's Choice in honor of the new president.

"Ever think about opening a distillery, paying the taxes and selling that stuff in states where liquor's legal?" Quin asked.

"Pay liquor taxes and income taxes on the profit?" Edwin frowned. "It's not right."

"Ain't that what Al Capone said before he went to Alcatraz for income tax evasion?" Wally recalled.

Doc Cooper treated ailing customers at their growing chain of drugstores financed by their burgeoning bootlegging business. He hired young druggists in white smocks to fill prescriptions and to sell the usual over-the-counter cures for common ailments.

If the end of Prohibition provided a sigh of relief, the Great Depression lingered on like an incurable national hangover. Presidential remedies and other inspiring solutions were no more miraculous than the cure-all nostrums sold in Edwin's drugstores.

But "the wonderful Great Depression," as George called it, still had its silver lining. The longer it lasted, the more car parts he sold to keep old clunkers clunking down the road. In his latest coup, he had negotiated a franchise from Gates Rubber Company. Buying direct from Gates boosted his profits on fan belts and radiator hoses by fifty percent, sparked Felix Rubinstein's infamous temper ("you god'am Irish spud-suckin' son 'a bitch!") and triggered another fistfight with the two brothers at Allied Auto Parts.

Bridie was relieved George's new enterprise was both legal and lucrative, "if only ye'd spare a few dollars now and then for food and clothes for the girls."

"I've got to get another truck on the road," he told her. "You might start collecting rent from these freeloading rogues hanging out here."

Bonanza Mine
Kennecott, Alaska Territory

Dear Bridie,

I am all right now after being out of work eight months. You surely must be having a hard time getting along. I have this job and I hope to God to do better in the future. Enclosed is a cheque for $166.88.

I have not been outside as we are right near the top of a mountain in a basin filled with snow. I step right out of the house into the mine. We have good food and steam heat and electric light.

I have not been feeling very good. I suffer from shortness of breath. When I walk in the tunnel about a thousand feet, my throat seems as if there was a red hot pepper in there. And I gasp for air and have to stop a couple of times. Next in the pit of the stomach there is a terrible pain with a feeling of exhaustion and weakness. My legs and knees begin to wobble and all the energy oozes out.

Every man that works in a mine for any length of time, his lungs are not in very good shape and mostly all died the same way. I have seen too many of them in my time to have any illusions about myself.

I was anxious to make all I could from 1920 to 1930 to save enough so that we would have something that would save us when times go bad. But there was something wrong all the time. George would not support you and our bonds are spent and we have nothing left. Thank God we still have one another.

Your loving brother,
Tommy
Erin Go Bragh

THE CURSE

Despite his disdain for the church, George found himself drawn to Mass several times a year at Saint Patrick's. And that's where he picked up Marion Summerfield.

A clerk for the Rubinstein brothers at Allied Auto Parts, Marion always pushed aside her other work to type George's weekly report when he returned from his sales route in central Texas. He'd wondered why someone hadn't already slipped a wedding ring on her finger.

"Didn't know you were Catholic," George said when they bumped into each other after Mass.

"Neither do the Rubinsteins. How about a ride home, George?"

With light brown hair and an engaging smile, Marion stepped nimbly into George's LaSalle. "Say now, this is some nice automobile." He admired her svelte, five-foot five-inch figure as he closed the car door. "Can we just ride around a little while?" she said as he started the engine. "Anywhere but home."

Marion told George she shared a two-bedroom house with her widowed mother, two married sisters, their quarrelsome unemployed husbands, and four squalling, squabbling children, including a six-month-old baby.

"You'd think they'd quit making babies bein' they can't afford the little demons they've got," she said, lighting a Lucky. "Say now, this is a doozy of a lighter." She inserted the chrome lighter back into the outlet. "Now, George, a car like this must have a Motorola?"

"No, those radios just distract drivers and they run over people or end up in the ditch, so I didn't get one. There's a heater under the dash."

"A heater? Say now, what'll they think of next?"

The LaSalle's whitewall tires thumped over the redbrick streets. George drove to Quality Hill and parked on Penn Street. It was a crisp, sunny morning. They admired the Victorian mansions overlooking the green valley—a picturesque view soiled by the river people's trashy camps along the banks of the Trinity.

"You gonna live in one of these fancy places some-day, George?"

"No, I'll have an address in Ryan Place," he said, a little too seriously, she thought.

Marion Summerfield smoked, told jokes and laughed a lot. George put her at about twenty-nine or thirty years old. If she was plain, youth itself teased a middle-aged man whose years registered in wrinkles, greater girth and the occasional gray hair.

George took her to FDR's Bar & Grill, a trendy post-Prohibition watering hole. "Strange just walking in, no goon guarding the door, no worrying about dry agents raiding the place," Marion said.

"Takes some of the fun out of it," George said as the jukebox crooned "Happy Days Are Here Again," the hit song adopted by FDR's presidential campaign. "A cold beer for the lady," he told the waiter. "And something a little stouter for me, if you have it."

"Two bits a shot, sir."

George recognized the singular taste of Roosevelt's Choice. *Edwin Brant always at work in the woodwork,* he chuckled to himself. He left a generous four bits on the table when they left to find a café.

"Say, George, that was some fine steak," Marion said, coming out of the fashionable Big Apple. "I've heard o' that place for years but never set foot in it."

George had had enough whiskey to invite her to his apartment for a nightcap. Marion was in no hurry to go home. She'd been wary going up the fire escape the first time. George told her he didn't want to chance bumping into the landlady in the hallway.

Several weeks later, as they came down, she said, "Say now, George, I'm getting the hang of these steps."

Then a woman called out, "That you, Sandy? Oh, God forbid...not ye, George."

George dropped Marion off at a small frame house on the south side and drove to Saint Patrick's. Statues of saints hid in the darkness, the familiar scent of incense and candle wax lingering in the cavernous church. A flame flickering in a red vase indicated the presence of the Host—the Body and Blood of Christ—in the tabernacle high up on the ornate marble altar.

George blessed himself and knelt at the altar railing, pondering his plight. Their plight. Their curse. The unwavering, unbending, unrelenting will of God—so said the priests.

Bridie had accepted her fate—their fate—as a cross to bear "in sickness and in health," she'd vowed. And what was expected of George O'Driscoll, a healthy man still in his early forties and a full decade younger than his lawfully wedded wife?

"Take up your cross with joy and thank God for your blessings," came the answer from priests—men never knowing the passion of the flesh between man and woman.

George had not touched Bridie or any other woman for more than a decade—not since 1921, the year

Anna was born. Bridie suffered "female complications that prevent conception," as the doctor at Saint Joseph's put it. Then Father James, the hospital chaplain, came in, closed the door and destroyed their marriage.

"I never meant to hurt her," George whispered at the altar. He implored the God of his youth for forgiveness, not for his sins but for breaking his marriage vow to Bridie.

Father Nolan suddenly appeared on the dark altar just before six o'clock Mass. George liked the white-headed old man, his humor and wit, as much as he despised him as a priest. In deference to his arthritis, Father Nolan only half genuflected to the Host and went down the far aisle to the confessional.

For a moment, George longed for the church of his youth—the church that comforted him before he fled the cobbled streets of Clonmel where Irish and English blood commingled in the gutters and flowed down the River Suir, and widows and children wailed in the funeral processions out to Saint Patrick's Cemetery.

Empty and numb, George felt nothing, however, for the church that had driven a forbidding wedge between him and Bridie and a stake through their hearts. He blessed himself and got up from his knees. Father Nolan listened in anticipation as footsteps neared the confessional and went out the double doors to the street.

"I'm so sorry, Bridie," George called at her door.

She turned to the gold shamrock on the shelf. The fairy's curse echoed across the years from the Tipperary County Fair. Nothing relieved the spiritual pain that wrenched her soul.

George packed his suitcase and hurried down the fire escape to avoid her in the hallways or the kitchen. As he passed her window, Bridie stood behind the pane, rosary beads dripping from her fingers like droplets of blood, her face washed in tears.

Startled, they looked into each other's eyes—across time, across the Atlantic to Clonmel, crossing Old Bridge together to the foot of Slievenamon Mountain, bicycling out to the fairy well where he had kissed her the first time, coming out of Saint Peter and Paul's on their wedding day in *cluain meala*, the meadows of honey. George bowed his head and went across the grounds to his big red truck.

TEN CENTS

"She's too old for you!" Quin shouted. He'd seen Mona leaving Jonathan's room again, buttoning her uniform as she rushed off to work at the hospital. "I know she's practically living here night and day."

"Jealous, old man?" Jonathan sniggered, crutch under his left arm, cigarette dangling from his mouth.

"I'll take my belt to your butt, little boy." Quin loosened his buckle.

"You wouldn't be talking to me like this if I had two legs."

"Well, you don't, dammit. And I'll call the police if I catch that slut up here rocking in your cradle again."

Jonathan's fist missed his father's chin by a hair and sent the boy in a spin. His crutch flew across the room as the tall, muscular athlete hit the floor with a thud. "Damn you," he cried, tears in his eyes.

Quin went to the door. "If I see her up here again, I'll call the cops, and I'll get her fired at the hospital. Hear?"

"And you, my holy father, breaking the Ninth Commandment, 'Thou shalt not covet another man's wife,' her children asleep under the same roof. And then taking Holy Communion on Sunday like you're some kinda saint."

Quin slammed the door and stomped down the hall. He had been driving Sunday mornings to Saint Mary's Church across town to confess his sins to Father Gillan and then taking Communion at Saint Patrick's.

The young priest didn't recognize his voice, as Father Nolan surely would have. And Father Gillan never threatened him with "the eternal fires of hell," which was Father Nolan's standing condemnation of sinners of the flesh. Indeed, Father Gillan laid on a paltry penance—three Our Fathers and three Hail Marys.

If others were aware of Jonathan's affair with Mona Lisa, Matthew Quinlan cashed in on it. "Yeah," he told Roger. "There's a hole in the closet wall next to Jonathan's room. You can see everything they're doing. It's what they call screwing. Ten cents and I'll let you take a peek."

Although Roger had acquired a rising passion for the women in bras and panties in the Ward's catalog, he refused "because what you're doing is a mortal sin. And you're going to hell, Matthew."

"No, Roger, Jonathan and that nurse are doing the mortal sin, and it's better than watching the dogs or Mr. Markum's cows do it."

If Roger feared dying in sin, other neighborhood boys considered robbing banks to acquire ten cents "to see the real thing." With repeat customers waiting, Matthew saved their dimes to buy a camera and sell pictures of the real thing at a nickel each.

DADDY'S HOME

Bridie feared Quin would fall and kill himself when he stumbled out his third-floor window to tinkle off the fire escape in the dark. He drank and smoked all night, slept most of the day and ate canned Spam in his room. When his bookkeeping clients phoned, Bridie told them he was down with a new strain of the old Spanish flu.

"If telling a little white lie troubles you, Bridie, ask God to charge it to my account," Quin said, his speech slurred. "The Man's been giving me hell for the longest time now, anyway."

Hunched over the banquet table in her kitchen, Quin fished a rumpled five-dollar bill from his silk bathrobe and shoved it toward her.

"Would you mind, dear Bridie, feeding my boys for a while?" Unshaven, eyes bloodshot, he staggered back down the hall in his bare feet.

"I'll look after them, Quin," she called, going to the door. "But they need their father. And don't forget Jonathan's back in the hospital for his last surgery."

"And sharing his hospital bed with that slutty nurse of his."

Bridie called Father Nolan. "He'll drink himself to death." Quin locked his door when the priest knocked.

Doc Cooper fared no better. "You owe me a drink, dammit. Open up."

"Go away, you old sot, or I'll call the cops."

Doc Cooper shook his head. "He'll have to ride this out, Bridie. This is living death. I've seen it before. Takes a man's soul and leaves him all hollowed out inside. Some make it. Some don't."

Why is it, she wondered, so often one person's joy becomes another's grief? Though it might have been foreseen, it hadn't been.

Jeremy had raced up the stairs last week, shouting, "Juliana, Juliana, our daddy's home! He's here, Juliana!"

Jeremy's sister came bounding down the steps two at a time. At the foot of the stairs stood a father who'd been missing a third of her life. Both held back. Les Bryant dropped to his knees and hugged the skinny, blue-eyed shrimp of a little girl in his strong, sinewy arms.

"Juliana," he sobbed. Taking her bony shoulders in his callused hands, he pushed her back to admire his daughter from head to toe. "You've grown so. You're beautiful, like your mother."

"She's at work," Juliana reported stiffly, uncertain of this stranger—tall and slim, thin nose, gentle mouth, warm brown eyes, sharp jib, black hair, handsome, suntanned face.

"I thought I'd never find you guys again." He reminded her of a soldier in his starched, tightly fitting denim shirt, khaki trousers, narrow brown belt, high-topped work boots laced almost to his knees.

"This place is as big as a palace," Les said, touring the convent.

"See, Daddy? There's lotta room for you," Juliana said when he looked into the meagerly furnished room where his wife and children lived.

"So what's the rent here, Bridie?"

"There's no rent at All Saints, Les. Space is the one thing we have in abundance." She almost invited him to move in before realizing it was for his wife to invite him, or not to invite him, to live here.

Over a cup of tea, Les—Juliana sitting on his lap, Jeremy leaning on him, one arm around his neck—told Bridie his train was leaving at noon.

"Ah, too bad, for noon's when Julie gets off at Saint Joseph's."

"I can't wait to see her again."

Les Bryant said he worked on a Texas and Pacific railroad section gang. "We replace broken rails and lay new track west all the way to the Mexican border. We live in a bunk car on rails, Bridie, so I've been saving my money. I make thirty-four cents an hour. Enough to take care of this little gang so long as they don't eat steak twice a day."

Bridie laughed with the likable, well-spoken young man and prayed he'd leave "before something dreadful happens."

Quin came through the back door, jovially announcing, "Hey, Bridie, picked up another bookkeeping job at the stockyards today," adding, "Oh, I'm Quin Quinlan" when he saw the stranger.

"This is my dad, Mr. Quinlan!" Jeremy shouted.

"Mr. Quinlan's Mama's best friend, Daddy," Juliana said. Bridie braced herself as if a stick of dynamite had been lobbed into her kitchen.

"Pleased to meet you, sir." Les Bryant nodded, standing to shake hands with the graying, broad-shouldered man in the expensive business suit. "I've gotta run and catch a train, but I'll be back." He failed to see that Quin looked like a man just sentenced to death by mistake.

347

"Tell your mom I love her," Les said, kissing his children. "See you in two weeks. Thanks, Bridie, for showing me around. Tell Julie I love her."

The back screen door slammed behind him with a bang that sent shivers through Bridie's heart and sent Quin slogging heavily up the stairs.

Bridie found him sitting in the windowsill, smoking a cigar and sipping a glass of whiskey. She knew he was watching for Julie to come from the streetcar line. Q.C., curled up under the bend of Quin's knees, cast his bulbous yellow eye on the sandwich and glass of milk in Bridie's hand.

"I see ye're in good company," she said.

"The devil's mascot," he said dully, rubbing Q.C.'s head.

She set the saucer and glass next to Sinclair Lewis' *Ann Vickers* on the table beside Quin's armchair. "Brought ye a sandwich and a glass o' cold milk, Quin."

He turned to Bridie vacantly and spoke quietly in a monotone. "I never meant to become involved again—certainly never to love again. Julie cheered me up, and I liked not being lonely anymore. She gave me permission to love her and Marion both. And I do. But Julie can't love both of us—me and that clean-cut young man, the father of her children."

He snuffed out the Montecristo in a coffee cup. Q.C. twitched and leapt to the floor as blue cigar smoke curled around his twisted snout.

"Jeremy and Juliana have gone to meet her at the streetcar," said Bridie.

"She…we…thought he was dead. It was easier that way. I can't let her break those kids' little hearts leaving their father. I'm going to free Julie."

"It'll break her heart whatever happens, Quin," Bridie told him, recalling Julie's question, "Is it hard to become a Catholic, Bridie? I mean if Quin gets carried away and asks for my hand."

He nodded. "I'll make it as easy as I can for her."

Bridie realized Quin had lost too much to believe Julie would leave him on her own to reunite with her husband.

"And what about yourself, Quin?"

He crossed the room and took the sandwich she'd brought him. "Thanks, Bridie," he said, returning to the window.

Q.C, sitting in the armchair, stepped over to the table and lapped milk from the glass.

ST. LOUIE

The pale predawn light etched out the figure of a woman in a long coat, a suitcase in one hand, high-heel shoes dangling from the other. Martin smiled, amused to see Mona Lisa tiptoeing quietly down the fire escape from Jonathan's room again.

The shadowy figure bent down, slipped on her shoes and stepped onto the wet grass. Startled when Wally Cox's rooster crowed in the new day, she looked up. To Martin's surprise, it was Sandra Scott.

"Leaving?" he asked, intercepting her at the front gate.

"Sam's outta jail, Martin. I gotta help him."

"Your business, not mine, but some people ain't worth helpin'."

"I got a letter from him. He just guessed I was here. He's sick, Martin."

"I see," he said, handing her a half-pack of cigarettes. "Take these."

"Thanks, Martin. Sam sent a little money, just enough for the bus fare. Tell Bridie I said bye and that I love her for all she's done for me."

"What? You ain't sayin' goodbye to Miss Bridie?" Sandra looked away and went out the gate. "Good riddance," Martin said.

Sandra Scott ran long Belle Avenue as a sudden gush of tears streamed down her face—tears for Bridie, the only mom she ever knew, and tears for Jonathan Quinlan, the only boy she'd ever loved. .

When Martin delivered the morning's milk and eggs to the kitchen, Bridie had finished her tea and returned to her room to get ready for Sunday Mass.

By noon, the churchgoers were home again. Wally had dismantled his truck motor to grind the valves. Bridie and Ollie boiled a chicken, their benefactor an aged hen that no longer laid eggs. They added water, a pinch of salt, a dash of pepper and an abundance of dumplings.

"The broth'll give the dumplings a real chicken flavor," Ollie said. "I'll cook up some vegetables." Her garden produced an abundance of vegetables since Wally had replaced the soil with dirt from their old farm.

By three o'clock, the Brants were up and about. Wally came in greased to his elbows. He washed his hands at the sink, dried them on his pants and sat down at the long table. After Quin gave thanks, Bridie ladled up dinner for the younger kids.

"What's worse on Sunday, church or chicken an' dumplings?" Matthew said.

"So, where's the chicken?" Richard asked, idly searching his bowl for a beetle.

"Be thankful for what ye have," Bridie said, "and remember all the hungry people in China."

"They must've gotten the chicken," Anna said.

"Oh, it's not so bad," Roger said, sitting on his Ward's catalog.

Josie served Jonathan a bowl of dumplings, including a coveted chicken leg, when he hopped into the kitchen, ignoring his father at the table. He called Josie his "redheaded woman" whenever she slipped him cigarettes and snacks.

"I'll save Sandy a bowl," Bridie said. "She loves dumplings."

"No need," Martin informed her, this being one of his rare visits to the kitchen table. "She up an' left at daylight with her suitcase. Didn't say bye or boo to nobody."

"Thank the Lord," Wally said.

"So my liquor cabinet is safe now," Edwin said. "A little safer anyway," he added. "Right, Matthew?" The boy pretended not to hear his accuser.

Bridie paled. "No, Sandy wouldn't leave like that, Martin. Not without a word to me."

Despite his misgivings, Quin drove to the Greyhound station at Bridie's behest. She remembered that a letter had come for Sandra a few days ago, the only mail the girl had ever received there. Though there was no return address, it was postmarked St. Louis, Missouri.

As Jonathan polished off his second bowl of dumplings, Josie asked him to help wash the dishes. "Sorry, Red, got a little pain in my leg, the one that's missing." He chuckled and hopped off on his crutch.

"*She* must be coming again," Josie said.

"Forget that boy, Josie," Lynn smirked. "There are more fish in the sea. And God help that little fish if Jonathan's father catches Mona Lisa in his room again. I'll give you a hand with these dishes."

At the bus station, Quin described Sandra to the ticket agent: pretty, slender, blue-eyed blonde, bright red coat, gold buttons. "Tell ya what, mister, I almost got on the bus with that babe. Too good-lookin' to be travelin' alone all the way to St. Louie."

Bridie, sitting on the back porch with Mulligan, saw no good news in Quin's face when he returned and got out of his car. She nodded and went to her room for a nap.

Bridie noticed the empty shelf when she awoke. She looked round the room, knowing she'd find it, on the nightstand, on one of the other bookshelves. "Must be somewhere here," she persisted, rummaging through dresser drawers, looking under her bed, under the pillows and pulling back the bedcovers.

"Looks like you've seen a ghost, Bridie," Edwin said as she came up the stairs, the evening sun slanting through the window on the second-floor landing.

"'Tis gone, Edwin. My gold shamrock's nowhere to be found."

"Sandra Scott," he blurted harshly.

"'Twas my last shamrock."

WITH LOVE AND
SHAMROCKS

My Dearest Delia,
    Forgive me, for I've lost our gold shamrock.

I t had taken Bridie most of the night to finish the
letter, as memories surfaced like an old movie:

Remembering how she and Delia Walsh had won
the coveted gold shamrock dancing at the County
Tipperary Fair of 1899, grandest of Ireland's ancient
fairs since the days of Tara and the Kings of Ireland—
before Saint Patrick and Saint Brigid, before the
Vikings and the Norsemen, before the English and
the Battle of the Boyne.

The shamrock had taken her to New York, to Broadway, home again to Ireland and to George and the lovely family they had had in Clonmel, before burying two of their little girls together in a single grave, unmarked for want of money for a headstone.

Then the war...another one...and the English coming after George, he and other lucky rebels fleeing to America, escaping the noose on Gallows Hill. Leaving her two daughters in the Irish sod had been the hardest burden of her life as she boarded the train for Queenstown and the ship to America to join George.

Leaving the homeland was the plight of all emigrants. She left forever the life she had known—family, friends, their accents and language, their bungalow at 9 Queen Street, the memories of childhood, the shops along the cobbled streets of Clonmel, the church where she was baptized and married, where the priest had baptized her daughters.

The gold shamrock had been her last link with Ireland. And though she would always long for the old country, its loss was an epiphany, a realization that America was her homeland and that she was never to see Ireland again.

People born here didn't know they lived in grand style even in these hard times compared with the desperate and wanting life she had known under foreign rule in Ireland.

And as refugees from this Great Depression, Bridie thanked God she and her guests had been blessed to find their way to All Saints. She was thankful they had food, shelter and one another. Together they managed to get through day by day. She prayed the shamrock would bring Sandra Scott a better life than the poor girl had lived thus far.

It had been a month since Bridie had addressed the envelope to Delia Walsh Butler, 31 William Street, Clonmel, County Tipperary, Ireland. In the meantime, her pride in another gold piece had helped relieve her grief. Josie had won a gold medallion for best essay in the annual Scripps Howard Writing Contest sponsored by the *Fort Worth Press*. When the *Press* editor presented it, he said he needed a good writer like her.

"I'll be at your door the day I get my journalism degree," Josie said, though the *New York Times* remained her goal.

The gold medal rested on the shelf in Bridie's bedroom where her shamrock had been, when Delia Walsh's letter arrived from Ireland. Crisp and brownish after the long voyage across the Atlantic, tiny gold shamrocks spilled from the envelope onto Bridie's lap. Delia wrote:

Clonmel, County Tipperary

Dear Bridie,

Let's not be worried over the whereabouts of our gold shamrock. Wherever it is, it'll be bringing God's blessings and Irish luck to someone who needs it, perhaps more than we do. And as you've always said yourself, we'll manage.

And manage we shall, my dear. For even though it's a time of porridge and potatoes (and butter for neither), Ireland is blessed with peace after these 800 years of war with the English, and famine in the land, and finally bloody strife amongst ourselves. Here in cluain meala, our own meadows of honey, we've christened Gallows Hill with a new name—Shamrock Hill, where I collected the shamrocks I'm putting in this envelope. God bless you with love and shamrocks, Delia

JULIE'S MEN

Les Bryant told Julie he'd written from Pittsburgh and Chicago, from Seattle and San Diego, from nondescript little towns and from boxcars rattling along the rails.

"I couldn't mail them, not without sending money. I just couldn't. And I kept thinking, next town I'll find work, send you a few dollars, settle down long enough for you and the kids to come to me. I missed you so much." He kissed her fingers as they sat on the front porch of a boarding house on East Daggett Street.

"No place for us to go here, Julie. Two guys in my room. I swear there was never another woman the whole time I been gone."

She averted her eyes, avoiding his loving gaze. Alluding to her work schedule, Julie had made excuses for meeting him here, instead of in her room at All Saints. En route to the streetcar, she'd noticed her bare finger and returned to get her wedding ring.

"I worked several months on the docks in San Francisco and thought, *Well now, this is it.* I sent the letter and fifty-five dollars, and it came back stamped 'Undeliverable. Addressee Not Here.' God, you don't know how that scared me. Took me over two weeks to get here.

"I went straight to our old neighborhood. People we knew on our street are all gone. A lot of empty houses. No one knew anything about you. I lucked out and landed a job right away. Trouble is, we work out of town for weeks at a time.

"Last time we were back in town again, I gave a guy two bits to drive me out to your cousin Wally's farm. A neighbor said they'd moved to town when the bank took their place. He'd heard they were livin' in Rosen Heights. I found the Rosen Heights Land Company.

"The woman there, a Miss Maggie, didn't have any Coxes in her accounting books. I was going out the door when she said there was an abandoned convent full of itinerant crazies up on Belle Avenue—bootleggers, orphans, homeless women, a whore and her pimp, a farmer with some cows. I knew Wally had cows. She said I ought to be careful if I went up there."

He laughed, fondling her hand all the time.

"God, Julie, you're beautiful in your uniform. Anyway, I walked up there—2115 Belle Avenue, she'd said. And this woman Bridie comes to the door and invites me in for a cup of tea. Kids all over the place. A goat trying to get in the back door. A fat ol' yellow dog asleep under the kitchen table.

"Bridie said you're at the hospital. A nurse, I can't believe. Juliana and Jeremy and Wally and Ollie and their kids are there. It was so unreal."

His train was leaving at six o'clock.

"We're laying new track on the Texas and Pacific's main line west of Cisco. I just passed an exam for assistant signalman. I'll be makin' fifty-four cents an hour. We can live on that, you know. And if you keep nursing at that hospital, someday we'll have an Oldsmobile and a brick house."

"He'll be back in five days, Bridie. He can't live here. It'd kill Quin. And me, too."

"God, the things that happen to people," Bridie said.

"If only he was a monster or something. Les is a wonderful guy. That's why I married him. And Jeremy and Juliana love their daddy."

"And he doesn't know anything about…"

"Oh no. Les has no idea about Quin. What am I going to do? Tell me, Bridie."

"You truly want someone else's opinion?"

"No, not someone's, Bridie—yours."

Bridie studied the tea leaves in her cup. "I sit in judgment on no one, Julie. For myself, 'tis a matter of faith. We have to believe in something beyond ourselves, something greater, even if it's not perfect, whether there's a cross to bear or a blessing to be gained. And so often one comes at the expense of the other. I've told no one this—no one, mind ye. It may help some."

Telling her greatest secret, Bridie omitted only her husband's infidelity with the woman on the fire escape. Twice since her surgery in 1921, she'd summoned the courage to speak out to priests behind the black cloth in the confessional. She'd told them the ban imposed on her was driving her husband away and destroying their marriage.

"You must steel yourself against the temptations of the flesh and pray your beloved husband does the same," the priests replied, in voices as cold as ice, as hard as granite.

"I don't understand, Bridie."

"It's Catholic doctrine, Julie. The Church says that the...the marriage act [she whispered the words]... is for procreation only...for the creation of souls to worship God. If for whatever reason, procreation isn't possible, then we must abstain. It's the law of God, according to the Church, you see."

Julie nodded. "We've all wondered why George slept upstairs and you live down in the library. It doesn't seem right or fair."

"'Tisn't fair to George or me. Nonetheless, we must abide by vows given before God. It was more than George could bear."

"And you, Bridie?"

"Except for burying two daughters in Ireland, I've never suffered more watching George drift away from me. 'Tis my cross to bear and his leaving my crown of thorns."

"Still, I don't know how you let them ruin your marriage, Bridie."

"I'm at peace with myself, Julie, and take joy in what I have, Josie and Anna and all the rest of you— here in this place in a time we'll all cherish one day."

"It comes down to what's right between you and God, I guess?"

"Between you and God, Julie, and then between you and yourself. Because He has given us free will, we are left alone to make the decisions we live with and die by."

"You're saying we're alone, Bridie, all by ourselves, in what we do, then?"

"Some seek God's guidance and abide by it...or not. Some never seek it. Either way, in the end, only you know what's right. No one else, not even God, decides whether you take the right path."

"I have to talk to him now, Bridie."

Julie emerged from Quin's room after midnight, shaking and whimpering like a wounded animal. She threw up in the bathroom. Bridie put her to bed. Doc Cooper injected Julie with a double shot of morphine.

Bonanza Mine
Kennecott, Alaska Territory

Dear Bridie,

I have been in the company hospital five days. I feel better as I have the best of care. They bring meals to me. The X-rays show my lungs affected with dust from the mines. Also the heart is affected. But I knew all that years ago. There is no cure so no use spending money on medicine. I may linger on for years.

I go back to the mine next week. My hope is to work as long as I possibly can. I will have to try and make enough to be eligible for a pension. It will not be much, $10 or $15 a month. But it's better than nothing. It will take steady work over 18 months before I will be entitled to that. All I need is a warm place to sleep. Our house at 1531 Bessie Street is good enough for that.

In our old home in Ireland, God was good to us all as we can look back on our childhood days with pleasure, and the love and affection we had for each other will never grow cold. This is something that cannot be weighed or measured. I thank God that He has given me something in life that will never pass.

I will have more money when I go back to the mine next week. I hope things are getting better in the States. There are no newspapers here.

Your loving brother,
Tommy
Erin Go Bragh

A DRESS FOR THE PROM

Sipping coffee at Terry's Grill, George O'Driscoll chuckled over the Sunday paper. "Cheer up, Terry," he said, reading aloud:

Mayor Urges All Citizens
'To Think and Act Happy'

The mayor of Fort Worth declared Happiness Day and called on all citizens to smile the economic gloom away.

"So how about serving up a big smile with my eggs?"

"The mayor's got egg on his face if he thinks I got anything to smile about," Terry mumbled, flipping two fried eggs on his grill.

George found more solace in a news story reporting that people were still buying fewer new cars than they did back in 1929. By his own measure, the Great Depression was greater than ever. His auto parts sales were growing like summer weeds as motorists patched up their old clunkers and went warily down the road until something else broke.

"Your daughter, Josie, was in here lookin' for ya yesterday, Mr. O'Driscoll," Terry said, placing a plate of eggs, bacon and biscuits on the counter. "More java?"

George held out his cup. "She's shopping for a ritzy evening gown. You'd think she was going to see the queen in London."

"Your daughter only graduates once, George," Bridie had told him over the phone. "All top marks and a journalism scholarship to Incarnate Word College in San Antonio. Surely you'll spare a few dollars to get her a dress for the prom. And, by the way, Tommy's in the hospital, so there'll be no more money from Alaska for a while."

George told her he'd spent his last dollar to buy another truck to run a new sales route to Broken Bow, Oklahoma.

Bridie grieved for her gold shamrock—both for its luck and its loan value at Zinn's North Main Pawnshop. Though she'd never been to a prom, she understood it was one of life's landmark ceremonies in America.

Josie had been describing in Jonathan's presence the forthcoming senior prom at Mount Carmel Academy, its festivities and cuisine, and the big-band orchestra. Their respective proms were a week apart. "So there's a chance he'll ask me," she hoped, until a sunny Saturday morning in May.

Jonathan had finished his porridge when he blithely announced that Mona Lisa was his date for the prom at North Side High. He'd been going to school there since the accident. Quin looked up from his paper and stared at his eldest son in blunt silence.

"Not just anyone can dance with a one-legged jack rabbit, you know. And since I can't work the clutch, Mona will drive your old chariot, which we'll need for the evening, ol' man."

Jonathan leaned back and waited, counting on Bridie to temper his father's fiery reaction. But she knew what the quiescent Quin would say.

Julie Bryant's departure from All Saints and from his life had left Quin stoic and silent. He reminded Edwin of shell-shocked soldiers in World War I. "All right, Jonathan," Quin said, "you may use my car, but I hope you have something to wear because—"

"We'll manage," Jonathan cut in, spouting Bridie's mantra and winking at her.

His prom outfit set Mona Lisa back twenty-six dollars and thirty-four cents—a third of her monthly pay—at the Monning's Men's Shop downtown.

Josie accepted another boy's invitation to the Mount Carmel prom, leaving the problem of her dress to her mother.

"Ollie offered to make Josie a dress, but it can't be made from flour sacks," Bridie told Lynn Brant.

"I failed cooking in home ec," Lynn said, "but my sewing got me a job with a dressmaker after I got kicked outta high school."

Bridie laughed. "I won't be asking why."

"I was very young." Lynn shrugged. *And so was the handsome new assistant football coach*, she fondly remembered, *though the school let him stay on after their little shower room scandal.*

"Follow me, Bridie," Lynn said, going to the basement.

They sorted through boxes among dusty furniture, rolled-up rugs and other furnishings stored there years ago after the White House fire.

"Smell the boxes. The ones we're lookin' for are packed with mothballs."

"'Tis here," Bridie said. "At least the mothballs are."

They found velvet, velour, Irish lace and Japanese silk in boxes, insulated, lined with tin and laden with mothballs.

Lynn borrowed Ollie's sewing machine, scissors and tape measure. She took Josie's measurements and cut up table linens and drapes that once adorned the

White House. She studied recent issues of *Vogue*, delivered by Quin from the Carnegie Library.

"You'll knock their socks off, my dear."

On a whim, Bridie took the streetcar across town to 1531 Bessie Street. "I was just in the neighborhood and thought I'd look in on ye," she said after her tenant asked her in. "And how is your husband doing these days, Mrs. Bentley, what with his war wounds and all?"

"Oh, you won't believe, Mrs. O'Driscoll. John's gotten himself regular work at the Purina Flour Mill."

"You mean the man's working, is he?"

"He gave up gettin' that war bonus and got a job, Mrs. O'Driscoll."

"Well, I know times are hard, but any chance ye might pay the rent? A bit of it, perhaps?"

"We got fifteen dollars. We could pay fifteen almost every month now, but eighteen's a little steep, don't you think, Mrs. O'Driscoll?"

Bridie lowered the rent to fifteen dollars, saying nothing about years of arrears. Mrs. Bentley counted out fifteen dollars on her kitchen table. The rent money bought Josie's shoes, a purse and a pair of stockings on a shopping spree in the lady's shops at Striplings and Cox's.

After a final fitting, Lynn Brant stitched an embroidered label in the dress: "Created expressly for Josephine O'Driscoll by Lady Lynn Fashions, Paris, New York, Fort Worth."

"Oh, it's lovely, Lady Lynn. I guess it's not too, you know, too tight or revealing or anything?"

"Not at all, kiddo. It's right out of *Vogue*'s April issue, with a few ideas from the *New York Times*. You're right uptown, Josie."

Ollie and Shirley Roberts stifled themselves when Josie entered the kitchen, regal and stylish, in her hand-tailored dress.

"My God, girl, if ye're not arrested for indecent exposure, you'll catch the Spanish flu before the night's out," Bridie cried.

"It is a little airy...and open, Mother, but Mrs. Brant says it's straight out of *Vogue*," Josie said in half-hearted defense of the backless, strapless dress—skimpy about the bodice, tight about the waist and hips.

"You look like a dance hall babe, if you ask me," Anna said.

"No one asked you, baby sister!"

"What'll we do?" Bridie said.

"I can alter it," Ollie said. "And don't worry, Josie. I won't make you look like you're goin' to a Baptist baptism, either." In an afternoon, she altered the dress to Josie's satisfaction and Bridie's relief.

"It's even prettier than before. But what'll I tell Mrs. Brant?"

"Just tell her you were the belle o' the ball," Shirley said.

THE GHOST FARMER

Wally Cox scooped up a handful of dirt, smelled it, rubbed it between thumb and finger and touched it to his tongue. He tasted sweet, rich, loamy, low-alkaline soil.

He looked out across the acres at the sagging barbed wire fences that hemmed in the black soil, heavily overgrown now with the ubiquitous Johnson weed. A rambling tin-roofed farmhouse nestled in a cloister of oaks, elms and cottonwood trees, rotting firewood stacked outside the kitchen door, a tricycle frame rusting next to the water well. Rooms had been randomly tacked on to accommodate a growing number of occupants.

Wally splashed water on his face as he worked a groaning hand pump at the well under the trees.

"Umm...so good," he said, slaking his thirst with the cool water. No longer connected to the well, a windmill, its blades riddled with bullet holes, slowly sliced a light wind.

The last occupant had carved "California 1933, Abe McGill" on a barn door. The barn, pigpens and a corral needed repairs, but the wood was neither rotten nor weakened by termites. A week's work with hammer and nails would fix it all.

In the kitchen, a 1933 wall calendar—courtesy of the "Azle Feed Store—All the Feed Your Livestock Will Ever Need"—was turned to June. It featured a rustic picture of a boy in a straw hat sitting on a riverbank with a fishing pole, a mongrel dog and a can of worms. Someone had circled 13 on the calendar and written in green crayon, "Go to Calif."

A family's detritus cluttered the gritty linoleum floor: a cracked Mason jar, a broken-handled broom, a coffee can, an oatmeal box, someone's soleless right shoe (shoestrings removed), a bent fork, both halves of a broken butter churn, a rocking chair (missing its rockers) and a photo of a very old man in overalls leaning on a pitchfork next to the barn.

Elsewhere in the house, Wally found bedsprings, three dilapidated chairs, a pair of patched overalls, a chamber pot, a child's doll without eyes, a dog collar and a large dusty mirror hanging on the wall in a bedroom. A pile of firewood was neatly stacked next to the rock fireplace that reached across one end of the living room.

The house was coated in dirt and dust. A broom, a mop, a bucket of sudsy water and a scrub brush would make it livable. There were no leaks from the roof, though rain had blown through several broken windows and warped the floor in the living room and a bedroom.

On the way home, Wally turned in at the Azle Feed Store. "Reckon I made a bad turn," he told the clerk. "Drove down an ol' washed-out gravel road that dead-ended smack into a wood gate, with a sign sayin', 'For Sale, First National Bank.'"

"The McGill place. All of 'em—Abe and Sandy, six kids, Granny and Grandpa—pulled out fer Califarny back in '33. The bank took ever'thing."

"Yip, I know the story."

The clerk laughed and said, "But at least Abe got away with his truck before the bank got out there to get that, too. And you know what? Those bastard bankers'll never catch up with 'em way out in California, neither."

"Let's hope not," Wally said. "How do I get back to town?"

Borrowing one of Clyde Markum's mules, he plowed and planted fifty acres on the backside of the McGill farm, a good distance from the gravel road. He dug out old drainage ditches to revive the peach orchard. He mended the barbed wire fences and repaired the barn, pigpens and corral.

Bridie gave him an envelope full of dried-out shamrocks Delia Walsh had sent from Ireland. "Scatter them for good luck." He scattered them over a row of potatoes, dribbling the remainder over the cabbage he'd planted for her.

Wally Cox had become a "ghost farmer," a common practice yet little-known outside rural America. Banks seldom gave their endless inventories of repossessed farms a second glance. If neighboring farmers noticed squatters working the land, they had no fondness for bankers.

The McGill farm flourished once again with green beans, purple hulled peas, corn, onions, radishes, tomatoes, potatoes and Bridie's cabbage.

When the first harvest appeared on the banquet table in her kitchen, Bridie bowed her head and gave thanks. "Bless us, oh Lord, in these thy gifts which we are about to receive through thy bounty and the labors of thy humble servant Wally Cox."

"And let us not forget the blessed First National Bank, whose soil he's robbed," Quin said, filling his plate.

HAPPIER DAYS

With fewer guests at her kitchen table now, Bridie missed Julie and the Bryant kids. George never called. She worried about Sandra Scott. And Jonathan Quinlan.

Only Bridie's pleas had kept Quin from reporting his car stolen and his minor son kidnapped by a mad nurse on his graduation night. He was dumbfounded they'd run off and gotten married ("like heathens," he shouted) before a justice of the peace in Ardmore, Oklahoma.

"I love her, and she's my wife now," Jonathan said when he and Mona Lisa returned the car and started moving her belongings into his room.

"In the eyes of the Church, you're not married. Now get out of my sight. And take your slut with you."

Jonathan and Mona, both in tears, cleaned out his room, borrowed Wally's truck and drove off. They found a one-room garage apartment near Saint Joseph's Hospital.

Bridie didn't tell Quin when Jonathan called to tell her about the job he'd landed at the *Fort Worth Press.* "They hired me as a proofreader after I took a little test. Doesn't pay much, but it's on a bus line."

"And Mona?"

"Believe it or not, she got promoted to head of Saint Joe's Physical Therapy Department. I'm proud of her and I love her, no matter what the old man thinks. How's everything out there these days?"

"Better, I think," she said. Indeed, Bridie felt the residents of All Saints were getting a foothold here and there, dealing with the lingering Depression in their own way.

"The trick," Wally kept saying, "is to forget what it was like in 1929 because it ain't never comin' back, and jest start over with whatever you can find to get your ox outta the ditch."

By fall, he was selling vegetables, milk, eggs, butter and bacon at the downtown Jones Street farmers market. Spurred by the war in Europe, meat prices inched up, and he sold a few cattle to Swift & Co. For the first time in years, he had money in his pocket when the fan belt broke on his Dodge pickup.

"If I could jest get enough together for a down payment, I could make that old McGill farm a goin' Jessie," he hoped aloud time and again.

Elizabeth Wellington put in six days a week as a seamstress at Williamson-Dickie making uniforms for the U.S. Army. The company was expanding in the expectation the United States would be drawn into another European war.

Martin's fear of leaving the convent abruptly ended when Edwin handed him a copy of the *Fort Worth Press*:

Gangster Jesus Cortez
Dies in Police Shootout

"Jesus is dead. I need you to set up a new still and run it for me."

Martin milked the cows every morning and took the streetcar across town to Edwin's newest Southside drugstore to tend the largest distillery in Texas. Edwin paid him a hefty salary.

Still desultory and distraught over Julie Bryant, Quin began keeping books again for Phil Donovan and other cattle traders at the stockyards. And he stayed sober most of the time.

Doc Cooper paid up the water bill, in arrears since 1932. And before the city came out to restore service, Wally removed the piping he'd installed to run around the water meter.

When the light bill came, Elizabeth Wellington and Shirley Roberts paid it. Quin and Edwin bought a load of coal before the first blue norther swooped down from the Great Plains.

If her guests' prospects were looking up, Bridie herself had little money since Tommy got sick in Alaska. Rent from the Bessie Street house was never a sure thing, though the Bentleys, true to their word, paid more frequently than ever, about every other month.

"We'll manage," Bridie told Josie and Anna.

ALASKA

When the letter came from the mine manager at Kennecott, Alaska, Bridie cried over the phone to Sister Vee, "Our brother died all alone ten thousand miles from Ireland. They buried him on the coast in a fishing village called Cordova."

When Delia Walsh's next letter arrived from Clonmel, Bridie took the dried-up little shamrocks from the envelope and mailed them to the priest in Cordova. She asked him to spread them over Tommy's grave "that he may rest in peace under the shamrocks of Ireland."

MATTHEW'S MOWER

"Coming, I'm coming," Bridie called, scurrying down the hall to the noisy beat of rapid rapping.

While neighbors let themselves in at the back door, a knock up front was usually a bill collector, a somber visitor coming to turn off the electricity again or some other ominous authority. But this was the first policeman, his right hand raised to rap on the front door again with his billy club.

"Oh no! Not you again, Matthew."

"You this kid's mother, lady?" the cop said, his left hand gripping Matthew by the back of the neck.

"No, officer, his mother's long dead," Bridie said, casting a reply to garner the greatest sympathy. "The lad lives here with orphans and others needing a place to stay."

"Orphan or not, this boy's a thief."

"I gave that ol' man back his ol' broken-down lawn mower."

"Shut up, punk," the cop said. "This stupid kid stole a man's lawn mower couple weeks ago, you see. Today he goes back and offers to cut the guy's grass for two bits."

"And he hasn't paid me for it, either."

"Shut up before I haul you downtown and give ya a lesson ya won't forget. So while this idiot's cutting the grass, the man calls the police station. Can you believe that, lady? I mean, this boy's too dumb to be a crook, so if you'll take him in hand, I'll let the little jerk off this time bein' he's so young and an orphan and all."

"I'll see to him, all right. And God bless you, my good man."

The cop shoved Matthew roughly toward Bridie, warning, "Next time, kid, I'll kick your butt and throw ya in the clink with all the other two-bit criminals." The officer went down the steps to his patrol car on the street.

"How could you do such a thing, Matthew?"

"Nobody let me cut their grass all day, Miss Bridie, and I needed money to go to the movies. I knew this man needed his grass cut because he didn't have a mower anymore."

She stifled a laugh. "But why did you take his mower in the first place is what I want to know, young man?"

"It was just an ol' broken-down mower that needed fixin' even before I could use it."

"No matter, Matthew. You know it's both a sin and against the law to steal from others."

"What else could I do after you got me fired from Blackie's blacksmith shop?"

"It was bootlegging, not blacksmithing, you were doing there, Matthew. And that was against the law, too."

"Well, you're not going to tell my dad about this lawn mower business, are you, Miss Bridie?"

"If you promise not to steal more lawn mowers or anything else and if you'll go to confession this Saturday and seek forgiveness for your many trespasses."

"Not that asbestos priest again, Miss Bridie?"

"Father Nolan, you mean? Indeed, we'll be taking the streetcar Saturday afternoon to Saint Patrick's."

"I guess I'm stuck," Matthew said.

THE BEST YEARS

B ridie had two boiled eggs, toast, tea and a sack lunch waiting when Josie entered the kitchen and sat down at the table.

"I don't have time to wait for the porridge," Josie told her mother.

"No rush now, Josie. You've plenty of time to get there."

At six-forty-five, Josie was walking double-time down Belle Avenue to catch the downtown streetcar. She had given up her journalism scholarship and gone to work instead of to college. It had become clear there was no other way to support herself, Bridie and Anna, still a student at Mount Carmel High.

To no avail, Sister Vee had begged George to support the family at a minimum level to free Josie to accept the scholarship. Then she badgered Eddie Duray to accept an application from Josie at Commercial Credit Company. "Josie not only had that scholarship, Mr. Duray, but she has three years of high school bookkeeping."

Eddie Duray, a devout Catholic, was one of the nun's generous supporters of the Dunne Home Orphanage. "All right, all right, Sister Vee, I'll accept her application, but I promise you nothing."

Despite her high scores on pre-employment tests, Eddie Duray reasoned the attractive redhead had no experience as an audit clerk in a regional finance office. Besides, the job paid a man's salary—a whopping one-hundred-twenty-five dollars a month.

Keeping his promise, he submitted her application and four others to the home office in Baltimore. A vice president there was taken by the originality and sincerity of Josie's answer to a question most applicants blew off with saccharine platitudes or ignored altogether: "What do you have to offer this company?"

"Enthusiasm and the best years of my life," she wrote.

"I'll be honest, Josie," Mr. Duray said. "Headquarters fixated on your answer to that question and practically ordered me to hire you over four other more experienced applicants. Don't let me down."

Ten percent of Josie's first paycheck went into Sunday's collection basket at Saint Patrick's. After the noon Mass, she walked with Bridie and Anna up to the Westbrook Hotel to celebrate their new wealth over lunch.

Bridie scowled at the life-size nude statue reigning over the elegant lobby. "What kind of place is this you're taking us, Josie?"

"She's the Golden Goddess, Mom," Josie said. "Oilmen kiss her for good luck when they drill a new well."

They marveled at the plush, ornate Derrick Dining Room. Tables were adorned in fresh flowers and bejeweled with silverware. China and glittering crystal glasses sparkled on linen tablecloths under an array of chandeliers.

"Never mind these prices, Mother," Josie said, scanning the menu. "I've got enough money to spring us without having to wash dishes."

Josie ordered the complete lunch: fresh Gulf shrimp cocktail, fruit supreme in a silver cup, garden vegetable soup, broiled top sirloin steak with smothered onions, green beans, apple cobbler and tea.

"Are you knowing," Bridie said, "'tis seventy-five cents and enough food for the three of us?" Bridie ordered the thirty-five-cent lunch special: broiled ham hock and new cabbage, string beans, apple cobbler and tea.

Anna said, "I want the filet mignon and mashed potatoes, string beans, a blackberry sundae and strawberry shortcake."

"The sundae or the shortcake, Anna, not both," Bridie said.

"I'll take the sundae."

Waiters in black coats and bow ties served them from silver platters, placing hot rolls and dishes of butter at each setting.

"Now, Anna, grace before meals," Bridie said.

"Here, in front of all these strangers?"

When Josie asked for the bill (which she'd parsed at two dollars and seventy-five cents), the waiter said it was taken care of—"with a generous gratuity not to reveal your secret benefactor."

As they crossed the great room to leave the hotel, Anna said, "Look, it's Mr. Quinlan. And he's with a...a woman!"

"Don't stare like you've never seen a man and a woman," Josie whispered.

"Come on over," Quin called, standing to greet them.

"Sarah Van Dyke," he said, nodding to the well-dressed lady at his table, "this is Bridie O'Driscoll—queen of that fifty-something-room castle where we live in the grandest poverty. And these are her lovely offspring, the Misses Josie O'Driscoll and Anna O'Driscoll."

"Quin's told me so much about you," said Sarah Van Dyke, an attractive, slightly built, blue-eyed brunette. A bit younger than Quin, Bridie decided. "So happy to meet you and your lovely daughters, Mrs. O'Driscoll."

"Likewise. And just call me Bridie." She knew from reading the society pages that Sarah was the widow of Thomas Van Dyke III, scion of one of Fort Worth's founding families. In the wake of the stock market crash, he'd gassed himself to death in their kitchen oven.

"And Josie and Anna," Sarah said, "you are as beautiful as Quin said you are."

Bridie turned to Quin. "You wouldn't be the one who paid for our lunch?"

"Me? A man who hasn't paid his rent in years?"

"So where are Roger and Matthew?" Josie said.

"Matthew's probably robbing a bank," Quin said.

"No, Mr. Quinlan, the banks are closed on Sunday," Anna said.

"Roger's up in Sarah's suite eating all the hotel's chocolate ice cream," Quin said.

"I live here," she explained.

Bridie hadn't seen Quin in a lighter, happier mood since before Julie Bryant left the convent. Also, he was sober.

THE LAST DANCE

The Brants sent a load of winter coal to All Saints the day after they moved to the Lucerne Apartments, a luxury high-rise on the south side.

"If people keep moving out at this rate, we'll be the only ones left next winter," Shirley Roberts said. "Wouldn't be surprised if Quin set up housekeeping with his new lady friend at the Westbrook."

"It's like family moving away," Bridie said, stirring her tea. "But everyone's leaving means times are getting better. None of us meant to live here forever."

Though the Coxes didn't know it yet, Bridie knew they were about to leave as well. She found the letter to Mr. Wallace C. Cox wadded up on the back steps where he had tossed it en route to the basement for a bottle of Roosevelt's Choice. She frowned over its three blunt sentences. Reading the letterhead, however, she nodded and smiled.

Bridie donned her Sunday clothes and went out. In the backyard, she passed Wally's twenty-dollar tractor under a tree—its oily innards and his tools laid out on a board—where he'd been working when the letter came.

Bridie walked briskly down Belle Avenue with a basket of potatoes, tomatoes, radishes and collard greens swinging from her left arm. As the streetcar trundled to town, she hardly noticed the putrid aroma of the stockyards or took pleasure at the burned-out KKK building, its white neon cross now blackened and warped.

"I'm Bridie O'Driscoll. I would like to see Mr. Connell, please," she told the funeral-faced secretary, a Miss Gertrude Grable, according to the nameplate on her desk. Bridie knew from the wrinkled letterhead in her purse that Wilson Connell was still president of the First National Bank of Fort Worth.

"We don't allow solicitors," Miss Grable said, gazing warily at the basket of assorted vegetables.

"Oh, this? A little gift for Mr. Connell."

"Then you have an appointment?" she said, wondering how this gray-headed little woman in a faded, once-fashionable dress and hat got past the guards.

"You might tell Mr. Connell 'tis an old customer who danced across the bank lobby with him one evening long ago."

"Dancing…in our lobby?"

"We're old friends," Bridie said, wondering if he'd remember her.

"I'll see if Mr. Connell is available," Miss Grable said, fearful of offending one of the old man's old friends. "Wait here."

Wilson Connell, well into his eighth decade, came bounding out of his office, his spindly, six-foot-six frame strutting like a racehorse across the waiting room.

"Bridie O'Driscoll," he said, his blue eyes sparkling, his baldpate shining. "We danced to George Gershwin's—"

"Rhapsody in Blue," Bridie said. "You haven't changed a bit over the years, Wilson Connell."

"And you've kissed the Blarney Stone again," he said, taking her arm and turning to Miss Grable, who was thankful she hadn't called the guards to throw this basket-woman back into the street.

"Miss Grable, this little Irish lady helped us save the bank in one of the darkest hours of the Depression."

"Now who's kissed the Blarney Stone?" Bridie said.

"You did put your money back after we danced and the bank didn't fold," Wilson reminded her. He lifted a bright red tomato from her basket.

"This would win a blue ribbon at the state fair. From your garden?"

"From yours, if the truth be known," she said as they entered his office with its bar, fireplace and a

menagerie of wildlife trophies mounted on the walls—
a longhorn, a bear, an elk and a Texas mountain lion.

"I won't take much of your time, Wilson. I know
you're busy."

"I wish," he said, gesturing for her to take a seat.
"I'm what's called president emeritus—an honorary if
not so honorable job. If I go to board meetings, they
hope I don't say anything. Beats sittin' home, though.
Well, never mind all that. What can I do for you,
Bridie?"

She handed Wilson Connell the letter from First
National Bank declining Wally's loan application on
the abandoned McGill farm.

"I shouldn't tell you he's trespassed," Bridie said,
holding up the basket of vegetables, "but you can see
what a fine farmer Wally Cox is."

"Another ghost farmer," the president said knowingly. "We chase 'em off now and then as a matter of
principle, 'specially if they're selling the fence posts
for firewood and things like that."

"Not Wally. He's even painted the house and fixed
the pigpens. He sells enough produce to make mortgage payments, if only he had a down payment. He
loves the land, and he's a good man."

Wilson sat back, rubbing his chin. "You know,
Bridie, the janitors and a few others around here still
think I have presidential clout. And I've probably got

just enough left to scare a lowly young loan officer into reconsidering a close decision like this."

"Bless you, Wilson," Bridie said.

"But a down payment is required. No exceptions."

"Oh, I see."

"Would you like to make that payment now, in vegetables, perhaps? I'd love to have those tomatoes in my salad tonight."

Bridie stood and put the basket on his desk. "I'll never be able to repay you, Wilson."

"Well now, maybe you can. Let me show you something." She followed him to a Victrola and a cabinet of phonograph records. "I play these after lunch while I smoke the one daily Montecristo my cranky ol' doctor still allows." He thumbed through his collection. "Here, 'Rhapsody in Blue'. So how about it, Bridie... one last dance?"

"One of my favorites, Wilson," she said as he spun the record and turned to her.

THE STRIPPERS

As meat prices stabilized, Quin Quinlan moved from part-time bookkeeper for Dan Donovan to manager of Grover & Sons Cattle Commission Company. To the ex-oilman, cattle were only a mean stepping stone to meaningful money.

Quin proposed the Grovers buy so-called "strippers"—oil wells that stripped out the last drops of black gold from old and dying fields. "We can pick them up cheap and make a buck or two during this European war," he said. "These strippers produce a piddling twenty to a hundred barrels a day, but even at that rate, any dog of an oil well will make you more money than a prize cow."

The Grover brothers winced.

"Get enough strippers together," Quin continued, "and you've got a steady flow of good money coming in every day."

After the Grovers saw the profits from a handful of wells, Quin began snooping around for a deal to buy up several hundred strippers to set up Grover-Quinlan Oil Company and to become its president. He began hanging out at the Westbrook Hotel with oil company landmen and scouts. Like undercover agents, these dowdy denizens of the oil patch sniffed out deals in the making, sold and stole secrets, spread rumors, lied, spied and hustled oil and gas leases for their masters.

Quin joined the slippery sleuths at the bar, played poker at their tables, said little and listened. The older ones remembered him now, some for better, some for worse, from the oil boom of the 1920s. Some remembered when he'd kissed the cheeks of the Golden Goddess—"all four of 'em"—and joined his drinking colleagues in a sloppy toast to the nude statue in the lobby.

Quin soon cut a deal with Gulf Oil for an aging field near Wichita Falls. The skeptical Grover brothers wondered "if them wells is so good, why's Gulf gettin' rid of 'em?"

"Because Gulf's a big-assed oil company with more profitable fields to produce," Quin explained again and again and then once more. "They want to sell, and I've beat 'em down to a hell'va good price."

Tad Grover said, "Look, Quin, we're cowmen at heart. We'll jest think about this a spell before we get any deeper in this awl bid'ness than we already are."

"Our option to buy expires in one week."

Sarah Van Dyke offered to buy all one-hundred-thirty wells from Gulf with Quin earning a working interest running the operation and marketing the oil.

"No," he said, pouring another drink. "I've got to do this on my own."

"Pride is one thing, Quin. Stubbornness is stupid. We're not getting any younger, either. And look at you. Drinking again like a sieve."

"I won't be known in this town for screwing a rich widow out of her money," he shouted. "Let's take a walk."

They stopped at the W. T. Waggoner Tower, the tallest building in town.

"I was right up there, Sarah, next to the Waggoner suite. I rubbed shoulders with Papa Waggoner, Sid Richardson, Amon Carter and your father and all of 'em." Quin paused as people began to stare at the couple. "Listen, Sarah," he continued, lowering his voice, "I'll have an office up there again, and then we'll get married."

When the Grover brothers bought twenty-five wells, he told her, "With my share of the profits, I'll buy a few wells on my own and then a few more. The price of oil will take off when the Brits drag us into the war. It won't be long now. Consolidated Aircraft's already building a mile-long bomber plant out on the west side of town."

OF WAR AND PORRIDGE

B y the time Jimmy Doolittle's raiders bombed Tokyo, Richard Levitz, Matthew Quinlan and Roger Quinlan were in uniform, assigned to combat units bound to the South Pacific.

"Thought my porridge days were over, but even the Navy serves the stuff," Richard wrote Bridie from boot camp. "So far I haven't found a beetle in it."

Frank Feldman, graduating with honors from North Side High, reported to the Army Air Corps flight-training school in San Antonio, Texas, one day after the Battle of Midway. German U-boats were sinking ships off the coast of Florida when Buster Roberts joined the Coast Guard. Brandon Reynolds, the last of All Saints' orphans, deployed from England with the 82nd Airborne Division to North Africa.

Jonathan Quinlan joked that "my missing left foot got me a job at the bummer plant"—the west-side factory that turned out a new B-24 Liberator bomber every sixty minutes, seven days a week.

"They knew a one-footed hop-along wouldn't get drafted, so they hired me as a clerk in the logistics department," he told Bridie on the phone. "Great pay. We bought a '32 Ford for ninety bucks—a hot V-8 like Bonnie and Clyde were driving when they got riddled by the cops."

"Your father will be proud, Jonathan," Bridie said.

"No, don't tell the ol' bas—uh, the ol' man a thing, Bridie. Let him think I'm a lost cause until I've made vice president. And I will before this war's over."

Bridie lost no time informing Quin of his son's success.

"The wages of war," he chuckled as he poured himself a drink, fired up an El Toro cigar and sank into his easy chair.

"And Mona's teaching at Saint Joseph's School of Nursing, as a lot of nurses are going to the Army. She walks to work so Jonathan can drive the car to the bomber plant."

"Drive?"

"She got him a new foot, a…what did he call it?"

"A prosthesis, an artificial limb. Well, I'll be damned."

At Jonathan's behest, Bridie didn't tell him Mona wanted to become a Catholic and be wed in the Church. But Father Anthony Marconi, the new pastor of Saint Patrick's, told the couple the Church did not recognize their civil marriage, and thus they were living in sin. He refused to baptize Mona unless the couple separated during the months she took instructions.

Turning to Jonathan, the portly, round-faced priest said, "And you, young man, will confess your sins of knowing this woman out of wedlock before I'll pronounce you man and wife at my altar."

Jonathan damned Father Marconi to the eternal fires of hell ("I went all out," he'd told Bridie) and stormed out of the rectory. "I'm never going back there or to any other church."

Although she bore the Church's destruction of her own marriage in silence, Bridie was distraught and angry that a priest would turn away a young couple at the door of his church.

BESSIE STREET

B ridie opened the letter and sat down with a cup of tea at the little table in her small kitchen. A postal clerk had scratched through 2115 Belle Avenue, stamped the envelope in black ink and filled in the blank space:

Forward: *1531 Bessie Street,* **Fort Worth, Tex**.

Dear Mrs. O'Driscoll,

Richard has told me all about you so I feel like we are friends. He told me about living at All Saints and what all you did for him when he was a boy and how you were always going to wash his mouth out with soap if he didn't stop cussing but you never did it and he still cusses like a sailor I guess cause he is one now.

He told me about all that porridge he had to eat and won't never let me cook none for him. Ha, ha.

Richard said you're just like a mama to him. I can tell he loves you a lot. That's why we named our little girl Bridget. I know she's safe with you. Richard said when he gets back from the war we will get married and go to Texas to get Bridget and I'll get to meet you then. I just wanted to thank you for taking care of her. I cry sometimes when I think about her. I hope the war ends real soon.

Love,
Molly Fraser

"Dear God," Bridie said to herself, "whatever's happened to this baby?" The letter, postmarked San Diego, Calif., bore no return address.

Richard had sent a postcard when he graduated from boot camp, telling her he was off to ordnance school to become a gunner's mate on a battleship. He had not replied to Bridie's note telling him everyone but Martin, Mulligan and Q.C had moved out of All Saints.

The final exodus of the convent's few remaining residents began when Jonathan told Bridie, "This bummer plant's crawling with women." Shirley Roberts applied for a job there the next day.

"They're going to train me to rivet those warplanes together, Bridie," she said. "And listen to this—I'll make three times the money I'm making at Kress's."

Wally Cox drove in from his farm in Azle to move her to an apartment she'd found on a bus line to the bomber plant. He'd moved after the First National Bank suddenly reversed its decision and approved his mortgage on the abandoned McGill farm.

After Elizabeth Wellington and Gabi took a duplex near the Williamson-Dickie plant, Quin said, "I'm thinking about moving myself."

"And where would you be going?" Bridie asked.

"With the boys gone, I certainly don't need anything on the order of a fifty-room convent."

"The Westbrook's even bigger, if you and Sarah are thinking of—"

"Not yet, Bridie dear. I've got to regain a lot of lost ground before we get married. We've all lost so much time."

"We survived somehow," Bridie said, remembering the noose she'd found in the basement. "Living in limbo perhaps, but we managed."

"Limbo? It's been hell, Bridie, a decade in hell."

"The renters left my house on Bessie Street, perhaps a sign the time has come for me to go home."

Like the nation itself, Bridie's old Bessie Street house suffered from a decade of neglect—sagging doors, peeling paint, a leaking roof and dangerously bad wiring. Bridie had sent Josie to ask her father to help make the place livable. They met at the Paris Coffee Shop, popular for its down-home food and waitresses who asked, "Whatcha gonna have today, hun?"

They ordered the twenty-nine-cent lunch, iced tea and peach pie included.

"If we can just get a new roof and new wiring, we'll manage, Dadda," Josie told him.

"A man's got to make it when he can, Josie, and as soon as Detroit turns from tanks to cars again, my business will never be as profitable." He paid for lunch, left a nickel tip, and dropped her off at the Commercial Credit office in the Fair Building.

Wally Cox moved Bridie's furniture to Bessie Street. "It's gonna be right cold in here with so many windowpanes knocked out," he said, looking through broken glass.

"With her job, Josie can get a loan from the bank to fix up the place. Just put those chairs in the living room, if there's space." Bridie laughed at the heavy 1920s art deco furniture the Brants had left at the convent.

Three days later, a tall, barrel-chested, beer-bellied giant knocked at Bridie's door. "Name's Foster, Randy Foster, ma'am," he said, tipping his paint-splotched cap. "Looking for Mrs. O'Driscoll, ma'am."

"I'm Bridie O'Driscoll."

"Mr. Edwin Brant sent us over," he said, turning to nod at a motley group of men gathered around three trucks in the street. "We fix up old drugstores for Mr. Brant, and he's asked us to fix ever'thing that needs fixin' on this house, inside 'n' out."

"Mr. Brant needn't do that, ye know."

"All I know, Mrs. O'Driscoll, is Mr. Brant said to fix up your house and to put in a water heater while we're here."

Seven men labored from dawn to dusk for two weeks straight.

"Looks just like it did in 1921," Bridie told Randy Foster. "And I've never had a hot water heater. It's a miracle."

REVELATIONS

The Westbrook Hotel baked the three-tiered wedding cake, courtesy of Sarah Van Dyke. The Brants sent a case of Dom Perignon, vintage 1922. Elizabeth Wellington made the wedding dress.

Ollie Cox stayed home to prepare the feast from the bounty of their farm, her husband's labor and his twenty-dollar tractor. Outside, Ollie May turned a side of beef over a mesquite wood fire and kept the dogs at bay, one of the chores she'd inherited after brother Cory joined the army.

Everyone else went to the double ceremonies at Saint Mary's Catholic Church. Father Joe Gillan administered both sacraments, moving from the baptismal font to the altar to celebrate the wedding Mass.

Rice and dried shamrocks showered Jonathan and Mona Lisa Quinlan as bride and groom dashed to a chauffeured black Cadillac (courtesy of Edwin Brant). The little three-leaf clovers—from Shamrock Hill in Clonmel—had arrived a day earlier, yellowed with age in a letter from Delia Walsh to Bridie.

Bridie, Josie and Anna rode with Wally to the farm. "Oh, it's a lovely place," Bridie said as she and the girls climbed out of his truck. Wally shooed off two mutts that came out to sniff the strangers.

The rambling white frame farmhouse, trimmed in bright green, stood in the protective cove of oaks. Wally had painted the barn red, the sun glaring off its tin roof. A new lean-to against the barn sheltered his tractor. A windmill, fitted with new blades, slowly sliced the cold breeze.

Two bleating goats thrust their yellow horns through the slats of the barnyard fence. "Bonnie and Clyde!" Josie called, hurrying to rub their heads.

"You've made it into a beautiful place," Bridie said.

"I'll never figure it, Bridie. The bank turns me down one week and gives me the loan the next week."

"Some banker made the right decision in the end, Wally."

"That's Edwin's driver over there," Wally told Bridie, nodding to a stoic-faced man in chauffeur's uniform resting against a black Cadillac. "His main job's to see nobody sneaks up and wires a stick o' dynamite to the starter."

"Let's go inside in case he falls down on the job," Anna said.

Ollie met Bridie at the door with a cup of tea. "Put the water on to boil when I saw y'all drive up," she said, noticing that despite a lively twinkle in her how Bridie had mellowed with age, a few wrinkles in her face, her hair silver gray. And turning to Wally, she said, "Time to carve the side of beef...before you touch that iced tea you just mixed. And put another log in the fireplace."

Shirley Roberts and Elizabeth Wellington set the table with borrowed plates and Mason jars for iced tea. Lynn Brant distributed crystal champagne glasses round the table. "You don't serve Dom Perignon in Mason jars," Lynn said.

Sarah Van Dyke, who accompanied Quin to the wedding, romped through the house playing hide-and-seek with little Michael Bryant.

"Michael's a good-looking boy, Julia," Quin said, sitting with her on a leather sofa that once furnished the White House. "Takes after his pretty mama."

"And his handsome father," she said quietly. "Your eyes, Quin, your hair, same broad forehead, quick wit."

Quin choked on his Dom Perignon. "You're sure?"

"Not a doubt, given the time of his birth, his looks, his walk."

"Has your husband, Les, said anything?"

"No. Michael was born just over eight months after we...after Les came back. It just happened that way. Michael's so much like you, Quin."

"But luckier, so much luckier."

"Luckier?"

"He has you." Julia looked down, stirring her iced tea with a finger.

"I shouldn't have said that. I'm sorry, Julia."

"Don't be, Quin. Michael was born of love. It was never a cheap affair. And it was right at the time. Then…well, things just changed, you know, like they always do. I love you, Quin. And you love me."

"Yes, Julie, I love you."

"And you love Marion, too."

"I do love her."

"And I love Les. Loving two people seems to be our dilemma."

Our damnation, Quin thought to himself. He looked longingly at Julie and sipped his glass of champagne.

Edwin tapped a spoon against a champagne glass and called for a toast to the "now twice-married newlyweds."

"Not yet," Father Gillan protested as he sauntered to the head of the table. "First, a toast to the newly baptized and then to the newly wed. In all the two thousand years of the Catholic Church, I'm surely the first priest ever to baptize and marry the same person on the same day. So, a toast to the one who made it all possible, the new Mrs. Jonathan Quinlan." He raised a glass of Dom Perignon.

"And God bless Father Gillan for making this day possible," Sister Vee said, lifting a glass of sherry.

"And I'll have you to thank, Sister Vee, when I'm excommunicated," the priest said.

The nun and the priest had met at Arlington Downs Racetrack when she begged there for the orphanage during the early days of the Depression. Slinking surreptitiously around the edge of the crowd, his white Roman collar hidden by a black turtleneck sweater, his black hat tilted to shadow his face, Father Gillan read racing sheets, chatted with bookies, placed bets, and finally introduced himself to the nun at the main gate.

"I pray you're having better luck than I am," he'd said, peering into the black bag at her feet. "I'm Father Gillan."

"Sister Villanova, County Tipperary. Pleased to know ye, Father."

"County Waterford meself, Sister. But my Irish luck hasn't paid off this afternoon."

"Well now, Father Gillan, you might put a prayer and a bet on Hot Biscuit in the ninth."

"A tip from Saint Patrick?"

"Saint Waggoner."

"W. T. Waggoner, owner of the track?"

"Himself."

Father Gillan, by his own accounting, became "almost as rich as a bishop" that racing season. Thus, he'd remembered Sister Vee when she poured out her story about Father Marconi's turning away a young

411

lady who wanted to become a Catholic and marry in the Church.

"You know," Father Gillan had said, frowning, "these Italian priests from the old country tend to act like little popes-in-waiting—holier than the Holy Father in Rome, they think themselves."

His disdain for the Italian wasn't entirely xenophobic. Father Marconi had been named pastor of the big church even though the late Monsignor Nolan had practically promised it to Father Gillian.

"As Monsignor Nolan used to say—God rest his soul—forgiveness is the biggest part of our business," Father Gillan told Sister Vee. "Ask this young couple to come see me."

After everyone sat down to the baptismal-wedding feast, Father Gillan gave thanks. Quin sat between Sarah Van Dyke and Julia Bryant, who told her son to sit "like a big boy" in the chair next to his sister.

"Auntie Sarah said I could sit in her lap," he informed his mother.

"*Auntie*, is it?" Julia said.

"Michael and I have become good friends," Sarah said. "And where's his father? I'd love to meet him."

Julia paled, reached for her glass of tea, swallowed and composed herself as Sarah watched across Quin's plate. "Are you all right, dear?"

"Sorry, something stuck," Julia said, touching her throat. "My husband's working today."

Quin delved into his plate, stealing a glance at his secret son, nestled in his fiancée's lap as she chatted with his former mistress, the boy's mother.

Doc Cooper and Martin huddled over a bottle of Roosevelt's Choice. Doc, living in an apartment over one of Edwin's drugstores, had stopped at the convent. "Get outta this musty basement for a while, you old groundhog you," the doc ordered. "And bring Mulligan with you." The old yellow dog lay under the table asleep.

Quin joined Jonathan and Mona Lisa at the wedding cake and raised his glass "to my lovely daughter-in-law and her lucky husband."

Mona kissed Quin on the cheek. "I love you," she said.

Their acrimonious relationship had melted in tears. Bridie had watched in sorrow and joy when Quin, Jonathan and Mona Lisa embraced as the bugler played taps in honor of U.S. Marine Sergeant Matthew A. Quinlan, killed in action on a blood-soaked beach in the Solomon Islands.

Bridie looked round the table. Everyone related to one another with the kind of easy kinship she felt for them. She wondered who among them had hung the noose in the basement and if anyone else noticed the striking likeness of Julia's little boy to Quin. And she wondered what had happened to Sandra Scott.

After Mona Lisa cut the cake and fed her groom the first bite, Jonathan kissed her and tapped a spoon against his champagne glass. "We have something else to celebrate today. We'll be asking Father Gillan to do another baptism in about six months. Right, Mona?" She nodded. "You see, Father Gillan, Mona's three months pregnant on this, her wedding day."

The priest paled. "I'll be excommunicated for sure now."

As everyone devoured cake, Quin stood and called for attention. "We have a fourth reason to celebrate today."

Bridie applauded lightly and waited to hear the date for his and Sarah Van Dyke's long-awaited wedding.

"Today is February first," Quin went on. "It's Saint Brigid's Day, after whom our own beloved Brigid... Bridget...Bridie O'Driscoll here takes her saintly namesake."

"I forgot," Josie said, her mother never having made much of the widely celebrated Irish saint's day.

"And for those few who just might not know," Quin said, "Saint Brigid, like our Bridie, also ran a convent."

"But I'll bet Saint Brigid didn't have a still in hers," Wally said.

"Thanks to you, Bridie, we always managed somehow," Elizabeth Wellington said.

"We all did what we could," Bridie said, "helping and loving one another day by day."

"Like family," Julie said, looking at Quin, holding their son in his lap.

"Things were never as bad as they seemed," Lynn said.

"No," Doc Cooper said, putting an arm around Martin's shoulders. "We always had plenty o' good drink, thanks to our man in the basement."

"And we didn't die from eatin' all those eggs," Ollie said.

"We laughed a lot," Shirley said.

"And Shirley cursed a lot," Quin said.

"Well, double damn you, Saint Quinlan."

"We lost a decade of our lives, as if we'd been standing still all that time and nothing changed," Quin said.

"We changed all right," Edwin said. "We all got older."

"But we're outta the ditch and goin' down the road again," Wally said.

ORDINARY LIVES

"Glory be, 'tis yereself, Martin," Bridie said, opening the door. "And Mulligan, too. Come in, come in, the both of you."

The yellow dog—old, fat, cumbersome—wagged his tail and struggled up the steps. He rubbed against her legs and plopped down.

"He don't move too good no more, Miss Bridie, and most of his teeth are gone," Martin said.

"And what's this in his mouth?"

"It's the other end of the rope, the one somebody used to make that noose ya found in the basement 'long time ago, remember?"

"Really, Martin! Where'd you find it?"

"Upstairs. Hard as it is for him, Mulligan goes upstairs once in a while lookin' for the kids and the other people who lived out there. Last week he come down carryin' this rope in his mouth."

"Ye wouldn't be knowing whose room it came from?"

"Naw, Miss Bridie, Mulligan's not talkin'."

"We'll always wonder."

"Mulligan likes to chew on the rope, but I threw that ol' noose in the furnace yesterday when I was packin' up." He handed her a box.

"Chocolate-covered cherries! My favorite. Thank you, Martin. Come, and I'll put on some tea. And a pot of coffee as well."

Martin turned to the front door. "Did ya see my car, Miss Bridie?"

"Ah, 'tis a big one," she said, looking through the screen.

"Thirty-nine Packard Eight. Bought it to go home in."

"And where would that be, Martin?"

"Kentucky. My ol' granny was more'n a hundred when she passed, so maybe Mom'll still be stittin' on the front porch when I drive up."

"You're coming back, though?" Bridie said, going to the kitchen.

"I'll probably go back to work at Jim Beam's where I used to make legal whiskey. Then Prohibition shut down the place and forced me to...well, to do other things. Not always good things."

Bridie put a kettle of water and a coffeepot on the stove. "You'll write, Martin, and let me know how you're doing?"

"Nice house ya got here, Miss Bridie. Josie live here with ya?"

"For the time being. She's met a nice young man. Lives next door with his brother and has a decent job with the railroad. I think it's serious."

"And little Anna?"

"Going to Incarnate Word College in San Antonio but mainly studying a young man in the Air Corps. And the Brants, how are they?"

"They's fine. I showed somebody how to run their stills. I play poker with Doc Cooper every day, least 'til he falls asleep."

Bridie gave Martin a cup of coffee and poured boiling water into a teapot for herself. She held out the box of chocolate cherries. Martin took one. "I ain't seen nobody else from the convent for a long while."

"Nor have I," Bridie said, slipping Mulligan a chocolate. "Except Elizabeth Wellington. Comes over now and then for Sunday lunch. Everybody's working and going about their business again."

"Tryin' to get back to normal," Martin said.

"That's all we ever wanted at All Saints—ordinary lives again."

"If this war would just end."

"God willing, it'll be over soon," Bridie hoped. "You've been living out at the convent by yourself all this time, Martin."

"I liked it down in the basement. I read that *Book of Gospels* ever' night—the one Sister Vee gimme, ya know."

"I'll tell her, Martin," Bridie said, smiling that he no longer called it the *Book of Gossip.* "She'll be pleased."

"Yeah, I know most of them parable stories by heart now." He finished his coffee and stood up. Bridie and Mulligan followed him.

"You're leaving Mulligan with me?"

"Yeah. I couldn't catch Q.C, but he ain't gonna starve. They's more mice in that convent than ever."

"I'm so happy you came to see me, Martin."

"Almost forgot," he said, taking a yellow envelope from his shirt pocket. "Western Union boy was gettin' back on his bike when I drove up yesterday. Said it's from the War Department. It's for you."

"Must be a mistake." She frowned.

"Well, better go," he said, opening the screen door. "Bye, Miss Bridie." He rubbed Mulligan's head, "Take care, ol' friend."

Bridie gave him a hug. "Fare thee well and God love ye, Martin."

He turned quickly and went down the steps to hide the tears.

Bridie sat down with a cup of tea to read the telegram.

> U.S. Pacific Fleet Command
> Port of Honolulu, Hawaii
> Territory of the United States
>
> Mrs. Bridget O'Driscoll
> All Saints Convent
> 2115 Belle Avenue
> Fort Worth, Texas

Dear Mrs. O'Driscoll:

I regret to inform you that Petty Officer Richard Levitz, who listed you as next of kin, is missing in action and presumed dead in the sinking of the United States Ship *Jarvis* in the Battle of Guadalcanal with the Imperial Japanese Navy in the South Pacific Ocean.

You will be proud to know that he, his fellow crewmen and his officers distinguished themselves, their ship and the United States of America with highest honor and greatest courage in giving their lives for their country. None was recovered from the sea. May they rest in peace.

We extend deepest sympathy and America's gratitude for your sacrifice in losing a loved one in war for the cause of victory.

We shall not forget.

Sincerely,

W. Thomas Tilson III
Director, Seagoing Personnel
Lieutenant Commander
United States Navy

Bridie sobbed quietly. She wept for Richard and little Bridget and a girl named Molly—raised her arms to heaven and cried out to the ceiling of her kitchen, "Dear God, all the lad ever wanted was a family to love him."

She knelt and asked Him to "watch over Bridget Levitz—wherever she be, her mother Molly as well— and keep safe the other boys from All Saints who've gone to the war."

⇒╬⇐

Word of Richard Levitz's death reached former residents of All Saints as they ran into each other on the streets of Fort Worth. At these chance encounters, they asked what one had heard about the others. And in farewell, they promised to "have Sunday dinner together soon." Yet the grown-ups never took time to visit, to catch up, to reminisce as they struggled to make up a decade lost in the prime of their lives.

Wally and Ollie Cox were in their mid-forties, their only bank account a mortgage at First National. "We'll get this farm paid for while we're still young—before we're eighty, anyhow," he laughed.

Quin Quinlan never gave up clawing his way back to 1929 and his office in the W. T. Waggoner Building. When he got there, he promised Sarah Van Dyke they would marry. They never did. When he died, Jonathan was the only Quinlan who knew why his dad had left ten thousand dollars to someone named Julie Bryant.

Edwin Brant operated stills under his south-side drugstores, his untaxed bootleg booze easily competing against legal liquor when it went on sale. Two of his fiercest competitors perished in failed shooting attempts on Edwin's life. The insurance company dropped arson charges when Edwin agreed to surrender his longstanding claim on the White House fire.

With eight trucks on the road, George O'Driscoll sold auto parts in three states, took a suite in the posh Forest Park Apartments and lived the American Dream, alone.

In her late thirties, Shirley Roberts shopped for her first car with her "war money," as she called her wages at the bomber plant. A used car salesman offered her "a real good deal for a little honey in the backseat." She slugged him in the eye and called him a "double son-of-a-bitch."

Elizabeth Wellington told Bridie that her husband, missing since 1931, would be back for her after the war. "I just know Dave's in the Army." As seamstress supervisor at Williamson-Dickie, she had money for Gabi's tuition at Saint Joseph's School of Nursing. Dave never returned.

Julie Bryant, a nurse at the hospital, raised her three children in a working class neighborhood with husband Les. Although they earned enough to live his dream of an Oldsmobile and a brick house, they lived in a modest frame home and drove secondhand Chevrolets, hoarding their money in morbid fear of another Great Depression.

When a lawyer delivered the late Quin Quinlan's check for ten thousand dollars to her at the hospital, Julie bought Les a new Oldsmobile 88, paid off their mortgage and deposited the remainder in their joint bank account. "My old auntie in West Texas left it to me," she told her husband. "I guess I never mentioned her to you."

No one heard from Martin after he left town, and no one ever learned his last name.

Bridie O'Driscoll lived in the Bessie Street bungalow bought with her brother's Nevada gold money. She took in ironing, "minded after" children for working mothers, sometimes cared for the elderly and the dying, and cleaned Saint Patrick's Church on Saturdays.

For the children of All Saints, the best years of their lives lay ahead. They would be called the greatest generation in a book of the same name. Yet like almost everyone who lived through the dark decade, they never escaped its shadow. Forever looking over their shoulders for the next Great Depression, they lived by their own mantra:

"It could all happen again."

Yet no matter how bad things got from time to time, they could hear Miss Bridie's voice when the lights went out, when the water was cut off, when the KKK came in the night, when porridge was the daily fare: "We'll manage." And so they did.

EPILOGUE

B oeing 707 jetliners spanned the Atlantic in a matter of hours when Delia Walsh mailed her first letter by air from Ireland. Thus, the three-leaf clovers she sent to Bridie were still almost fresh when they reached Fort Worth. The next afternoon, Josie sprinkled the green shamrocks, from the meadows of honey, over her mother's grave.

Bridget O'Driscoll
September 5, 1881
Meadows of Honey
Clonmel, County Tipperary, Ireland
January 13, 1961
Tea with the angels
Fort Worth, Texas

AUTHOR'S NOTE

The abandoned All Saints Convent and Girls School became, in succession, home to the South Central Bible Institute, the Baptist Southwestern Bible Institute, the Wilkes Convalescent Home and, finally, Rosen Heights Apartments.

Half a century after Sam Rosen donated the land to the Sisters of Charity, the building was razed to make way for Masonic Lodge No. 942. A black and white picture of All Saints Convent hangs in a meeting room there, 2115 Belle Avenue, Fort Worth, Texas.

Bridie O'Driscoll's house, 1531 Bessie Street, Fort Worth, looks much as it did when she, George, Josie and Anna moved into it in 1921. Another family lives there now.

Gretta Brittan, a widow, invited me in to have a look at her little two-story row house at 9 Queen Street, Clonmel, County Tipperary, Ireland, where Bridie grew up, married and gave birth to three daughters.

Seventy-six letters and a diary (early 1900s through 1937) written by Bridie's brother, Tom, reside in museums in mining towns near his gold claims or near company-owned mines where he worked in Nevada and California as well as the Hoover Dam, where he helped build the great tunnels. The material is kept under his name, Tom O'Driscoll, at Northeastern Nevada Museum, Elko; the mining museum in Tonopah, Nevada; and the Hoover Dam Museum in Boulder City, Nevada. His Alaska letters are available at the McCarthy-Kennecott Historical Museum, McCarthy, Alaska, and copies of these are kept at the Cordova Historical Museum, Cordova, Alaska, where he is buried.

When the Westbrook Hotel in Fort Worth, Texas, was demolished, the revered Golden Goddess statue eventually found a home in the Fort Worth Petroleum Club. She greeted Texas oilmen in the foyer until their blue-haired little wives condemned the bosomy nude to the men's room, next to the urinals.

ACKNOWLEDGMENTS

The Last Shamrock is a story I heard most of my life from my mother, Josie; my aunt, Anna; my grandmother, Bridie; and later from others who lived at All Saints or were neighbors and visitors to the convent during the Great Depression.

Others who encouraged me and provided information include:

North Carolina: Greensboro: Retired Chief Warrant Officer Roger Quinlivan (former resident of All Saints) and wife Mayme. **Hendersonville**, Joe Gillan, author, *For Her Sake (Sine Qua Non)* and *Just Before the Dawn.*

Fort Worth, Texas: Diane Quinlivan Redmond, Earlene Quinlivan; Sam Rosen II, grandson of Rosen Heights developer Sam Rosen; Sgt. Kevin

Foster, historian, Fort Worth Police Department; Zoranna Williams, TCU Department of Nursing; Susan Prichitt, former director, Tarrant County (Fort Worth) Historical Commission; the late Bill Fairley, columnist, *Fort Worth Star-Telegram*; Jim Evans, editor; Fort Worth Public Library; *Fort Worth Star-Telegram* and *Fort Worth Press*, 1919–1942.

Clyde T. Markum, Hardy Tadlock, Rosen Heights neighbors; Mr. Green, secretary, Masonic Lodge 942, 2115 Belle Avenue; Lawrence Curtin and Pat Curtin, Bridie's nephews, frequent visitors to All Saints; Rev. Dr. Katherine Long, United Methodist Church; Mike Long, editor; Billy Jones, Patrick Pitts, Johnny Pitts and Clyde Schrill, playwright; Jill Scott, copy editor.

Dallas, Texas: George Salih, orphan at the Dunne Home for Boys, Sister Villanova's twelve-year-old chauffeur, now owner of Sole's Restaurant; Betty Hudson, proofreader supreme.

San Antonio, Texas: Dean Collar, Anna O'Driscoll's childhood beau and owner of the Christmas donkey; Sister Mary Alibi Heavener's master's thesis, *The Depression Era in Fort Worth, 1929–1934*, University of Texas, 1974; Sister Francisca Eileen, archivist, Incarnate Word College; Library, Incarnate Word College; Brother Edward Loch, SM, archivist, Catholic Archives of San Antonio; Sister Margaret Patrick Slattery, author of *Promises to Keep—A History of the Sisters of Charity of the Incarnate Word.*

Houston, Texas: Dr. Lily Ann Cunningham, University of Houston, and Richard Cunningham, author and photographer. Bleu Beathard, editor.

Iowa City, Iowa: Dr. Thomas Dean, University of Iowa.

Riviera Beach, Florida: Gil Gillivan, who taught me about writing, and Jean Gillivan, who encouraged me to write.

Iowa City, Iowa: Dr. Thomas Dean, University of Iowa.

New York City, New York: Ellis Island immigration records; *The New York Times*, 1900–1909, 1919; New York Public Library.

Clonmel, County Tipperary, Ireland: Eamonn Lonegran, historian, author of *Saint Joseph's Hospital*; Eileen and Michael Moran, Moran's Pub, Parnell Street; Mrs. Gretta Britton, 9 Queen Street; Mrs. Mary Butler Kerr (daughter of Bridie's lifelong friend, Delia Walsh Butler), 31 William Street; Father Michael J. Ryan, Saint Mary's Church, Irishtown; the curator, Saint Peter and Paul's Church; the ladies in the archives at *The Nationalist* newspaper; Clonmel Town Hall records staff, and the shy, nameless gravedigger at Saint Patrick's Cemetery, resting place of George and Bridie's two young daughters, Norah and Brigid.

Thurles, County Tipperary, Ireland: Pat Bracken, researcher, Thurles Public Library.

Rock of Cashel, County Tipperary, Ireland: Dierdre Walsh, genealogy researcher, Bru Boru Heritage Centre.

Tipperary Town, County Tipperary, Ireland: Ann Maloney, Tipperary Heritage Society, The Bridwell, St. Michale Street.

Dublin, Ireland: Office of the Registrar-General, Births, Deaths and Marriages; David Snook, the Marine Institute of Ireland.

Great Britain: The Cunard Steamship Company; long-lost Irish-Anglo relatives John Lambie and Shirley Edwards and their families in England; Liam Ryan, Irish-Scottish relative, and wife Pat, Edinburgh, Scotland.

Books*: Fort Worth—Outpost on the Trinity,* Oliver Knight*; Hell's Half Acre,* Richard F. Selcer*; Gamblers and Gangsters* (of Fort Worth), Ann Arnold*; North of the River,* J'Nell Pate; *Fort Worth—The Civilized West,* Caleb Pirtle III; *St. Patrick's (Cathedral)—The First 100 Years,* William R. Hoover.

Since Yesterday (the 1930s in America), Frederick Lewis Allen; *Hard Times* (an oral history of the Great Depression), Studs Terkel; *The Great Depression,* T. H. Watkins; *The Great Depression,* David A. Shannon; *The Great Depression,* edited by Dennis Nishi; *The Story of the Irish Race,* Seumas MacManus*; Ireland* (the Oxford History), edited by R. F. Foster.

Made in the USA
Coppell, TX
25 August 2024